Phil Hogan lives in Hertfordshire with his wife and four children. *The Freedom Thing* is his second novel. His first, *Hitting the Groove,* is also published by Abacus.

Also by Phil Hogan

HITTING THE GROOVE

PARENTING MADE DIFFICULT (non-fiction)

the
freedom
thing

PHIL HOGAN

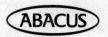

An *Abacus* Original

First published in Great Britain by Abacus in 2003

Copyright © 2003 by Phil Hogan

The moral right of the author has been asserted.

A CIP catalogue record for this book
is available from the British Library.

ISBN: 0 349 11556 7

Typeset in Erhardt by M Rules
Printed and bound in Great Britain
by Clays Ltd, St Ives plc

Abacus
An imprint of
Time Warner Books UK
Brettenham House
Lancaster Place
London WC2E 7EN

www.TimeWarnerBooks.co.uk

For Sue

'I've got no strings' – Pinocchio

b&s

Nick (dealing cards): I mean, it's not rocket surgery, is it? What it comes down to, right, is whether you've got what it takes to break loose and grab life by the horns.

Monty: What if your life doesn't have horns?

Jas (puffing on small cigar): What Nick means is, do you want to be master of your own destiny or lose your identity in the comfortable bosom of someone else's life?

Bart: Comfortable bosom sounds pretty good to me.

Nick: Yeah, right, but haven't you tried that once?

Bart (shrugs): I might want to try it again. Next time it might be different.

Jas: That's what everyone thinks. It's that kind of thinking you have to escape from.

Monty: Maybe some of us don't want to escape. Maybe some of us don't like it out here.

pause

Nick: Are we playing this game or what?

one

A beautiful white space. What did it mean? Well, of course, it could mean anything. That was the joy of it. It was only when you started filling it with rubbish that the possibilities started to diminish. One thing you learnt: when one thing led to another, it reduced your options of it leading anywhere else. You had to get it right. This was no time for rash gestures or incontinent splashes of colour but contemplation, a bit of thought. You had to treat a room like a blank canvas; the world before God got his hands on it; the full untriggered bomb, packed with the seeds of its own promise. A space like this had its life to look forward to, that's what Bart liked about it. That, and the size of it: two thousand and twenty square feet of unblemished possibility. Beautiful.

But it couldn't stay that way for ever. A man had to eat, watch TV, install a medicine cabinet, floss his teeth and so on. So there was a bathroom shell, a curve of brushed metal where a whole kitchen would one day materialise, a stereo in permanent use (Ry Cooder, he had discovered, was the perfect music to sleep to), a statesmanlike American fridge, a cat flap leading out to the communal court below so Bird could come and go, and poke about in the bins, and look for other smart pussies to have sex with. And in the end, Bart had just positioned the new futon slap bang square at neat parallels to everything, even though now when he awoke in the morning, light strafing in from all sides, he was never sure, especially in the absence of Natalie, which way he was facing. But then he would fumble for his little Muji alarm on the floor beside him (or, by process of elimination, at the other side) and his Armani specs, with which he could then locate at a distance his psychiatrist's couch (that is, not *his* psychiatrist's couch, as he had hastened to add, laughing rather too loudly, to Jas and the others at last month's beer & sausages - things hadn't got *that* bad; no, just a nice Italian job in orange leather and aluminium he'd picked up on Brompton Road in the sales. A pound short of three grand. A comfort purchase). So, although he was happy to take what spiritual solace he could from a room whose sense of provisional repose so exactly mirrored his own – in so far as it, too, looked like it was in no hurry to make up its mind about what it wanted from the rest of its life – there were times when the practicalities of not having blinds or furniture would intervene with their own insistent logic. Like, actually, some mornings you didn't want to wake up on the floor at dawn. One thing, for instance, he hadn't quite factored in – and on reflection this did suggest a lapse in his professional judgement that couldn't only be ascribed to emotional duress – was that dawn arrived at different times depending on the time of year. You couldn't set your clock by dawn. And, since today was the first Friday in May, things were bound to get worse before they got better; which wasn't helped by the second unfactored-in thing – namely, that in all likelihood, tomorrow would dawn on a hangover similar in weight and intensity to the one he'd woken up with on the morning after the first Friday in April. Not that waking up feeling bad was the chief purpose of beer & sausages, but you didn't need to be Arthur Koestler to see how this could turn out to be one of its more reliable side effects.

The point was, Bart was beginning to realise, one thing led to another at the smallest provocation, even if the one thing in question was nothing more than to put everything on pause. Interior design couldn't be expected to have all the answers. Something had to be done. The rest of your life could only wait for you to choose the right paint for so long.

He lay on the couch stroking Bird, *Astral Weeks* rolling through his mind without touching the sides, reluctant to stir, though he'd done no useful work since breaking at three to pop up here, and it was now pushing four-thirty and he had an appointment at five-thirty, which was when Suzanne's private sessions began. *Doctor* Suzanne. After that, a quick Victoria line down to the West End to see a film. And after that, back to Jas's in Smithfield for half-eightish. Nick would be there and Monty, unless he'd thrown himself under a bus. So that should be fun.

A breeze moving between the window and the door to his flat, still open behind him, cooled his cheek. And down below, in the street, against the warm outdoor hum of ordinary daytime, he heard a motorcycle pull up and the buzzer go in the office. A courier with something. Jim would get it. Or Christian. He paused the music with the remote, opened his eyes and angled his head to listen better. American accent faint up the echo of the twisting stairwell. Jim, god of efficiency in human form. Jim, discreetly admiring the leathered biker's arse in retreat. Bart closed his eyes again, unpaused the remote to let the waiting music back in the room.

Rooms were Bart's field, though with other people's rooms he didn't get paid to leave them beautiful, empty and white but to study their idiosyncrasies and to transform them in a way pleasing to the imagined imagination of the client and the client's other consultants and financial partners along with the functional requirements of health, safety and fire authorities and the fleeting aesthetic whim of the paying public. First thing today, this had meant motoring to the outskirts of Cambridge with Christian to look at a project to convert a crumbling flour mill into a characterful but smart waterside restaurant with moody subterranean bar and blonde East European waitresses paying their way through EFL school. 'What do you think?' the client – a Tristram, Bart's first – had said, touching his neat goatee, glancing anxiously round the ripped-out interior, the hillocks of builders' sand and cement, improvised tabletop scattered with teabags and spilt sugar and spoons, scaffolding up there, visible through the hole where the roof would be. 'New wallpaper for sure,' Bart had replied, telegraphing his joke with a reassuring grin. Because you could never be certain with clients where a joke might land. Tristram had nodded seriously, the arm of an unmanned digger up there like an erection above his shoulder, its piston unsheathed, the beaten jaw of its thick bucket catching the sun with a flat gleam. Christian, being reassuring in a Scandinavian way, had roamed earnestly, muttering into his digital voice-recorder with lapel-mike, grimacing, sketching elegantly, looking up, listening intently when the client Tristram spoke, running a measure down a wall or across a ragged lintel. Christian, a man of clear-eyed solid virtues, hewn of pale ash and strapped with honest leather and corduroy, a man whom Bart imagined rising at five to make a sled for daughters, little Cari and Astrid, both ice-blondes, that they might all hunt in the pine forests for wolves or bears or whatever. A craftsman/philosopher/miracle-worker like Christ himself, serene in the presence of English humour, blue woodsmoke twirling from the chimneys of his quiet mind. Tall and able. A proper grown-up, though five years younger than Bart. He was down there in the office now, probably thinking about the Cambridge job, while Bart was up here where he shouldn't be, musing, stroking, listening to Van Morrison. 'Just got to pop upstairs for a minute, feed the cat . . .'

He'd said that more for Jim's benefit, in case anybody rang, though it was a courtesy, too, to Christian, with whom Bart not only shared office and admin costs but now collaborated on jobs where Bart needed an architect or Christian needed a designer. Good man, Christian, as well he might be. And of course you couldn't keep a good man down. Which was why there was talk of Christian being offered an associateship (or whatever it was that Americans offered) with one of the big Manhattan firms. Mortensens. Fantastic, Bart had said, immediately thinking the opposite even as he swivelled his chair and pumped Christian's hand and said this called for a drink, which it didn't. That would be a bit careless, Jas said later, to lose two partners in twelve months, meaning Natalie. Self-pity wasn't encouraged at beer & sausages, where house therapy was confined to raising matey toasts to long and happy divorces. To liberty. To sexual emancipation.

Natalie. Bart swung himself off the couch, popped a multivitamin from a jar on the counter, took a carton of orange juice from the fridge and stood by the open window taking gulps from it. Bird followed, stepping out on to the balcony, stretching his long, lithe form in the sun, yawning, licking his paws, settling himself on the sunwarmed concrete. Born to idle. Bart stooped to brush the velvet of Bird's fur with the back of his fingers. 'Lovely kitty,' he murmured into the abrupt quiet, as the music stopped.

The trouble with a white room was what it stood for. Sometimes it just stood for Natalie. Or rather it stood for what she had thought they both still wanted. An ordered life, clean lines, no clutter, no children, no pets, nothing to impinge on clarity. Room to think. Of course they'd had all that, more or less, at the maisonette in Finsbury Park but you could only go so far. It would always look like a Victorian terrace from the front. Here they would start, they said, from first principles and do it properly. Natalie had loved the new place, pulling Bart excitedly from one end to the other, pictures flooding into her mind of how it might be, the two of them spilling on to the bare floor like newlyweds. 'Space, light, smoothness, depth, continuity,' she'd said afterwards, in between mouthfuls of spicy noodles – it was their first (and last) time together in the Bangkok Palace across the road. (Bart was now practically their best customer. Often, especially at weekends, their only customer.) 'That's the important thing. We don't need the history of it. It detracts too much.' They had deliberately not looked for somewhere with exposed girders and gantries and industrial hooks embedded in the walls. They wanted somewhere that was up to the job of encapsulating the present. This was really Natalie's thing. When they'd first shared a house in Canterbury, as students, he'd been amazed at how little she possessed in the way of, well . . . *possessions*. No memorabilia, no keepsakes, no favourite toys, no yellowed letters or birthday cards or stuff girls usually hung on to. She didn't even have any old records. 'I can't get sentimental about things,' she said. 'If I don't use it, it's out. I don't want to reflect on what was.' Big smile. Her big smile was fixed with certainty, and in time Bart came to share her certainties in the same way they shared everything else. He had no strong opinions of his own to bandy with, but Natalie had enough for them both and anyone else who happened to swing into earshot. She was the engine; he was the wheels. The perfect couple.

He selected another album – the Smiths – and put it on autoplay. He owned old records, but the Natalie in him had made him whittle them down to those he still wanted to hear. What he didn't have was books, which was a growing nuisance. Their mini-library of reference works and specialist periodicals – art, design, architecture, aesthetics, cultural stuff, photography – was still shelved in the study, back with Natalie in Finsbury Park. Any fiction they'd bought – his James Ellroys and Carl Hiaasens, Natalie's zeitgeisty reading-group choice – came and went like yesterday's newspapers. 'Books aren't supposed to be decorative,' she would argue. 'I mean, you wouldn't put your old cereal packets on the wall.'

You might, of course. And books could be decorative. They were decorative for other people. This was all too random a notion for Natalie, and it was hardly worth arguing about. He didn't care either way. And maybe she was right. How many people read a novel more than once? Why did people hang on to them? Intellectual vanity? Nostalgia? Nostalgia was a sort of sickness. It came from the Greek, she said, meaning 'pain'. With Natalie, everything she came up with was an article of faith and there was no point arguing against someone's faith unless you had one of your own that you cared about more. And when you lived the faith, everything became a holy war. No boundaries, no prisoners. It would never have occurred to Natalie to defer to Bart's expertise on interior design matters just because he happened to be an interior designer. 'Listen to this,' she'd said once, stretched out on the floor working her way through the weekend papers. 'Ford Jackson. He's a top chef, right, with two Michelin stars and never cooks at home.' She rolled over and looked up. 'I mean *ever*. Not so much as a boiled egg.' She looked back at the paper. 'He lets his wife do all the cooking. Don't you think that's weird?'

Bart smiled. 'Do *you* think it's weird?'

There was no point waiting for her to dwell on an irony, not being an habitual user of irony herself, irony being the tool of people who were happier saying the opposite of what they meant in the hope of being thought informed rather than committed to something. And if he himself fell into that category it was another irony lost on her.

All the same, it was Bart who had discovered their two thousand and twenty square feet of perfection. He who had seen the loft boom coming and got in at the bottom, plundering all his early ideas from raids on New York in the early nineties, made some money and a name for himself among the developers while Natalie was busy building up her graphics firm and being cutting edge in a more aesthetic, less obviously money-grubbing way. So understandably it was ages before they finally got round to looking for a place for themselves and when they did this was what they found: half of the second floor of a former hospital on the fringes of upcoming Clerkenwell. No girders, no industrial artefacts. Bart had landed the design contract, and as part of the deal had put his name on a piece of the project at little more than cost, plus first option on rented office space on the ground floor. Two years later the builders were out. By which time, of course, everything between them had changed. Now there was just Monty to help him slap on the Dulux white, a bottle of Tiger beer on the floor beside him, painting over his own woes.

It was obvious now, when Bart thought about it, that it wasn't just the past that he and Natalie had been standing against, shoulder to shoulder, hand in hand; it was the future too. Modern had only one moment and that was the now. Natalie was very now, so he'd been very now too. Long-term planning, they agreed, drained life from the now. They saw it all around them – friends who had had a kid, then two, moved out to the commuter belt to find decent schools, grow their own vegetables, allow their sensibilities to turn to jelly. They wouldn't make *that* mistake. That much they had set in stone; signed and sealed with their heedless laughter. The trouble was, the more the *now* progressed – the more it speeded up – the scarier not having a future seemed. And it was this thought that was the hardest to share. It was this thought that had soured things between them until everything they had turned bad. He could see how he'd let her down. Though she'd let him down too. And although, actually, disappointment was the worst it ever came to, it was enough to tip the scales the wrong way.

Bart had gone ahead and moved in alone, but not until he'd spent six months submerged in his own dark unmeetable longings at Aunt Marian's in Cockfosters. He bought the couch, the TV, the fridge, put in the hours with Christian, a stable influence, waited to be inspired by some as yet latent but real desire that would pull him forward again, tried to keep at bay the reveries that slipped under his defences of him and Natalie having frantic sex in their squeaky leather armchair, or, more often now, Natalie and someone else having frantic sex in someone else's squeaky leather armchair. It was in these moments of panic that the white room – his ward – became a symbol of sterility, scrubbed of its past, just as Natalie had wanted it. It became associated in his mind with morbidity, oxygen tents, life running out.

But then he'd stopped to chat to one of the cleaners on his way back up from the patisserie one morning. A tiny, ancient Spanish woman, Maria. 'I *khaff* my three sons right *heeere*,' she said pointing at the floor, grinning. After ten minutes of polite, ear-straining conversation he realised what she was talking about: this had been the maternity wing, a lying-in place, a labour ward, antenatal, postnatal clinics, midwifery, obstetrics, paediatrics – a whole child factory. He almost laughed out loud at the spookiness of it. Then one night he'd half woken to the sound of a baby crying. He thought it was a dream, but the echo of it stayed with him till morning. Not life running out, but just arriving. An augury. Potential.

Five to five. He grabbed his dark linen jacket, turned the Smiths down a couple of points and went out. Twenty seconds later he came back in, spooned food into the cat's bowl. *Miaow*, Bird said.

● ● ●

Fuck. Nick took an involuntary step back, banister post against his shoulderblade. Tried a smile. 'Olivia . . .'

'I mean it, Nick. Key. Now.' Her hand outstretched, waiting.

'Look, I'm sorry, I thought you'd be out.'

'Yeah, and that makes it OK, right? Key. Now.' Her hand. Bare, familiar, even without the wedding band.

He sighed, fumbled with his BMW keyring, detached the key.

'I just needed my suits.'

'Excellent, now you've got them. Off you go.'

'How are the kids?' His eyes twitchy with nerves.

'They're fine. Why wouldn't they be? They hardly know who you are.' Cold grimace disfiguring her looks. Hair tied back. Sunglasses on her head. Standing to one side, the door open behind her, inviting his exit, her green Polo in the street across the road from the house, parked on the kerb, slight dent front nearside. Five months since he'd moved out. Not ideal, in the run-up to Christmas. Weakness of the flesh, spirit, drinks parties and everything else. Briony. Whom he never saw again, not intimately. Who didn't want to get involved. Nice name, Briony, from Forward Planning. Olivia hadn't wasted her time asking about the whos and whys of his protracted absences, didn't need to. More or less kicked him out, so not his fault really. He'd left the suits behind. Still there, snuggling up to her grey coat in the wardrobe, polythene-wrapped as if expecting him back any moment. Paul Smith, both dark, one a soft wool mix, one sharp with a butcher's stripe. Too nice for her to burn.

'Come on, Livvy, that's a bit unfair . . .'

'Bye.'

'Look, I'll be at Jas's.'

'Of course you will.'

He left her standing in the hall, arms folded against him, as he hurried out to his prize Beemer, draped the suits over the back seat and drove. Forty minutes later, still crawling along the Embankment, sweating, swearing. Fuck of an idea to try and get over to Fulham and back at lunchtime. Stupid impulse. Bastard Hugo. *You might try wearing a suit.*

Copywriters don't wear suits.

'Think of it as an experiment,' he'd said. 'Half a dozen graduates or, you know, graduate calibre. Helps put some

13

distance between you and them. You're the expert. It's just psychology. You've got to take this seriously, Nick, I'm not kidding.'

'Seriously? Teaching kids how to write radio recruitment ads? Am I missing something?'

Hugo, palms face up, playing the reasonable cunt, fret lines across his head saying otherwise. 'It's an enabling role. Tutorial. Showing where ideas come from. You know what to do. What does it say over the door? *Communications*. That's us, remember. It's what we do. Why not try and see it as a challenge?'

'What, as opposed to constructive dismissal?'

'Nick, Nick, humour me, all right?'

Pause. Blood starting to thump, hands shaking, nerves hammering. *Don't say it, just don't.* 'Jesus Christ, what is this, I'm the best fucking copywriter this agency has had since fucking . . .'

Hugo, pissed off now, across his big architect-built desk. 'Actually, Nick, you're fucking not. And anyway this isn't about that, and you know it. For Christ's sake, take it easy. Do yourself a favour.' Samaritan now. Talking him down.

'Meaning?'

Meaningful pause. 'Meaning, Nick, take what's on the table and try to clean up your act.'

Nick sighed, defeated. Beyond Hugo's twin reddening ears entire fucking department rubbernecking, pretending to chew pencils, look thoughtful. Long, silent walk back to his desk.

Nick left the suits in the car in the car park and vaulted up the steps, past moustached Dave on security, lift to third-floor reception, sweating. Three o'clock. Switched on his winning smile for Anita. Nice condition for the year. 'Hugo back yet?'

'Haven't seen him. Shall I say you're looking for him?' Cheeky grin.

Grin returned, even cheekier. 'Don't you dare.'

He spent the afternoon looking busy. Chickenshit campaign for a dating agency. Tube ads for God's sake. Key word: UNATTACHED? Series of pix showing young people who have become humorously 'unattached'. One: skydiver losing his parachute. Two: swimmer losing his Speedos. Three: rider going over jump without horse. Perfect. Time taken: thirty seconds. Bill them for a week. Crime to be doing this for a living, he thought. Five-thirty. Time for an early evening tootie-rootie. Patting his back pocket en route to the toilets. One and a half wraps left. In and out of No. 2 trap, sniffing robustly, washing hands. Fat presence swinging in behind him.

Des. Shit.

'Need anything, Nick?'

'Fuck's sake, Des, don't creep up on me like that,' he said, not turning round, just plunging his hands back under the tap as if washing for Britain, knowing what the real question was.

Des pausing. 'Wondered if you'd got the, um . . .'

Awkward for Des, being a minion, having to ask. Felt bad for a mo. Made a show of splashing water on his face. Looked at himself, as advised by Hugo. Beaky. Drawn. Haircut required. *Do yourself a favour*. Sniff. Start tomorrow. Jesus, how are the fucking mighty. He yanked on the towel roller like a man in a hurry to do something more life-enhancing than exchange credit-related pleasantries with tradesmen. 'Sorry, mate, didn't manage to get to the bank.'

Coke coming on-stream now. Fuck Hugo. Nerveless Nick. A year ago he was the agency's performing dog. No job too big. No marketing high-ups too hostile. Class-A bollocks talked while-u-w8. Send 4 Nick. Their busiest and best boy by a long mile. Blue-chip clients, good share of the telly work, high-end poster roll-outs, automatic invite to all the awards parties, unquestioned exes, champagne, nice drugs. Complete round of duty. Credit to the uniform, which was, strictly: designer togs for creatives, suits for everybody else. He had nothing *per se* against suits, which he might happily wear for civilian functions – wedding, smart eating, remortgaging the house – but, please, not at work. Not here in this agency, where a suit meant you *were* a suit. Point being that's what this suit shit was about. Public humiliation.

'S'OK, I've got time – I'll come with you now,' Des said.

'What?'

'Sorry, Nick, got to push you on this one.'

Des's double-chinned face. Piggy eyes. Desperate and embarrassed at the same time. Obviously didn't want to insist but had to. He probably had this pay-up malarkey with half the agency. Probably did too much of the stuff himself. Probably up to his eyes in it at the thug end of things. Be a shame to have Des lose his fingers, or whatever it was they did to you. Smile, Nick.

'No probs, old chum. How much was it again?'

'Two twenty.'

Fuck's sake. 'Cool. I'll just nip down to the cashpoint. Wait here. Well, obviously not here. You wouldn't want to get yourself a reputation,' he chuckled. Des, chuckling too, starting to follow him, head shining from the glare of hard surfaces.

'God's sake, Des, wait *here*. I'm not gonna leave town, am I?'

Des flummoxed now, alarm bells in both eyes, like someone who's got to the front of the queue and now can't find his ticket.

'I'll be back in five. Fuck's sake relax.'

Nick scooted down to the first floor, picked a card from his wallet, stuck it into the machine, went through the motions of waiting for it to tell him how much money he didn't have till the twenty-eighth. Credit cards just about hoicked up to the gills. Damn. He looked round. Fuck it. Sorry, Des. He slammed downstairs to the ground floor, trainers slapping the steps, echoing, mind permutating risks of an early departure vis-à-vis Hugo. Fuck him. Dave on security flagging him down, wary. Dave it was who had twice stumbled upon him in the office, in the early hours, once snoring on the floor, once (slightly more delicate) shagging a girl he'd met at the Mirrorball. Dave, moustached, silent disapproving type you could never find the key to with a joke. 'Gentleman came in five minutes ago, left these for you,' he was saying. Nick's eyes registering. Ominous brown envelope, Beemer reg scrawled kiddilike on the front in blue felt-tip. Suits, polythene-wrapped, butcher stripe showing through, Dave still talking in his lugubrious TV police-inspector way, explaining what the gentleman had said, though Nick was already ahead of him, sprinting for the doors, racing round the back of the building, heart pounding, to where the car had been. And now, of course, wasn't.

● ● ●

Willkommen, as they used to say in Berlin, and indeed any-where else the humble bratwurst might be teamed with a foaming stein of Hofmeister or whatever. *Prost!* Beer & sausages. b&s. Jas always found himself looking forward to it, though the novelty should have worn off by now. Maybe it was the slow rotation of personnel that made it still feel like an unexpected pleasure. Or perhaps he was still impressed by the number of relationships to be found gently crumbling apart in the same social currents during any given period.

It had started as a kind of a black joke, with Roger, who'd been recently separated, and he had introduced Jools, who had invited Pete the next time they'd met, and he had brought along Nick, who by coincidence Jas already knew from art college years ago. And that was how it came about. Friends, and friends of friends, who washed in and out with tales of woe from their respective conjugal theatres of war, egos in splints, eyes still gazing into the burning wrecks of relationships that had once seemed so full of passion and optimism. Of course, one by one they had moved on (except Nick, who had moved in), like cured patients, shriven souls, purged of their rancour and self-pity (this was the idea, as Jas saw it), redeemed, born anew in the heat of this big steaming kitchen, with its aroma of seared meat, its clash and clangour of joy and misery amid the companionable glug of strong beverage and drift of smoke, overlooked by a Victorian print of a mustachioed swashbuckling pirate Jas had picked up at an auction, mainly for the accompanying legend, handwritten in black ink, from Byron's 'Corsair':

> *O'er the glad waters of the deep blue sea,*
> *Our thoughts as boundless and our hearts as free*

The pirate, laughing heartily, was standing on a wooden dock, his sunlit ship looming in the background, his white shirt slashed to the waist, an ample-bosomed wench on each arm. It made Jas smile. He liked the idea of it. Uncomplicated. Fellow rovers. Salts of the earth.

Old boys were always welcome back to b&s. First Friday of the month. Open house. They tended not to come, though. Jas's rousing song of singleness was less compelling out there in the desperate pursuit and retention of long-term girlfriends

18

than here in the comfy, dark den of kindred, convalescent wife-sufferers. It seemed most men were either romantics, cowards or just pragmatists, preferring to try their luck a second or third time on the treadmill of monogamy rather than face the uncertain returns of new bachelordom in their late thirties. But that was cool. There were always enough for a quorum. Four to six was the optimum spread of bodies. Fewer than that looked a bit sad; any more and they looked like extremists.

Because it was like a group, Nick had to call it something. Slaughterhouse Four, he suggested, because of Smithfield right outside, and butchers all over the place. But, as Jas pointed out, sometimes it might be five or six, so that was no good. And anyway it wasn't the group that necessarily stayed the same but the event – in so far as you could call it an event. It was more like a chatroom – the non-virtual kind, obviously – or a male version of the sort of thing women got up to when they set up a reading circle only to spend the whole evening getting drunk and telling each other how crap their boyfriends and husbands were. 'OK, how about the Men's Room, then? No, I know – how about Swordsmen of the Aporkalypse!' Nick whooping, delighted at himself.

The others had groaned and rolled their eyes in a way they mightn't have if Ivy hadn't been there marauding that evening, busying herself behind the stainless-steel counter. She elbowed the fridge door shut, walked through carrying a wilting carpet-tile of pizza and a bottle of Becks. 'How about Shites of the Round Table?' she said. Everybody laughed, nervously, as if she might have a point, glancing at Jas for his reaction. It was difficult with someone's daughter.

'Ivy, have some proper food,' he said. 'Come and join us.'

'Dad, I'm a vegetarian? Anyway, I thought you had to be, like, embittered and divorced to join in. And a bloke.'

He smiled. Poison Ivy. She must have got that from her mother's side.

Anyway, they'd decided a name was a bit unhip. A bit unspontaneous. On the other hand, they'd had to call it *something* – i.e. something that differentiated this occasion from others where they might just go for a pint or a curry. So beer & sausages had somehow happily invented itself, sounding both banal and amusingly phallic in a knowing, self-effacing way that suited the times, as Nick had said, in a suspiciously rehearsed way. The best thing, of course, the amusingest thing, was that no one ever brought beer and Jas had only actually done sausages once. But beer & sausages it was. Say it with an ampersand in the middle, Nick said, drawing one in the air with his finger. b&s for short.

Humming a snatch of Led Zep he'd heard on Capital and now couldn't get out of his head, Jas turned off the gas, forked sizzling T-bones off the grill and slid them on to the waiting hot plates heaped with deep-double-bronzed chips, melting butter-fried onions and best brown mushrooms. '*Voila!*' he said, casting his tea towel down dramatically and bowing to the resulting smatter of indulgent applause, Nick, fag in his mouth, squinting against the smoke, Bart smiling wryly, halting in the middle of his account of some Scandinavian comedy he'd seen on his own earlier, doleful Monty doing his best to enter into the spirit, banging on the table with his left hand, right arm bandaged up and in a sling, the result of falling off a ladder at the shop. Monty: what a case. One minute responding to the treatment, and then suddenly going downhill. Glutton for punishing himself.

Still on his feet, Jas gulped down half a glass of Rioja. 'Hang on – music,' he said. He pushed through his salvage-yard waiters' swing doors into the room beyond, his live-in studio, disarrayed with books, portfolios, cuttings files, blow-ups of his best eighties war pictures covering the walls, big comfy sofas, widescreen TV. He flicked though a rack of vinyl albums and picked out a Tom Waits. He could hear Nick barking away back there. He put the record on at a low growl and joined the others.

'Pardon my ignorance of point-of-sale marketing . . .' Nick was saying, as though anyone present knew or cared more about point-of-sale or any other kind of marketing than Nick, 'but what's the sense in having books up so high your customers can't reach them? And what is someone six foot five doing up a ladder anyway?' He stubbed out his cigarette with a hard twist, grinning at the others, fringe flopping forward.

'Well,' Monty said slowly, trying to saw through his T-bone with one hand, sending chips skittering across the table, 'it's a long and uninteresting story.'

'Why don't you let me help you with that?' Bart said.

'These steaks were running about in a field this morning,' Jas said, topping up glasses with wine. 'A toast . . . Nick, your turn, I think.'

'Right,' Nick said, standing up, thinking. 'Here's to unat-tachment.'

'I'll drink to that,' said Jas, sitting down in the big carver's chair.

Jas had been drinking to unattachment for twenty years. Unattachment in the broad sense, which meant only attach-ing himself on an ad hoc, short-term basis, like strapping yourself into a car, he said, knowing that you were going to get out again after a mystery tour of unspecified duration. At the moment, he was strapped in with Stella, the weather was fine, the road was clear, and the rest of the metaphor was self-explanatory – eventually they would run out of petrol in the middle of nowhere, or jump the central crash barrier while engaged in lewd practices. Or perhaps one day he'd have to leap out on impulse to help another hopeless female change a tyre and afterwards, through no fault of his own, find himself strapped into the wrong car. It could happen. The bottom line was, if necessary, he could get out at the next traffic light, leave the door open and the engine running, carry on walking and never look back.

'I did a tube ad today for a dating agency,' Nick was saying.

'Tube? I thought you were on commercials now?'

'Yeah, that's right, I've been seconded to a sort of guru role. Hugo's idea. It's kind of a promotion. Well, you know, leading to it. Management side, creative.'

'Does that mean you'll be moving out of my spare room?' Jas said.

Nick ignored him. 'Anyway, so I take *unattached* as my word, see . . .'

The twenty years was how long Jas had been unattached from Ivy's mother. Or Barbara, as he used to call her. He'd had precisely one proper conversation with her in the past eight years and that had been two years ago, an awkward lunch at Chez Victoire round the corner. She'd looked drawn, fatigued, a proper, stern grown-up wearing an olive mac and a touch of make-up, which did little but accentuate the fact that she probably didn't normally wear any. It seemed odd that from the same starting point they should both arrive here. It was as though, he thought, she had drifted effortlessly into middle life, while he had effortlessly avoided it. Sitting there, looking exactly like you'd expect some-body's mum to look, she made him uncomfortably self-conscious about his still unruly mane of hardly greying hair, buggered leather jacket, his ageless metro-boho world view, his rambling converted office slum overlooking the meat market wisely acquired for next to nothing during the property doldrums of 1990 – uncomfortable about his studiously not looking like somebody's dad. He tried not to think about the girl he had barely known long before that and got pregnant and married – back when he was James not Jas, and was trying to do the right thing. And now here she was, Ivy's mother, sitting here with anxious questions to ask about student life in London, which he knew something about, with his informal ties with colleges here and elsewhere – the odd guest seminar or open lecture, lucrative ad work, photojournalism. Understandably she wanted to see where he lived; she wanted to know what Ivy was getting herself into. What the catch was. When she drank her coffee, she held the saucer as well as the cup. Her hand trembled a little.

'No catch,' he said. 'She's my daughter, isn't she?'

The deal was a rent-free living and working space on the floor below that used to be one of his two spacious studios. 'She can come and go as she pleases,' he says. 'My door's always open if she has any problems.'

'Please don't tell her I've been here,' Ivy's mother had said, getting up to leave. 'She's very independent.'

'Just like her dad,' he beamed, to her obvious annoyance.

And, actually, it had worked out well, he thought. Ivy came and went – mostly to and from his fridge, but she sometimes liked to loiter if he had people round, making acerbic, studenty comments, pointing her Polaroid at people, or circling with her video camera, eyebrow pierced, magenta hair tied in rags, flaunting her unfashionably bra-less independence. She disappeared off somewhere every weekend, no questions asked. Of course she wasn't very happy about the Stella thing, but that was something she'd have to be more grown-up about. You could hardly give your daughter power of veto over whom you slept with. Even if who you were sleeping with happened to be your daughter's tutor. Which, Jas was forced to admit, was not exactly brilliant family politics.

'I'll match your two quid and raise you two of the same,' Nick was saying, a cigar jammed into the side of his mouth. It was ten-thirty. Jas smiled and folded his cards. The poker part of beer & sausages had been Nick's idea. Hardly anyone else had the faintest clue how to play, but Nick had been adamant. 'If you're going to do this properly, you've got to have poker,' he'd said. 'And cigars.' Naturally poker appealed to Jas's sense of what postmodern man should have in his social armoury. The poker thing always materialised among British press photographers hooked up together in foreign parts – the Balkans, Chechnya – along with the office flak jacket, three-day beard and squashed pack of Gitanes, so he knew what Nick was talking about. But you weren't supposed to take it seriously. Nick took it slightly too seriously. You could tell he loved nothing more than slapping down a fiver he'd just borrowed off you and demanding now to *see* you or announcing his intention to *raise* you, his splayed fingertips just touching the table, his face wearing a permanent half-smile borrowed from old Westerns. Nick would always spend the poker phase of the evening amassing a heap of everyone else's money, only occasionally chipping into the conversation as the rest of them pieced together from memory the byzantine plot of *L.A. Confidential* – book, not the film – or moaned about Arsenal's current drawing streak or made clucking noises with regard to Monty's ex, who had by all accounts abandoned him so cruelly after fifteen months. Once in control of everyone's finances, he would relax and offer the ten best ways to meet a woman on the internet or explain to Monty why he was better off *out* of it, mate, adding, his arm round him now, 'No offence, old chum, but she does sound a bit of a nightmare.'

And the thing about the current b&s configuration was that they *were* all old chums, reunited through adversity. Or at least old fellow students, which was near enough. As Nick told it, he had ducked into a cool, designery bookshop to shelter from a downpour on his way to meet some woman at the Eagle, and there was old Monty standing behind the counter, even taller than he remembered him and that was pretty much giraffe-tall. They swapped numbers, and when they'd eventually met a couple of weeks later for a pint, Monty had brought Bart along and the rest was history, with a side order of hand-wringing.

'Women can be so difficult . . .' Nick was saying.

'Except that Catherine wasn't difficult. She was perfect,' Monty said. 'And, actually, it was my fault.'

'Monty. Mate. Trust me. It wasn't your fault. Bart, fucksake, have you played this game before or what?'

Bart surrendered his cards with a yawn.

'Ha!' cried Nick, slapping the table, triumph glittering in his eyes. 'Saw you coming.' He raked in the pot, started dealing again, in his element, cards and girls. 'I mean, going back to old Bart's problem here. What difference does it make what a woman talks like? Shag's a shag, surely? You don't have to have a bloody conversation about it.'

'I wasn't saying you had to have a conversation, I'm saying that part of what makes a woman attractive is whether she's capable of having one. A conversation, I mean.'

Jas topped everybody up. 'I could drink to that,' he said.

'Well, yeah, I mean obviously, I agree you wouldn't want a complete mental blimp,' Nick said. He stubbed out his cigar and lit a cigarette in the candle flame, his face angled side-ways, yellowed and lean.

'I saw her yesterday,' Monty said. 'She didn't see me, of course.'

The three of them looked at him. 'Oh, right – the ex,' Nick said. 'I know what you mean. One of the weirdest things to get used to when you split up is, like, suddenly not being able to touch someone who you've always been able to touch whenever you wanted. I just had that feeling today, seeing Olivia, first time in months. It just struck me that I'd never be able to, you know . . .'

'Have sex with her again?' Jas said.

'Well, yeah, but not just that. Just touch, I mean.' He coughed.

'This "just touching" doesn't sound like you, Nick.'

'No, what I mean is, it's like suddenly someone doesn't belong to you any more, so you're not *allowed* to touch.'

'And that's weird?' asked Bart, breathing on his glasses.

'It is when it happens. It's like a permanent version of your missus being pissed off with you for, you know, leaving her with no petrol in the car or . . .'

'Or not coming home for two days?'

'Or, or . . . you know, after a big row. Only this time you haven't had a big row. Well, not recently.'

'Me and Natalie didn't really do rows,' Bart said. 'We did hold talks occasionally, followed by ten-point plans. She wouldn't have allowed a row in the house. Rows were a form of untidiness. She was very organised like that. I think that's why it took us so long to split up. We kept thinking we agreed with each other.'

Nick looked impatient. 'Yeah, well, with your more normal *rowing* couple, that's what happens. But seeing Olivia today . . .' He stopped.

26

Monty was starting to do his staring thing, eyes welling up, drink taking over, Prozac not doing the job, about to go off, head bent forward, hand going up to cover his face. Jas shot Bart a glance. Bart gave Monty's uninjured arm a tentative pat. 'Come on, Mont. Hey, I was thinking – why don't I try and get some tickets for the Chelsea match? Last game of the season . . .'

'Can you do that?' said Nick, taking a sudden interest.

'You know me, friends in low places,' said Bart. 'Monty?'

Monty blew his nose on his paper napkin and groaned loudly at the spectacle of himself. 'Sorry, you must think I'm a complete twat . . .'

'Hey, don't worry,' said Jas. 'That's what friends are for.'

Monty snorted out a laugh, Jas too, realising what he'd said. Bart smiling grimly, Nick holding the pack of cards, waiting for normal service to be resumed as soon as.

'More wine,' Jas murmured, administering refills, though he could see nobody needed one. Everyone declined another cigar.

Monty inhaled, exhaled, cheeks puffed out, his teary eyes glittery in the candlelight. 'Sorry, chaps, wrong time of the month . . .'

The door banged and Ivy sloped in, video equipment slung round her shoulders. She took a beer out of the fridge, swung the door shut with her elbow. Monty clammed up and blinked at his cards.

'Ask for one,' Nick said.

'Ivy, do me a favour, babe – load the dishwasher, would you, there's a darling,' said Jas over his shoulder.

'Bloody slave,' Ivy said, clattering plates and knives into the machine.

'Are we still playing or what?' Nick said. Monty sniffed.

Ivy lit a cigarette, came round the kitchen counter, camera rolling, smoke trailing. 'Smile everyone,' she said.

two

A beautiful blue sky. What did it mean? Bart, specs perched on top of his head, lips pursed in contemplation, was thinking about temperature control, ventilation and lighting. Cost implications thereof. He was thinking of a bright, twenty-cover mezzanine brunch room open to the azure heavens (assuming LA-style weather, rather than East Anglia, for the purposes of this projection), an open-tread metal staircase with high rails, aircraft-style maybe, though obviously without the wheels . . . ground floor encompassing lively dining space, exposed kitchen with atmospheric steam and sizzling and clattering pans, access to basement chillout

29

area occupying the footprint of the building. Emergency exits here, here and here, blonde East European waitresses from the EFL schools weaving up and down here and here, struggling with heaps of dishes, struggling with English as a culinary language. Envisioning a scene with detail, he thought, was crucial. He put his glasses back on.

A developing plan came and went on the wide screen of Bart's Mac, flipping into 3-D at the click of his mouse while he sat swivelling, doodling, thinking, adding measurements from a doodle pad. Trying things out. Thinking about temperature control, ventilation and lighting, but also about what Suzanne had said on Friday. Or rather what she hadn't said. What Suzanne hadn't said about Natalie. He breathed on the lenses of his glasses and polished them on his shirt. It was hard to think of a restaurant in winter when it was blistering outside.

Jim came in with afternoon iced tea. 'Home-made,' he trilled, looking at the image on the screen. 'That the Cambridge job?'

'It will be, one day.' Bart took the glass from him. 'I need some reference drawings. You know those metal stairs for aeroplanes? You know, the ones they wheel about?'

'Sure. I'll make enquiries,' Jim said, turning smartly, camp secretarial manner. 'By the way, the girl from Montgomery's called to say your books have arrived.'

'Ah.' Bart looked at his watch. 'Actually, maybe I'll call it a day, take a stroll down there now.' He downed his iced tea, swapped his glasses for dark ones and went out, crossed to the sunny side of the street.

Thinking.

Thinking about what Suzanne *had* said.

*

'So,' Suzanne had said, 'are you seeing someone?'

'Well, no. Not at the moment. I mean I *have*, obviously. Quite a few actually. Well, one or two. But not, you know. Serious.'

'I see.'

Doctor Suzanne: clipped, professionally stethoscoped, glancing at his records on screen, pale lipstick. Doctor Suzanne. Not the plain old Suzanne who had lived opposite the flat in Finsbury Park with husband Pete and dog and fifteen-year-old twins Ed and Polly; not the plain old Suzanne whom they'd met at a party shortly after moving in, discovering what she did for a living only when Bart hobbled into the local surgery a week later with a suspected broken toe and looked at her with amazement. 'Suzanne?'

'*Doctor* Suzanne to you,' she'd said.

'Bloody hell. You're a doctor?'

'I'm in big trouble if I'm not.'

He'd got used to the idea, but then up to this point he'd kept his ailments well to the uninteresting side of intimate.

'So what makes you think you need a sperm count?' she was saying, angling her head in a puzzled way.

'Well, because it occurred to me that . . .' He gave a small cough. 'Well, you know Nat and I were trying for a while before we split up. For a baby, I mean. Obviously. Anyway we tried for about six months. So, you know. I just wondered whether I might be, you know. Firing blanks.'

'Oh . . .' She looked at him over her glasses, as if something still wasn't adding up; thinking quickly to *make* it add up, but still failing, drumming her fingers on the desk.

'What?' Bart puzzled back at her over his glasses.

'Sorry, mental block.'

She smiled too brightly. What was it?

'Well, yes,' she said, 'I suppose you *could* have a sperm count if it makes you happy. And you don't mind spending your hard-earned cash.' She pulled something up on-screen and tapped at her keyboard.

'I don't mind,' he said. This was Suzanne's idea of persuading her better-off patients to come after hours with their imagined luxury ailments and pay for treatment, with all the profits going into extra services for those who were really sick and had no money. This was Suzanne being a brilliant doctor in a way that made everybody on the street look like heartless sharks if they didn't go along with it. Which they did. She printed a letter out, enveloped it and handed Bart a plastic bottle. 'Fill her up. Usual method, or any other you can think of. Take it to the clinic and we'll get to hear in a week or so. But I really wouldn't worry. There's absolutely no reason to suppose it's a sperm problem. You're probably teeming with the little buggers.'

'Thanks.'

He hovered.

'So,' she said. 'How are things? I'm sorry the two of you split up.'

'Yeah, well, you know.' He paused. 'Suzanne.'

'Bart?'

'What you were going to say. Just now, I mean.'

'When?'

'Just now.'

'Oh, you know, nothing. Perhaps I just had the idea that you and Natalie had decided not to have kids. I seem to remember you were dead against it. I seem to remember you thinking about them as luggage. Or baggage, was it?'

'Clutter, I think we might have said. That's what we used to think. Well, Natalie did. But we had a change of heart. We decided to give it a go. Well, it was more me really. I wanted to give it a go. Obviously we didn't want to broadcast it. Well, Natalie didn't want to broadcast it.'

'Right.'

'And then she got cold feet. And then . . .' He shrugged.

'Ah.' Suzanne pressed her lips together, took her glasses off and rubbed her eyes.

Bart inhaled, took off his own specs in what he realised what an empathetic response to her discomfort. He put them back on. 'Was it because she suddenly went on the pill? If it is, I did actually know about that. But that was just at the end. We'd been having sex for ages before that without contraception. Was that it? Had she asked to go on the pill? Is that what you were thinking? Just now?'

'Bart, I'm not really supposed to have this kind of conversation. About another patient, I mean.'

'Can't you just kind of . . . nod?'

'*Bart.*'

'OK. Sorry. I don't want to have you excommunicated or whatever. I just wondered, that's all.'

Suzanne gave him a smile. 'Give us a ring some time. Come up for lunch one Sunday.'

Bart crossed the road, past the little Budgens supermarket and into Exmouth Market. He stopped to look at chairs in a designer shop. It seemed an act of sheer provocation the way Natalie had suddenly gone on the pill – not, he noted, back to her cap-and-spermicide ensemble, which she'd been quite happy with before all this – but the *pill*, which along with everyone else her age she'd given up years before, for the usual reasons of not wanting to get a coronary thrombosis and die in her twenties. It was now as if, somehow, anything less than fully armoured, lead-lined protection against having a child with Bart wasn't enough. That was how badly she didn't want one. Being prepared to flee their impending new life together in a much-longed-for white, pristine loft apartment was how badly she didn't want one.

'I just can't do this,' she'd said.

'What can't you do?'

'Any of it. It's such a mess. I'm sorry, Bart. It's got to end.' She left it hanging there, wanting him to fill in the blanks.

'What – you want us to split?'

That's what she wanted. It occurred to him that maybe that's what she'd wanted all along. He wondered whether trying to convince Natalie that having a baby might not be such a terrible idea after all had provided her with the perfect exit in the absence of a more compelling reason – say, him getting fat and unhygienic or even her arriving home one day unexpectedly to find him in bed with someone of that description. But the idea that Natalie was looking for an easy exit suggested an unhappiness and restlessness prior to his ominous talk of babies and cots and clutter, and she had shown no signs of that. The prospect of an infinite future full of earning money and subscribing to an expensive gym and buying designer clothes and attending gallery openings held no fears for her. The unhappiness and restlessness, he realised, were all his. His fault, then. He, it was, who had driven Natalie away with his irrational yearning to reproduce, with his jolly, chivvying insistence on preparing their bodies for seed-planting and conception with pints of Guinness and multivitamins and oily fish. Whatever Doctor Suzanne wasn't saying didn't really make any difference in the end. Life was emptying out even back then.

He waited for the lights to change on Rosebery Avenue, the lingering tang of iced tea making his mouth sour and dry. He crossed.

34

Life could still be refilled, of course. Bart had readjusted, coped, tried (as Natalie might have advised) to dismiss the past as clutter, had had energetic sex with an unsuitable woman whom Nick had introduced him to at a drinking club. And he had eventually moved into the white room with Bird, a cat bought and named after Charlie 'Bird' Parker by Aunt Marian, a lifelong lover of jazz, a woman who had made sacrifices in life so that Bart would grow up happy and well adjusted. And he did feel well adjusted, and if not exactly happy, not bitter either, not an emotional burden to anyone, not too transparently seeking a permanent relationship with someone of childbearing propensities, not too fucked up that he couldn't be a friend in need to those less fortunate than himself, meaning Monty, who would drop in at the office with a view to allowing himself to be persuaded to come out and drink too much and eat too little at the Bangkok Palace, one moment laughing and joking, the next in mourning for his lost Catherine, sometimes both at once. 'You, know, I think those evenings round at Jas's actually help,' he said.

'Bloody hell, it must be worse than I thought,' said Bart.

Monty's shop came into view now, pale modern wood-work, gold metal lettering and large double-fronted display – photography and art in one window, moody spread of architecture and design in the other, neon 'Coffee' sign advertising the café and browsing area. He walked towards the shop, the effect of the walk in the afternoon heat prickling his back with sweat. He slowed as he saw the door swing inwards, a woman coming out. Pale, almost doll-like she was. He stepped back, took in the bobbed dark hair with a short fringe cut at an angle. The woman registered Bart's eyes with her own. He thought she was about to speak – he *did* think this, though perhaps it was the other way round, that it was him who was about to speak – but she swept past, walking quickly. She was wearing something blousy and trousery in cream, Japanese looking. She reminded him of someone, in her efficiency of movement, the cut of her clothes and the way she followed her chin like a model. But whoever it was, whatever was at the back of his mind, or on the tip of his tongue, his legs were on the move, and though Bart was categorically not the kind of person who followed strange women in the street, *somehow* – and he knew this to be the act of someone in a dream, or a film, or worse, someone in a perfume ad – following a strange woman in the street was exactly what he seemed to be doing. Though even in the process of being astonished at himself, he saw in this a pattern begun in the months following Natalie's departure, though he couldn't put an exact moment on it – perhaps the day he had found himself uncharacteristically being stirred by the proximity of his dentist's breast, her crisp white tunic rustling softly against his cheek as she busied herself unplugging an old upper filling and tamping down a new one. Or when he found himself loitering on the perfume floor at Selfridges, just to see if one of the assistants spraying out samples looked as good from the front as from the back (she didn't). Or there was the girl in the glasses on the tube doing the crossword. 'Give us a clue,' he'd smiled, before he could stop himself. The girl had just blanked him, as though happy to rely on the rest of the passengers to look at him as though he was a man likely to take his penis out on public transport.

'Actually, what you've rediscovered,' Nick had said, at beer & sausages, 'is sexual curiosity. Which is what you've been repressing all these years, no doubt erroneously thinking it was tantamount to mentally cheating on your missus. And, no offence, mate, but now that you've been dumped, what you're doing is falling back on nature. Way I see it, it's like the old bloke who dies in his flat and eventually gets eaten by his dog. Inevitable. In the same way that you've got no regular sex, poor Fido's got no Winalot with essential minerals or whatever. Same thing. You're not getting nourishment, instinct takes over. It's Darwinian. Red in tooth and claw and all that.'

'Yeah, thanks, Nick.'

The church rose up on the left, its thick gold lettering burning in the sun against the red brick above the black railings: CHRISTO LIBERATORI. The woman stopped at Farringdon Road, turned right, shading her eyes against the glare, looking for the light of a vacant cab. If this had been a dream, Bart might now have walked up to her and contrived an accident whereby her unwieldy armful of brown paper packages tied up with string would spill on to the pavement, perhaps as a prelude to him asking what she did for a living (something artsy for sure – no point going into Monty's looking for holiday reading), or whether she'd like to get a coffee somewhere, or go 'catch' a movie with him sometime or – in a different dream – whether she had any firm views about rolling around naked on a futon with someone she had only just met. A cab was coming up the other way. Bart saw to his surprise that *his own arm* was now in the air flagging the driver down, saw to his ridiculous excitement the cab slowing, the driver's expectant face at the open window awaiting bidding and bearings. Bart, his audacious, improvised gambit deliciously and spontaneously unfolding, turned to look at the beautiful strange woman, expecting to see her own arm held aloft in vain, her look of frustration quickly melting to gratitude as Bart – eyebrows arching into a gracious apology, his open hand employing the international semaphore for *sorry, please, no, take the cab, it's yours, I insist* – prepared to do the gallant thing. But no . . . what he saw instead was a second taxi throbbing at the kerb and a short but unmistakably hostile glance in his direction as she disappeared into the back and slammed the door on him. His heart thumping, he watched the cab perform a U-turn and pull away north towards King's Cross. Across the road, the first driver parped his horn, his expression having already slipped from expectant to the brink of pissed off. Bart smiled and gave him a cheery thumbs-up, as though to indicate how a woman suddenly remembering she had a mind of her own was somehow a measure of success for them both. And if his phone had not immediately erupted with a trilling passage of Mozart, obliging him now to legitimately ignore the man's scowl, fish his Nokia out of his pocket and clamp it to his ear with an air of corporate urgency, he would have had to ritually disembowel himself on the spot.

Jim calling.

'Jim.'

'Aha, Mr Barton, guess what . . .'

'I can't.' He turned to watch the taxi rumbling away.

'Breakdown in communications. Mr Montgomery *himself* is here at the office with your books. As you may already have guessed by his absence at the shop. And of course the absence of your books.'

'He's there now?' In the warm air, the sea-effluent scent of prawns and cockles reached him from a street stand, mingling with the clinging sourness of the iced tea in his throat. He moved away.

'As we speak. Blaming his assistant Gail for the mix-up, regretting the inconvenience caused, suggesting a drink to make amends.'

'It's an old trick but it might just work. Tell him to hang on there.'

'Don't worry, I'll look after him,' he said.

You wish, he thought. He walked back, paused at the

shop selling designer chairs, measuring form against comfort, ornament against functionality, rerunning the last seven minutes in his head, wondering whether it was the heat that was turning his mind to mayonnaise, or just thoughts of sperm and of what Doctor Suzanne hadn't said.

• • •

Fuck . . .

Nick sprang to the window bare-arsed, clutching the duvet to his southern territories, scrutinising the street below, his heart thudding. A winding jam of taxis and deliveries, couriers and the like, office workers crowding the boiling pavement outside the pub in the fumes. There was the door-banger: white van parked on the kerb opposite, beefy, bullet-head driver carting red crates into the 24-hour supermarket.

'For God's sake, Nick, relax. I've told you he won't be back till three at least. No need to leap about like a nutter every time you hear a car stop.'

He sloped back into bed, Ivy still circling, *completely* naked, pointing her video camera. Which could make a man nervous, though obviously he couldn't say as much without seeming a bit unchilled and anti-creativity and inhibited and so on. Cracking body. Beautiful freckly shoulders. Nice little tattoo. Some kind of flower. No, ivy leaf. Of course. He lit a cigarette. Still didn't quite believe his luck, her and him here like this, though fear had to come into it too. Usually husbands or boyfriends, it had to be said, rather than blood relatives.

'And even if he does, so what?'

'Well, it wouldn't be ideal.' Dead spliff there in the ashtray, smoke hanging on the ceiling in the heat. Minx. Hair in rags like that, sticking out. Quite artistic. Under the striped duvet an erection stirring. Time 1.58. Should make it: two stops on the tube, presentation at three. Death by firing squad to miss another. Travel agent campaign: *Get out of here!* tag line delivered in a bad American accent. Shite to be sure, but good enough for radio.

'Why? Do I dictate to him who he sleeps with?'

'Well, no, absolutely not. And, I mean, obviously, you're your own person and that, but it might not look, you know, too good.'

'What, because you're nearly as old as he is? Because Dad wouldn't like me having sex with an older man?'

'Something like that.'

'Ha. You think I'm stupid, right?'

If only.

'Ivy. Why don't you come back to bed . . .'

She came closer with the camera, smiling, knelt on the bed, slowly straddled his chest, writhing gently as she filmed, one hand behind under the quilt looking for his chap and finding it. *Isshhhh*. He gave a moan, stubbed out his fag. 'I don't suppose we could lose the live coverage?'

She laid the camera on the bedside table. 'I thought you had to get back to work,' she said, leaning forward, nipples dipping into range, favourite kind, summer berries. Lifting herself up a bit now, positioning for re-entry. Yes please.

'*Nnnnnnn* . . . hang on,' he said. That condom moment.

'Actually, maybe we'd better not,' she said, starting to climb off. 'I've got a few things to sort out this afternoon. Stuff from the library.'

'*Ivy* . . .'

'What?' She disappeared off to the little en suite that Jas had had installed for her. He heard water thudding into the tub, watched his tent slowly collapse, sighed. Time to start feeling a bit bad about all this. Post-coital death or something, the French called it, and they should know. Still, her idea to invite him down for a smoke in the evenings when Jas was out. Hardly his fault she preferred a man with a bit of experience. Plus, he was only thirty-six to her twenty, so only *just* legally old enough to be her father, whereas Jas was five years older due to him having been a proper grown-up by the time he went to college, someone who had pretty impressively done enough living to have been to a war zone and been married and divorced at the age of twenty-three and had a little daughter somewhere. To whom, as fortune would have it, he, Nick, was now listening as she sang in the shower. Quite weird when you thought about it, though he preferred not to. Jas's old pics from the eighties blown up on the far wall. Refugees and the like. New Romantics queuing up outside a club looking like transvestites.

Ivy came back in steaming and pink, big fluffy towel up to her armpits. 'Besides,' she said, 'Dad never comes down here without ringing first. That's the deal. And it's not as if you don't live here. Well, up there.'

'Yeah, but if he sees me coming out of the wrong door . . .'

'He won't. I've told you, he's at Stella's. Doing his best to fuck her life up.'

'What, you think she can't look after herself?'

'She doesn't know what he's like.'

He threw back the duvet, sat on the edge of the bed, peeled off one sock, then the other. 'I thought you got on well with your dad.'

'Did he tell you that?

He shrugged, took himself off to the shower, sluiced, soaped himself, stood with the water running over him for a while, turned off the tap, dripped, looked around. Student towel facilities, i.e. none. Re-emerged cautiously, wearing the bath mat, fretting about the camera, but she'd packed it away and was busy lacing herself into her artist's boots. Suit trousers looking up at him, one leg balled up, on the floor, dark shirt, three of the buttons still fastened, flung inside-out on the chair. Tie. He gathered it all up to his lap, sat down.

'Don't sit on the bed!' she shouted. 'You'll soak it.'

'Sorry.' He looked round, found a hard chair, café type, water making a little puddle under his balls where he sat.

'People like Dad just shit on women,' Ivy was saying. 'He doesn't know he's doing it of course. He's all very entertaining and hospitable and generous with his money, and likes to make people laugh and all that. Nice *bloke*, no doubt. But look at his life, one dumped girlfriend after another, most of them half his age. He just avoids everything.'

'How can you say that? I mean you don't win major national press photography awards by avoiding things. Your dad was in Beirut getting shot at before you were born.' Nick struggled to get his left foot, still damp, into a sock. He would have preferred her at the weekend, when time wasn't quite so pressing, or, in truth, when time could drag a bit, really, for a man in his position. She didn't do weekends, she said. He didn't ask why.

'Escaping to Beirut more like. And *after* I was born, funnily enough. Leaving Mum to cope with me. He came and went as he pleased, until one day he just went. And now he thinks he can just walk back in and everything's fine when, actually, it's not.'

'Maybe he's trying to make up for it.'

'Yeah, right. By shagging my tutor. Does that strike you as a great move?'

'Well, I don't know – I never met the woman.' He grinned. 'But, look,' he said, smoothing down two gears to match Ivy's glare, 'all daughters hate the idea of their dads . . . you know, having sex. It's in the genes. It's all to do with envy.'

She stopped buttoning. 'Oh right, like deep down I really

want to sleep with my dad. It's Stella I care about, you idiot, not him.'

'What – you mean you and her . . .'

'Fucking hell, Nick, what planet are you on? No, I mean I just like her and care about her. You know, like, friendship, respect and all that?'

'Well, yeah, obviously that too.'

Jesus. He knotted his tie. 'Nice mirror,' he said. 'Rennie Mackintosh?'

She snorted. 'Dad's transparent attempt to remind me that he went to art college too. He thinks a mirror's art.'

'Right.'

Ivy behind him fiddling with an earring, breast swaying inside her shirt as she moved. Wave of desire, regret, love, arousal, whatever. Bollocks.

'Are you getting the tube?'

She stopped fiddling. 'Why?' she said. 'Where's the car?'

'What? Oh, right, yeah, it's in for a service.'

Her green eyes giving him the annoyed bit. 'Can't you get us a cab? I'm going your way.'

'Er, possibly. You couldn't lend me a tenner, could you?'

Car door banging in the street. Nick shot to the window. Jesus Christ. Jas's old droptop sitting across the street. Jas coming out of the super with a paper, squinting up. Nick leapt back from the lifted blind.

'What?'

'It's your dad! Shit. I think he saw me.' Fucksakes, calm, calm.

'Well, don't just stand there, *go* – down the back stairs,' she hissed, pushing him across the room. 'And wait till you hear his door before you leave.' Nick fell over something, stumbled, all thoughts about a last kiss spooked by the idea of Jas catching him up his daughter suddenly mattering to *her* now and not just him. 'Come on, hurry *up*.' She bundled up his jacket and shoes, pushing them at him, clicked opened the door, pushing him out. He caught sight of himself as he passed the mirror, shirt collar still up, half-dried hair standing on end. Two thirty-six. *Fuck*.

•••

A little *quelque chose* . . .

Jas stood in front of the open fridge muttering to himself, touching his sandy stubble. He liked Stella, but wondered if perhaps he liked her too much. And he wondered whether he had started liking her too much for the wrong reasons. Such as, because she kept him guessing. He snapped open a beer and rummaged anew through the top chiller compartment iconed with an open-eyed fish in profile and a joint of meat, the little blue graphic swirl to suggest rolled pork perhaps. *Poulet, poulet* . . . He thought, as he often did, of ringing down to see if Ivy fancied popping up for a chat, because he'd seen her from the street flitting past her window, but resisted the impulse, as he always did, respecting her privacy and adulthood, respecting the distance between what he hadn't been as a father and what he was now. Because that's what made their relationship tick over so well. He put the radio on loud so she'd know he was in. Capital FM, 'Golden Brown' by the Stranglers.

Swaying to the music, he glugged a green slick of olive oil into a pan, put it on the gas, turned it up high, slapped in some chicken pieces, squashed up some garlic into the sizzle with his palette knife and squeezed a lime over it from an unnecessarily theatrical height followed by a gloop of Madeira, tossing and stirring, singing along quietly, *golden brown* . . . enjoying the bent note on 'brown'. He put his face above the steam and sniffed the cooking smells before sawing open a loofah-sized ciabatta he'd bought at a deli on the drive back from Stella's place in Mile End.

Stella's place, where he had arranged to meet Stella at one, where he had found Stella deep in thought – not, that is, deep in thought about a spot of lunch with himself followed by spontaneous sex on the floor of her studio, but deep in thought about two canvases leaning against the wall, both traced similarly with tentative brushstrokes, the first rough guides to what was stirring in her mind in the absence of anything more pressing. Their date, for instance.

'Oh,' she said, when she saw him in the doorway. 'Shit . . .'

'Hey, nice to see you, too.'

'Oh God, I'm really sorry, Jas, I completely forgot.'

She grimaced, her hand up to shade her eyes from the light pouring in from the stranded windows of the upper floor, a second bedroom that had been sledgehammered to create empty vertical space, the stain of a little fireplace and mantelpiece visible up there too, its dirt ghost against the wall, the body of it gone the way of the floorboards, and a doorway, a visual joke in red bricks. Stella's platinum hair, held in place with some sort of wooden knitting needles, looked hot to the touch. She was dressed like a man on holiday, khaki shorts and a short-sleeved shirt, brown arms, long brown legs, turning inward at the knees, Bambi-like. She came to kiss him on the cheek, fingers smudged with black paint, as tall as him in her bare feet. 'I can't leave this now,' she said. 'I really can't. I've only just got started. You don't mind, do you? Ring you later?'

She didn't see him out.

This was how she kept him guessing. Guessing about how much any of this meant to her. It wasn't that he wanted it to mean a lot. He just wanted to gauge more accurately her level of interest. You couldn't just stumble around in the dark about these things. Because strictly speaking, the boot *was* supposed to be on the woman's foot. How could you relax into a relationship with someone who seemed as deliriously happy not to see you as vice versa? 'You decide' was one of her favourites. 'I don't mind' was another. 'Great!' was another. 'No problem' she said quite a lot. It wasn't that she was frivolous. She could be serious about art and work and student fees and a country's treatment of asylum seekers. But when it came down to him – that is, him and her, as an item – nothing ever seemed to matter more than anything else. Which could be unsettling for a man who needed to know whether a girl was in his passenger seat or he in hers. It was as if her 'mystery' button – the one women used to mesmerise and entrap men – had been accidentally left on.

'So I'll pop round, shall I?' he'd say.

'Yes, why not?'

'Eight OK?'

'Great! Whatever.'

'Or half past?'

'You decide.'

'I've got to have my leg amputated tomorrow.'

'No problem.'

He'd lost count of the number of times in what was barely three months together that she'd either not turned up (once, actually), or only in response to his phone call (once again), or had been ridiculously late or had rung to cancel (more than three). So was she being cool, or devious, or just mentally absent beyond the call of professorial duty? Because it wasn't as if she was backing off. She always seemed genuine – lavish, contrite, affectionate even – in her apologies when she left him standing like a dorkish Johnny-no-mates outside or inside some place of entertainment. And she was a kitten in bed.

But how was he supposed to respond? Clearly, not by being pissed off. That would be a mistake. For a start that would suggest a dangerous loss of faith regarding the abundance of other fish in the sea, and would in any case inevitably lead to a *squabbling* relationship, which was of course a step towards either a bust-up or choosing kitchen equipment together.

And he could hardly get his retaliation in first. Playing someone at their own game only worked if the other person knew there *was* a game. What it boiled down to was, he knew she wouldn't ring later because she never did. So he would ring her as usual, she would greet him like her long-lost twin stolen from his incubator by gypsies at birth, they'd go out for a drink somewhere and end up at her place having a rather splendid fuck in the big jangly Victorian bed she'd inherited from an ancient Welsh relative. A circumstance much to be envied, yes . . . But it shouldn't work like this. How could you ever get tired of a woman who was so unreadable? How could you move on? Perhaps he should move on. But that would be like starting your next course while you're still tucking into your first, to use an analogy more suited to Nick.

He frowned, waited impatiently by the pan, pressing down the chicken with the spatula. An ambulance siren outside. He wandered to the window, watched the traffic squeeze outwards to let it by, engine roaring as it got stuck down the narrow street then blaring away at last, past the bistro with jazz in the evenings and the Coffee Republic and the plain café doing grills and fry-ups, customers gawping out over their cups of tea, and the gates and domes and dragons of the meat market, that green and purple ironwork, rubbish piled outside, pigeons always tossing it about in the shade under the old hanging numeralled clock where it gets hosed down every morning, blood down the gutters.

47

And then there was the question of Ivy. Jas got on brilliantly with Ivy, no question, but he could never get her to talk about how things were at college. So, naturally he'd occasionally bring up the subject with Stella – Stella, who was nominally in charge of Ivy's needs as a student, pastoral and otherwise. Stella, whom he knew Ivy adored and admired, and therefore presumably confided in or at least had a tutorial sherry with from time to time.

'Oh, Ivy's fine. A bit distant at the moment, understandably, but otherwise . . .'

'What do you mean, distant? Understandable why?'

But then Stella would invariably occupy her speaking faculties with a forkful of fishcake, or look hard at something and say hmmm, or distract him anew in some pleasing sexual way, depending on whether they were having a meal or walking around a gallery or enjoying post-coital social intercourse.

She had once managed to touch on the project Ivy was working on for her end-of-year show. 'Conceptually very sound. Mmm. There's been a bit of dealer interest since Peter Augie was picked up the year before last. Quite strong year again, I think. And no doubt Ivy will be up there in her group next time. Not that that's what it's about, obviously. But it's good for the school if anyone gets noticed in a prominent way. Doesn't happen often, but when it does it has an impact.'

'And this conceptually sound thing is . . .'

'Quite promising. You should ask Ivy.' She smiled brightly in that vacant, enigmatic way that was always on standby, just below the surface waiting to be uncovered. She started talking about the possibility of curating an exhibition looking at the depiction of horses in the history of painting from Lascaux to Stubbs to Picasso. 'There's something about horses,' she said.

So that was it. The more a woman could deflate your expectations of her, the more you became a slave to her mystique. Look at Monty, who had – through some act of stupidity so dire he couldn't bring himself to disclose it – brought upon himself the wrath or contempt of a woman he was crazy about and getting crazier. Look at Bart, leaving his records playing in his flat even when he was out, trying to keep the silence out of his life. That kind of thing didn't happen by accident. It happened because you got in too deep in the first place. Falling in love. What was that except cutting yourself off from rationality, blinding yourself to the rest of life and experience? What was commitment if not a magnet for misery?

Steam rose from the pan. He turned the chicken with a fork. *Parfait.*

Avoid regret was his motto. Learn through adversity was another. Not just by not repeating a mistake, but by making a virtue of it. As he had done, after he'd met Barbara and got her pregnant and married her in the space of their first year together at university. Yes, it hadn't worked out, but it did give him the opportunity of dropping out of modern languages – which he felt had proved too severe a drain on his social life anyway – and dropping into a job on a local newspaper in Norfolk, selling ad space, covering council meetings, learning how to operate the office camera. He loved taking pictures. And six months into the job, out of the blue, he sold a photograph to the *Guardian* – a bunch of moody, pansticked New Romantics queuing outside a club in Covent Garden. A month later another picture – a shot of pickets at a steelworks in Yorkshire – then a third. He spent time in London schmoozing other photographers and picture editors. He blagged a free air ticket and went to Johannesburg for a week and sold two pictures. Exhilaration. He went freelance.

49

He loved 'freelance' for its sound of freedom. He loved to go abroad. He was willing to go abroad and *not* make money. But a marriage in Norfolk could not thrive on his absences. He went abroad until he was abroad more than he was at home – until he was abroad as a way of not being at home. That he did regret. Though not until it was safe to do so.

'Airport' came on the radio. He joined in on the refrain – *Airport! Oo-oo-oo-oo*. Who sang that? He couldn't remember. He loosed a clot of mayonnaise on to the bread with the palette knife, wedged a handful of baby spinach leaves into the V of the bread, piling steaming chicken pieces on top with sticky scrapings from the pan. The door opened and Ivy stuck her head round the door.

'Hi, babe,' he said. 'What's new?'

She glanced around the kitchen as if expecting someone else. 'No Stella?'

'Oh, bit of a mix-up, that's all.'

'What's cooking?'

'Chicken sandwich. Do you eat feathered animals? There's plenty here for two.'

'No thanks.' She came over to the counter, picked up a stray spinach leaf and chewed it. She turned the radio down, flicked through his six months' bills and letters and rubbish from the Inland Revenue bulging from a bulldog clip on the wall, sauntered over to the window and looked down on the street, humming.

'Drink?'

'Better not. I have to go.'

She hovered by the window. He noticed her hair was damp.

'So, how's things?' he said. 'How's college?'

'Great.'

He cut the sandwich and transferred it on to a plate with

the palette knife, licked his fingers. 'So . . . what then? Were you looking for something?'

She smiled as she turned to leave. 'Isn't everybody?'

'Christ, don't you start,' he said.

three

A beautiful free kick, quickly taken, just outside the D with two minutes of stoppage time already gone. A whipped-in, curving ball that whistled inside the far post and billowed the net while Chelsea were still getting their wall together. A jubilant Dennis Bergkamp wheeling away fists clenched, the Dutchman's face contorted into that brutal expression of triumph more redolent of having just smacked someone in the mouth than having snatched an exquisite equaliser from the jaws of a disappointed tube ride for fans travelling back to north London. Goalkeeper rooted to the spot. Furious defenders pursuing the referee like yapping dogs all the way to the centre circle. One–one. Not a win, but enough to get Monty jumping up and down and punching the air. A result.

It was the second game Bart had been to with him. The other had been a dismal nil–nil at home to Southampton, a Sunday match the same week Monty had blown back into the present after his years in the wilderness. Bart and Natalie had had the odd postcard from him when he'd been out there – some voluntary thing in Africa somewhere, and a Christmas card once from Lyons with no return address, but even that had been ages ago. Other friends from college who had shared the student house in Canterbury recalled how Monty had gone straight off after graduating – how he'd wanted to 'find himself', rather than plunge himself into the commercial feeding frenzy of eighties Britain. Very unfashionable at the time. Very Monty.

He had been back in London a year before Bart heard from him. An invitation arrived at the office one day for a launch party to celebrate the opening of a trendy art and design bookshop in Clerkenwell. Of course there had been no reason to associate this Montgomery Books – very cool and new millennium – with the unfashionable Steve 'Monty' Montgomery Bart had once known, but there he was, all six-foot-five of him, doling out glasses of white wine. 'I came back when my mother died,' he said as they spoke afterwards, flopped in twin leather chairs set aside for browsers while his assistant cleared up. 'She left me the money to open this place.'

'Up and coming area. Good for business, all these old buildings sprouting bars and restaurants every five minutes.'

'I'll keep an eye out for you,' Monty said. 'Give me your card.'

Eventually he had asked about Natalie, whom he remembered mainly for her advanced sense of tidiness. 'Bit unusual for a student . . .'

'We split up,' Bart said, picking from the tray of canapés on the table between them. 'Quite recently.'

'Ah. Sorry. You could say we're in the same boat though.'

'You're married?'

'Just about. It was one of those whirlwind romances you think only happens to other people. I suppose it was inevitable that we'd have a few problems. I still have hopes of us getting back together.'

That was six months ago, before things got worse. Whatever Monty said about his ex-wife these days it didn't feature them getting back together. It was because the hope had faded that the pain of it had started to eat away at him like it did. 'What you need is closure, mate,' Nick said at beer & sausages. 'Beat it out of your system.'

Bart had never had that experience with Natalie. Their one neat life had ended as two less neat ones, but at least they knew why. It had come to them slowly, like subsidence. Admittedly it had taken Bart by surprise but only because he wasn't looking properly, or thinking the cracks were something else. For years they had done the right thing, striving for and finding accommodation in each other, because that's what well-matched couples did, dealing with subsidence here and there, putting in new anchors to hold things up. But even the best-matched couples could be forced apart when what they couldn't say to each other got too much to bear – when no amount of anchoring could hold them up. Gradual slippage. That was him and Natalie.

He was sitting with Monty in a pub half a mile from the ground.

'Are you sure this is a good idea?' Bart said, feeling that at least one of them ought to be thinking aloud on the subject of how the place was filling up with disenchanted Chelsea fans,

tattooed and fat-necked in replica shirts and boat-sized trainers, loudly fucking and cunting it on the inconsistencies of
English refereeing with particular reference to being on the
arse end of the whistle.

'Why not?' Monty said, lighting a cigarette. 'Free country.'
He took a sip of his pint and looked round casually, amiably,
relaxed, as though waiting for the curtain to come up on *The
Merchant of Venice*.

'Yeah right,' nodded Bart, having already decided to adopt
the standard survival procedure for hostile post-match envir-
onments of confining major eye movements to a study of his
own feet, allowing himself an occasional reconnoitring glance
into the neutral middle distance, adding a judicious yawn to
denote a man at ease with his surroundings. Much as Bart
enjoyed a live game, the places he most hated to find himself
on a match day were – in no particular order – a public house
near a football ground, a public convenience near a football
ground, any public space set aside for the purposes of civilian shopping near a football ground, any mode of public
transport leading to or from a football ground. Anywhere, in
fact, he might unavoidably find himself sharing too much
breathing space with fans of either persuasion, any one of
whose number might suddenly announce himself as duty
psychopath for the day by inaugurating an exchange of abuse
with the nearest person careless enough to have left home
without a valid accent or wearing the wrong colour face paint;
the kind of psychopath who would spend the rest of his
week posing as a respectable plumber or estate agent or bar-
rister's clerk or derivatives trader; the kind of psychopath who
got so much grief from the world during the week that he felt
the least he could do was try to give some of it back to the
community at weekends.

'Another drink?' Monty said.

Bart adjusted his glasses. 'My round, I suppose.'

'I need a pee. Keep an eye on my stuff,' Monty said, getting up. He propped his bag up on the table and took the stairs to the basement. Bart squeezed in at the bar and ordered two pints of Guinness and a bag of corn chips. There was a sudden ominous quiet to his left. He wasn't so paranoid as to suppose whatever conversation there had been had stopped because of him, but with football you were instinctively aware of the conditions in which the devil made work for awkward silences. Five or six of them at least, blue-shirted, some baseball-hatted, restless, pints in paws, fags smouldering. Bart felt their interest shifting to him, their eyes taking in the tiny red enamel badge he wore on his lapel, the only obvious sign of his eligibility to be publicly beheaded on the pavement outside. He waited.

'Your lot took a liberty today, didn't they?'

Bart turned and smiled agreeably at the man facing him: short, wiry, cocky type wearing wraparound shades, vigorously flicking ash into the ashtray. 'Yeah, we were . . . they were pretty fortunate,' said Bart. 'Lucky, I mean. To get the decision.'

'Bergkamp was well out of order taking that fucking kick before the ref had blown,' said a second scowler at the back. 'What a cunt.'

'Yeah, well he, er . . . I suppose he can be a bit of a cunt sometimes. Quite a nice curling effort though, don't you think?'

The wiry, cocky one turned to his mates. 'This guy's taking the piss.'

'No, no, not at all,' Bart said, flashing his best nervous smile. The Guinnesses were ready. He turned with relief to pay the barman, clamped the bag of corn chips between his teeth and picked up the drinks (you couldn't kick a guy in glasses with his mouth full, he figured). "Scuse me, lads,' he mumbled. They stood aside, satisfied it seemed, at least for the moment, to adopt a standpoint of malicious amusement, having failed to goad him into defending the honour of his team. Perhaps one of them would stick his foot out as he passed, by way of consolation. But in the time it took to pick the drinks up and turn to the table, three other beefheads were already sitting at it. They were affecting to be engaged in some raucous interchange, but were clearly clocking Bart for a reaction. He felt the gap at the bar closing behind his back, leaving him in a no-man's-land of scrubbed pine floor holding the two dripping glasses, the bag of corn chips dangling from his jaws. He took a step forward, feeling useless for having lost the table but wondering whether saying something in a muffled comic voice might be too provocative. He hardly noticed Monty stepping in ahead of him. 'Sorry, this table's taken,' he heard him say, with disbelief. 'We were sitting here.' Bart was hardly prepared for this. Monty was unfeasibly tall but he wasn't Clint Eastwood. Or at least he didn't used to be.

The trio looked up, leaning back in their chairs. 'Yeah, but you left it, didn't you?' said one, rocking slightly, shifting his weight from one buttock to the other, close-cropped head, emphatic double earrings in each ear, *easily* in his late thirties, possibly married, kids to bring up and teach the way to. What was *wrong* with these people?

Monty stood, and blinked patiently. 'I left my bag here.'

'It was on the floor, mate. Don't count, do it?' He looked round smirking at the others.

'It was on the table when I left it.'

The group shrugged, half smiling at each other, looking up at Monty towering above them, not moving. Double Earrings scraped his chair back a fraction, eyebrows arched. 'So, what . . . you wanna make something of it?'

'I'm saying the bag was on the table.'

'So, you're saying I'm a liar?'

Bart hung back, not because his legs were shaking – though they unmistakably were – but because he knew that the sight of an obvious reinforcement stepping up and sticking his oar in, regardless how absurd a spectacle he presented, would be unlikely to improve things. Monty paused for a moment longer then picked the bag up. 'Forget it,' he said. He turned to Bart and took one of the drinks. 'Come on, there's room at the rail.'

One of the halfwits at the bar shouted something across to the trio at the table, prompting laughter and snorting. Monty's face and neck were burning. He drank his Guinness steadily, saying nothing, responding to Bart's efforts at conversation with painful monosyllables. They finished their drinks and Bart started to lead the way out. As they passed the table, there was a short silence. 'Wanker,' someone shouted. 'Poof.' Bart felt something hit him on the back of his head. Something small. A dry roasted peanut perhaps. Yes, just keep going, he thought. But he sensed Monty was not quite behind him and in the moment it took to scent the changing air, to hear the first syllable of incipient uproar, the table and drinks were going over and he turned round to see Monty laying into the earringed one like a man possessed, punching and kicking. A second came into range and got a headbutt for his trouble that sent him backwards. Bart's inner organs immediately turned to liquid, but his legs were filling with adrenalin. Before he knew it he was thundering down the street. Monty, he saw, was close behind, blood on his face. There was shouting and clattering – the slam of a car door, he thought – but Bart kept going, his thundering legs threatening to buckle at the unaccustomed punishment,

Monty overtaking him with his long strides. A bus flashed across in front of them on the King's Road. Bart risked a backward glance. Three or four of the bastards half a street back, staggering to a halt in the road, knackered, shouting after them, jabbing fingers. *You're fucking DEAD, mate, you're fucking DEAD . . .*

Thirty seconds later they were on the top deck of the bus, panting their lungs out and laughing like teenagers, Monty, his lip bleeding, searching in his bag for tissues, a dull lump bubbling the middle of his forehead. The only other passengers – two boys, fifteen or sixteen – sat stiffly close by, wary in their seats, silenced by the sudden turbulence with its gust of fear and excitement. One of the boys dared a peek. Bart, exhilarated, fixed him with a level stare that made him turn back.

He smiled. 'Fucking hell, Monty, you're a maniac. You're supposed to be a bookshop owner. Where did you learn to punch like that?'

'Where did you learn to run like that?'

Bart leaned back, the road unravelling fast behind them as they travelled towards Sloane Square. 'Coward school,' he said.

They weaved further eastward, relieved to go where the bus went, until it turned abruptly south, when they jumped off and took a cab back to Clerkenwell. It was gone eight by the time they were sitting in the window at the Bangkok, wolfing down the entire menu. The place was almost empty. A tired-looking couple Bart had seen in his block pushing a buggy were holding hands across the table. A man – Oriental – sat by himself reading a book and sipping tea, an empty noodle bowl in front of him. Behind the bamboo confines of the bar, the waiter sat motionless, his head angled towards an overhead TV, the applause of a game show just audible above the house muzak.

Bart pointed his chopsticks at Monty. 'I've just noticed –
what happened to the sling?'

Monty looked down. 'Yes, that would have made things a
bit more difficult. I've just got the bandage now.' He peeled
his jacket cuff back to reveal a frayed strip of crepe.

'But didn't you say it was fractured or something?'

'No, no, just a scratch.'

'It's funny, something like that,' Bart said.

'What, my arm?'

'No, tonight. What happened. I mean, admittedly I was
only really there at the escaping end of things, but it does
pump you full of something. Look at me, I'm starving. Thing
is, most of the time, people like us get on with our lives not
really needing to be cavemen. I mean, we might regress a bit
when we're having sex or playing five-a-side and so on. And
we go to gyms to make ourselves look the part because we see
our bodies withering away through disuse . . .'

'Speak for yourself, buddy.' He scraped gluey prawns and
chicken on to his plate from the iron skillet.

'But it's true. We use our heads to do all our work so we
have to think up artificial ways of keeping physically in shape.
Unlike, say, builders or gas fitters or other manual-labouring,
high-calorie-burning professions. I mean as an interior
designer I might be theoretically conversant with electrics and
plumbing but I've never actually struggled with a pipe
wrench or blown myself up installing a ring main. I mean I
just don't have those kinds of hunter-gatherer, worker-bee,
mountain-climbing skills. I'm a finely honed product of
advanced evolutionary economics. If my car breaks down, I
get someone else to fix it.' He motioned to the waiter for
more beer.

'Bart, not even a builder fixes his own Porsche.'

'So am I talking rubbish?'

'Yep.'

'Why?'

'Because most blokes are white-collar anyway these days, working in call centres or boring office jobs or whatever. They're the ones who create havoc in town squares on Friday nights after a few buckets of lager and flavoured vodka.' Monty took a mouthful of food, carefully avoiding the split lip.

'That's just an accident of employment history,' Bart said. 'They're not temperamentally *suited* to being white collar. Anyway, probably everyone *we* know is insulated from this stuff. We've learned to transcend the physical side of what it is to be a man – or what it used to be for most men. Now the only time you notice it is when trouble flares up – say on the tube or in the West End when the pubs are turning out. And when it happens you just feel . . . I don't know, useless? You know backing off is very much the right thing to do, but it also seems the wrong thing.'

'What, you think we should all go out brawling every night just to keep our hand in as proper men? It all sounds a bit *Fight Club*. Have you forgotten everything they taught you at coward school?'

Bart laid his chopsticks sideways and put his crumpled napkin on the plate. 'I suppose what I'm saying is, I think you did the right thing earlier by doing the wrong thing. I haven't felt like this in ages.'

'Only because we got away with it.'

The waiter brought more beer, plus whisky chasers, at Monty's insistence.

'Do you know why I went overseas after college?'

'To help people less fortunate than yourself?'

He shook his head. 'Actual bodily harm.'

'Actual *what*?'

'It was a while after I'd left the house. After our finals and everything but I was still hanging round the union bar. I'm sure we'd lost touch by then. I got into a scrape with some rugby club idiots. Anyway, something just kind of snapped and I hit someone with a bottle. I didn't really mean to – I mean not with the bottle. I just happened to be holding one and it sort of got in the way. It didn't break. Cracked his cheekbone though.'

'Fuck . . . And you ran away to Africa?'

'No. I got three months, suspended, following character references, psychiatric reports. And *then* I ran away to Africa. Saw an ad in *Time Out*. A month later I was on the plane with my new criminal record.' He pushed his plate to one side and lit a cigarette.

'So . . . what was the fight about?'

'Nothing really. I think someone called me a nancy boy for drinking tomato juice or something. But to be honest I'd had a few emotional problems. I was on antidepressants at the time.'

'Right, hence the tomato juice . . .'

'With three parts vodka. I'd brought my own bottle. I had it under the table. I don't think they would have got me for hitting someone with a tomato juice bottle.'

'I suppose not.'

Monty smiled grimly and they clinked their bottles together. 'Here's to coward school,' he said, glassy-eyed.

When they'd finished eating, they carried on drinking and reminiscing about college. They were drunk by the time they came out and crossed the road, and sat on the wall outside Bart's office. Monty smoked a cigarette and, unprompted, told Bart about the split with his wife – a trial separation that escalated into a permanent one when she'd dropped by at his flat above the shop one Sunday morning and found a strange girl leaving the premises.

'I tried to sort things out, but it was impossible after that.'

'Yes, I imagine it was.' Bart looked up, one eye closed, searching for stars but finding none.

'I'd had a lot to drink. I suppose I was a bit sad and desperate.'

'What, for a shag?'

'No, no. I don't know. Another woman. It's too hard to explain.'

He stopped what he was saying, as he had in the pub earlier, as though he'd said too much and yet somehow not enough. They sat for a minute, Monty staring at the pavement, Bart leaning back, propped on his hands, squinting at the glow of the streetlights through half-closed eyes, the blood pulsing in his ears. You could lose yourself to a silence like this, letting it grow like something not turned off, flowing and widening until it was a big enough world to swim in and to fathom. Monty here, circling and sending down lead markers like clues, Bart himself peering vainly into the secret hollows and black openings, the two of them in this great, deep unsaid, leaving their trails of bubbles, their eyes round behind their face masks as the sky of their brilliant day vanished, curtained by this new green darkness.

There was a speck of rain in the air. Monty burped loudly.

'So what are you going to do now?' Bart said.

'Get her back.'

He jumped down from the wall, kissed Bart hard on the forehead and went swaying off into the night.

Bart watched him for a moment, then trudged up to his flat, the last soft strains of an Elvis Costello track he couldn't quite place soft in his ears as he turned the key. Bird met him at the door, miaowing and skirting his legs. He was suddenly tired, his spirits dragged under by nagging currents. He picked up the cat, stroked his ears, deposited him on the couch, tail in the air. Strange how Monty had suddenly gone weird about things, thinking his last chance had gone like that. But then how that turn of events must have made things easier for the ex-wife. How a clean, hard decision could be neatly forged in the heat of that unwelcome disclosure.

Then he sat down and picked up the phone, his heart and mind beating as he dialled. He hadn't planned it, and it was a bad time to ring but he knew he would never make this call sober. Though he had run it through in his head, it was always with bad results.

'Hello?'

'Suzanne, hi, it's Bart.

'Bart, what a surprise. How's the sperm count?'

'I just want you to tell me the truth,' he heard himself say, blinking at a version of himself that had appeared like a pre-sentational slide in the dark of the window, his face a wilted caricature under the hard kitchen spotlight, his glasses tilted forward on his nose.

'Bart, are you drunk?'

'I want you to tell me you don't already *know* about the health of my sperm. Probably teeming with the little buggers, you said . . . right, right.' He had imagined an almost jocular tone here, but he felt it turning into something not funny at all. He heard the tremor in his voice as he spoke, and knew this would be something to regret.

There was a pause at the other end. 'Have you been talking to Natalie?'

What Suzanne said came to him ready filtered, like one of those dreams in which you can see and name an animal with absolute clarity and only afterwards remember it wearing the stripes and horns of another. 'She came to you about an abortion, didn't she? And you thought I knew about it. Which is why you wondered . . .'

'Bart, I'm sorry, but I really can't discuss this. What did Natalie say?'

'. . . which is why *you* wondered why on earth I'd want a sperm count. Because how could I have got her pregnant without sperm, right? Tell me I'm wrong.'

'Oh God.' She gave a long sigh. 'You haven't spoken to her, have you? Look, I'm going to put the phone down now, Bart, OK? You really need to talk to Natalie about this, not me. I'm sorry. I'm a GP not a marriage counsellor. I'm not *allowed* to join in like this. It's not fair to expect me to. I'm going to put the phone down. OK?'

The phone clicked at the other end, and he put the receiver down. Bird jumped into his lap, Elvis Costello's 'Stranger in the House' playing now, faintly, in the background. He leaned back, eyes closed, stroking the cat, feeling its warmth. Whatever rubbish Jas and Nick hymned together about the unencumbered life, he wondered what kind of freedom this was that felt so much like tyranny. Everything you'd ever done in the past had you in its tentacles for ever. There was no freedom, only new ways of being locked into the same old thing. He felt Bird abandon ship and the white walls close in as he slid out of consciousness and the day's grip, thinking about Monty trying to punch his way out of things, only to find himself punching his way into something else, about Nick shagging his demons away with ferocious abandon and Jas always one stepping stone ahead of his women, none of them good enough to wait for.

'This is the life,' Jas loved to say, looking round at them all, turning a fat ribeye on the flaming and sizzling grill. 'Isn't it?'

• • •

Fuck, damn. How did he do that? Nick saw a drop of sweat fall from his own nose to the playing surface. Say what you like, Jas carried his weight lightly. Didn't matter where you put the fucking ball, he was waiting to twock it down the tramline or lob him. How could you play tennis without actually moving? You had to admire that. Lot of grace for a big bloke, swishing it just so, having him, Nick, dashing all over the court like a bloody lemon. He mopped the sweat off his head with his sleeve. '*Cunt*. How do you do that?' he panted.

'Positioning. Let the ball do the work.' Jas pointed the racket. 'Your serve.'

Up . . . He smashed the first ball into the cord, it hopped over cartoon-like. Second too loopy. Jas swatted it back over the net like something annoying. Nick turned to see it thud inside the line, smack hard against the fence with a bang and up at a sharp, pleasing angle. 'Love–fifteen,' Jas said, not for the first time.

Jas, smiling, pointed his racket again. 'You should work on your toss. You're having to step back instead of forward.'

'Work on my toss. Right.'

They played for another twenty minutes, then walked back to the changing room, Jas looking crisp enough for the full fortnight at Wimbledon, him drowning in his own perspiration. Not his idea of course. You managed to wangle a morning off work to do some urgent flat hunting and the first thing that happened is you got pounced on at breakfast and forced to do double fucking games. Could hardly say no, Jas having been so fantastically laid back about everything. Well, everything he knew about. Hardly a sniff of Ivy since last week, except a brief walk-on part during TV dinner on Wednesday. In and out of the fridge for a beer, ignoring him completely. Understandably a bit jittery now, doing it right under her dad's nose, so to speak. Hence urgent necessity for room of his own, as Virginia Woolf so eloquently prescribed, though obviously she wasn't prescribing it with blow jobs in mind. Thinking about it, you could do an ad — someone forever nicking someone else's beer out of the fridge, last frame being bloke actually *in* fridge guarding beer. Or maybe beer *monster* in fridge — door suddenly opens, thief gets pulled inside, turning tables in humorous way. Not an ideal one for radio, admittedly.

'The great thing about Stella is that she's totally undemanding,' Jas was saying, sitting on the little bench under the coat hooks undoing his laces. 'Which means when we see each other it's great, and when we don't she's not always in my face, wanting to know what I'm up to.'

'And what *are* you up to?'

Jas winked. 'Actually, not much,' he said.

'So . . .' So what he really wanted to know was what Ivy was up to, and whether he thought she might be available for, say, half an hour of being joined at the waist Thursday lunchtime. 'So, how's business?' he said. 'Hear any more about the vodka job? Or Bacardi, was it?'

'Billboard and press campaign launches some time in the autumn.'

'Impressive.'

'Gives me a bit of space. I'm giving a little talk at Ivy's college this p.m., which is good. Do my bit for the community, meet the students, look at their work, keep up with events.'

Nick grinned. Yeah, and the rest.

'What?' laughed Jas, marched off to the shower, bath towel round him.

Big as he was, you wouldn't call him fat. Probably because he wouldn't see himself as fat. Well-fed, yes. A sensualist. It was a confidence thing. And posture. Funny how it made a difference. Good facial structure helped. Some people turned to suet the minute they put a couple of doughnuts away. *Apply directly to abdomen*. He thought of Olivia, before and after pregnancies. Looking sharp enough now, of course. The divorce diet. You could market that, all right. He could talk. A bit undernourished himself at present.

They walked back towards Smithfield. Stopped at Farringdon tube. Usual snarl of traffic, shoe repairs, leather goods, keys cut while you wait. Chemist. All films processed.

'So, where are you looking?' Jas said.

'Sort of west Islington.'

'What – King's Cross?' He made a sour expression.

'Well, yeah. But what can you do, having to fork out rent as well as paying a fucking giant mortgage in Fulham for Livvy and the kids? Not that I begrudge them a roof over their heads, obviously.'

'Mmm, tough. Of course, any other time, you'd have been welcome to the studio. I think Ivy's a bit attached to it now. You can't blame her, rent free in the middle of London. Perfect for her. She's trying to get some money together. She won't take a penny off me, needless to say. Well, not in readies. There's plenty of bar work in London, I said. Or waitressing. Anybody can do it. "Well, I'm not anybody," she said. I don't think she much enjoyed working at Monty's at Easter. Something a bit more challenging than making coffee and washing up, she said. Bart said maybe she could do a month's holiday cover with him while his admin man is away.'

'Bart said?'

'Yeah, why not? Creative environment. Right up her street I would have thought.'

'Well, except . . .'

'What?'

'Oh nothing.'

'What?'

'I just think he might have a soft spot for her, that's all.'

'Bart? You're kidding? He'd better bloody not have.'

Nick tapped his nose. 'Trust me. Your speccy, wry, schoolboy types are the worst. Course, I'm not saying he'd do anything about it, but a chap can see the signs. Now, *you* might not see the signs. Fathers hate the idea of their daughters, you know . . .'

Jas striding off, puzzled look, a freshly planted thought sprouting in his head.

Down into the tube. Smiling to himself. Some things you hated yourself for, but had to be done none the less. And fair's fair, you'd have to be the biggest fruit in the tin not to fancy her anyway. Ergo: a white lie justified if only on common-sense grounds, self-preservation being nine points of the law. Or was that self-defence?

Travelcard in the slot. *Ftttt*. Out again.

Heart of hearts, he had to admit she was getting to him. Never learn. Briony all over again. Nice name Briony. Completely wild for her too, same stupid story. Completely self-destruct. Messy way out of a perfectly tolerable marriage. But where was Briony now? That was it. He didn't care. Another day, another delusion, like Kleenex. Pull one out of the box, another pops up. Knowing didn't make a crumb of difference. Ivy now. Couldn't stop himself. *Whoooshhh*. Sucked after her like papers and rubbish chasing a train. Thought about her every sex seconds. Biological clock dick-dicking away. Thinking about her now, her red ragged hair and little ivy tattoo and summer-berry nipples. Except it was more than thinking. It was hurting and aching and churning. And yearning. And burning. But not, when you get to it,

70

learning. You couldn't teach an old dong new tricks. Not his anyway. Down, boy. Good copyline for porn site. Give the dong a bone. She could, just by sitting there on the end of his thoughts.

Ivy, oh, Ivy, Ivy, Ivy . . .

The tube doors crumped shut. One stop. He scanned the ads. Every one a loser. Walking, his shoes echoed on the platform, nearly empty now. Up the escalator. Worst thing was being stuck in Jas's spare room, knowing she was only about six foot below him, writhing hot and naked in bed. Obviously it wouldn't do to repay Jas's hospitality by drilling a spyhole in the floor. Or a bigger hole. Stick his head through. Or his penis. *Hello, remember me?* Hence, the morning off, room of his own, or at least one with a new proprietor. If anyone asks, emergency dental work, he said to his crack team of graduate-calibre underachievers. Sweating up Caledonian Road now. He checked his *A to Z*, glanced again at the letting details. Compact studio, galley kitchenette, FGCH. Close to shops. In fact, right above one. Bookies. And very convenient for newsagent, hairdresser's, kebabberia, funeral director's, railway line. Mixed neighbourhood: pub with boarded-up window, public library full of old drunks, social services hostel featuring woman slouched refugee-style on step, peasant headscarf, baby attached at the front, hand out in supplication, waiting to be captured in oils by wandering nineteenth-century Russian Reformists, if memory of art history served, which it probably didn't. Beauty parlour: sunbeds, non-surgical facelifts.

He recognised the bloke from the agency, pacing at the front, looking at his watch. Switched his grin on when he saw Nick. 'I'm Warren,' he said, sticking his hand out. 'Lovely day for it,' he added, looking up between the crumbling blocks of high-rise crack dens opposite.

'Not late, am I?' Nick said.

'No, no, not at all. Entrance at the rear, if you'd just like to . . .'

He followed him round the parade of shops. Cheap suit to go with the rest of him. Nick waited with his best tight smile while the poor halfwit struggled to work out how the gate opened.

'Apparently they've just had a new fridge put in,' he said.

He followed him across a rubbish-strewn concrete yard hemmed by the windowless sides of adjacent buildings. To his credit, Warren resisted the temptation to say 'Shared patio', but kept his mouth tight shut and unlocked the door. Staircase going up. 'Ah . . .' Warren said, meaning *why's the fucking light not working?* They went up in the dark to a landing. 'Here we are,' he said. 'Number two.' He turned the key, pushed the door open. On the left, a modest bathroom with dripping shower head, nicotine enamel, jigsawed lino. 'Reasonable to average decorative order,' said Warren. Main living space: three walls colour of gherkin, one bare plaster, seventies sitcom sideboard, chair and Marmite-varnished coffee table, TV with indoor aerial, early example of sofa bed. Dusty, Chinese lantern shade (large with small sellotaped split) taking half the fucking room up.

'New fridge,' Warren said, opening catflap-sized fridge door and closing it again. 'Da-da . . . Electricity and gas fully metered, month's rent in advance plus returnable deposit up front for any damages.'

'What's there to damage?' asked Nick, thinking about his fridge monster.

'Say again?' said Warren.

'I'll take it,' he said.

Little horrible Honda parked near by. Warren gave him a lift back to the office, weight off his mind, tuppence-ha'penny commission, just waiting for Nick to check the small print and do the honours, gibbering away with relief about how colourful and vibrant King's Cross was, presumably referring to the lively local drugs and prostitution scene. Across the lights, down St John Street, they squealed to a halt, bumping up the kerb, making leeway for some blaring old fanny leaning on his horn behind. Nick looked back. Cabbie throwing a hissy, making a meal out of having to pull out into other lane. 'Plenty of room for everyone,' Warren cooed affably, rather than just rolling the window down and shouting *cunt*, as he might on his day off. Nick glanced into the back of the taxi as it passed. Hugo staring back at him, eyes shifting rapidly out of neutral and into bulging recognition, dropped jaw filling the rear window as the cab swung down towards Sadler's Wells. I'm dead, Nick thought. Excellent.

● ● ●

Stella was watching from the back, her arms folded and wearing a benign, proprietorial expression that Jas found comforting and disconcerting at the same time. He surveyed the class from the thinker position, one foot on the seat of the chair in front of him, a blown-up image of a burnt-out Iraqi tank on the screen behind him. He was winding down now, inviting questions.

'Anyone?' he said. '*Personne?*'

Question time was his favourite part, personal interface being the lifeblood of an informal talk. He liked the rhythm and banter of it, the to and fro of it, getting the measure of these young turks – the familiar array of badly handprinted T-shirts, skateboarding trousers, facial ironmongery, some of them lounging back twiddling with their straggly beards or bleached dreadlocks, others leaning forward with notebooks –

helping them crystallise their ideas, hoping to inspire, notwithstanding the hard truth that only about one in five of them would ever actually become a photographer. Two girls with identical lavender eye-makeup and matching nail polish at the front, one of them leaning on the desk, chin cupped in her hands. No sign of Ivy, which was a shame but – and he didn't know why – also a relief. Perhaps because she had heard it all before the year previously, and would catch him repeating himself, perhaps because she was proving herself too much a virtuoso of the awkward question these days.

A hand went up. 'What do you like best – war photography or advertising?'

'Ah, I'm glad you asked me that,' he said, if only because someone always did. He took a couple of paces to his left, as if having to think about it, and then turned, looking hard at the floor. 'Because the two are not unconnected. For me, at least, purely commercial work is a means to an end. A necessary evil. That's not to say that it has no aesthetic merits – of course it does. You're always striving to be true to your own vision of things. But the bottom line is you're working to a client's brief. Money calls the shots. You're part of a collaborative effort to sell something. So, no, you never forget they're the enemy.' He chuckled. '*But* . . . this kind of work pays for the stuff you really want to do – photojournalism, photography as fine art, whatever it is that you're trying to express creatively – the thing you always keep with you right here' – he touched his chest, held the gaze of his audience – 'the thing that first gave you that desire to freeze the world on film.'

'Yeah, but what about global capitalism?' said one of the beardies. 'Aren't you kind of helping that?'

Stella had opened the door and was slipping out, signalling to him, lunch, ten minutes, in the cafeteria.

'Well,' he said, turning to his questioner with a grin, 'the trick is to choose your enemies carefully,' adding that of course when he was a student, back in the eighties, practically *everyone* wanted to get into advertising.

'Why didn't you?'

'Ah. I was a *mature* student.'

Didn't anyone here today want to work in advertising, he asked. No. Though one of a trio of dandies lounging together near the back said he wanted to do fashion shoots, an admission that created a short but predictably circular exchange with two beardies about whether artistic probity was automatically forfeited with the involvement of models and obscenely expensive clothes.

'What's the difference?' the dandy said. 'Everybody gets paid by somebody.'

'Absolutely true,' Jas said, seeking now to be more even-handed. 'Even war photographers – well, eventually. It depends which paper you're working for.'

There were a couple of questions about being shot at, which he tried to answer truthfully on behalf of all the photographers who might have been shot at, without quite formally excluding himself from their ranks. Someone else had a technical query, which spawned subsidiary technical queries and had everyone staring at the floor for the remainder of the session. At the end he packed his kit away as the students scrambled for the door, eager to get to the bar for a spliff and a game of pool. One of the lavender girls hung back. 'Hi,' she said, tucking a lock of hair behind her ear. 'That was really interesting. I really like your pictures of the mountain people. And your tricks of the trade – that stuff about using an old twin reflex lens so you can look the other way when you're taking a picture. That was funny. Do you really do that?'

'All the time. Though obviously you can end up with a picture of a goat.'

She laughed. They walked out into the corridor together.

'Look, I know you must be hugely busy,' she said, 'but I don't suppose you could spare five minutes to look at my portfolio.'

'Which is . . .'

'Just in my room. I could go fetch it and meet you in the union bar maybe?'

'I'm a bit tied up right now,' he said. 'But . . . Hang on.' He found a scrap of paper and scribbled his phone number down. 'Why don't you give me a ring some time? Pop into my studio when you're passing. I'm in Clerkenwell.'

'That'd be brilliant. I'm Lois, by the way.'

'Lois. OK, great, look forward to that.'

Professional. Proper, he thought. No jokes about Superman.

They stood for a minute, Lois telling him about her trip to Cuba last year. He glanced up and saw Ivy at the noticeboard at the end of the corridor watching them. He was about to wave, but she quickly turned and disappeared down the stairs. Something in her expression reminded him of her mother. A memory came to him unexpectedly of her – Barbara – waiting for a kettle to boil as he walked in unannounced, of her turning to see him in the doorway, unshaved, fresh from some lowly paid adventure, backpack slung by his side. Ivy tucked up for the night in her cot. Barbara's hair was scraped tightly back and fastened with a rubber band.

'I tried to call,' he said.

'The phone's been cut off.'

Her eyes reproving, like Ivy's. The scene seemed like a photograph itself now. A long-yellowed moment captured in the harshly lit compass of a small kitchen; it was the moment he realised that this would probably be the last time. Not the last time he would go away, but the last time he would come back to her. In effect it was the moment of abandonment; the moment he stopped being merely an absent father and became the estranged one who would, in years to follow, turn up on birthdays or at half-term; who would send toys at Christmas and – as Ivy was growing up – postcards from abroad. Six months later he had left to go back to study – to art college – too buoyant with optimism and youthful enterprise to risk the burden of duty. And because of everything he had seen, strangely fearful.

Jas went to dump his audio-visuals in the boot of the Merc. He came back to find Stella at a table overlooking the car park. She was eating fish and chips and had a text-heavy periodical open in front of her, art-prof glasses on the end of her nose. Jas set down his tray and sat opposite her.

'That seemed to work quite well,' she said, one eye still on the magazine.

'Yeah, it's nice to get back in the thick of it every now and then. Knock some ideas about.' He paused, his fork knotted with tagliatelle. 'I saw Ivy just now.'

'Mmm?'

'Do you think she's OK?'

Stella carried on reading for a moment, the small cleft of a frown appearing between her eyebrows, which could mean she had a problem with some topic of burning importance in the field of aesthetics or just with being interrupted. She closed the magazine. 'Hmm,' she said. 'You know what you were saying in your talk back there, about art and morality . . .'

'What? Oh, right. Well, of course it was more Oscar Wilde who said it really. I was just putting it forward as a kind of broad *modus operandi*.' He took a mouthful of pasta and chewed, but it was Stella's fried fish he could smell, the pure white of the remaining cod in its weird identical layers as they fell away from each other like crafted pieces of a game, its salt and vinegar tang scenting the air between them.

'But do you actually believe it? Do you believe morality has no place in art?' she said, tucking into her food, glancing up at him.

Clearly there were only two possible answers, but he wasn't sure which one the occasion called for. The stiff batter with its spongy underside preserved in its whole curling length reminded him of lizards that shed their tails to avoid capture. 'Well, to an extent, obviously,' he said. 'For an artist. In principle. Especially way back then, in the er . . . late Victorian era. Repressed sexual appetites and all that. Why is this important?'

She shook a cigarette out of a packet of Camel and rolled it between her fingers for a few moments before positioning it at the side of her plate like an item of cutlery. 'It puts me on the spot if you keep asking about Ivy,' she said. 'Sorry,' she added. She gave him the smile of a parent having to impart bad news to a child.

'Right, right. I can see that,' he said. He wondered what Ivy had to do with morality and art, but he didn't want to seem to be missing the point in addition to being insensitive in some way that was glaringly obvious to all interested parties but himself. Stella smiled. He felt a sudden urge to kiss her. Or even just to take her in his arms and hold her to his body.

'Have you finished eating?'

'Yes, I think so. I had a big breakfast.'

She lit the cigarette. 'She's doing really well under the circumstances,' she said.

They were quiet for a moment.

'How was the tennis?' she asked. 'With your lodger?'

He thought of Nick puffing and panting all over the court. He thought of Bart eyeing Ivy's breasts over a hand of cards. 'Instructive,' he said.

four

A beautiful car, the Boxster, Bart thought, unfolding his sunglasses. Beautiful lines. Thirty-odd grand. Barely four thousand miles on the clock in two years, most of that from pootling around town or shooting off to Aunt Marian's on a Sunday, plus a couple of weekends away with Natalie and that trip to the hypermarket in Calais the Christmas before last, when life still looked like the finished article. Satisfyingly deep whirrs and slow clunks when you unlocked the doors or adjusted the seat in its numerous different ways. Expensive, but not ridiculously, ostentatiously so. Monty said it looked like a footballer's car but there was nothing vulgar about it *per se*.

And, as Natalie said, you had to spend the money from your bonanza years on something. You couldn't turn up at a client's in a Mondeo, she said. Unless, of course, something double-glazed in white PVC was part of the spec, she said, switching from her professional frown to her sunny weekend smile.

But then Natalie said a lot of things, all of them full of certainty. That *was* her. It wasn't as if he hadn't known her properly. Furtiveness was foreign to her until the something she couldn't be upfront about came along and made her into somebody else entirely for the rest of their time together. He understood more clearly now why it had to end for her. Someone like Natalie couldn't carry on being somebody else indefinitely. He was hurt, but perhaps he shouldn't be surprised. It helped, at least, to know that *something* had happened. Though the something made him catch his breath every time he thought about it.

He eased the car out from his space near the dustbins in the courtyard below his window. He tried not to rev it too much, and flashed to let a BT engineer go first at the junction and resisted the temptation to go squealing off when the lights changed. If you owned any kind of Porsche you learned to be an exemplary driver, a gentleman of the road, if only to confound other people's expectations of you as an inconsiderate tosser.

Normally he would have gone with Christian in his Saab – stylish without being showy – but Christian was at Mortensens in New York, planning to turn Manhattan into Stockholm. Bart snaked through the City until he found signs for the A12 and Cambridge. The traffic thinned as he left the eastern suburbs behind. By mid-morning he was bowling through the sunlit countryside with the top down, music blaring, the wind whipping his hair, a free man made by circumstances beyond his control.

An hour later he found the village and turned into the site by the river opposite the newsagent's. There was a big old Citroën van with corrugated sides and rusty French plates blocking the entrance to the little asphalt car park where he could see the back end of a red Fiesta and the bonnet of Tristram's navy Jag protruding. A small pickup was squeezed between a yellow skip and the site toilet, the driver slumped back in his seat with his eyes closed. His mate was reading a paper and eating a sandwich. Bart pulled up behind the Citroën, swapped his sunglasses for see-through ones and got out. He squinted up at the gutted mill and took a breath of air. The big door was open but there was no sign of activity. Nothing much looked different, though there was a ditch and signs of drainage having been laid. He stuck his head inside. Someone had left a radio on somewhere, just audible. He came back out and climbed the wooden steps to the temporary office erected on blocks alongside. Tristram was sitting on a desk, barking down the phone and looking harassed. He motioned vigorously to Bart to come in. A woman was already waiting, standing by a trestle table leafing through a samples catalogue of some sort, a big canvas holdall at her feet. She glanced up at Bart. She was wearing a carpenter's brown bib-and-brace with a black T-shirt underneath, her pale face, pixie featured, was framed by a cut of thick dark hair with a short, angled fringe. Chic, but with overtones of scruff.

He twinkled her a grin to acknowledge Tristram's high-volume conversation. 'Sounds like someone's in trouble,' he said.

'So it seems,' she said flatly, and carried on turning pages.

'Sorry, were you . . .'

'No, he's all yours,' she said. 'I'm just about done.'

He noticed a light Irish accent. Husky too.

He looked at her again. It was her, wasn't it? It *was* her. He turned away as she glanced up. She didn't recognise him. He found himself staring at a year planner tacked to the wall, his face getting warmer. She wouldn't remember. She wouldn't remember some imbecile in the street stealing a taxi from under her nose. Christ. He sneaked another look at her, pursed lips, her eyes flicking over the catalogue.

Tristram put the phone down. 'Bloody contractors,' he said. 'No one turns up for a day and a half, and now he's got problems matching the bricks. He's had two chaps sitting out there over an hour waiting for him. Appalling manners if nothing else.'

He took a deep breath and exhaled, like a diver come to the surface. 'Sorry. One of those days. I was hoping to be well into the structural stuff by now. Can't even raise the damned surveyor.' He turned to the woman. 'So . . . Kate, brilliant. Can I leave that with you?'

'I'm on the case,' she said. 'Give me a couple of weeks.' With effort, she hoisted the holdall on to her shoulder.

'This is Bart, by the way,' he said. 'Interiors.'

'Kate,' she said, accepting Bart's handshake. 'Floors.'

Kate. Kate. She moved away.

'You might have trouble getting out,' said Bart, suddenly finding his tongue. 'Some idiot's blocking the car park.'

'I'll manage,' she said, not looking back. He watched her go. Kate.

He and Tristram sat down with coffee at the trestle table and began to go over Bart's exciting sketches and Christian's elegant drawings – a nice impression, Bart thought, of uninhibited passion and functional beauty. He heard himself talk, selling the ideas, surprising even himself with his sparkle and professionalism and aura of craftsmanship. Christian would have been proud of him. Tristram had a few things to say, as clients must – how otherwise could they be masters of their own dreams? To this end Bart had left minor anomalies of style to be spotted, commented upon and tweaked, providing Tristram with a modicum of creative input, or at least the illusion of it. Where he didn't take the bait, Bart would nudge him towards it – polished aluminium rods for the upper handrail rather than reclaimed ash spindles, thus drawing the eye to the metallic tumult of the kitchen; perhaps rounds of frosted glass for the mezzanine, picking up the shape of the building and allowing natural light to filter through to the lower levels. Yes, that would be an improvement, and actually not that much more expensive. Kate. Bart's thoughts drifted back to her – it wasn't every woman who could make dungarees work – while Tristram pondered and pointed at this or that feature, and stroked his greying goatee a good deal. There would be levels of discussions with the listed-building people and his chef and his French girl-friend Lisette who was doing the marketing, but on the whole he thought it was a plan that could fly. Bart nodded and agreed with everything and promised a final quote and revised specifications. He polished the lenses of his glasses and, with skilful nonchalance, manoeuvred her – Kate, Kate – into the conversation. 'So where did you find, er . . . sorry, what's her name again?' He pointed at the door.

'Kate? She worked on my last place,' Tristram said. 'She's a salvage scout. That's what she calls herself. Basically, she finds nice old stuff and sells it – a lot of restored single pieces go to the bigger upmarket shops in the West End. But she works for private clients too, if you're looking for something in particular. She's not cheap but she is good.'

'So, she's not just floors.'

'This time she's floors – well, the main floor and basement. But no, she's not just floors. She's everything.'

She's everything!

The phone rang while they were concluding business. Bart left Tristram giving his surveyor the benefit of his grievances and headed for the car. The pickup had gone. He noticed the big Citroën van still there but the bonnet was in the air now. He saw her – Kate – pacing in the entrance to the little asphalted area, talking into a mobile.

He waited on the step for her to finish, then called to her. 'Can't you get out?'

She looked at him coldly. 'My van's broken down.'

He was puzzled for a moment. 'Oh. So . . .'

'Yes, I'm the idiot blocking the car park.'

Excellent. He sucked air through his teeth and gave her his best goofy expression. 'Sorry about that.'

She looked away, across the road, her arms folded, as if fascinated by a dog sniffing the display board outside the village newsagent's.

'I'd like to help,' he added, 'but I'm hopeless with cars.' He wandered over to the van and stared hard at the engine. He waggled one of the pipes mired by a hundred years of oil and grease. 'Hmm,' he said.

'I *know* what's wrong with it.' She walked towards him, holding up a hank of frayed rubber. 'It needs one of these. Snapped as I was starting it up.'

'Fan belt?'

'My, aren't you the quick learner,' she said, only marginally less coldly, arms folded again. She looked away again, watching the traffic trickle through the narrow street. 'The main dealer in Cambridge has one but they can't get it out to me right now. I have to go pick it up.'

'I could give you a lift.' He nodded sideways at the Boxster, his heart beating out the tattoo of hope.

She made a doubtful face. 'That's your car?'

'It is. You got something against Porsches?'

She gave a half-smile, or perhaps a half-smirk. He dipped into his top pocket for his sunglasses but changed his mind. 'I'm not going to apologise for driving a Porsche,' he said smiling.

She shrugged. 'Why should you?'

'OK,' he said, 'I know that people who drive fast cars might understandably come in for a bit of flak, for reasons of hatred and envy and resentment and bitterness and so on. But, you have to admit, looking objectively, that it's an exquisite bit of engineering. Look at those gentle curves – look at those wheel arches and sloping headlamps and that interior and that lovely little dash with those dinky little clocks. It's not about speed and pissing people off who think you're showing off, which, actually, I'm not. As I see it, beauty is neutral. Beauty has no context,' he added.

'Buying a car has a context,' she said.

'Well . . .'

'I mean you can't be neutral about context. I mean you either don't *know* that some people are bound to think you're a wanker for driving a car like this, or you *do* know but don't care what people think. Or, third option, you could of course just *be* that wanker.'

'Right. Thanks for the warning,' he said, satisfied that *this* Porsche owner always made a point of stopping at pedestrian crossings, even waiting that extra few seconds to allow slow, annoying people to reach the kerb. 'Given the choice, I think I'll take the second category, if that's OK.'

'Trouble is, you don't get the choice. Which is why you end up explaining to people like me why you're not apologising for driving a Porsche. Nothing personal,' she added.

'Absolutely not,' he said with an open pleasantness, mentally preparing now to allow himself to be irritated by Kate, thereby softening the disappointment of her being irritated by him. Those cute pixie looks could get irritating. And that sexy Irish voice.

She stooped to look inside the car now, as if having reached the brink of rudeness she was ready to take a step back. 'On the other hand, I do like *old* Porsches. If that's any consolation.'

'So maybe you'll like this one in thirty years,' he said.

'Not necessarily.'

'That's usually how long it takes modern things to turn into nice old things. Once they've been pronounced cool by enough people. Which is fine.'

'Meaning?'

'Well, you know, modern things can be a bit challenging.' He cast a glance at her van. 'Your old Citroën was probably modern once.'

She pursed her lips, her hands deep in her pockets as she walked round the Boxster, inspecting it. 'I take your point about modern things,' she said, 'but this Porsche is no more modern, in any real sense, than an old Porsche.' She nodded at the car. 'It might be technically more up-to-date, but all the things you were going on about – those curves and little clocks and so on – first made their appearance decades ago. It might be a new car but it's not actually saying anything new. It's just a parody of an old modern classic. The reason modern classics don't lose their status is because they were there first.'

'So what are you saying – it can't be beautiful because it's not truly modern?'

'No, I agree it is quite beautiful in a conventional way.'

He looked gloomy. 'So it *is* the wanker argument.'

'As I said, nothing personal. And as for old Citroëns – mine is purely functional.'

'It's not looking too functional at the moment.'

'*Touché,*' she said.

He followed her round to the front of the van. She lowered the bonnet and wiped her hands on her overalls. There was a triangle of rusty indentations against the radiator grille where the Citroën chevron badge had once been. 'I suppose we'd better push it out of the way,' she said. 'You'll have to move yours first.'

He reversed the Boxster into the gap left by the pickup next to the toilet, and together they rolled the Citroën back a few feet. 'Jesus Christ, this thing weighs a ton.'

She gave him the idiot look. 'All cars weigh a ton.'

'Yes, I know,' he said, panting. 'I was joking.'

They stood for a moment. 'I travel in France a lot, buying old furniture and stuff. If they see you coming they just put the price up. This way they don't see you. This is my disguise.'

'Don't they notice the Irish accent?'

By way of an answer, she gave him a burst of rapid-fire French, gesturing comically with her hands and eyebrows – something about *meubles* and *tables* and *chaises*. Bart's French vocabulary wasn't bad. It was the stuff that made it all hang together that he had trouble with.

'Did *you* notice it?' she said, very nearly smiling.

'Not bad,' he said.

'I keep the Irish accent for speaking English.'

'Is that a disguise too?'

She locked the van door. 'I think I've seen you here before – with a tall, blond guy. Drives a Volvo estate?'

'Ah. A Saab, actually.'

She nodded. 'I thought I recognised you.'

'So . . . do you want a lift or not?'

'That's my taxi just arriving,' she said, directing her glance over his shoulder. He turned at the crunch of tyres on the gravelly site entrance. 'Unless you were maybe thinking it was yours,' she added.

He sighed and looked at the ground. 'I was afraid you'd say that. Do you believe in fate?'

'I don't even believe in coincidences,' she said. He noticed her blue eyes for the first time. Irresistible Irish combo of blue eyes and black hair. And pixie looks.

'Why don't I give you my card,' he said.

She waited for him to dig one out of his wallet. 'Barton,' she said looking at him with those eyes. 'Is that you?'

'Yes, Barton. Bart.'

'Don't you have a first name?'

He hesitated. 'Arthur.'

'*Arthur?*' she repeated.

'My aunt's idea. Hence Bart,' he said smiling.

She left without offering him a card of her own, following her chin as she walked to the waiting taxi, a brown dungaree strap looping from one shoulder, like a model on dress-down Friday. Bart got into his car, turned the ignition and squeezed the gas gently, bringing the engine to growling point. He did like his Porsche, the sound and the smell and the feel of it – no reason why he shouldn't – but realised that his defence of it had been a spurious, uncooked version of the argument Natalie would have used, an act more of frozen habit than conviction. And though it was hardly Natalie's fault, he blamed her now for loading him with her thoughts and then doing a runner, for sending him into battle so fully baggaged as to be put to the sword by the first beautiful stranger who came along.

Still . . . He smiled and turned the radio off. Sometimes all the music you needed came from your own muddled heart.

Later, he met Monty at the Red Horse.

'I saw this fantastic girl today,' Bart said, bringing the drinks.

88

Monty was stooped over the pool table at eye level with the white ball, chin resting on the pale grain of the cue. 'Don't tell me about her,' he said, carefully teeing up his shot.

Bart slapped him on the back. 'Sorry, mate. Forgot.'

• • •

Fuck. Cold shudder to the sphincter. Nick stared at Hugo, uncertain of how to play this, immediate assumption being that he'd been called in for a bollocking over non-attendance of some joke 'ideas' breakfast, or wearing an unironed shirt, or for coming skipping in late this morning flushed with – as fortune had it – a fresh promise of Ivy. A naked Ivy swam through his thoughts now, a flicker of warmth amid the treacherous currents of Hugo in full corporate flood.

'It's not absolutely certain how it's going to pan out, but if the merger goes ahead – and, at the moment, I'm obliged to say it *is* still very much an if . . .'

'It sounds more like a takeover to me,' Nick said. 'And then it'll just be their agency against ours, won't it? And they'll win because SBO Young's are bigger than us.'

Hugo looked at his watch pointedly, point being if Nick had been in at ten-thirty he would have got the same briefing as the rest of the team and Hugo wouldn't now be wasting his valuable having to say everyfuckingthing twice. '*If* the merger goes through, I'm guessing that the more conspicuous idea would be to synergise the two agencies into one, skimming the cream from each. Otherwise what would be the point? We all know this is a people business. I'm telling you this so you don't hear it from anyone else and get the wrong end of the stick, and so you know what you're up against. As I told everybody else, I wouldn't blame anybody for wanting

to stay ahead of the game and making alternative arrange-
ments. Depending on how strong they feel their position is,
obviously. Part of the cream or otherwise.'

Nick suddenly saw himself in very much the non-cream or
otherwise position. 'So we're not talking about random blood-
letting here.'

'The board would be asking department heads for their
recommendations, I imagine. Should the occasion arise.'

'Based on talent and creative track record, right?' Twitch
starting its radar blip under his left eye.

'Based on everything. What can I tell you?' Hugo looked at
his watch again and stood up. 'Your team's yoghurt presentation, this p.m. Try and be there, eh?'

So, hey. How a day could shape up. Up with a lark, trains clattering past the bottom of his bed every five seconds into King's
Cross an hour before dawn. No hot water, yesterday's clothes.
First bus in the vague direction of Smithfield. Coffee, fags and
toast in the café opposite Jas's for an hour and a half, reading
the print off the paper while he watched for her blinds going
up third day running, this time with required result for teeth-
gritted exultations behind his steamed-up pane.

Yes . . .

Another three-quarters of an hour before she'd finally sur-
faced on the street, student-scruffy, but how his heart had
raced out to her! How he had leapt to his feet to follow it,
pausing in his haste to thrust money at the unshaven man of
Mediterranean appearance at the till, risking Jas being up at
his kitchen window wondering what the fuck *he* was doing
out there. Sprinting like a bag snatcher, then slowing to a
half-walk as he suddenly caught up with her outside the
French place clocking herself quickly in the glass looking
moody as she walked past.

'*Ivy* . . .' (Fucksake, calm *down*, you needy sap.)

Her turning in alarm. 'Christ, Nick, what are you doing?'

Falling into step with her, her moving up a gear like an answer in itself.

'Phew, thought I might just catch you,' he said.

'Well, now you have.'

They carried on in silence, cutting through the market, iron arches all over the place, past the old red phone boxes, pigeons, forklifts, traders' noticeboard, hard hats for sale, union meeting, driver required, resuscitation classes at St Bart's.

'How are things?'

'Fine.'

Cyclists must dismount beyond this point.

'Aren't you going to ask me about my new place?'

Speeding up again. 'How's your new place?' she said. Voice croaky.

'Great. You'll have to come round some time. Quite homely.'

He heard the pitch of desperation in his own voice, saw himself for the first time as she did, as a person of possible declining appeal. They stopped between the entrance to the tube and the fruit man standing by his scales, wino asleep under a blanket next to the chemist's. Tiring, all that begging and drinking. Paper coffee cup on its side rolling this way and that with the breeze. She pushed her tangle of red hair back with her hand. Looked like she hadn't slept for a week herself, no make-up. True beauty that was, shining through, as it were. He gazed at her as she looked the other way, tried to discern a hint of compliance in her expression, fathom something hopeful in her mood before the instant was gone and her with it – felt his stomach tighten, as though he'd asked her for money and *no* was already on her lips. Please, please.

But then – fuck! – it worked ... he didn't know what. Something collapsed slightly about her. Like she was weakened by a low thought that came to her and not because he was poodling up on his hind legs in front of her with his big brown, bloodshot eyes.

OK, she said, they could meet for lunch. His heart flapping in its cage, astonished that she had now somehow given him the money without being asked. He felt impelled to make a run for it before she realised what a mistake she had made. She'd got a lecture at twelve, she said, so just after one, outside the college gate. No enquiry about his own plans. It was take it or leave it. Yes again. Joy, desire, expectation. What else did you need on your timetable?

And ... action. After his briefing with Hugo, he spent the next hour overseeing the emergency yoghurt meeting he'd convened to give his graduate-calibre rookies a fighting chance to remember the name of the product, simultaneously trying to find Des, leaving messages at the courier's office in the basement, on Des's mobile, on Des's voicemail at home. He'd just about given up when his phone went and Des's number came up. He left Kirsty, Will, Charley and whatever the fuck the other one was called running through their pitch, which actually was better than anyone deserved: organic frozen yoghurt on a stick being seen sucked at the opera and other centres of upmarket entertainment ('Ice-Bio. Get some culture into *your* life.').

Out in the corridor, standing by the lift, Des's new impatient, barky voice in his ear. 'Nick. Talk to me.' Des had lost all respect for the upper floors in general after getting fucked over courtesy of Nick's last trick, and introduced a new 'get tough' retailing strategy based on not trusting anyone under nineteen stone and being unsympathetic to pleas of negative liquidity. He'd had to sell his new, massive, fuck-off BMW motorbike at a substantial loss to square things at his end, he said, and even then only just avoided a slapping. Shame. Still. That was crime for you.

'Des, Des, what you been up to?'

Sullen bastard, playing hard to get.

'Trying not to give them an excuse to fire me.'

'They've got it in for all of us, I think.'

'What do you want, Nick?'

'Get me some stuff?'

'When?'

'Yesterday?'

Des snorted. 'You must be kidding.'

Nick sniffed to let him know he was still there. One, two, three . . .

'OK. Cash up front,' Des said after a pause long enough to satisfy his new way of being pissed off with life as a fetcher and carrier in general and with Nick in particular.

'Pound notes guaranteed. But I'm a bit pushed, old chum. You might have to run me into the West End.'

'Do I look like a minicab driver?'

'I don't know, mate. Are you wearing that jumper with the bobbles on it?'

'Funny.'

'Couple of grams?'

'Fuck, it's Christmas already.'

'Car park, quarter to one?'

'See what I can do.'

The phone went dead. Thank you for your custom.

He paused at the lift to check his watch. The doors opened like an invitation. He stepped inside and pushed the button. There were times, he thought, when excitement got the better of fear and apprehension; times when you couldn't return to yoghurt; times when to buy a crisp new shirt seemed the only way to proceed, the A to B of enhancing love and career prospects in one serendipitous short cut. Past Dave on security, disapproving moustache visible above the front desk. Out on to the pavement. The nearest menswear emporium was a brisk, sunny walk to High Holborn, made all the sunnier with his pockets metaphorically bulging with credit, thanks to the Bank of Free Money offering a spanking new platinum card in return for letting them mop up his old debt and providing tons of fresh pocket money to put on top. It was eminently possible, he was beginning to realise – by the simple expedient of exaggerating the truth in all formal declarations of income and outgoings, paying the monthly minimum and transferring to a new card once or twice a year – to comfortably live beyond his means until he died. Or at least until something better came up.

He spent twenty-five minutes in Next choosing patterns and colours. Candy stripes, he thought, pass for a Paul Smith. Mentally awarded full points to the assistant for remaining unfazed by his decision to wear his purchases back to the office, unblinkingly allowing Nick himself to parcel up his own used shirt, boxers and socks and pop them into the proffered bag.

And . . . inhale. Sun on his face. Shopping finished, fucking yet to come – and enough time on the clock to put Ice-Bio products firmly on the consumer's map of dairy necessaries, thus offering up the symbolic lucrative contract of atonement for transgressions past. It could all happen.

Just after one, they pulled up at a cashpoint machine, him riding pillion gripping the seat of Des's old wreck of a Yamaha, which the dealer had been happy to let Des have back for just slightly more than he'd allowed on it when

Des'd bought the new one, which the dealer had been equally happy to buy back for slightly less than he'd sold it to Des three weeks earlier. All in all, not a triumph for the consumer, Des said. Nick was attentive to his plight, even jocular ('What – do they still make Triumphs?'), though only up to the point where Des palmed him the coke in exchange for a straight ton in twenties, still warm from the machine. He left him strapping the spare helmet to the bike, and panicking about needing to get to Brentwood in five minutes to pick up some artwork.

Nick found a pub, a toilet stall, a white cistern to chop a quick line. Out again. Cut through the alley of antique books, maps and old stuff, sniffing. Not bad. Though not great. Obviously something Des kept back for his worst customers.

Ivy waiting outside the college as arranged. Peck on the cheek. Sleeveless in the sun. Her warm freckled shoulders.

'Sorry I'm a bit late,' he said.

'So,' she said, unsmiling. 'Where shall we eat?'

Eat . . . He flashed a smile. 'Ah.'

It wasn't just the money, of course, it was the time window.

'Right,' he said, mind whirring. 'Actually, there is this place I've been wanting to try out,' he added. Though, truly actually, what he'd figured was a fast cab back over to his place, a vigorous, coke-fuelled shag with a bit of leisurely post-coital to chill and smooth things between them for next time, and a fast cab back to the office. You couldn't fit food into that. You couldn't fit the unpredictable rhythms of chefs and waiters into that, with their insistence on making you look at menus and keeping you hanging around for hours while they fucked off and served somebody else. No.

'Where is it?' Ivy asked. 'This place?'

His mind was now rapidly thought-processing the tourist

slump issue, which had appeared in his head, and for good reason. Hotel rooms. Were they not absolutely *surrounded* by cheap, empty hotel rooms? Admittedly he faced the immediate difficulty of squaring the idea of a double deluxe en suite with the more conventional expectations that the word 'lunch' might encourage, but it wasn't inconceivable that a hotel might have a sushi or tapas bar, or other instant pre-something that could pass as lunch and wasn't sandwich-based and thus patently haste-orientated, and which would leave the necessary three-quarters of an hour for the main purpose of their visit, as at least he saw it.

He was lightly steering her across the road, arm gently around her, through the traffic, the electric from her running right through him as they breached Covent Garden borders. 'I thought it might be fun,' he heard himself saying. 'Bit unusual, but I've got this client, who . . .'

'Who . . .'

Tapped his nose. 'Wait and see.'

Hotel. Expensive-looking with an awning and brass frontage and little tailored shrubs growing in pots and proper restaurant with people eating and slurping. No sushi counter. 'Let's have a drink first,' he said. 'Just got to have a word with . . .'

Bar. He left her sitting on a high stool with a large G&T and big bowl of cashews. Reception back through the big doors, first on the left. Tiny woman looked up, smile, good sign. Singaporean, Thai, Filipino, somewhere like that. 'Can I help you?' she was saying.

'Well, yes. Hope so. We just had this crazy idea. Me and my girlfriend.' He jerked a thumb back at wherever. 'We've got a transfer out of Heathrow this evening. We were just going to do a bit of sightseeing, but then we thought it might be an idea to get a couple of hours' sleep instead. I don't suppose you have a room? Double?'

Smile disappeared, frown in its place. 'One night?' Black eyes reading him for terrorist connections, then flitting across a computer screen down there below the desk. Name-badge: Krissie. Not obviously South-East Asian.

Maintain grin consistent with crazy idea. 'Well, just the afternoon, really. It's my girlfriend's birthday, you see. Our flight's at six, and we're going to Peru. Couldn't get a direct flight from . . . Brussels,' he said, falling into a slight French accent, being unacquainted with a Belgian one.

She glared at him. 'Afternoon makes no difference, sir. Full day rate is hundred twenty pounds.'

Fuck.

'Perfect. And could you organise a bit of lunch in our room? Something really, really quick. Something cold maybe, save time. Salad. My girlfriend doesn't eat meat. Something fishy perhaps?'

'We do have room service, sir.'

'Would you mind organising that for me? Anything will do. Really.' Hopeless grin now. Charm. 'Krissie?'

She resisted another smile, but amazingly produced a menu from behind the desk. 'I can ring for you,' she said, glasses now perched on her nose. 'Salad. We have tuna . . . or warm lobster salad.'

'Whatever. But don't bother to warm it. Plus a bottle of house champagne. Straight away if possible. We're just having a drink in the bar first. Could you give us a call when it's all ready?'

He handed over his credit card and scribbled in the register.

'You have luggage?'

'Probably on its way to Barcelona by now.' He laughed.

'Excuse me?'

'Sorry. Joke.'

Whoops, there goes the Belgian cover.

Triumphant dash back to Ivy, blood up. 'We've just got to wait for our table.'

'It didn't look that busy in the restaurant.'

'Ah yes, but *our* table's not ready. We're getting one with a view.'

'Nick, a pub would have done. Or a café.'

'No problem. It's all on the house anyway. Client, as I said.'

'So, if they're your clients, what are they doing offering you free lunches?'

'Well, you know, usual reason. Valuable word of mouth, from their point of view. They need people like us – media people, advertising people – to tell everybody else. And this new kind of service they're marketing – this *day service*, as they call it – you can't just advertise it. You've got to let people discover it. It's like one of those water-cooler jobs. Couple of weeks and it'll be in all the style supplements and every hotel in London will be offering day service.'

'Day service . . .'

'Yeah. It's for busy travellers really, but also brilliant for anyone who's in town and needs a bit of relaxation between art galleries or shopping marathons. Sounds almost Japanese in concept, but really it's just a way of plugging into the tourist crisis. Course, they're only piloting it at the moment. People like me and you. Lucky us, eh?'

She looked unintrigued. 'Right, so what is it?'

'Ah, wouldn't want to kill the surprise.' He winked at her over his drink, checked the time. One twenty. Same price as room. Lucky omen. Yoghurt people at three.

Fifteen, twenty minutes went by. Touching knees at the bar. Gazing into her eyes, making the effort to pay proper attention as she went on about the sanctity of art and moaned about Jas, the two things being inextricably linked somehow.

'And really,' she said, 'he's just trawling for women students, who think he's some kind of fucking legend just because he's had a couple of books out. And all this bollocks about commercial work freeing him up to do what's really important. When, actually, it's the absolute *opposite*. Do you know what he told me?'

'What did he tell you?'

'When I first came to stay with him. My first week. He said the best way to get highly paid advertising work was to have some war pictures and hardboiled social realism in your portfolio. And that's why he still has his annual fortnight going round trouble spots and scenes of tragedy and misery pretending to be a working photojournalist. I mean, that's the only reason – to get the right kind of moody shots of people looking lost and defeated so he can make heaps of money doing commercial work. Because, as he put it, tragedy is a powerful aesthetic in advertising and you have to have it in your repertoire. It's obscene! Can you believe he actually thought I'd be impressed by that?'

A uniformed flunkey, late teens, appeared in the doorway.

Nick leapt to his feet. 'Ah, lunch is served, I believe.'

He took the key off him quickly, ushered Ivy through the doors, slipped the boy a fiver. 'We'll find our own way, thanks.'

'Everything's ready, sir,' the boy said, thrilled at his own efficiency, rushing ahead to call the lift for them, standing back to let them in as it dinged its arrival. Soft carpet underfoot, promise of intimacy, shoelessness.

'And – you know,' Ivy was saying, ignoring his fingers accidentally brushing her thigh as he stood unnecessarily close to her as the doors closed, 'the way he just trots out this Oscar Wilde stuff about not mixing art and morality and how we mustn't pander to bourgeois sensibilities and how art is supposed to answer only to itself. I mean, bourgeois sensibilities, for fuck's sake. He thinks it's still 1975.'

Up. Third, fourth. *Ding*. 'Right, art and morality,' he heard himself say. The doors opened. 427. Arrows left, no right.

'I mean, do you believe that?' she said.

'Um . . . do you?'

'Of course *I* do. But he doesn't. It's just bullshit. He's the one pandering to bourgeois sensibilities. He's pandering to bourgeois sensibilities every time he picks up a fucking camera.'

Smile. 'Well, you have to remember, he does have to make a living.'

'Exactly. So why does he keep harping on about artistic integrity? I mean, you guys. You were all supposed to have been at art college together. There must have been some point where all you wanted to do was *make* something.'

Polished door numbers counting down. Take-off. He wondered where the old seductive Ivy went. He wondered where this new, intense one had sprung from who cared so much about this stuff, babbling on so much she'd hardly noticed where they were going. Which was no bad thing, under the circumstances. 427. Yes. Key. He swung the door open. 'At your service!' he said.

She looked at him. 'A hotel room? Hey, wow, Nick, that's subtle.'

'No, no – day service. Lunch, as promised, but with added-value, post-digestive relaxation facilities.' He grinned, escorted her to the table in the little bay, flapped open a napkin for her, made a deal of popping the cork, busied himself peeling shrink-wrap off the tastefully arranged platter of fish and fresh greenery, pouring champagne with a flourish. 'I ordered tuna – can you eat tuna?'

Shrug. 'Has it been caught with a line?'

'Guess what? This *is* line-caught. I checked. Lobster, too, I think.' He took a big forkful and plunged it into his mouth. 'Mmmm – actually, that *is* good,' he said, one cheek exaggeratedly distended in a way intended to make her laugh, which two weeks ago it would have done, along with everything else he did, up to and including the old party trick of wearing a sock on his large and impressive erection. But that was then.

She started eating slowly, looking sideways and out, subdued now, emptied of rant. View of the dirty top windows of the shops opposite. He talked quickly, filling the void with his own witterings – office successes, TV ads, the advantages of his new flat – urging her on with the spur of his irrepressible cajolery. But even as he laughed and assailed her with badinage he saw the hour of his need ticking by, disappearing, in the way she prodded her food around, not touching her bubbly while he poured himself a second and then a third, setting a pace that he could see she was disinclined to follow. The coke was wearing off and he felt himself sinking into the opposite of alert, felt the uncomfortable warmth of the room, the damp of his armpits, the fatigue of it all. Perhaps another snort was in order, rubbish as it was (thanks, Des). He made a pantomime of struggling out of his jacket, yanked his tie free, undid another shirt button and asked if she fancied a line or two – perk herself up a bit? 'Got some excellent stuff,' he said. 'Fresh off the boat.'

She pursued a flap of cold pasta with her fork around the neglected chunks of glistening seafood, slabs of sweating flesh on her plate. 'Thanks, but I'm not really feeling up for it,' she said.

'Exactly! Isn't that the best time to do it?' He reached across and speared a piece of her lobster with the point of his knife, pulled it off with his teeth, chewed sensuously (Woody Allen in what was it – the one with the hair dryer and Humphrey Bogart?), trying to catch her averted eyes, praised the food lavishly, using the language of waved cutlery. She sighed, told him about her mother, who had been ill with something and was now at home on her own. He beetled his brow and nodded, but the details of it were lost in the churn of his own mind, calculating the odds of moving the feast from table to bed, flitting back to the point only after he'd missed it. Parkinson's, was it she said? Varicose veins? Hip replacement? As she spoke – something about her mother's finances, because she'd had to jack in her job at the town hall – his eyes settled on the outline of Ivy's budding nipple pressed against her sleeveless coral-coloured top, roved to the dipping curve of her breast you could just see as she leaned forward to pattern the avocado and garlic mash with the tines of her fork, the ambient buzz of Covent Garden filling his head like a warm, narcotic haze, blunting the sharper sensations of the immediate situation, the artificiality of the meal, the full tenor of Ivy's preoccupations. Lunch was over, in so far as neither of them was eating. The champagne was gone, except that still pointlessly releasing the last of its fizz in Ivy's glass, half full from when he had topped it up after her first sip.

'So . . .' he said. Because there *was* still time. At least half an hour. But one of them had to do something about making this an occasion to remember.

'Trouble is,' she was saying, 'I need someone to help me take some stuff up to Norfolk at the weekend.'

Weekend!

'I'll take you,' he said. 'My car's still under the mechanic but I can arrange transport, no *problemo*.'

Did she mean going *for* the weekend? Did she mean the two of them? The possibility of a Norfolk weekend reared its mighty head above the fading possibility of the here, right now in this room, and with it his hundred and twenty quid plus whatever this lot cost, not to mention the new shirt, socks and boxers.

'Thanks,' she said, as if she couldn't bring herself to be surprised by the offer. 'You'll have to pick me up Saturday morning when Dad's at the market. Ring first to make sure.'

'It's a date.' He grinned at her, but she was looking at her watch. His heart sank again. One last throw. He got up from the table, stretching and yawning, walked across the room and flopped on the bed. She gave him a pitying stare. Which was a start.

'Well, I think we ought to test it for comfort. Least we can do, surely,' he said, tone just the right side of ambiguous, leaving space to reverse out quickly if necessary, tail lights protected by small buffer of humour. 'Don't you think?' He lay there on his back, uncertain, like someone in Selfridges with the salesman hovering, levered off one shoe, then the other, heaved sigh of contentment, patted the bed beside him. 'Come on, Ivy, try it out . . .'

She shook her head, sniffed (tear in her eye?), turned away, went off to the bathroom. Jesus. What the fuck now? Closed his eyes for a mo. Heard the door lock, echo against the tiles. Her period maybe. Had to be. But if not today, weekend. How long did periods last. Thurs, Fri, Sat. Norfolk, though . . . flint cottage overlooking the beach, evening in the pub, as much sex as he could eat. The low thrum of engines from the traffic below came to him now through the window, open only the fraction allowed in hotels, people chattering on the street, occasional far shout, music from the piazza beyond. Take the noise apart, find millions of smaller things, scuffing of a tyre against the kerb, a car key turning, locks popping, rustle of a newspaper, scrape of a chair, clop of heels, they all counted, like atoms, no real silence, more of a whirr so soft we're used to it. Mmmm . . .

Yes.

He *was* making something. Saw himself holding a welder's torch, mask up, standing legs triumphantly apart in front of a towering structure, only partly completed but nevertheless of undisputed artistic worth. An allegory of political struggle (or whatever) surrounded by admirers – Olivia, that Briony girl, Ivy, Jas, Jackson Pollock (or the bald guy who played him in the film), Francis Bacon for some reason wearing Jas's leather jacket – bright shafts of daylight streaming in through long windows like a cathedral or a fire station. Himself, smiling, heroic. Renaissance man. Ads, design, fine art, stand-up comedy. Call this number.

He opened his eyes suddenly, acclimatising to the strange room with its Oriental wall prints and tall canvassy lampshades, and wondered where he was and then, remembering, wondered at how the day had so suddenly changed its look – the angled blade of sunlight across the ceiling and, out there, on the building opposite, the dazzle of top windows like mirrored aviator shades. Oh, holy fuck. He leapt off the bed and looked down the street for the second time in as many weeks, it occurred to him, in panic. Where was Ivy? How could he have slept for *four fucking hours*? Oh Jesus. He grabbed his jacket, *where were his shoes?*, phone to his ear. Hugo. Hugo. Arm stuck down other sleeve. Voicemail giving out Hugo's mobile. Redial. Wait. *Fuck*.

'Yep.' Background noise. Bar somewhere. Sundowner.

'Hugo, it's Nick. You won't believe this but I'm, I'm . . . down at the hospital. I had a . . . an incident on the tube. I'm OK but, um . . .'

Laughter behind him, glasses clinking. *Shh*, Hugo was saying, it's *Nick*. Hugo with drink inside him.

'There was this guy, right? On the escalator—'

'No explanations necessary, old chum. Kirsty and Will and the others ran the presentation, and you know what? They were fucking great. They're all here now. So the good news is – we won the business. Bad news is . . . well, things aren't looking too bright for you, mate. Jonathan dropped by with one of the partners from SBO's. Obviously impressed but he *did* wonder what the hell I was doing letting the juniors run the whole shebang. Had to tell him. No choice really. Anyway, talk tomorrow. Sort everything out. Don't rush in or anything. You take it easy. I mean, obviously, easier than usual . . .'

● ● ●

In an ideal world, Jas believed, freedom was to be found as much in life's routines as in its wilder excursions. Freedom on a Saturday morning, for example – routinely between ten and midday – was to be found in a leisurely peregrination round Clerkenwell and environs, hunting and gathering. Organic kebabs and pork ribs from Lenny's; bread and whatever else smelled good at Flâneur; something fragrant from the Italian deli on Farringdon Road; chorizo, olives and probably more bread from the Spanish shop on Exmouth Market. No shopping list, just shopping. And then he would stop off at Al's for the all-day big *petit déjeuner* with tea and the *Guardian* from the newsagent's opposite before heading home in time for *Football Focus*.

But not today. His canvas war-photographer's bag was brimming as usual, but his heart wasn't in it. And the problem was not, as might be expected, the result of last night's episode of b&s – which he hadn't really had the heart for either (though the show had had to go on) – but of the business preceding b&s, the kind of business that might have given rise on previous episodes of b&s to an oblique, even prurient, allusion to events with the intention of eliciting weary applause or show of envy at his success with women. He didn't do real kiss and tell. After all, he wasn't an adolescent or – worse – Nick. But if you didn't flicker a light on your private life every now and then, people might be forgiven for thinking you didn't have one. This time, though, he had not been actively looking for the business to happen – had even taken steps to avoid it. Which was why, he supposed – as he passed Al's by on the other side, studiously denying himself the pleasure of bacon, a couple of sunny *oeufs*, chipolatas, black pudding, fried mushrooms, toms, tea and toast – yesterday's business had left him with precisely what every connoisseur of freedom at the age of forty-two should have long learned to avoid: regret.

She had rung yesterday morning from Leather Lane, where she was looking for cheap CDs. 'Hello, is that Jas?'

'In the flesh.'

She hesitated. 'I don't know if you remember me – Lois? You gave a talk at my college?'

'Yeah, right, of course. Lois. You wanted me to take a look at your stuff.'

'You said to call if I was passing. Have you got time now?'

The truth was that, no actually, he didn't have time. He had a batch of contact sheets to look at, he had to catch the post and he was supposed to be meeting a Sunday magazine editor for lunch with a view to pitching the first UK rights to *Finest*, his NYPD coffee-table oeuvre, out this summer in all good bookshops. But he'd said yes, called to reschedule his magazine editor, rearranged the cluttered flat in an aesthetically self-flattering way, put another bottle of white in the fridge, and waited for the doorbell to ring. What did he think he was doing, if not laying the foundations for some outcome consistent with his status as a bachelor of the parish?

But he hadn't pursued it, though this Lois was the regulation half his age and good enough to eat in a light summer dress down to her ankles and a straw hat and basket in matching lavender. Very unstudentlike. So, what was his problem – weariness? One routine too many (albeit a routine gone unpractised in recent months)? Were the cold feet in deference to the imagined disapproval of his daughter? Certainly no one liked to be disapproved of, but he didn't not like it *that* much. Or was it the one reason he didn't want to hear himself think about – Stella. Stella, who he couldn't even be sure wanted or expected sexual fidelity from him and certainly couldn't be imagined demanding it. So why give when nothing is asked for? And more important, from the world view of the twenty-first-century voluptuary, why abstain from pleasure when no one is there to witness the sacrifice?

He didn't know. The point was, he wouldn't pursue it. No, no, no.

He offered his guest tea, put on his glasses to leaf through her portfolio of photographs of farm labourers from her trip to Cuba, offering praise and critical pointers such as the importance of timing and holding your nerve. She produced an apple pie from her basket, which they ate as they drank the tea. It surprised him when it turned out that she was a fine art student. 'I just want to keep my options open,' she said. 'I've done a film piece too,' she said. 'Do you want to see it?'

'Sure.'

He loaded the videotape. 'Eden' the label said, 'Lois Goodwood, 10 mins.' The film opened up on an indoor swimming pool, the surface of the water still, the figure of a girl poised motionless on a diving board, arms at her side, wearing a lavender dress, bare-shouldered, a clock above her head showing ten o'clock.

Jas leaned forward, adjusting his glasses. 'Is that you?'

'In the flesh.' She sat on the arm of the sofa next to him where he could smell her. Same girl, same dress.

The film cut away to underwater images of her circling, shark-like, the lavender dress swirling and ballooning in the water as she swam, her face serene, her arms and legs moving languidly, the water returning slowly to calm as she swam out of shot, becoming turbulent again with a flurry of air bubbles as she returned after a few seconds of expectant stillness, swooping, rising, revolving and falling. It was beautiful to watch – or at least she was. If the reference behind *Eden* was in the invitation to work out whether she was naked beneath the dress, thus transforming viewer into voyeur, innocent to corrupted – the purity of the water as tainted by the dark purpling of the dress serving to amplify the point – it worked like a wet dream. But then didn't the conceit, supported by the smooth editing that kept Lois's secret teasingly ambiguous, falter with the final view of her, from the back, wet dress clinging to her body now, deeper in hue, ripe buttocks clearly outlined? No. That was the QED, the *fait accompli*, both the answer to the question and the question asked of the viewer – the putative Adam to her Eve: does it work for you? What would you give up for this? How quickly is your paradise lost? Ten minutes had elapsed on the clock above the pool, as it had on the display in the VCR, as if filmed in real time. The time it took to change your mind. Christ, he thought. 'Would you like some wine?' he said, his eyes on her like food in a window.

'Why not?' she said.

*

He stopped at the record shop opposite Monty's. It would be easy to stroll over, chew the fat for ten minutes. He imagined, for a moment, persuading Monty to leave the shop with his assistant and come out for a quiet coffee or an early pint somewhere, and bending his ear with details of this whole unnerving song and dance. There were times – maybe not too often, but certainly occasionally – when it was no doubt mentally healthy to discuss this kind of thing properly with somebody. It was what kept therapists in business. Having spent yesterday evening sitting through Nick's coke-fuelled fantasies about gambling for a living in Vegas, or trying to read into Bart's unforthcomingness on why he was looking so pleased with himself ('Oh, it's nothing . . .'), he realised that while beer & sausages might pose as a kind of intimacy, its real purpose was to pronounce favourably on a particular way of life. It was probably a disappointment to Monty that b&s was too much fun and not enough misery. He would be a good person to talk to if only because he was in too many pieces himself to find amusement or irony in other people's unexpected vulnerabilities. But though Monty wasn't the type to delight in the misfortune of others, you didn't have to be around him long to see that he did take other people's happiness pretty badly. (What would you call that – *Freudenschade*?) Which would account for Bart not wanting to be too explicit about whatever or whoever was putting him in such la-la spirits. It couldn't be drugs. Bart didn't do drugs, except out of politeness when Nick insisted on bringing some weed along as a variation on cigars. It had to be a woman. But Bart wouldn't be drawn. Perhaps Monty already knew about her. He was, after all, quite chummy with Bart, often dropping by at the office, according to Bart, hanging out there, or waiting for Bart to turn up if he was out on site somewhere.

109

Jas turned and headed back towards Farringdon Road. In this hypothetical world of him confessing all, the meat course would have been his determination to resist the opportunity of having sex with Lois, followed closely by his remorse at having had sex with Lois. There would have been much emotional confusion and puzzle as to his motive in this, but at least no shame – even, perhaps, some residual satisfaction in 'admitting' to what under normal circumstances would have been rather a triumph. And so, even if Monty had, say, let slip to Bart or Nick the rough outline of events, it would hardly have been a tragedy.

But the truth was worse than that. The truth was that the second, quite crucial part of the song and dance in question had not – strictly speaking, if adhering to the literal rules of full sexual penetration – occurred. And it was this part of the affair that occupied the most regrettable proportion of his regret – not least the burned-on image of himself with capacious Calvin Klein's still suspended from one ankle, labouring like an old vehicle towards the hard shoulder of indignity, the sound of his own mocking words (yes, the ones in which he emphasised the importance of timing and holding your nerve) reverberating above his grunting efforts. But equally unbearable was the return to his mind of anxieties so vivid and palpable as to be only viewable with 3-D glasses, anxieties not least about how this sorry mess must have looked to the poor girl herself, this Lois whom he didn't know from Adam, but a person young enough to be his daughter's fellow student at college (a happy coincidence that he had pointedly failed to mention). What did *she* think? Who *was* this fat, middle-aged bloke on top of her who couldn't get a hard-on?

And the odd thing was that, although he wasn't lying when he'd said 'God, I'm sorry, that's never happened to me before', it sounded like a lie, even to himself, and one of the most pathetic kind.

'Hey, don't worry, it can happen to anybody,' Lois said. And then she smiled, which made things worse in a way he couldn't begin to define.

There were some things you couldn't tell. Like defecation, the act of sex was a comedy for anyone not directly involved. Which was why people did it in private. He moved on, Clark's jellied eels, shuttered for the day, Videoworld, the church – CHRISTO LIBERATORI – and turned left ahead of the dirty sycamores casting their summer shade on the flagstones and the spattered communal benches and builders skip outside the derelict Penny Black, its guts ripped out, corrugated iron at the windows, soon to be five luxury apartments, all sold.

By the time Jas raised his eyes to see Bart's car outside his flat, it was already moving away and gathering speed. He stopped, still a good hundred yards away, and watched as the brake lights flared briefly at the junction, and the gleam of silver as it turned and disappeared. It *was* Bart's car. The Porsche he was always slightly embarrassed about driving; the Porsche that he'd all but admitted his ex had made him buy. But what did he want? Perhaps he'd left something in the flat last night. Or no . . .

Jas was frowning now and walking more urgently, as if the heat he could feel growing inside him was directly fuelling his legs, as if arriving sooner at his front door would quickly solve the mystery in a way that didn't involve Ivy. Because now he was trying to remember what Nick had said about speccy schoolboy types always being the worst. He hurried up the stairs, dropped his bag in the kitchen, strode down the corridor and tapped on her door.

'Ivy?' he called, forcing a cheerful note into his voice at the last moment.

No answer. He stormed back to his kitchen, picked up the phone and dialled Bart's number, but slammed it down quickly again. No. What was he doing? If it was Bart's car – and it *had* to be Bart's car – they wouldn't be back at his flat yet anyway. And maybe it was something perfectly innocent. Had he not himself asked Bart whether there might be some holiday work for Ivy? Maybe he, or even she, had followed it up and . . . and what? Bart had come to pick her up on a Saturday morning to discuss it? No. Even if he was right, ringing Bart and giving him grief down the phone was probably not a brilliant idea. It would only make things worse with Ivy. He slotted two slices of bread in the toaster and switched the kettle on, then wandered into the living room opening junk mail from the morning's post. He didn't quite comprehend things at first, his mouth opening in wonder at the odd sense of unfamiliarity as his eyes took in the bare floor space, a space that seemed all the barer for having a short snake of brown cable ending in the middle of it, a space occupied until now by a quite new, matching JVC widescreen television, DVD player and VCR. He blinked at the copy of the *Radio Times* lying limply on the rug near by like a burglar's dropped glove and he stopped in his tracks, drawing a sudden breath. Jesus Christ.

He stood, listening hard, not moving. If someone else was breathing, he would hear. He waited. Just his own heartbeat and the murmur of cars on the street below. He reached for an empty wine bottle on the floor and edged towards the bedroom, pushed open the door slowly, the bottle raised to shoulder-height. A dribble of wine ran down his sleeve as he peered into the room, preparing for the worst. But the bed didn't look as though it had been pissed on. There was no excrement smeared up the walls. Everything was in the same state of elegant chaos he had left it in. He exhaled slowly. But then a sudden clatter behind him made his heart leap, made him wheel round and he gripped the wine bottle and dashed for the kitchen roaring loudly. There was no sound of panic at his approach, or doors opening or anyone making their escape. Just the toast sitting there in the toaster, where it had popped up. He let his breath out and his brain back in, the old pirate on the wall laughing at him. It wasn't burglars. It wasn't breaking and entering. It was unlocking the door and entering, and then exiting. Clearly, Ivy and Bart. But why? He tried to set things straight in his mind, separate fact from conjecture, locate truth. On the one side there was his daughter and his so-called friend – for whatever reason. *Perhaps* in view of her prospect of temporary employment. On the other, *his* TV, his VCR and his DVD. So far so inexplicable.

There was no answer. Unless she was moving out . . . Unless she *had* moved out and had, for whatever reason, decided not to discuss it with him and had felt it only fair to take some of his material possessions with her. He was angry now. He now had to do something he was never going to do. He took the spare key from the kitchen drawer and went back down to her room. He tapped at the door again, listened, called her name, just to make sure. Then he turned the key and opened the door. He didn't need to go inside – he could see Ivy's badly made bed, book on the pillow, make-up, coffee mug, college stuff all over the place, clothes on a rack of hangers. She hadn't gone. He locked the door again and went back to his kitchen. He thought about the way Ivy had glared at him at college when he'd been out with Lois in the corridor. Had she seen Lois leaving the flat yesterday? No, Stella had been lecturing, and Ivy never missed Stella's lectures.

Anyway, he had gone out ahead of Lois and – to his shame – looked up and down the street.

He sighed again. He was holding the wine bottle from yesterday afternoon. 'Shit,' he said, his eyes closing against the probing light of another thought. The thought of how afterwards (after *what*, exactly?), when things couldn't get worse and he was making such tragic chit-chat with Lois while his dignity burned, he had turned the conversation back to her work, as though the other thing had been some kind of silly misunderstanding and was all but forgotten now. How he had said her pictures were good and the film too, though he suggested that perhaps it suffered conceptually from being rather gender-specific. He smiled ruefully as he said it.

'What do you mean?' she said.

'Well, obviously, as an analogy of temptation, it only really works with men. You being a woman.'

She looked puzzled.

'You know, *Eden*,' he said. 'Eve.'

'Oh,' she said, laughing and putting a hand up to her mouth. 'I never thought of it like that. It was just supposed to suggest innocence and, you know, nature and holiness, with the flowing water and all. And beauty, sort of. But not *that*.'

He suddenly felt numb with the stupidity of it all. And then at the bottom of the stairs, he had remembered. 'Hang on,' he said, 'did I give you it back – the video?'

'Oh, keep it,' she said gaily. 'It's only a copy.'

And then she was gone. Of course the last thing he wanted to do was keep it. But he had kept it. And when he'd woken in the night, after b&s, unable to sleep, he had run the tape again, as he knew he would, perched on the edge of the sofa in his dressing gown, eyes fixed on the images flickering in the quiet of the dark room, an erection the size of Denmark just asking for punishment. Afterwards (after *that*) he should have ejected the tape and dumped it then and there. But he hadn't. Which was why it was still in the machine. Wherever that was.

five

A beautiful day for visiting, though there was no obvious scenic route for this three-mile hike across one of the least visually compelling parts of London. Gray's Inn, King's Cross, then a north-westerly zig-zag of crumbling Victorian conversions blighted by the occasional strip of sixties-built, low-rental retail outlets, concrete, urine-scented municipal facilities, small ethnic restaurants held together by string and offering all-you-can-eat lunches at all-you-can-spare prices. But Bart had read that walking was the new running, and was especially suited to over-thirties who needed to avoid exposing their bones to long periods of high impact. Plus, he didn't have the car, Nick having appeared unexpectedly on the doorstep at the barely acceptable hour of half past eight to relieve him of it, a request made no less bizarre for his having said goodnight to him not six hours earlier.

'What – you're seriously asking to borrow my Porsche?'

'Come on, Bart, what do you think's going to happen to it?'

'Er, let me see – you might wreck it? Anyway what's wrong with your own car?'

Nick sniffed, glancing to left and right, like a comedy chancer, the collar of his suit turned up as though he'd spent the night sleeping in a shop doorway. 'Long story. Any coffee going?'

The long story was as advertised, though its chief characteristic was not so much longness as tallness, even by Nick's standards. 'OK,' Bart said, pushing the plunger down on his cafetière, 'you're out motoring in the Scottish Highlands, miles from the nearest town – and, of course, this is why you can't possibly get the train now . . .'

Nick, mouth stuffed with toast, sitting on Bart's psychiatrist's couch, nodded vigorously, his eyes lighting up. 'Exactly!' he spluttered, not so much as if this thought had occurred to him previously as materialised this very instant as a stroke of luck to support his story.

Bart put the tray of coffee on the floor and sat on a cushion, arranging the folds of his dressing gown round his legs. '. . . and you've just taken this hairpin bend when there's a cow, believe it or not, standing in the road, large as life.'

'Yeah, one of those with the long horns?' Nick said. 'The bloke who came to pull me out of the ditch and tow me to the garage, he said . . .'

'On his tractor.'

'Right. The bloke with the tractor said it was always

happening. Bit of a hazard in those parts apparently, wandering longhorns or whatever they call them.'

'And you were in the Scottish Highlands for what exactly?'

'Business,' Nick said, nodding seriously.

'Business.'

'Uh-huh. Do you mind if I smoke?'

'Yes, I mind if you smoke. You were saying. Business.'

'Right. Tell you the truth, it's to do with a takeover of the agency. Some of us had to meet up at a big country hotel near, whatsit . . . Inverness. Few weeks ago. So it's all a bit hush-hush. Which is why I couldn't mention it before. The story about the car I mean.'

'Ah, yes. I was wondering about that. It does seem to have come slightly out of nowhere. I mean, I don't suppose you could have mentioned it last night? I only ask because of my exciting new role in all this.'

'To be honest, I got let down badly by this guy – Des – at the office. Des is the one who's supposed to take me up there, but his car's just got pranged too. One of those new Audi Cabriolets.'

'Oh, bad luck. Another longhorn?'

Nick took another piece of toast. 'No, no. Just some cunt at the traffic lights on Fulham Road. Swedish halfwit in a Volvo thought he was still in fucking Helsinki.'

'Stockholm, I think that would be.'

'Whatever. Fortunately, he does feel pretty bad about putting me in a spot – Des, that is, not the aforementioned Scandinavian gentleman – so he's still coming up with me. Because, of course, someone's got to drive my car back.'

'You seem to have thought of everything.'

Nick grinned. 'It's what I do best.'

So he'd given Nick the keys, not because he believed a word of it, but because he was in a good mood and because that's what friends were for. Plus, he had the feeling things were not currently happening for Nick, for whatever reason. Apart from the news that he could get his hands on some 'really good coke', he'd hardly said a word at Jas's last night, even after he came out thirty quid ahead at poker. Preoccupied would be the word. Jas, too, had been a bit thoughtful, mumbling about life being a series of 'interlocking phases' and how 'taking stock' occasionally saved you from becoming stale and predictable, which was a weird thing coming from someone whose life had gone happily down the straight and narrow path of unapologetic self-expression for the past twenty years.

Still, Bart had kept his good mood to himself, not least because he couldn't have explained it in any convincing way. It was the kind of good mood that could spring from a single event – say, the right football result, or the arrival of an awaited package on a Friday morning, or a bright idea that could bring a little hope to your weekend. Nothing more concrete than that, though hope, like a tank of petrol, could get you a long way – maybe even as far as you wanted to be. He pondered on the inaptness of the metaphor as he trudged on in the midday sunshine, a Budgens plastic carrier bag slapping his leg as he walked, inside, a silver trophy unearthed from the Internet. Camden Town announced itself as a destination by virtue of its pavement life of spilling pubs, cafés and market stalls and promenading body-pierced circus of goths, punks, frightened tourists, locals, asylum seekers, pickpockets and wandering homeless, every littered passage and opening exhaling the same primary jangling of rap, psychedelic rock and world rhythms, the same mingled waft of chilli sauce, dahl patties, baltis, falafels, riceballs and other varieties of snack cuisine provenanced in the conquered dominions of imperial history. Over the canal bridge and towards the overhead railway bridge, Bart was looking for street numbers when he spotted the big Citroën van parked in a bay outside the gold- and red-painted frontage of a workshop-cum-showroom set back from the road. 'Lost & Abandoned', the sign said. He moved closer to the place, one of three premises of the same kind carved out of a former railway depot grimed with the original soot. And then there she was. The glass on one half of the double doors had been broken and neatly boarded up, but through the big window he could see her, at the back, half in shadow, standing at the workbench, brush in hand, a chair held in a clamp in front of her, souvenir Piet Mondrian coffee mug standing to one side. He watched her work for a minute or two, admired the careless expertise with which she applied varnish to the wood and reloaded the brush. He didn't give himself more time to feel nervous or foolish, but walked straight in, a warm cave, sweet-smelling of worked wood, glue, paints, oils.

She looked up. If she was annoyed that he had come here, deliberately sought her out like this, she didn't show it. 'Well, well . . .' she said, laying down the brush, wiping her hands on a cloth, 'Mr Barton.'

'I just thought I'd pop in to say hello,' he said. 'Tristram mentioned you had a place up here.' She stepped into the curtain of sunlight that bisected the room now, making the darkness at the rear newly impenetrable to the eye. 'I've just been looking round the antique shops,' he added.

'Antiques? That doesn't sound like you,' she said.

'I was looking for something for my aunt.'

'Ah yes, the aunt.'

Her brown shoulders were bare under the straps of the dungarees, which he could see without enquiring too deeply were worn over nothing much more than a bra. 'Got time for lunch?' he said.

She sniffed, hesitant. 'I usually just work through. There's no one to mind the shop.'

An ornate wooden garden bench was hanging on the wall, a carved balcony with legs. Her hand reached out to touch, as if testing its dryness. She rubbed her thumb and forefinger together.

'My treat . . .' he said.

She frowned. 'I'd better just wash my hands then.'

They walked to a place two minutes away called Tunis. It was full, but the waiter fussed around her and found a table for them at a side window overlooking the canal. He came back quickly with menus and mint tea in a hexagonal pot, two cups without handles.

'Shall I just order for us both?' she said. 'The couscous is always good. And the lamb?'

'Sure.'

The waiter wrote down the order and disappeared with a short bow.

'I thought you didn't get out much,' Bart said, pouring the tea.

She smiled for the first time and glanced out of the window at a narrowboat moored by the lock, filling up with sightseers. 'Cheers,' she said, raising her cup. 'Here's to the old mill by the stream.'

'So you've worked with Tristram before?' he asked.

'Did he tell you that?'

'I suppose he must have. Was it a secret?'

'No, not at all. Sorry, I'm just a bit . . . I don't know.' She gave a little shudder. 'I met him in Brittany. I was working in France at the time, shipping stuff to the UK, Ireland. He was over there looking at wine and food suppliers for a place he was opening in Cornwall. My husband bumped into him at our local vineyard, and brought him home to lunch. He was interested in the kind of work I did and asked me to find a set of 1930s iron chairs for him – not for the restaurant but for his own house. So I tracked some down, and when we came back to London, I started doing the odd bit of scouting for him.'

'So what does your husband do?' Bart asked, looking over his cup, seeing – not for the first time – no wedding ring on her finger.

'We don't get to talk about him,' she smiled. 'The two of us called it a day a little while ago now.'

'I'm sorry,' he said, warmed by the news.

'It happens. And it was amicable. Well, it was to start with.'

They both inspected the view for a moment, children running along the canal bank, parents with buggies, lager drinkers sitting on the fence, legs dangling, heels banging against the wooden posts.

'How about you?' she said.

'I'm separated too,' he said. 'Divorce going through.'

'No, I mean, how did you come to be working on the Cambridge job?'

'Oh. I've no idea. I think it must have come into the office. I suppose we were asked to quote for it. My partner Christian usually takes care of winning new business. Unfortunately, he's likely to move to New York soon so I'll have to start taking a bit more interest. Or starve, of course.'

The food arrived. He wanted to know more about the husband who couldn't be talked about. He wondered whether Natalie discussed their own marriage and pending divorce over couscous and mint tea with men she'd just met. If she didn't now, she would eventually, if she started seeing someone. That was understandable. At some point you'd want to make sure it was the other half who was impossible to live with, who slept around, who introduced irreconcilable differences to the marriage and made it a trap you eventually had to escape.

But Kate was asking how someone born in the sixties came to be called Arthur. So he started to tell her about his Aunt Marian, who had adopted him after his mother – her sister – had died during childbirth. It was a story he had told before. Everyone, he figured, must have a story that made them seem interesting. This was his.

Kate winced. 'That must have been tough for her – losing a sister and gaining you. What happened to your father?'

'He disappeared before that. He probably never knew about me. Aunt Marian was in showbiz, in a sort of modest way. She was a session singer at the tail end of the big bands. My mother was about ten years younger – about twenty-two, I think. She used to hang around the clubs and dance halls with her big sister. That scene. But then disaster struck and she got herself pregnant by one of the musicians.'

Kate stopped eating. 'Really? What instrument?'

Bart laughed. Most people he told this story to wavered in their reaction between sympathy and embarrassment. But it was obviously all a long time ago and equally obviously he had never known any mother but Aunt Marian. There was something about a girl with an Irish voice and nice blue eyes and black hair who could ask insensitive questions with such sensitivity to what *was* obvious that you had to find yourself being smitten by her. 'Aunt Marian never found out who the man was,' he said. 'The musicians moved on. He was married and my mother had no interest in pursuing him, so that was it. This was the sixties, remember. She was a woman with an independent mind who'd been to university and started a postgraduate degree, so she knew the score. It could have turned out a real mess but my grandparents were prepared to stand behind her, support her. The whole family were pretty enlightened types really. But then . . .' He shrugged. 'Apparently childbirth was still a relatively risky business in 1964.' Out of the window, small children were chasing panicking ducks off the bank and into the canal, their parents coming to intervene, pointing at the water, deep green in the sunlight. 'Anyway, to answer your question, Aunt Marian got to call me Arthur. And still does. I think she hoped I'd get called Art and be an alto sax player when I grew up. She's a jazz fan. She probably imagined me one day leading the Art Barton Quintet or something. There was a lot of jazz in the house, but I never liked it much – I just remember being into the Clash and Elvis Costello and U2, like everybody else.'

'And your mates called you Bart, did they?'

He nodded. 'Just as well. I mean, you can't go through art college calling yourself Art.'

They walked back to the shop through the crowds. She unlocked the door and stood on the step. 'I ought to get on with some work,' she said, 'but thanks for lunch.'

'What happened to your window?'

'Someone smashed it a few weeks ago. Some drunken fool. I was in bed at the time, above the shop at the back. Scared me to death. Anyway, I've been too busy to get it fixed. I don't suppose you do glazing?'

Bart smiled. 'Sorry. I did bring something for you though.' He handed over the carrier bag he'd kept by his side since he arrived. 'It came from an old wreck in a scrapyard. It's a bit rusty but I thought it would go well with the rest of your van.'

He watched her eyes light up as she put her hand in and pulled out the Citroën chevron badge. 'Hey, that's brilliant. And so thoughtful.' She looked at him. 'Thanks.'

They lingered on the step, her clutching the metal Vs in front of her, him holding the empty bag, fluttering slightly in the breeze.

125

'I don't suppose you'd like to meet one evening,' he said. 'Dinner or something – a drink even.'

'Ah . . .' She took a deep breath and slowly let it out while she found the right words to turn him down. 'To be honest, I'm not really seeing anyone right now. That is, I'm kind of avoiding any sort of, you know, involvement. I'm not quite over it, as they say.'

'What, the husband?'

'Things are a bit tricky.'

'Let me ring you, and ask again,' he said. 'When you've had more time to think about it. You still get to keep the badge.'

'OK,' she said.

'I know this is a bit corny,' he said, 'but . . .' He gave her a pen and asked her to write her number on the back of his hand.

'Talk to you soon,' he said.

She gave a small wave, stepping inside the shop and wedging the door open for business. He looked back and she waved again.

Kate, Kate. He turned her name over in his mind as he walked to the tube, smiling to himself. He bought a paper at the kiosk and leaned against the railings in the sunshine, scanning the headlines, seeing her face in his mind. Then he folded the paper, took out his phone and punched in the number.

'Hello?'

'Hi, it's Bart. Have you thought about it yet?'

There was a long pause. 'You don't give up easily.'

A bus rumbled to a halt at the stop, giving out a hiss of brakes as its doors folded back, the clatter and low shudder of the engine making him turn towards the station entrance.

'I'll take that for a yes, shall I?'

• • •

Fuck. Nick swivelled. 'What was that sign back there?'

'I don't know, I had my eyes closed.'

'I don't want to seem like one big, long moan, Ivy, but you must have some small inkling of where your mother lives.'

'I do, but only from the railway station – I can't drive, remember? Anyway, we're not going to her house.'

'Where are we going then?'

'She's staying somewhere else at the moment. Just pull over, and we'll look at the map.'

Pull over, look at the map. He could smell the whatever it was she put in her hair. Loved it, being this close to her, snug-fitted in this car. He hadn't mentioned Bart's role in its ownership. Better to gain points for renting a classy motor than for possessing the grovelling skills to borrow someone else's. She'd almost squealed with delight when he'd turned up, though he had been a touch late, and admittedly getting a fucking huge TV in the boot was a worry that might have been averted with the kind of vehicle that slept six rather than two.

'I don't suppose you could have mentioned the removal job earlier,' he'd said.

'I didn't want to spoil the surprise,' she said.

'And are you sure this is OK with Jas? I mean, why do we have to do it while he's out?'

'Because I don't want to give him ideas about me and you, of course,' she said smiling, looking up from the map.

Me and you. He liked the sound of that, though admittedly there hadn't been much me and you in evidence when she'd fucked off and left him in a hotel room to get fired. Still, an ill wind and all that. Three months' money in lieu of notice plus a month's goodwill voluntary redundance payment, as Hugo put it, before they made him clear his desk and had him escorted from the building. A lean, downsized life was the thing now. Nice fresh slate. Which was why in the end it'd been simpler to move out of the new flat under cover of darkness than continue to dodge calls from the halfwit agent, who was losing patience vis-à-vis the initial cheque for advance rent and deposit, which the bank had for some reason failed to honour.

As a temporary measure, Des had been good enough to let him have a sleeping bag and exclusive use of the living-room floor of his squalid flat in Stockwell once he'd heard the bad news, or rather once Nick had ambushed him outside the office and, in terms just short of physical violence, all but blamed his lack of current employment on having been supplied with what could only be described as low-grade charlie, unless somehow sending the user to sleep for hours was a USP of that particular drug hitherto undiscovered in previous reputable consumer tests and anecdotal market research. Which then gave Des the brilliant idea of their going into partnership together.

'Ha, ha, ha. You're kidding, right?'

'There's money in it, Nick.'

'With respect, mate, you do live in a shithole.'

'Yeah, but it's all to do with critical mass, isn't it? Economy of scale. See, personally, I've never built up enough cash to get on top, but by pooling our expertise we'll have synergy – you with the capital, me with the supply line. Plus you've got access to a higher class of punter network, whereas I've just been selling to scallies and wasters. No offence, Nick.'

Cue Des to go rabbiting on – almost to the point of being interesting – about how the more you could afford to buy, the more you got for your money and the better the quality of the product, so you'd have people queuing up for it and he,

Nick, wouldn't even need to get his hands dirty because Des would do all the biking round town to swish parties and clubs, etc. It was a self-fulfilling prophecy, wasn't it?

Obviously, he didn't want to shoot Des down in flames while he was putting a roof over his head, so he didn't say no, but instead put a couple of hundred his way to see if any of it came back. Beggars, choosers, gift horses, etc.

'Left at this junction,' Ivy said, head in the map. 'And then we just carry on till we get to Millston. After that it's a bit fiddly but I think I know the way from there.'

What the fuck this was all about he didn't know, but being alone with Ivy now, deep in this adventure, speeding towards some unknown destiny like wild runaways taking life by the horns, had to bring them closer together, didn't it, if only for the weekend. He dreamed about her all the time now, woke up with her face and body filling his thoughts. It was about sex, but he was crazy for her too, in a way he hadn't been when they were actually having sex, which seemed ages ago, the memory of it having been transmuted in his mind to a symbol of potency and possibility. It was like he was clinging to something, but clinging was better than falling off and could even mean climbing back on. Amazing that women had the discipline to say no to great sex, when on previous occasions they seemed to be having so much fun. But if it had happened three times – as it *had*, albeit in the good old days of only a month ago – there had to be decent odds of it happening again. Until it did, every time he saw her now he just wanted to touch her, but instead found himself taking deluded comfort in her silences and moodiness, as though they were like intimacies in themselves, a ladder of loyalty points to real intimacy, a time soon when he might bury his own life in hers, away from everything – from the financial nightmare, the job, grief from Olivia, guilt about the

129

kids. He knew it was bad and could only make things worse, but he couldn't help it. Ivy.

She was pointing through the windscreen towards a big house coming up on the right. 'This is it, straight up the drive. You can park in front of the door.'

'Saint Mary's Garden?'

'It's a hospice. This is where my mother is.'

'A hospice?' He brought the car to a halt, slow, careful, bit of respect for the gravel. 'So is she . . .'

'Wait here.' Ivy disappeared into the house and came back a few minutes later followed by a short but hefty male nurse in a white buttoned-up tunic and jeans. He helped Nick carry the TV into the house, up a flight of stairs, down a dinner-smelling corridor and into a small, bright room where a woman was lying propped up in bed. 'Hello, Barbara, just LOOK what we've got for you!' the nurse said, grinning like she was a kid. 'A new TELEVISION.' She didn't respond. 'Her old portable conked out,' he whispered. 'It's all she can do now, really.'

Outside of Pathe News concentration camp footage, Nick had never seen anyone so thin who was still alive. Skin on her arms sagging like leathery sleeves, cheeks and eyes hollowed out, what wisps of hair she had pasted to the skull. She looked a hundred years old. He could smell her, a sort of scented decay.

'This is my mum,' said Ivy, standing in the doorway with the VCR and DVD player.

He managed a tight smile. 'HELLO!' he bellowed.

'We've brought you a TV, Mum.' Her eyes flickered a bit at Ivy's voice, and she turned to look, smiling, mouth open, bits of food in there. 'The cancer's in her brain now. She doesn't know who she is any more or who I am or what she's doing.'

130

'I'll try and set it up, shall I – the telly?'

'Aerial socket's just here,' the nurse said. 'Give me a shout if you need anything else. See you LATER, Barbara,' he said, standing, hands on his knees, leaning towards Ivy's mother.

No smile for you, mate, Nick thought. 'There's a video already in the machine,' he said. 'I'll just try it out, shall I?

He set the tape running, found the channel. Girl on a diving board in a purple dress. Nice looking. In the water now, whirling round. Ivy's mother clapping her hands, eyes like saucers. 'I don't know what this is. Jas's tape, I suppose. Maybe it's not suitable for proper adult viewing.' He reached for the eject.

'Leave it,' Ivy said, eyes narrowing about something.

Innocent enough as it turned out. Some arty thing. Nice body. He looked out of the window. Inmates being pushed around the garden in wheelchairs. The film finished.

'Let me see that,' Ivy said.

He ejected the tape, read the label. *Eden* by—'

She snatched it off him. 'Lois Goodwood. Fucking cow.'

'Steady on, Ivy. Probably some student thing.'

She put the video in her bag. 'That's the trouble.'

They put *Grandstand* on, Ivy holding her mum's hand, watching with mother. Hard to believe, he thought suddenly, this wrecked woman being Jas's ex. He caught himself imagining the two of them together, but stopped himself before it led to Ivy. Tragic, bowing out of life like this, watching the golf, not knowing what the fuck's going on, or who's winning. Through the window there was just an old bloke now, standing by himself in the middle of the lawn like something left out by accident. A forgotten boot upright on the grass, waiting for someone to notice him and put him back in the cupboard.

Nick dozed off in the chair with the drone of the TV.

Woke up with Ivy shaking him. He was flustered for a minute, blinking, wondering where he was. Like the last time, in the hotel. He jumped up, feeling bad about being asleep on duty, dry in the mouth.

'Let's get a drink somewhere,' she said, as if she was the one with the dry mouth. He looked at her. She looked like she ought to get a couple of hours' kip herself. Her mother was propped up in bed fast asleep, mouth gaping, drooling a bit. Ivy kissed her on the forehead, teary now, eyes glistening.

He put his arm round her. 'Come on.'

They found a nice pub in the village with Oriental cuisine as edible as you could probably get in the middle of nowhere. Ivy had been starving. Displaced grief or something, probably. Makes you eat like a horse. Brasses, hunting horns, pictures of cricketers, reclaimed agricultural tools. He was on his second pint of Carlsberg now, Ivy downing gins and tonics, smoke from their cigarettes twining between them like a sign.

'She's been through all the chemo and the drugs and look where it's got her,' Ivy was saying. 'She's dying, Nick.'

Nick gave her a sympathetic smile, reached out and put his hand on hers. 'So how long has she been ill, then? It's funny your dad not mentioning it.'

Her eyebrows dipped into a scowl. 'He doesn't know. He can find out when it's too late.'

'Don't you think you should tell him?' Nick said gently. 'He'll want to help. He's bound to.'

'He should have thought of that twenty years ago when he dumped us.' She pulled her hand away. 'Mum doesn't want anything from him now.'

The woman of the house came to take away their plates, to change the ashtray and wipe the table, trying somehow to divine with the quickness of her movements and glances the secret of why they had come here, arriving from the city by Porsche to murmur cheerlessly over the Chef's Sizzler Special of crispy chicken in black bean and lemon sauce with Chinese vegetables and egg fried rice.

'So what did you tell him about the TV?' Nick said.

She looked mutely into her glass and began to stir the ice with her finger. Excellent, he thought. Bonnie and fucking Clyde.

'He can afford it,' she said. 'Anyway, I can pay him back once I've got myself a job. Bart said he'd give me a job.'

'Did he?' *Cunt*.

'Well, I haven't actually spoken to him yet. Dad asked him ages ago and he said yes. He said I should ring him nearer the time. Dad'll get his money back.'

She was drunk by the time he got her home to her mother's place, a ground-floor flat in a purpose-built block on a street leading to the seafront. They got out of the car. He could hear the waves. Ivy leaned into him as they walked up the little path, gave him the door key. 'This is where I grew up,' she said. 'Mum looked after me here after Dad left. She never went back to work, except part-time jobs when I was older. She never had a proper career. Wasted her education and her possibilities. She said he was James back then, not Jas. Jas is an affectation, like the rest of his life.'

Nick didn't say anything. The flat was warm. He switched on the light. It was neat and homely with cushions on the sofa and yellow dried flowers in a vase, photographs on the mantelpiece. Ivy and her mum as a younger woman, Ivy as a little girl at the school gate, same age as his own little father-less daughter. No wedding pictures. Ivy kicked her shoes off, shook her hair loose from its clip. 'Let me make you a cup of coffee,' he said.

'No,' she said. 'I just want to fuck. Let's just fuck.'

Fuck?

Fuck.

●●●

Jas followed Monty into the little café at the back of his shop. 'I'll take over in here for half an hour,' he said to Gail, his assistant. 'Give me a call if we get a coach party in.'

'Yeah, right,' she said, smiling. She untied her apron and went to read her copy of *OK!* at the till at the front of the shop. Saturday wasn't Clerkenwell's busiest day.

Monty took her place behind the counter. 'I don't really like her reading trashy magazines in the shop. It makes us look like frauds. Sustenance,' he said, towering behind the counter filling mugs with coffee and milky froth, transferring two giant flapjacks on to plates with pastry tongs, still frowning. 'She told me she was interested in cinema. I'm starting to think she must have meant film stars.'

'*Bellissimo*,' said Jas. He picked up the tray and took it to a low glass-topped table flanked by leather armchairs. He sat back stretching, legs out, ankles crossed. 'I had a thought after you'd left last night,' he said over his shoulder.

'What's that, mate?'

'I've got a new book coming out this summer. New York cops. Lovely big colour pics. I wondered if you might be up for doing the launch here in the *magasin*.'

Monty came to join him wiping his hands on a tea cloth. 'Yes, why not. I'd love to.'

'Nothing too ambitious – wine and nibbles. Should bring in a few customers – fellow professionals, journalists and the like. I'll get Stella to invite some of her students along. They're usually up for a free drink.'

'Not the biggest spenders, though. Biggest *shoplifters*,

134

maybe, if our own college high jinks were anything to go by.'

Jas smiled. 'Those were the days. Nick trying too hard to be a bad influence. Art books should be free at point of delivery, I remember him once saying. Can't imagine him saying that now. He's not that crazy about students. Anyway, the point is, you have to think ahead. Today's freeloading layabouts are tomorrow's millionaire creative geniuses.'

'It'll be nice to meet Stella anyway. You two are obviously still pretty keen on each other.'

'Absolutely. Well, actually, to be honest, I haven't seen her for a week or so. She's pretty busy at the moment. Exams and so on. College politics. How about you? How have you been?'

Monty's eyes widened as he exaggerated a mellow smile. 'Back in therapy. Taking the pills, working on my unresolved issues. Still trying to attract the attention of my estranged wife in a variety of inappropriate ways. Against legal advice, I might add.'

'I suppose sometimes the only thing you can do is move on.'

'Yeah, right, but how? Where?'

Jas shrugged apologetically, spooned the whorl of froth on his cappuccino one way and then the other. He had no idea. Even for people like himself – people who could come and go as they pleased – life sometimes offered more choices than you could reasonably carry. You thought you were free, but in practice you patterned your days with behaviour every bit as uniform and predictable as that characterised in your mind by less free individuals, falling back on traits and habits that in other people seemed poorer in imagination, lacking in instinct, less vital to an appreciation of the world at its fullest.

A young couple in matching black T-shirts were outside, arm in arm, looking at the display of film books and paraphernalia in the window.

'Do you ever feel lonely, Jas?' Monty said.

'Me? God no,' he said quickly.

'You're lucky,' Monty said. 'I don't want to be out here on my own. I don't want the world at my feet. I want someone to love, and to love me. Like most people.'

There were some things Jas didn't really want Monty opening up to him about, and not only because it might end in tears. He took a sip of coffee. 'Speaking of which,' Jas said, more brightly than he felt, 'what's Bart up to these days? He seems very chipper.'

'Yes, I suppose he does. He was in earlier this afternoon looking for a book on post-war French auto design. Which was a bit of a tall order, I thought.'

'This afternoon? Was he alone?'

'I think so. I did catch him whistling to himself though. Maybe he'd just had sex. I didn't ask. I thought it would be a pity to spoil our friendship by turning into someone too transparently twisted and envious.'

Monty was smiling now, but Jas wasn't. 'Monty, I know the two of you are mates, but just answer me something. Is Bart sleeping with Ivy?' The question took himself as much by surprise as Monty, whose mouth was now open, his eyebrows up.

'Are you kidding? I mean, obviously, she's a very attractive girl. Objectively speaking. In a young way. But . . . I mean, well, what makes you think he is?'

The couple outside were kissing now, which Jas found irritating.

He shook his head. 'Just one or two things. I really hope not, that's all. I really hope not.' He fixed Monty with what he hoped was a pregnant stare, one that would compel Monty to run to Bart with this suspicion, make Bart see the recklessness of his ways, perform this small service by means that would promise an agreeable outcome with no harm done and

136

no harsh words spoken. Jas looked around the shop for a way out of this now, his eye roaming the aisles of books, the display tables, the smart seated nooks for browsers, the top shelves accessible to customers, the modern sunken lights that gave the low ceiling more height, which seemed a sound idea given Monty's monstrous perpendicularity. Which struck him as a reasonable enough opening to escape the previous subject. 'So where were you going when you fell off your ladder?' he asked, looking up. 'Through the roof?'

'Did I say I fell off a ladder?'

'I thought you did.'

'You're right, I did say that . . . Yes, I must have been cleaning my sign outside. On the pavement, above the windows.' He bent his elbow and mimicked a fisherman casting a line. 'I'm all right now, though,' he said. 'Well, you know. In a physical way.'

Jas came back from Monty's following a meandering route, the better to contemplate and then reject the cheer and companionship of the pubs and bars he knew would be starting to fill up with lively early evening drinkers, some standing in groups out on the pavement to absorb the last of the day's warmth. Half past six on Saturday was like an orchestra tuning up. He let himself into his flat, listened for any messages but there were none. He stood in the kitchen in the fading light. He didn't have the stomach for the pork ribs or sausages he had bought that morning, even though he had abstained from food all day, most recently the flapjack at Monty's, which was probably still intact on the plate, on the glass table, next to his empty coffee mug, and would be till Monday morning when Gail came in to prepare for the lunchtime rush and read trashy magazines.

When Ivy had stood in over the Easter period, she'd hated

137

serving choco-lattes and frappuccinos with Portuguese custard tarts to media wankers, as she put it, but loved being surrounded by books on art and film. No *OK!* break for Ivy. There was already too much in the world to despise without seeking it out. All the same, he found himself envying her integrity, and recalled his days on the local paper in Norfolk when he'd disappear off in his minivan at weekends to London or Brighton or Bradford, taking pictures just for the love of it. There was ambition there, yes, but it was driven by a passion. His marriage couldn't survive it – perhaps was never intended to – but that was life, wasn't it? He'd accepted the financial and other duties incumbent on him and the repercussions that were still evident in Ivy's occasional barbed asides. But what wouldn't Ivy herself sacrifice for whatever it was that kept *her* burning with commitment? There was no moral aspect to art, Stella had said. Or rather *he* had said it (because it seemed the thing to say) and she had tried to find out how much he believed it.

There were times though, like now, when whatever you believed in might be held up and shown to be see-through. If he was free to do as he pleased, then so too was Ivy or Bart – putting aside for a moment any subsidiary questions concerning the theft of his TV. Why, then, the anger? Was it some sense of betrayal? Freedom-seekers believed in the sovereignty of the moment, the decision taken on a whim or violent compulsion to follow one path rather than another, even if the path you took was the one you always took. He poured a glass of wine. At this sovereign moment, Stella was the key to his feelings. Whatever he wanted from the remains of this day was now distilled into a strong desire to talk to her, if only to arrange to meet some time soon, maybe when she'd stopped being busy. He dialled her number, but she'd left her machine on, as she always did when she was working. 'Hi, it's me,' he said, trying to keep everything out of his voice but the moment. 'Just thought I'd give you a ring ahead of next week. Quick chat. Give me a call back when you can. Missing you already,' he added in a way that suggested he was missing her but not missing her so much that he wanted to put it into his own words.

He went out into the West End to see a film, ate a hotdog and a bag of M&Ms as he watched, drank a large Coke, hunkered down in the dark, shielded by George Clooney from the forces of uncertainty. Walking back afterwards, he looked into the windows of restaurants and modish bars and the backs of taxi cabs waiting at traffic lights to see if he might, by cruel chance, spot Stella, not hard at work at all but pursuing interests outside of his understanding of what her life was. She was free too. And, at this moment, at the end of this day, after the empty hours he had spent trying to fill it, he realised that's what scared him most.

six

A beautiful morning, charged with expectation. Christian waited till Jim was out of the office, buying mid-morning cakes for them all at Cake – 'the most *gorgeous* little place on Exmouth Market' – before announcing his news. Bart could tell he had news to announce by the way he was pacing around the office and sitting down again, gazing out of the window, sharpening his pencils, showing unnecessary concern about jobs in progress, leafing through architectural journals, rearranging the paraphernalia that surrounded his already fastidiously tidy workstation and being inscrutably Scandinavian in general.

'So, Bart,' he said, once Jim was out of the way.

'So, Christian.' Bart smiled, swung round in his chair, took his glasses off as if to give him the attention that seemed to be called for. 'I guess you have something to say,' he added, in broad imitation of Christian's American-inflected English, which made his partner pause benignly and lower and raise his eyelids, an indulgent teacher waiting for giddy spirits to quieten. He was dressed in khaki, as if ready to lead an expedition. Compass, binoculars.

'Mortensens is settled,' he beamed. 'They want me to start in the fall.'

'Hey, congratulations, well done.' Bart's heart sank as he shook Christian's hand. 'That's really fantastic,' he added, making his face live up to the words.

'They made it hard to say no. My own department, stock options, seat on the board a couple of years down the line.'

'Sounds brilliant. Though, obviously, I don't have to tell you how much you'll be missed round here.'

Christian poured coffee for them both. 'Ah. I want to talk to you about that.' He looked out of the window, took a sip of coffee. 'Obviously, there's a lot of redevelopment going on in lower Manhattan – not just around the Ground Zero site but also SoHo and the financial district. Which will mean plenty of opportunities for people of talent. So, I was thinking . . . perhaps you'd like to think about coming too.'

'Me? New York?'

'Why not? We work well together. You know your way round the place. Mortensens have already told me to start building my team. So, I'd like to start with you. What do you say?'

'Gosh. It's nice to be asked, obviously, but . . . well, I don't know what to say. I mean, I'll have to think about it.'

Christian looked serious. 'Of course you must think about it. And then you must say yes.' His blond eyebrows bristled.

'I will. Think about it, that is. Thanks.'

'And remember,' he said, his face breaking into an uncharacteristic, unScandinavian grin, 'American women love British men. Now that you are single and fancy free.'

'Yeah, I've heard about that.'

'And now,' Christian said, clapping his hands, his appetite sharpened with thoughts of the future, 'where is our young man of the cakes?'

So what was there to think about? New York, even for just a couple of years, would be great. It would broaden his experience, give him the chance to work on much bigger, more technically and visually exciting jobs than he could expect to take on here alone, and without the added grief of having to search for new business. Then, revitalised, he would return in triumph, a share-option millionaire, a stable of American girlfriends begging him not to leave – flame-haired lawyers perhaps, or something else that involved wearing short skirts and offering top sexual and conversational skills – to set up a twenty-five-storey London joint venture (Barton-Mortensens had a nice ring to it) clearly visible from the grubby windows of Natalie's little graphics firm on the hill near Alexandra Palace. It was the kind of opportunity an unattached man of the world might expect to take *without* thinking about it. This was what Nick meant by taking life by the horns. He had Aunt Marian to think about, of course, though she would just tell him to go, and be sure to give her regards to Harlem or somewhere. But what about Bird? He could get one of those cat passports. Anything was possible with the right kind of corporate backing. Anything was possible, full stop. Or, as they said over there, period.

He took a late lunch and sat in the park with a sandwich from the deli and a James Lee Burke that Monty had lent him. When he got back, Jim met him at the door. 'There's someone waiting for you up there,' he said.

'Man or woman?'

'Woman, I believe,' he said. 'Christian let her in. He said to tell you. I'm just off to the gym for an hour.'

Bart took the stairs two at a time, caught sight of her in profile through the window as he passed. Natalie, like a ghost, sitting there on the cream sofa reading a magazine. She stood up when she saw him, and came over to meet him, smiled weakly. 'Hello, Bart,' she said, allowing him to peck her awkwardly on the cheek. 'Sorry to barge in on you like this.'

'No, no, that's fine.' He was breathless, and felt the disadvantage of not knowing why she was there. But she seemed diffident too. She was wearing a long summer dress, which somehow made her look less like the Natalie he knew, less brittle and sure of herself.

Christian, working at the far end of the studio, gave a brief wave.

'Shall we go up to the flat,' said Bart, 'or we have a sort of conference room . . .'

'Could we get a coffee outside somewhere?'

They walked to a nearby deserted café. She ordered mint tea, which surprised him, and reminded him of the mint tea he'd had with Kate.

'Detox,' she smiled, in answer to his unasked question.

'You look well,' he said, though actually she looked quite pale. A soft beading of moisture gleamed above her upper lip. His stomach was tight with nerves. He wondered if she had spoken to Suzanne. Whether Suzanne had told her what he'd said.

'How have you been?' she said.

144

'I'm fine.'

They talked about the nice weather, about their respective businesses. He didn't mention New York. He told her about old Monty being back in London, and his bookshop on Exmouth Market. 'What made him go off abroad when he did?' she said. 'He used to sometimes send us a Christmas card, didn't he? Is he still weird?'

'He's fine. He's had a few emotional problems,' Bart said.

'There were rumours that he tried to kill himself,' she said.

'Really? I don't remember that.'

'After he'd moved out of the house. Maybe even after we'd left Canterbury. Overdose, I think.'

'Well, he's still alive. You should pop in and surprise him.'

'I probably won't.'

'No, I suppose not. Natalie . . .'

She looked at him, took a deep breath, as if fuelling up for something.

'All that time we were trying for a baby . . .'

'What about it?'

'Did you have an abortion?'

'Did I have a *what*?'

'I went to see Suzanne. A few weeks ago. I asked if I could have a sperm count . . .'

'What on earth has she been telling you?'

'Nothing. She didn't say anything. It was just something in the way she reacted. Afterwards, I rang her when I was drunk. I asked her if you'd been to her wanting to get rid of . . . well, our baby. Is that what happened? Did we get pregnant? Nat?'

There were tears in her eyes now. She spoke quietly and emphatically. 'No, Bart. Believe me, I would never, ever have done that.'

'OK. I'm sorry,' he said. 'I suppose Suzanne was just being professional by not denying it. I don't know, maybe I pushed her into it. I shouldn't have assumed the worst. I'm sorry.' He touched her arm. She put her hand on his and pressed it gently, but her eyes were closed to further inquisition. They sat in silence for a minute. There seemed to be no neutral territory left to move on to.

'I'd better go,' she said, getting up. 'I'll call you.' She kissed him on the cheek and pressed his shoulder, the sign that he should stay, not follow, finish his coffee, pay the bill. There were still things left unsaid. What Suzanne hadn't said back then. Why Natalie had come and gone today without declaring the purpose of her visit. But the result he thought he might have pressed for, the closure he thought he needed, was lost now in a confusion of feelings he imagined had been dealt with, but which had rushed unexpectedly back to the surface at the very first sighting of her, sitting on the cream sofa, wearing a dress, leafing so casually through a magazine. And now, in the balance of things, further questions seemed more a threat than a force for good, an extinguisher of hope. What closure brought was an end to openings. Was that what he wanted?

'Yes, call me,' he said.

He watched her through the window as she walked in the heat of the day to the end of the street, stood on the corner looking for a cab, then turned down the hill, out of sight. He sat for five minutes, staring, his mind milling with thoughts you couldn't catch, like specks of dust in the light.

He was still trying to pin things down that evening. 'Come on, Bart, New York!' cried Monty when he told him, midway through noodles at the Bangkok. 'Why the long face?'

'I don't know,' Bart said. 'I'm suffering from white room syndrome – it's like, where one single decision reduces the possibilities of everything else. Do you know what I mean?'

'I do,' said Monty out of the side of his mouth, laying down his fork while he chewed. 'But isn't that just designer bollocks?'

●●●

Fuck. Nick put the phone down, pondered, consulted his organiser and punched in another number. Tea, toast plate on the floor beside him. Fags, lighter, *Sun* open at sports pages.

'Feel free to pay for the calls.' Des, fat oaf supreme, struggling into his courier's outfit. 'Some of us have jobs to go to.' Nick flashed him a grin, winked, listening to the ring tone at the other end.

'Yo.'

'Frank! Hey, it's Nick.'

'Nick . . .'

'Nick Murrow.'

Des in the doorway zipping up against the sun, pointing to the sink. 'Feel free to do the washing up.'

Best flatmate grin. Go on, fuck off then . . .

Frank, fake breathless. 'Nick, right, hi. Listen, mate, I'm a bit pushed right now. Pitch meeting in about a minute. Give you a call back, say, this afternoon?'

'No prob, Frank, look forward to it.'

Shit. Forgotten to give him the fucking number now. Not that he'd ring back. Redial. Voicemail. 'Frank. Me again. Sorry, I'm working from home at the moment. Kind of free-lance,' he said, immediately wishing he hadn't. F-word, kiss of death. Des's number on the scrap of card wedged in the phone written in disappearing ink. Fucking perfect. 'Tell you what, Frank, I'll call *you* back,' he said. Shit. Mental note to pay bill for mobile, eighty quid.

He spent the morning ringing so-called friends round the other agencies, gun for hire. No takers. Industry downturn. Everybody shedding staff like dandruff. He picked up his jacket, fags and left the flat, pocketed spare key Des had kindly had cut for him. On to the high street, towards Stockwell tube. Portuguese area, Stockwell. Fuck knows why. Into Ladbrokes, quick bet, two-fifteen Doncaster, twelve to one, 'Green with Ivy'. You never know your luck, he thought. Tenner each way. Set him off again though. Horrible groaning inside for her, like hunger except you had it in your head too. Ivy, Ivy. Hadn't got a peep out of her all the way back from Norfolk. Dropped her off as near to Smithfield as he'd dared, Jas's light still on, presumably very much *not* watching TV. After which, car returned to Bart's as per arrangement, or at least only a day late and with no petrol in the tank, followed by cab back to Des's, wait on doorstep for hours till he got home with, as it happened, eye-opening return on his investment. 'See?' he said. 'Ye of little faith.'

Dirty money, though it did seem to spend OK. He thought of the kids, grumbling Matthew and little Lucy, waiting for him on Sunday. His pathetic phone call from Norfolk. 'Sorry, I'm stuck in Scotland . . . bloody car broke down.' Olivia livid. He peeled a twenty off his wad. *Father of two Nicholas Murrow was sentenced to six months today for . . .*

Man seeks position. Anything legal and well-paid considered.

Woman behind the counter quite nice-looking in a tarty kind of way.

She smiled. Mmm, teeth could do with some work. Ivy, Ivy. He smoked two fags watching yesterday's racing highlights, then a tube to the West End. Woman in front walking up the steps squeezed into some horrible pink pant things. If women realised how often men looked at their arses, they might make a bit more effort.

Fresh air of Oxford Circus. Lit a cigarette, dawdled down to the college. He knew Ivy had a tutorial that finished at one, curricular detail tricked out of her before she stopped communicating in words. Must have been something he said. Must have been something he said about it hardly being Jas's fault that her mum had cancer. There had to be a statute of limitations on leaving someone in the lurch, he'd said. You had to be free of it one day. It was only fair. He hung around the iron gate, out of place in his suit among the young beardies and tattooed hordes milling in and out pretending to be undiscovered conceptual fucking geniuses. Then he saw her heading his way, laughing (laughing!), crowded by three ragged students, talking in her own language, predatory males, boys of her own age. He retreated into a doorway as they passed, pretending to be taking an unhealthy interest in fifties American sci-fi comic books. He felt sick.

An hour later he'd found a pub that had the racing on, settled at the bar, drank two pints of cooking lager, read the print off the *Standard* and waited to watch his horse come in second. Leapt off his stool with a big cheer, fisting the air. People looking round. Fuck 'em. More like it. Enough luck in his locker now to walk briskly across town to Clerkenwell, glorious sunshine. Worse ways to spend the day. Drop in at Monty's first, he thought.

Clerkenwell, quite a dump really for somewhere supposedly up and coming, full of skips and pigeons, hardly the new Champs Élysées. Exmouth Market. Monty there, half hidden behind the counter, hair damp, eyes scanning something, sales figures probably.

'Excuse me, but have you by any chance got the latest Dostoevsky?'

Monty, looking up. 'Nick, what a surprise. To see you in a bookshop, I mean.'

'Intellectual pursuits are the luxury of the fucking idle, mate, as I believe Oscar Wilde said. And look at that weather. Too nice to be stuck in here. How do you manage to get your hair wet in a job like this?'

Monty giving his hair a rub with his hand. 'Lunchtime workout,' he said. 'Good for the endorphins.'

'And if it's good for them, it's good for anybody, right?'

Monty smiling, not sure if joke or pig ignorance.

'I was just passing. Thought I'd pop in.'

'It seems to be the season for it. I had Jas just passing and popping in Saturday.'

'Saturday? How was he?'

'Much the same as Friday. Started off well, then hit a strange low. Not really himself. Bit worried about Ivy, I think.'

'Why's that?' Casual enquiry. Heart going. He picked up a philosophy of art book from the display, turned it, read incomprehensible blurb, put it down again. Monty, frowning, wavering, torn about whether to tell. Come on, for fuck's sake, out with it. Deep breath.

'He thinks she's sleeping with Bart.'

He missed a breath. Not that. She *couldn't* be. Calm. Keep face in neutral. 'Blimey,' he said, picking up philosophy of art book for second time, intrigued now by jacket design, spine, title page, size, weight and volume. 'Do you think he is?'

Monty grimacing, reluctant deliverer of tittle-tattle. 'I don't know. I mean it's not inconceivable. Jas seems to have convinced himself. And, much as I love him, Bart does seem to be in a slightly irksomely cheerful mood these days . . .'

Right. Cheerfulness being unmistakable mark of sexual conquistador, English, mild-mannered, non-strutting, loosetrousered variety with own loft accommodation. QED.

'Better ask the man himself,' Monty said.

Nick gave a deep chuckle. 'I'm not sure I need to know. Divided loyalties and all that, respect to Jas. Though, as it happens, I was on my way to Bart's anyway. Business proposition. I'll try not to mention his love life. It'll be our secret, Mont. My mobile's just gone on the blink. Mind if I just use your phone?'

The sun was not so much glorious now as getting in his eyes and giving him a headache. Longer walk than he thought. Nice offices, though, Bart's and the Swede and Jim the fruit who answers the phone with that American accent. Civilised way of life, notwithstanding sudden devastating Ivy rumour. Don't think about it. He found the entrance, buzzer, up the stairs. Deep breath. Sometimes wished he'd stayed in design. Steady, reliable, if a bit overdisciplined for the freer spirit. Ads had seemed the place to be, late eighties, nineties. Very champagne, drugs, money and fun-based, ideal for committed applicant not interested in hard work. Creative, with just the right level of shallowness. Probably job-hopped a bit too much in the end, bit of a downward spiral, losing focus, respect of peers, home, family, car, salary, sense of rectitude in personal appearance, occasionally hygiene.

Still, onwards and upwards. He pushed open the door. Jim springing to action. 'Nick, hi, take a seat, I'll get you some coffee and cake. I'm sure Bart will be back soon. He just had to slip out for half an hour,' he added, stage whispering. 'He's with a female.'

'Female?' Heart starting off again. 'Anyone I know?'

Jim pursed his lips, turned on his heels. 'I'm sworn to secrecy.'

*

They sat in the little conference room. Bart, beetle-browed, twiddling with a pen, not looking especially like someone who might have spent lunch shagging Ivy. Faced by a multiplicity of signs in a changing world, always believe the last one you see, thought Nick. Motto. Concentrate, now. Revived fortunes, respectable occupation, modest reduction in excessive behaviour, status renewed, win the girl.

'To be honest, I'm looking for a change in direction,' he said.

'What – you want to be an interior designer?'

'I did study design, Bart. You were there too, remember? And I did do that year and a half at Adam-Bluchner.'

'I do remember. You hated it. Anyway the business has changed beyond recognition in the past fifteen years. Plus, you know, I'm not really looking for a partner.'

'I thought the Swede was off to New York?'

'*Christian* is a trained architect. It's not something you can pick up on the job, Nick. And, yes, I know you made the transition into copywriting but that's different. Putting buildings up is more hazardous than thinking of advertising slogans. They don't just let anyone do it.'

'Hang on, you think anyone can write advertising slogans?'

'No. I didn't mean that. I mean slogan-writing is precisely the kind of thing that *can't* really be taught. And is therefore more open to people with flair rather than training. People like you. Happy?'

'OK, Bart. Listen. I think I can help you. I'm not talking about the practical side of things. I'm talking about the commercial aspect. Bringing in new business. Schmoozing clients. Strategy. You provide the expertise, let me sell it. That's the kind of thing that can't be taught either. OK, you've managed without a project manager up to now because of the Swede. But once he's gone . . . You know that's a weak side of your game. Let me ask you a question.'

'Go ahead.'

'Can you imagine ever using this conference room to hold a conference in?' Pause. 'Yes, well spotted. A rhetorical question. I can do this, Bart. Trust me.'

'Trust you?'

'Why not? I brought your car back, didn't I?'

'Nick . . .'

'What?'

'Have you lost your job?'

Bart. As brainy as he looks.

'Do you mind if I smoke?'

'Yes.'

'Cool. Let's just say I'm looking around. Let's say I'm someone who constantly craves new challenges.'

Bart gave a big sigh, rubbed his eyes. 'To tell you the truth, I'm at a bit of a crossroads myself at the moment. Things are a bit up in the air.'

'What, personal life or . . .'

'Both. I can't really consider this right now. I appreciate you've got many glaring qualities, Nick, but I'm not sure I can take advantage of them at the moment. Sorry I can't be more, you know, *here* for you.'

'No problem. I'm not trying to put you on the spot. Have a think about it.'

'Right. Think about it. I will.'

Jim tapping on the door. 'Sorry to disturb. Call for Nick, someone by the name of Des?'

'Put it through into here, Jim, thanks,' Bart said, getting up.

'Don't go, Bart . . .' The phone rang. Nick picked it up. 'Des, I'm in a meeting for fuck's sake . . .'

'Well, get out of it. Someone's been in the flat and turned us over. All my stuff's gone.'

'What, they broke in?'

153

'No, Nick. They didn't need to break in. Because some stupid *cunt* left the door unlocked. So that'll be a grand you owe me, plus the grief I'm going to get from clients. Now just get back here now. And for fuck's sake get yourself a bloody phone.'

He hung up.

Bart frowning. 'Bad news?'

'Temporary blip, mate, nothing more. Temp blip.'

● ● ●

They lay together in Stella's big bed, the big wooden ceiling fan she'd brought back from the Amazon slowly revolving, stirring the air above them, his right cheek seeking out the softness of her left breast. There were worse ways to end an afternoon, Jas thought. Worse ways to greet an early summer evening, the mingled *tristesses* of Ivy, Bart and Lois now dissipated in the narcotic release of urgent sex and soothing post-coitals. He snuggled closer to Stella now, closed his eyes, inhaled her scent, her warm body smell.

She sighed. 'Well, I'd better get moving.'

'What's the rush?' he murmured.

'Things to organise, ahead of my meeting with Mark. We've got to get our policy submissions in for next year.'

'Mark who?'

'Mark of the faculty, of course. Mark McCaulay. I work with him. I'm meeting him for dinner. To sort out our—'

Jas sat up. 'Stella?'

'What?'

'We're supposed to be going to that Brian Eno thing at the ICA tonight. That's why I'm here. We were going to go for a Chinese afterwards. Remember?'

She looked up at him. 'Is that tonight? Oh God, you're

right, I'm sorry. I had to fit Mark in before we went off to this poster thing. Damn.'

'Poster thing . . .'

'In Bologna. Did I not mention it?'

'What – me and you?'

She laughed. 'Me and *Mark*. Well, there's a small group of us from the two schools – fine art and graphics. Conference on poster art. Should be quite enjoyable. The downside being that tonight is the last chance we'll have to agree our submissions strategy. I know it's boring, but I think poor Brian Eno will have to wait.'

'I was thinking of me rather than him.'

'Sorry,' she said, getting up abruptly and putting an arm through the sleeve of a bathrobe. 'Maybe we could go out another night soon. I'll call you when I get back, shall I?' The shower started up in the bathroom.

'Maybe I could just wait here,' he said, watching the ceiling fan.

'Sorry, can't hear,' she shouted.

He tried to count up the things he knew about Stella. She was half Welsh. She was a *great* shag. She didn't put on weight regardless of how much she ate and drank. She was thirty-four. She was an advocate of Old Labour social values. She had done her first degree at Camberwell and doctoral research at the Courtauld. Surprisingly, she paid to have her toenails done every six weeks at an expensive beauty salon in Covent Garden. She knew his daughter better than he did. Her parents lived in Herefordshire. Or Hertfordshire. Or Hampshire. She had a brother and a sister. He didn't know their names, or what they did for a living, or how old they were. He didn't know where or when she had been in the Amazon, or for what purpose. He didn't know if she had a driving licence or had ever broken a bone or acted in a school play.

155

He realised he had now moved into the list of things he didn't know about Stella. Which was a much longer list. And, thinking about it, a longer list even than those he might have theoretically compiled for the previous women in his life, who tended to be younger and not as intelligent and therefore had less for him to be ignorant of or, for that matter, interested in.

She came out of the bathroom, arms and long legs glistening and steaming, hair piled on top of her head, and started to rummage in drawers, searching for fresh clothes.

'Stella, what's your brother called?' he asked.

'I don't have a brother,' she said.

When he got home, Ivy was in the kitchen. 'Hi,' he said.

'We're out of milk,' she said, meaning they were out of milk because she had just used the last of it on a bowl of cereal.

'Right.'

'I'll get some when I go out.'

'Fine.'

Communications between them had not been helped by the discussion about the TV, during which she had found it impossible to acknowledge that it might conceivably have been wrong to take it without permission or consultation, or even the courtesy of leaving a note. 'It was a spur-of-the-moment thing,' she had said.

'Oh right, so how did you get it out? In your rucksack?'

'A friend helped. Someone with a van.'

He waited a beat. 'Oh, a *van*. Right. Not a smaller vehicle . . .' He paused again, wondering whether this was perhaps not a good moment for taking things to the brink.

Her narrowed eyes looked at him. 'A van. My friend Lois has a van.'

He took a breath and tried to fix her glare with one of his own but she looked away and started buttering bread. 'Do we have cheese?' She went back to the fridge for cheese and tomatoes, and came back, paring and slicing. She cut the sandwich neatly, saying nothing more.

For Christ's sake, what was this *about*? He followed her into the sitting room, scene of the crime, *Radio Times* still on the floor, the sofa still angled mockingly towards the bare corner where the TV had stood.

'Anyway,' she said, 'if I'd asked, you would have just said no, wouldn't you?'

Either she and Bart *were* at it, or it hadn't been Bart's car and she and Lois were up to something, which had to be worse. Depressing as it was, a romantic alignment with Bart was to be preferred. It could be addressed. Confronted with evidence of his inadvisable dalliance, Bart would come to his senses, apologise for transgressing the usual decencies between friends, put it down to a temporary imbalance of hormones, shake hands, look stupid for a while. The alternative alignment with Lois, however, was too fraught with unreadable conspiracy or hideous coincidence to contemplate without some element of mental torture. Had he been set up? No, that way an improbable cruelty lay. Did Ivy even *know* Lois? She would have seen her around. He knew Ivy had seen him and Lois chatting together in the corridor at college. She had no doubt found the video and had probably watched it and for some reason jumped to the right conclusion. So even hypothetically he didn't get to choose the lesser evil of Bart over Lois. Whatever the truth about Bart, the reference to Lois would remain slung between Jas and Ivy like barbed wire, leaving them nothing to do now but stand at either side of it, playing ethics tennis in the no-man's land of TV ownership.

She sat down and bit into the sandwich.

'Well, of course I would have said no,' he said. 'Your mother is perfectly capable of saving up and buying her own TV and video and DVD with remote controls. She goes out to work, doesn't she?'

'Ha. Well, that's the point – you haven't got a clue whether she goes out to work or not, have you? You don't know anything about her.'

'Of course I don't. Why should I? We split up twenty years ago. What do you expect me to do – follow her around making sure she's OK for the rest of our lives?'

'I'll pay you for the bloody TV,' she muttered. 'If it means so much to you. I'll pay you for everything – the milk, the bread, the cheese—'

'I don't want your money, Ivy, even supposing you had any. I just want a little . . . you know, consideration, a bit of normal respect.'

'Consideration? Well, why can't you consider Mum? Is that so out of the question? You don't just dump someone and walk away. It's all right for you. You've had your career. She had to give hers up when I came along.'

'Well, yes, but I did pay for it. I mean, I paid for you. Once I'd got on my feet. I've always done my bit financially. That's not walking away, it's doing the right thing. She can't complain about that.'

'She's not complaining, I am.'

'Anyway it's never too late,' he said. 'She could go back to university. Or even just get out more, by the sound of it. Live a little.'

'Fuck you,' she said.

'Well, I'm sorry, Ivy, but fuck you too.'

That had been a low point.

Now at least they were talking about milk. She ate her

cereal standing up while he read the paper and listened to the six o'clock news on Radio Four. He wondered where she was going 'out' to. He wondered where the video was now. He wondered in precisely what sense Stella and Mark would enjoy Bologna.

seven

A beautiful redhead, semi-reclined, knees forward, bronzed arms supporting her body, eyes closed, face and breasts angled at the clear sky, legs only slightly parted – Bart didn't subscribe to the shaven-pubed, gynaecological school of soft pornography (although its prevalence in the two magazines hastily chosen at random and brought home ill-concealed in a copy of the *Guardian* encouraged the suspicion that he might be in a minority on this) – the whole pleasing arrangement of limbs, firm torso and prominent bush arrayed against the turquoise mosaic surround of a Mediterranean pool. The girl even looked as though she might genuinely be enjoying a few rays, perhaps having taken a well-earned break from teaching English as a foreign language or nannying for a well-heeled family holidaying in a Tuscan hill town or the Greek islands. Not a tart anyway.

Thinking positively while masturbating into a plastic bottle required more imagination than Bart had . . . well, imagined. But the day seemed to be right for it. He'd be passing the hospital on the way to meet Kate. And, though he refused to allow his hopes to be infiltrated by the wild possibility of a modest Sunday date ending in *actual* sex, he did remember reading somewhere (perhaps in one of the *Men's Health*s or *GQ*s stacked up in Suzanne's waiting room) that those embarking on a new relationship anxious not to allow the tail of excitement to wag the dog of performance and timing during that first tricky act of coition would be well advised to enter into the proceedings with a recently emptied tank – at least until such time as you could be reasonably confident about the expected duration of foreplay, precise location of orifice and how much help you might get with the important inserting bit. He screwed the cap on the bottle and held it up to the light, favourably impressed at how much he had produced. He tapped the bottle. 'Anybody in there?'

Elvis Costello's *My Aim is True* played in the background. Bird miaowed, agitated at the brief flurry of effort and vague sense of waste that remained in the air like an invisible vapour, circling Bart's bare legs, his fur on end with electricity.

The hospital was open, but the reception to the clinic in charge of counting sperm was closed. He stood at the door for a minute peering through the window. Damn. He wondered whether the contents of his bottle would still be alive on Monday. Otherwise he'd have to go through the whole thing again. He got back in the car and drove to the northern entrance to Regent's Park. She was waiting outside the gates to the zoo, cream linen dress, bare arms, trainers, bag slung from one shoulder, half-smile for him.

'I've already bought the tickets,' she said. 'My treat.'

'Have you been here before?'

'First time,' she said. They clicked through the turnstile. 'Never quite got round to it. Seen the monkeys often enough, though, driving past on my way out from the shop. My dad took me and my three sisters to Dublin Zoo once or twice. That was pretty grand. Took us all round the place. I remember him telling us that during the Rising in 1916 they had to kill the little animals to keep the lions and tigers alive.'

'Just like real life,' Bart said.

'He told us all kinds of stuff – you know, like elephants not being able to jump. That kind of thing. Did you know a donkey can see all four of his feet at the same time?'

'Do they need to do that?'

'I've no idea.' She laughed. 'I guess it explains why they're so good at going up and down mountains in the old Western films.'

They were walking slowly up a tree-lined path.

'Is your dad still alive?' asked Bart.

'Sure. And Mum. Dad still has his carpenter's business out where we lived in Sandycove.'

'Ah. Did he teach you everything he knows?'

'He gave me my first chisel, showed me how furniture was put together. I suppose I got to hang out with him because I was the eldest and there were no boys to muscle in. So, yes, I grew up with the smell of sawdust and glue. I've always liked wood, other natural materials too – slate, stone.'

'What about your sisters? Were they good at woodwork?'

She laughed. 'You must be kidding. No, they all went into primary teaching. Then they all went into having babies. I've

163

been a bit of a disappointment in that respect.' They stopped to look at the map. 'How do you feel about ungulates?' she asked.

'Dunno,' he said, 'I've never eaten one.'

They spent the morning wandering on and off route: the big cats, the reptile house, Russell the sad-looking ape who'd had to be separated from the others for antisocial behaviour.

'Poor Russell,' Bart said.

'Hey, you didn't have to live with him,' she said.

'That sounds like experience talking.'

She smiled, but stood back and frowned at Russell for a moment before moving on. Bart wondered about the husband, the one they didn't get to talk about. They stopped for lunch and afterwards went to watch the penguins racing around underwater as the keeper threw wet herrings from a bucket.

'Now this *is* a modern classic,' he said, running his hand along the crisp, curving wall. 'And a listed building in its own right. I know concrete isn't your thing but you have to admit you'd be pushed to make a decent pool out of wood.'

'It is lovely. I've heard of this, I think.'

'Lubetkin. He was the one who famously said architecture was politics pursued by other means.'

'And what, famously, did he mean by that?'

'I've no idea. The penguins seem to like it, though. Maybe the white reminds them of home.'

They watched for a while. 'I have to find a loo,' she said. 'Looking at water for too long does it for me.' She unfolded the map and located the nearest toilet block. 'I may be some time,' she said.

Bart went to sit on a bench to wait, the sun on his shoulders. The place was pretty busy – a party of gangly, rucksacked foreign sixth-formers jostling round the café, a couple of Japanese tourists hung with cameras and camcorders, a pair of nuns among the penguin crowd, which struck him as amusing, a lone dad crouching to wipe ice cream from the mouth of his daughter, while a second child, a boy, stood and watched absent-mindedly, his own ice cream dripping down his hand. Bart looked closer at the man. Unmanaged, swept-back black hair, beaky features, crumpled short-sleeved shirt, jacket draped over one arm, trying to lick a tissue and dab the little girl's face. It was unmistakably Nick.

He was only twenty or thirty yards from where Bart was sitting but faced in the other direction. Nick's attention had turned to the little boy now. He helped him finish his cone, struggled to find another tissue in his jacket pocket, repeated the wiping procedure, licked the stickiness off his own fingers. Bart was about to call out, follow his immediate impulse to go over, but something stopped him. It wasn't to do with Kate, who on her return and finding him gone would have to be shouted over and introduced to Nick – and this wasn't the best time for that, for sure. But no. It was more that he didn't want to intrude on Nick's moment, which seemed both pathetic and heroic at the same time. He was surprised and touched to see him in this role as nurturer, taken by his tenderness, his gentle solicitude and rudimentary sense of what had to be done. Of course it shouldn't be surprising at all – Nick had presumably had plenty of practice. But, nevertheless, it seemed like some kind of instinct being enacted, something quite apart and alien from the other Nick – the Nick of glittering-eyed bluster and chance and provisionality. This was Nick when no one was watching; it was Nick showing what else he was. The children, cleaned up, clothes straightened, tucked in, were ready to resume their adventure – perhaps the snakes and spiders next, Bart thought, or Russell the gloomy ape. Nick was saying something now to make them both laugh, smiling himself – not grinning his shark's grin – and kneeling to hug them, comically, both in his arms at the same time, planting a kiss on each little cheek before they moved off, hand in hand, the three of them, up the leafy path.

'Today's been really nice. Thanks,' Kate said. 'I wasn't joking the other day when I said I didn't get out often.'

They were sitting in a quiet pub a short walk from the zoo, studiedly scruffy with secondhand card tables and armchairs, old photographs of sports teams on the wall, blackboard chalked with the lunchtime roasts and puddings. A grand-father clock with the wrong time on it ticked deeply in the corner. The landlord was leaning on the bar with a Sunday paper, reading by the light from the window, the only noise coming from a group of locals sitting outside.

She took a sip of beer. 'To tell you the truth, I've had a bit of a time of it recently. Not much of a social life.'

'Is this the divorce?'

She nodded. 'Final papers should be going out soon, thank God,' she said. 'It hasn't been easy. Stephen was never a man to go down without a fight. Emails, letters, scraps of notes through the door. Then he started waiting outside the shop, watching me come and go. My fault for ignoring him, I suppose. I was angry, but I really didn't want anything to do with him. Then there was the night the window went through. Now that *did* get to me.'

'My God, you think that was him?'

'Pretty certain. I ended up having to set my solicitor on him.'

'So is he violent?'

'Frustration, I think. He wouldn't hurt me.'

'Right,' he nodded. 'Actually I was thinking of me.'

She laughed. 'Why do you think I didn't want you to pick

me up at the shop today? But no, he's not *that* bad. I just don't want to make things worse, that's all.'

'No, let's not do that,' Bart said, anxiously glancing out of the window. 'Do I recall you saying he was quite a big man?'

She smiled. 'No, you just made that up. Though, actually, he is.'

'I'll bring a bodyguard next time.'

'Next time?'

He smiled. 'Zoos are only a fraction of my repertoire.'

They finished their drinks and walked back to where he'd left the Boxster.

'Mmm, nice car,' she said.

'It's always a big hit with girls,' he said.

He unlocked the doors, expertly removing the white envelope containing his specimen bottle from the passenger seat, figuring that a first date probably wasn't the best time to explain why he kept extra supplies of sperm in his car.

They drove the short distance to Camden Town in a comfortable silence. He pulled over just ahead of the canal bridge. The market stalls had closed but it was busy on the street. She looked at him and he leaned over and gave her a kiss on the cheek, lingering for a few seconds. She drew him towards her and kissed him properly. After a minute she pulled away from him, smiled and released the door catch.

'Did you know crocodiles can't move their tongues?' she said.

'Everyone knows that,' he said.

• • •

Fuck. Olivia on the warpath now. Nick took a step back.

'Where have you been? You were supposed to be back at six.'

'*We've* had McDonald's,' Lucy said.

Wide eyes. 'HAVE you? McDonald's without me!' Olivia, hand on hip, pretending to be cross, Lucy running off delighted. Mock disapproval for the kids, real stuff for him. Lucy, just like her mum, full of it. Matthew traipsing in past her, pausing to have his hair ruffled, head kissed. Moody, quiet. Suffering maybe. Couldn't always tell. Heart went out to him. Had to. Little fellow, little baggy designer jeans Olivia had bought him, ears stuck out. Like to follow them in there, say goodbye properly. Olivia in the doorway, coat hanging like a noisy statement over her arm.

'So what happened?'

'Sorry, but, you know, we were having a good time, then they were hungry, then the tube was full of football fans and we had to wait. You didn't say you were going out.'

'You didn't say you were taking them on public transport.'

'No. Well. Needs must. I've lost the car.'

'What do you mean you've lost it?'

'I mean I got in trouble with the payments. The leasing company took it back. Listen, Livvy, I need to talk to you.'

'Well, I can't talk now.' Tight-lipped, looking off down the street, waiting for someone.

'Where are you going?'

'Out. None of your business. Katarina's sitting for me.'

Slimmed-down Olivia, make-up, dress, heels. Nice.

She looked at him, pitying or something worse. Scorn, that was it. 'Nick, have you seen yourself recently?' she said.

'I'm in a bit of a spot, Liv.'

'When were you ever not?'

A study of beauty and cruelty. Never been one for taking prisoners, Olivia. Looking at her watch, wishing him away. Put his hand out to touch her arm, thought better of it.

'Where's that taxi?' she said.

*

Closed his eyes for a second on the tube, woke up at Tower fucking Hill. Shite. Slept more out of bed than in these days. Not that he had a bed, strictly speaking. He crossed to the other platform, waited, lost fifty pence in the chewing-gum machine. Thought about giving it a kick, though perhaps not a good idea right in front of the camera nosing down up there in the girders. Enough on his CV without adding criminal damage. The train came. Set off again trying to stay awake, trying to rework the rubbishy ads into something clever and funny, but couldn't get his head round it. One for Tate Modern, one for blue chip finance house. Art and money. Ivy and Livvy. Funny. Chalk and cheese but common ground namewise. Ivy plus LV. Luncheon Vouchers.

His eyes closed. Rattling under the bridge. Where did your life make a turn – what pivots or points sent you down this track or that? He saw himself sitting in Olivia's parents' drawing room way back whenever, sipping sherry, him wasting his best jokes, them trying to put her off marrying him, her the smiling go-between, introducing investor to long-term prospect, public-school best girl turned venture capitalist, liked horse-riding, tennis, Queen's greatest hits, dinner parties. SuperNick, gabmeister, who had pitched perfect for their advertising account, won the business and her too. Loved him for his mouth she did until she started hating him for the lies that came out of it. But they couldn't get enough of each other back then. Once had it up against the sink in the utilities room at her parents' house, surrounded by ironing, the skivvy having just left, mother out there through the slats in the blind, not twenty feet away, snipping roses, red gardening gloves, carrying one of those little willow baskets. Wiped themselves off on clean, fluffy towels. Turned Olivia on like an animal. True love that was, despite occasional tiffs. Livvy's bio clock running down a bit maybe, too, truth be suspected. Still, big frothy fuck-off wedding back in Surrey, parents now desperately reduced to talking him up to big-hatted friends and relatives. Hard as nails, Olivia could be, background like that to push her along. But softie moments too. Lovely with the kids, though hadn't quite reckoned for being stuck with them day in, day out, only the Slovakian au pair with no English verbs for company. And yes she might have gone back to work, but the bank had a thing about women who fucked off and had two babies in two years and then wanted to come back and work part-time with special undeclared holidays for diarrhoea and chicken pox. Fuck *them*, she said, 24/7 venture-capitalling being out of the question because she wasn't having *her* kids brought up by nannies, which was admirable, if slightly financially negligent, in the light of her having overestimated his own, often erratic, on-target earnings, currently running at nothing.

Now she was out of the work loop. She had never been, and never would be, the kind of wife, mother or daughter who would give her wealthy parents the satisfaction of being asked for money, a virtue best appreciated by a husband on his way up, Nick thought, which kind of counted him out. The rest was bad luck, carelessness and possibly flawed character on his part.

All he ever wanted was . . .

Had to hand it to Jas. A philosophy for living, starting point being men are never satisfied. Solution: hey, don't be satisfied, keep moving, fresh and alive, one step ahead of the enemy, the enemy being convention, settling down, paralysis, death. No point looking for 'the one' because the one stopped being the one and turned into everybody else. Period. Trouble was you had to be mentally strong and for God's sake not get stuck on the next 'one', like he was stuck on Ivy. Of course, if he'd got Ivy knocking on his door for sex every five minutes it would be different, moving on made easier, having had enough. Mystery of women, that was. Sweet-shop syndrome. Because, actually, contrary to common opinion you can have enough M&Ms, though it helps if you live in the M&M factory.

Something would happen. Something that wasn't Des, who was now chasing the game, having had his mind concentrated with the help of two leather-coated Afro-Caribbean gentlemen who had arrived early one morning and talked purposefully with him downstairs, Nick being meanwhile naked, quaking, locked in the bathroom, ear pinned to the flimsy door for sounds of blood being shed. But no.

'Five hundred should be enough as start-up,' Des said afterwards, animated, almost evangelical, as if gentlemen in leather coats had called with an urgent job from God. 'That's about . . .' Des working out on his fingers how many 'rocks' that was. Crack was the thing, a drug that was quickly moving into respectable circles, and madly profitable because of the high-octane addiction factor, which translated into multiple visits from desperate punters with money, as opposed to those who murdered pensioners in their own homes for their wedding rings and electrical goods. 'You don't have to stand at Piccadilly with a big sign,' Des said. 'Just drop the word here and there. You know plenty of people. Seriously, it's starting to be the recreational smoke of choice, especially among your set. You can do it, Nick. You know it makes sense.'

Woke up with a start at Gloucester Road. Shit. Leapt from the train just in time, doors banging shut behind him. Passengers in the yellowed light clattering rapidly off, young couple laughing at him. He stood on the platform, bearings lost, panting, unaccountably sweating like a pig.

Fuck.

•••

Avanti! You could just stand there and let the pull of events in Bologna suck you under or you could look inside yourself for a way out. It was when Jas looked inside himself that he found a compelling urge to do something real. Not with a national poster campaign or stylish coffee-table book in mind; just something that made a connection back to a time when what he saw as real things mattered to him. He went out before dawn and waited for the light, not knowing what he was looking for or where to find it. No bags of heavy equipment or screens or tripods, no commission to execute, no subject in mind, just him, his beautiful old Leica, a pocketful of film and whatever instincts he had for catching a moment as it happened. He walked along the South Bank, found some ancient steps leading down to a small beach washed up with rubbish and filth, where he took shots of the river, big and massy, pale sky just breaking over it. He stood in the wind coming off the dark water and inhaled on the sour air. He found a girl asleep under Hungerford Bridge, hair matted, closed eyelids milky and violet-veined above the frayed blanket. He stepped close up, stood above her and took photographs while she slept, her grubby hands, black, bitten fingernails, big empty brown plastic bottle behind her, white screw-on cap lying nearby. He knew that, strictly speaking, this counted as a violation of some kind, but didn't he keep telling people that photography was about seizing what was there and worrying about the rights and wrongs afterwards? He loaded new film, shooting quickly, the soft *schhh* of the shutter echoing his movements around the girl. And still she slept. He tucked a five-pound note under the bag she used for a pillow and left, exhilarated. At eight-thirty he stood on Holborn Viaduct and trained his lens on the crowds of City workers below, surfacing at Blackfriars and streaming up towards Ludgate Circus. Later he took a distance shot of tourists queuing for the London Eye, a snatched one of a uniformed ticket vendor holding up someone's twenty to the light, and later still, in the morning sunshine, a boy and his mother throwing crumbs out over the water for the gulls swaying on the air, the woman's hair blowing in her face. Cabs on the move, Big Ben striking the hour at ten, eleven, midday, one, counter staff serving lunches in the café attached to the Festival Hall, resting promenaders in the act of drinking Coke through a straw or forking quiche or pasta into their mouths, fatigue on their faces, their eyes fixed on the pages of newspapers or guide books. He stopped for a bite himself, wolfing down a quarter pounder from McDonald's, and then carried on shooting throughout the afternoon and into the evening, roll after roll of black-and-white, up and down the river from Lambeth to the Tower and back: policemen, doormen, boatmen, barmen, cyclists, typists, flautists, economists, artists, theatregoers, diners, drinkers. A life in its variety.

He found a pub, and sat by the window with a glass of wine, watching the colour and shadows on the water change as the sun fell towards Hammersmith. It was still light as he walked back, breathing deeply, feeling alive enough to make a difference, not turning off at Cowcross Street for Smithfield but marching on to the top of Farringdon Road, along Exmouth Market, past Monty's, closed and shuttered for the night, and beyond, stopping short of Islington, traversing a square, seeing a loft development, corporate space below, one unit bearing twin vogueish signs side by side: one Barton, the other Svenssen. A desk lamp had been left on in the office but there was no movement in there. He skirted the building, found a lane that took him to the rear entrance leading to a smart courtyard and parking area. He saw Bart's car, and two floors up the bare windows of a first-floor apartment that took up half the depth of the building. He'd only been here once before but the design was distinctive – the original vertical panes set in metal frames at either side of bigger more modern windows with reliefs in the stonework between each storey depicting the story of Victorian medicine. A former hospital with converted wards.

It was too high to see in from the ground and was at an angle from the other buildings in the immediate locale. This side of the building was now in shadow but he could make out the head and shoulders of someone with their back to the outside, someone leaning against the frame. He held his breath, knowing it was Ivy even before he'd raised the camera to his eye. She walked out of shot but then returned, looking out of the window now, arms crossed, talking. He stepped back, shot off three, four pictures before she disappeared again. A church bell was striking – eight, that must be, he thought – when he heard someone coming out, at the hidden side of the building, then a car door slamming. He retreated and walked down the lane, glanced back to see a shabby little Fiat Uno emerge at the entrance and turn right to go down the other way, rattling, pumping out fumes. Nobody he knew. His heart was beating, angry now about everyone.

Back on the main road, at the other side of the square, he saw the tall figure of Monty walking in the direction of home. Jas slowed down to let him get ahead. Perhaps he had been looking for Bart at the office to lure him out for a drink, though it seemed late for coming over on the chance of him still being there. And, anyway, having bothered to come wouldn't he have just gone round the back and buzzed the flat? Perhaps not. Even among friends, turning up at someone's place in London without warning was a step beyond casual. Maybe Monty had arranged to drop off some books and put them through the letterbox. Bart had mentioned how he was trying to replace all the design stuff he had let his wife have when they'd split up. He tried to gauge Monty's mood by the way he was walking, but he was too far ahead, striding into the distance.

At home Jas checked his voicemail. Nothing. He made coffee and took it into his old darkroom. These days he used pro labs or plugged the pictures straight into his Mac – it was quicker, less bother and, in terms of his time, cheaper. But tonight he found himself taking the wraps off his old enlarger, clearing the sink of rubbish, feverishly emptying the drawers and cupboards of boxes of paper, tubs of developer, stop solution and fix, plastic tanks, tongs, working methodically into the night, processing his work through the trays of chemicals, hanging out prints to dry in the dim red light, absorbing himself in the work. This had been part of the experience of being a young photographer – waiting, watching an image that had not yet died in his memory materialise anew, waiting to see if his eye had been right, a vindication in black and white of his judgement, technical, visual, aesthetic.

Afterwards he stretched himself out on the sofa, light spilling through on to the floor from the kitchen spots. He knew they would be good pictures. Good in the way that they had come about. He wanted to show them to Stella.

He thought about an old email from her, still sitting in his in-box like an indictment. It was a message she had sent him a few months after his first lecture at the college asking if he might be able to offer a couple of weeks' work experience to photography students. He'd replied immediately. Yes, he'd love to help out – maybe he ought to meet her for a quick drink, he suggested, work something out. But really – what

175

was there to work out? But they'd met in a members' club in one of the little streets off Piccadilly Circus, and he'd given her his address and suggested she pass it on to anyone who was interested. They had stayed on and had dinner and talked for hours – she enthusing about a trip she'd been on to the Hermitage in St Petersburg, he about being nearly caught by a bomb that took out the museum in Grozny; they'd had a lot to drink, ended up in that big jangly Victorian bed of hers. Afterwards he had received two or three letters from students but hadn't got round to replying. By then he'd started to see Stella, who had pointedly reminded him about his promise until eventually, even more pointedly, she had stopped reminding him about it. But that was life, he thought. He didn't feel too terrible about it. Disappointment went with everyone's territory. The truth – and, surely, she must realise it, he thought – was that the last thing you needed as a professional photographer was to have a gormless first-year trailing around with you, getting in the way and insisting on explaining how a light meter actually worked as opposed to just holding it in the right place – students tended to be drearily well clued-up on all matters technical. Giving a talk was one thing; being stuck with someone was something else.

The other truth was that the two or three letters had come from male students, and what the hell use was that?

Integrity. An effortless integrity, unpremeditated, casual and, yes, free. That's the way he thought about Stella. That's why he wanted to show her these pictures. To show, in a subtle way, that he could be like her, and go off and express himself in a way that wasn't tainted by money or career or sex; show that he hadn't completely lost the idealism that made her youthfulness seem so real and carefree when contrasted against his own attempts to hold back the years by wearing a leather jacket and sleeping with his daughter's imaginary friend.

176

What else did it show – that what Stella thought about him mattered in a way he could never have predicted two or three months ago? That against the unstoppable tide of his own previous opinions, and through no fault of his own, he was sick with love for her? That such madness in love affirmed itself in such bizarre acts of moral cleansing as taking pictures of orange lifeboats in black and white on the Thames on a fine June afternoon?

eight

A beautiful tone. Distinct. Magisterial. That was the key to the great Charlie Parker, the man was saying, leaning on the counter at Hot Dog Jazz, glasses propped up on his forehead. 'Listen to it,' he said with a wink, proprietorial, though pleased enough to let the knowledge be seen, a smiling goblin at the gates of cool, the secret beat and blue light of the interior beckoning for all. Yeah.

Bart strained his ear in polite appreciation. 'Sorry, it's a bit wasted on me,' he said. 'But you're sure this is new stuff?'

'New?' The smile dropped off his face. 'New on CD, remastered and remixed with many extra tracks from the original sessions,' he said, indignation and pride rearing in his voice like fanning peacock feathers, as though he himself had unearthed the originals and taken charge of the remastering and remixing, perhaps in a back room right here in the shop. He was almost as old as Aunt Marian herself, and actually reminded Bart of her slightly, despite the beard, as he placed his glasses on the end of his nose, tilting his head back to get the sleeve notes in focus. Maybe jazz people developed a similar look. 'Uptown House, New York, 1942,' he said.

'Excellent,' Bart said. 'I'll take it.'

The man popped it in a plastic bag, tore the receipt off the till roll. 'Wish her a happy birthday from me.'

Kate was waiting for him at Camden and they headed off in the car for Aunt Marian's house in Cockfosters, the house he'd grown up in and still thought of as home. It seemed weird, after all this time, taking a new girlfriend back there to meet Aunt Marian, to eat cake and drink tea along with whoever else might be there on an occasion like this – Pa, now ninety-one, a couple of uncles and aunts, Bart's cousins and their young children. Weirder still – at least measured against the usual yardsticks of bringing girlfriends home – to bring a girlfriend home he didn't even know well enough to have sex with, who in fact he had never even taken back to his own place.

They were working on the sex bit, though, at last, having met the previous evening for that difficult second date – she looking casually edible waiting outside the Curzon on Shaftesbury Avenue, poppies on her long floaty dress, flat shoes, thin summer cardigan draped over one arm, a fleck of white paint in her black hair, him breathless and damp, having driven at speed across town and run from the parking meters at Soho Square after getting stuck for half an hour with Ivy. ('Actually, I'm just on my way out,' he'd said when Ivy had turned up unexpectedly at the office well after close of play, video camera slung over one shoulder, saying something about standing in for Jim while he was on holiday, big smile on her face, ignoring his subtle attempts to look busy leaving the office. 'Did my dad not mention it?')

Jas had mentioned it. And with Kate on the bright horizon of his evening, Bart had been more than delighted to say yes, no problem, he'd square things with Christian first thing in the morning. Which had made Ivy delighted too, talking excitedly, asking questions, following him round the office as he switched his lamp off and checked his messages, waving to Jim at the other side, who'd got some work to catch up with before he flew off to Barcelona or Casablanca or wherever next week.

'Anyway,' he said, 'if you don't mind, I've just got to . . .' He was pointing upstairs.

'I've heard about your brilliant loft,' she said. 'Would it be all right if I just came up and took a few shots?'

'What – now?' he'd said, when clearly 'No' would have been the answer for a man in a hurry.

'It won't take more than a minute.'

So they went up, Ivy alive with curiosity ('You forgot to turn your CD off . . .'), and of course it had taken more than a minute, all the time her chattering away about college and art as she wandered round his flat, filming the walls and furniture and the cat, taking pictures of his psychiatrist's couch, standing there with her eyes on him while he'd self-consciously pulled on a fresh shirt and brushed his teeth, thinking seriously about having a door put on the bathroom. But he was surprised at how likeable and animated she was, in contrast to the abrupt, saturnine performances he'd witnessed at Jas's – how full of charm and almost innocent enthusiasm. She made him laugh – though, of course, she also made him late, eventually obliging him to bundle her out of the flat and then surrender to her pleadings for a lift to a pub in Covent Garden to meet student friends.

'This is *your* car?' she'd said, reminding him of the day with Kate in the yard next to the mill job in Cambridge, just a few weeks ago, but already seeming like an age. Getting to the Curzon seemed like another.

'Sorry I'm late,' he'd said, kissing her quickly on the cheek, and then, more carefully, on the lips. But the film – something about Brazilian peasant sugarcane growers that had been liked by the critics – didn't start till 8.50, so they'd had time for a beer. He told her about Ivy holding him up, which then meant telling her about Jas – a quite highly thought of photographer in his field, he said – and then, remembering the launch party coming up for Jas's book, asking if she'd like to come along, but then wondering whether she might think he was rushing ahead too much, wanting to show her off to his friends this early in the relationship, which might make him seem shallow and . . .

'That sounds nice,' she said. And then, after the film, they had gone back to her place for coffee and talked for a long time entwined on the sofa, music on faintly in the background in a way that brought back to him a distant epoch from his life – as a seventeen-year-old, babysitting in a strange, badly decorated brown and orange flat with a girl from school, then later, at college, sharing the big house with Natalie with the high, peeling corniced ceilings . . .

It was odd how, with her, last night, he'd been barely aware of their surroundings, nothing more than a blunt impression of books, cushions, a screen, a wooden blind, candles, comfort; too immersed in the moment to imagine for a second what a place like this would be like stripped and emptied of its possessions and colour, to see into its corners, plot its spatial dimensions, number its salvageable features, put a shape on its possibilities. These were the routine tricks of his mind. But none of it mattered, as things didn't when your body sensed an emergency and seized the wheel.

They kissed. They kissed until they knew where it was heading and Kate came up for air, the blue of her eyes glittering beneath the sloping thick fringe of her black hair. 'Not now,' she said. 'Not here.' Which meant another time, somewhere else. So he had to see her the next day, even if a third date meant rushing ahead of himself again and taking her home to meet Aunt Marian and all the rest of his living relatives. 'It's just a birthday tea,' he said. 'Will you come?'

'I'd love to,' she said, smiling at his uncertainty with her, smiling because she knew what he was thinking.

The time sped by in their stories of failed marriages. He told her about Natalie, though not about his sperm count or the business leading up to it; not about the specimen bottle, currently the only item in his freezer. She told him about Stephen, whom she had met in France. 'It all happened quite quickly,' she said. 'It was like a holiday romance. And it *was* terribly romantic. That was the problem,' she smiled. 'We got married over there. My parents came out with my sisters for the wedding. A few months later, we moved back to London. Stephen's mother died about that time – they weren't close, but he had to sort out her estate and all that stuff. The other thing was I really needed to be nearer my clients in the UK. Stephen wanted to start up a small business for himself of some kind. It seemed like a good idea.'

She poured a glass of wine for herself, no more for him.

'But we were heading for the rocks. Anyone could see it coming. When I was away in Europe – or even here, if I had to stay overnight somewhere – he used to get absurdly possessive and fall into terrible moods when I got home. I remember once taking a phone call, here in the flat. Next day he followed me all the way to a client's offices in Essex. I could actually see his car parked right across the road. I think he thought it was endearing. We had a row about that one. The other thing was we hardly ever went out. It was as if he wanted to keep me all to himself. He'd cook romantic candlelit dinners for me and say he loved me and I know he did. But it wasn't a healthy thing. He was doing my head in. It was a mess. A big mistake. We tried counselling for a while, but in the end I felt I'd given it my best shot.'

She shrugged. It was gone two. 'Come on, Mr Bart,' she said. 'Confession's over.'

Bart swung the Boxster on to the North Circular, slipped into the outside lane. 'Are you sure you're OK about this?' he said.

'I'm fine about it. You?'

'Great, looking forward to it, absolutely.'

Half an hour later they stopped outside a small terrace house with balloons outside the door. 'This is it,' he said, giving her hand a squeeze. 'Probably be a full house. Uncles, cousins . . .'

'Bart,' she said.

'What?'

She looked at him, her chin dipped, showing her eyes above the rim of her sunglasses. 'Relax.'

He pulled her to him as they walked up the path and opened the door to the sound of voices and a piano, the smell of something in the oven. The front room was dotted with relatives, some turning to greet Bart's arrival – a couple of neighbours, too – listening, murmuring, nodding their heads to the music, standing or seated around the slight figure of

Aunt Marian, her back to everyone, banging out one of her old boogie-woogie numbers, her knotty fingers travelling up and down the keyboard of the funeral-black Victorian upright that Bart remembered had somehow magically appeared one rainy day while he was out at infant school. Pa in an armchair, dressed in his best snazzy waistcoat, tapping his foot, raised his eyebrows in greeting and opened his mouth in a part-toothless grin. They waited till she had finished and was turning to receive their applause.

'Happy birthday, Aunt Marian,' Bart said.

'Arthur!' she said. She came to hug him, kissing and hugging Kate too, even as he was introducing her. He gave her a card and the present he had bought, ill-wrapped and sellotaped.

'Just a CD,' he said.

'You're not supposed to say what it is,' said Aunt Marian.

'I brought you these,' Kate said.

'Irises!' Aunt Marian said. 'Beautiful. I'll put them in some water. Come through and talk to me, love,' she said to Kate, bustling off to the kitchen. Bart made an apologetic face at Kate, who smiled and followed her.

He poured a cup of tea for himself, bantered happily with his uncles and their wives and his two cousins, Tom and Michael, and their wives (Sophie quietly breastfeeding in the corner, Janice short-skirted, legs crossed on the sofa, laughing, nursing a large G&T). His three little nephews hauled him into a wrestling match, ending with him chasing them squealing into the garden, round the old swing, where they dodged him this way and that, leaving him flat on his back before they escaped back inside laughing. He stood up panting, adjusting his glasses. Kate and Aunt Marian were standing at the kitchen window, watching, cradling cups and saucers. He waved and came inside.

'Having fun?' Kate asked, plucking a leaf from his hair.

'Too early to say,' he said.

The boys eyed him expectedly from the foot of the stairs. He made a sudden move for them that sent them scampering up to the landing, red-faced, drunk with laughter. 'You win,' he called to them. 'You're too quick for me.'

'I'm just going to show Kate the garden,' said Aunt Marian.

'What about me?' he said.

'I see enough of you,' she said.

In the sitting room, Pa was sitting with a heavy black photograph album in his lap, his eyes watery with memories. Birthdays reminded him of Betty, the daughter who couldn't be here. Bart had seen lots of old black-and-white pictures of his dead mother, as a gap-toothed girl with her older siblings on camping holidays, in pyjamas holding a baby doll on Christmas Day in the family's small living room (large-pattern rose wallpaper, her own mother in attendance, Pa as a younger man, teacher, amateur artist, author of two books on watercolour, father of a young, still healthy family). In another she faced the camera alone, a bold young woman wearing a loud-checked sleeveless dress, hair beehived up, lip-sticked, perhaps setting out for the dance hall – perhaps *that* evening – smiling out from a distant time; an earlier portrait captured a new graduate in a formal gown, wearing heavy-framed spectacles, holding a scroll. In a way the pictures were too familiar to touch him deeply. It was only through the rest of the family – Aunt Marian, Pa, Uncles Roy and Stephen, their wives Sylvia and Maureen – that he sometimes felt her loss and a non-specific emptiness, not least for his part in it. Aunt Marian had always been his mother. As for a father, he very occasionally felt a difference there between himself and the boys at school, who all had one, but, again, it was not a difference he could put his finger on or find himself yearning for. He had uncles who lived close by, who seemed to vie for the pleasure of taking him off at weekends to see matches at Highbury with one set of cousins or the other. He was their sister's boy. Their dead sister in whose memory they rallied with such unhurried, unforced grace. Together they were all his parents. He realised this now, though it had seemed a normal, natural and unremarkable thing then.

The anonymous father was never spoken of unless Bart himself raised the question, innocently as a young boy and then more tentatively as an adolescent, understanding more as his understanding of the world grew. But though he had asked (Aunt Marian, Pa, his uncles all had a similar recollection of events, culminating in an outcome which in its unbearable magnitude seemed totally to eclipse the question of paternity), he had never sought or desired 'closure' in respect of his father's identity. A one-night stand. A musician. A slip-up with much unforeseen sadness. 'Your mother was a remarkable girl,' Pa had once said, eyes glistening. 'Always one to handle things her way. She said it was over. There was nothing your grandma or I could do about it. We have to learn to respect that now as we had to back then and let the past be the past.'

Bart was as satisfied with a gap in the story as everyone else seemed to be. It didn't seem to be part of who he was. But still there were things unsaid. The question of the sacrifice made by Aunt Marian – something Uncle Roy had once started to tell but didn't finish (the two of them unexpectedly thrown together in a bar, unguarded in suits and loosened ties, during the long winding down of a christening or wedding) about a man she had been seeing whom she might have expected to marry but, in the circumstances following Betty's death and Bart's birth, had not. An enjoyable showbiz career, too, that had been curtailed, though the big bands were start-ing to disappear with the advent of the Beatles and the Stones and the Kinks. The Uncle Roy conversation had been a puz-zling, half-drunken one about continuity and family that also touched on Aunt Marian's hopes for Bart and Natalie, but for Bart it had been a moment of epiphany in which for the first time he saw Aunt Marian – his 'life' mother, as the caring professions would call her – as someone who had forfeited her future for his. It seemed *such* a big thing, it was a shock even to think of it in that way. If only for this reason it seemed a betrayal of everyone's wishes to dwell on his mother's big mistake, which after all had been a tragedy for everyone but himself. But it was a moment that made him see himself in a different light – as part of the greater whole that involved those who had casually caught the baby before he dropped, stepped quietly in to take the place of his vanished parents and cushion him from his own catastrophe. It made him see the idea of family, of connectivity from back then, as a boy, forward to infinity. It came to him as a new-fledged thought that sat uncomfortably with Natalie's and his joyful isola-tionism, their minimalism of heart and soul, their freedom thing, their avowed war against clutter.

Bart sat on the sofa next to Aunt Sylvia and fielded un-subtle questions about Kate – when and where they'd met, what she did for a living. 'She's divorced,' Bart said, sipping his tea. 'Well, as good as.'

'Nothing wrong with that,' Auntie Sylvia said. 'Sign of a woman who knows what she wants.' She smiled, inviting further confidences. 'Serious?' she asked.

'I've only seen her three times,' he said.

She lit a cigarette and opened the window. 'No rush then.'

'We seem to like each other,' he said.

Much as he treasured them, Bart had seen probably more

of his aunts and uncles than was necessary for a grown adult when he'd come back to hide himself in his old room at Aunt Marian's. He had tried to match their show of support with a level of stoicism that not only sustained him through his troubles with Natalie but helped him suffer their love and best wishes with patience. And if he couldn't quite bring himself to be grateful for their concern – and for a willingness to become indignant on his behalf regarding the rights and wrongs of events as they understood them – he could at least accept that they were probably entitled to express it. Today he was happy to see that they were happy to see him happily recovered – sufficiently so, at least, to be seeing someone else, to be shaking off his sorrows and starting afresh.

His cousin Tom's baby was crying. Just a bit of wind, someone said. Auntie Sylvia stubbed out her cigarette. 'Shouldn't really be smoking this,' she said.

'Where's our birthday girl?' Pa was shouting. 'I'm ready for some cake.'

They left the family drinking sherry and went back to London to eat at the Bangkok Palace, Bart faintly anxious, Kate full of warmth, enthusiasm and everything else you got from standing too close to Aunt Marian. 'She's *so* lovely,' she said. 'Though she does ask questions. I'm starving.' Bart hardly touched his tiger prawn noodles, but watched Kate talk and eat.

Afterwards they went back to his flat, an alt. country compilation barely audible as they crept in ('Hey, you left your CD on . . .' she said) and had sex on his kingsize futon, the first time quickly and desperately, struggling out of their clothes and into contraception like comic adulterers; the second time handling each other with care, easing themselves together with a sense of something that called for tenderness.

They lay in each other's arms, hearts beating, light filtering in from the street, softening the skin on her shoulder, casting shadows.

He hadn't dared to expect something this good and delicious from the start. With Natalie, whatever they'd had had arrived with stealth, unannounced, a pair of students living in the same house with similar interests, imperceptibly growing in and out of each other, like vines on a wall. This, now, with Kate – you could see it growing while you watched. He found his glasses and switched a lamp on. She was looking at him and he kissed her. 'Don't worry, no one can see us,' he said. 'Don't go away.' He got up and tiptoed quickly over to the fridge, and came back with half a baguette from yesterday and a bottle of Coke. 'Hunger.'

She raised herself on one elbow and looked round. 'Nice place you've got here,' she said. 'Ever thought of putting some furniture in it?'

'It's in progress. Or rather I'm in progress,' he said. He offered her the Coke bottle. She shook her head.

'Your aunt said you've been through a difficult time.'

'She can be a bit overprotective,' he said, brushing breadcrumbs on to the floor. He turned back to face her.

She sighed, though not unhappily. 'It's been a long time for me,' she said. 'I mean longer than you might think.'

'What has?'

She paused, looking at the ceiling. 'I mean Stephen. The two of us. He couldn't do it, or wouldn't. We never had a full sexual relationship. Our marriage was never, you know, consummated.'

'Wow. That must have been . . . weird.'

'It was worse than weird, though to start with I suppose it seemed sort of endearing. I told you he was romantic, and he was, in that old-fashioned way. I'd never met anyone like him before. I'd just broken off from another relationship, which had been fun but kind of wild – too much drinking, too much partying, too druggy. Too much for a Catholic girl, even one like me. Stephen seemed the perfect antidote to that. Very gentle. Undemanding. Very attentive in all the other ways. He said he wanted to wait for sex.'

'Blimey.'

'That's what I thought. But we waited. And waited. As you might have guessed, our wedding night was not a success. Naturally, I put it down to nerves. Perhaps he wasn't one for the big occasion, I thought. Perhaps it was the in-laws staying in the same hotel. I don't know. I told him it didn't matter, though to be honest I was beginning to think it might.'

'But couldn't he . . .'

'No. Not when it came to it. Whatever progress we made faded away when it came to the moment. And we did try. All the usual methods. Without going into details.' She laughed.

Bart smiled.

'It wasn't funny, of course. It was what was behind all the other obsessive behaviour. The way he kind of put me on a pedestal. And all the stuff that had seemed romantic and sweet in France now just seemed dysfunctional – the way he wouldn't let me pay my share when we went out, the way he insisted on calling me Catherine instead of Kate. It got worse. He thought I was having an affair, begged me not to, and then said he wouldn't blame me if I was. Though I wasn't, of course. And would never have. Eventually we agreed to a temporary separation, a breathing space. Our counsellor thought it was a good idea. So I went back to my place over my shop and he stayed put at his.'

'So, what happened?'

'A couple of weeks went by. It must seem odd, I suppose,

but I was missing him. I did still love him. I did want everything to be OK between us. I went over on Sunday morning even though I wasn't supposed to see him. Anyway, this girl was coming out of his flat just as I was about to ring the bell. I'll never forget the smile she gave me. He was still upstairs in bed.'

Bart was listening but his mind was backpedalling, trying to process what she had said even as she was adding to it. There was something . . .

'I just went crazy with him,' Kate was saying. 'I threw some stuff around. Walked out. Maybe he was just trying to prove something to himself. I don't know. I didn't want to know.'

She turned to Bart, smiling. 'Sorry about all that.'

He was quiet for a moment. His mouth was dry. 'When you said you went back to your shop and he stayed at his, did you mean . . .'

'His shop. He has a bookshop. Art, design, photography, that kind of thing. On Exmouth Market. You probably know it,' she said. 'Montgomery Books?'

Her eyes accused him only with their unblinking, blue trust, an unwarned innocent on the threshold of a forbidden room. 'Montgomery Books,' he repeated, nodding, seeing in profile the smooth, upturned weight of her small, perfect breast, the pale strap mark on her warm, browned shoulder that, even at a moment like this, called to be kissed. 'It does ring a bell.'

• • •

Fuck. Nick looked at his watch, hurried along, caught his reflection in a shop window on Old Compton Street as he passed, winced. Haircut at some point. He touched the patch of stubble on his face where he'd cut himself and had shaved round twice. Disposables. Worst a man can get. Crumpled suit by Paul Smith, grooming products by Des. Must buy a toothbrush, he thought. He stopped into a newsagent's for a tube of extra strong mints, popped one, then two, chewing and swallowing as he walked. Coach and Horses. He peeped over the frosted glass into the bar. Packed. Frank hemmed in at the furthest end trying to read the *Standard* amid the noise and ruck. Hawaii shirt, shorts, shaved head, goatee. Nick wiped his mouth, lit a cigarette and swung in, shouldering his way through, old pals act. 'Frank, Frank . . .'

Always make an entrance. Never apologise. Frank looking up, folding his paper, glass of wine on the bar, touch of a frown with possible regard to being kept waiting twenty minutes.

Puffing and panting beyond the call of credibility, he shook Frank's hand, touched his shoulder. 'Sorry about the lateness of the hour. Bloody cabs. Same again?' He pointed to Frank's glass.

'It'll have to be just the one. I can't hang about too much. Sandra's got some tennis club people coming round.'

'All the more reason, eh?' Don't wink.

'Well, no, they're friends of both of us. Matt's a writer. Well, journo. *Sunday Times.* Quite high up, editorially. TV stuff.'

'Oh, right, sure. You still in Camberwell?'

'Muswell Hill.'

'Nice and leafy.'

'We like it.' Frank looking at the suit. 'So what's with the suit?'

'Oh that. That's Hugo wanting me to take on a more strategic role. Top brass were crying out for a sort of conduit to link with the creative end, for better client interface and so on. My name came up and before you know it, presto, I've got meetings coming out of my ears. Hence the corporate stripes.'

Drinks arriving. Glass of Stormy Cape for Frank, large Guinness for himself. 'Cheers. Nice to see you again.'

'But didn't you say you were freelance?'

Freelance?

'On the phone the other day. You left a message.'

Fuck. 'Ah, yes. More consultative really. Contractual, retained basis. Makes more sense for me that way, from a fiscal point of view.'

Frank nodded. 'So . . .'

'Having said which, I do find myself sometimes yearning for the simple life. You know, the more creative, less suit-wearing kind of life, if you see what I mean. A new challenge, but . . .'

'But doing what you were doing before?' Frank eyeing him.

'Well, yes, but maybe an opening somewhere else. And, since we're mates from the old days back at Shoutt, I thought I'd give you first refusal.'

'So, you're looking for another job?'

'Well, not exactly looking, exactly. Just putting out a few feelers. Unless you had something in mind . . .' Casual, boy, casual.

'We're pretty much stocked up with talent at the moment,' Frank said, glancing at the time.

'Course you are. I'd be amazed if you weren't. Agency like PTBO. Tell you what. Think about it and I'll give you a bell in the week, OK?'

'To be brutal, I can't see it happening, Nick.'

'As I say, you don't have to decide now.' Grin. 'Another?'

'More than my life's worth, I'm afraid.'

194

'Sure. Busy man.' Pause. 'Do you ever see old Rod from Shoutt? Or what's-his-name – Randolf, who turned out to be a shirtlifter? Remember that party of his we went to in Camberwell when he came out with the biscuit tin full of drugs? Toot, toot! he says. Speed, weed, whatever you need! Say what you like about the old fudge bandits, they do know how to enjoy themselves.'

Barman at three o'clock. Another pint.

'Sure you won't?'

'No, but let me get this.'

'Remember those two girls, completely out of it, arguing about whether men or women gave the best blow jobs? Then Randolf says prove it and she gives him one right there and then in the front room with her mate cheering her on. I didn't know where to put my face. Those were the days, though.' Another cigarette. 'Fag?'

Frank shaking his head. 'It seems a long time ago.'

'Speaking of which. I don't know if you're in the market for something special. Make your own party go with a bang.'

'What do you mean?'

Nick fished in his back pocket, laid a little plastic bag on to the bar.

'What is it?'

'Don't worry, it won't go off. A pal of mine gets it. One of his samples. Special introductory price. Little rocks of pleasure. The ultimate smoker's requisite. Improve your tennis at a stroke.'

'Crack?' Frank taking a step back.

'Shh, not so loud, everybody'll want some.'

'Bloody hell, Nick, are you fucking mad?' he hissed, horrified mug. 'For Christ's sake put it away. You'll get us both arrested.'

'Just a thought,' he said, retrousering the offending. 'How is Sandra, by the way?'

'Pregnant.'

'Wow, right . . . bad moment then.'

'How's that?'

'To try out new drugs, I mean.'

'Are you serious?'

'No, no, just kidding. Congratulations. You must be chuffed.'

'I am. You've got kids, have you?'

Nick blew smoke down his nostrils. 'Matthew and Lucy.'

Frank shook his head, looked at him in a funny way.

On the tube. Late-night drunks propped up all over the place. Trouble with being toxed-up was the occasional inappropriate stuff that might come out, and someone would suddenly say *Are you serious?* Like when Monty had once wondered at b&s what was the worst thing he'd ever done. As though he was always doing bad things. Not that he'd minded, though you'd only really ever ask someone that question who had no sense of dignity, someone you knew would take a crowd-pleasing pleasure in confessing bad things. So, predictably not being able to resist, he'd reached for his wicked grin and told them about the time he'd abruptly abandoned Olivia and the kids at her mother's one bank holiday weekend, pretending to be taken ill. Livvy halfway between bewildered and pissed off as he dragged himself to the car, doing his best to look pale and weak, starting the engine with an unnecessary cough.

'I don't see why you can't just let Mum call Dr Price,' she said. 'He could be here in twenty minutes. You're mad to drive home.'

'No, it's just a virus. I need to be on my own.'

'I thought it was a migraine.'

'Yes, a viral migraine. I can tell. I need to lie down.'

'I'll ring you tonight.'

'No, I'll ring you.' Livvy, exasperated in the rearview mirror, standing on the road outside her mother's, watching him disappear.

Then excitement hurtling through his veins as he picked up the hire suit and black tie on Fulham Broadway and drove out to Heathrow and got on a plane to Zurich. Zurich! Six hours later, five minutes to seven p.m. local time, walking into the lobby of a big apartment block – one of those like a hotel with liveried servants on the desk to call ahead and find out if you were expected. Tenth floor, plush lifts with gold fittings. Surfacing at the top looking like James Bond, padding down the carpeted corridor, fingering his cufflinks, heart thudding as he got the mask out (a nicely foldable latex one, as instructed, from a shop in Soho – Old Compton Street as it happened) and put it on outside the door before ringing the bell.

This was the point where Monty said, 'Are you serious?'

'True as I'm smoking this cigar,' he'd said. 'Woman answers the door. She's wearing a mask too, but more feminine, if you can imagine that – sort of Catwomanish – and a really sexy evening gown and heels. Anyway she *shakes my hand* and invites me in. She speaks really good English and asks how the flight was and stuff like that and takes me into this sumptuous apartment with dinner laid out for us both. So we had dinner and chatted away . . .'

Bart shaking his head slowly in disbelief. 'Didn't you feel a bit odd, chatting away wearing a rubber mask?'

'That's the weird thing. It was really sort of . . . liberating. You could be who you wanted. You could say anything. It was like being in a film. Her name was Hildi and she talked in this sophisticated European accent. Told me about her husband, who was in banking and always away on business and how he had mistresses all over the place. I didn't ask her whether she went into chatrooms often and organised business-class

197

plane tickets with a view to flying strange men in for a shag, but only because it might have spoiled things a bit, destroyed the illusion. Anyway, we hadn't had a shag yet, though obviously we did pretty soon after. The deal was we weren't allowed to touch each other until we were both naked . . .'

'Apart from the masks?' Jas with his photographer's eye for detail, almost drooling, he could tell.

'Apart from the masks.'

'What was she like?'

'Fucking hell, Jas, I can't tell you that. What do you take me for?' Laughs all round. Jas pouring more wine.

He'd had to be out by ten. She'd made him wear a red condom that went with the mask. On the plane back to London he tried to recapture the images from the sex, but it was already slipping away – body in its mid to late thirties, skin gleaming in the candlelight, great Teutonic breasts heaving up and down as the two of them pumped away, substantial thighs, touch of cellulite wobble, impossibility of kissing nipples properly with mask on. Laptop winking in a corner of the room as they entered the final thrust. Her wicked window on the world. Then the noise of it when she finally came – wailing, shrieking. Alarming really, wondered for a second whether it might be a signal for the *Polizei* to come bursting in. Gratifying all the same. Vote of appreciation, bit of feedback.

He didn't tell them – unblinking Jas, sceptical Bart, watchful Monty – how she didn't invite him to stay for a shower or a nightcap, her retiring to the bathroom, him picking up scattered clothes, retrieving a cufflink that had rolled under the bed, head sweating in that mask, arse in the air. It was all a mess suddenly, post-shag, smell of rubber and sex in the room. Stripped now of promise, desire, greed, whatever, it all seemed absurd, humiliating even. 'You must go,' she said, with a tone of regret that made him think she must have been through this very anticlimax on previous occasions, wrapped in a silk dressing gown, sounding like Greta Garbo or whoever but looking like someone who had absent-mindedly gone to bed and woken up in fancy dress.

Olivia came home that Monday afternoon to flowers, bought in panic, mood of self-disgust, at the airport. 'Sorry about ruining the weekend,' he said.

She kissed his cheek. 'I suppose it could have been worse.'

There was always something worse.

Nick got off the tube, swaying up the bright tunnel. Man there holding a briefcase, forehead against the cold tiles, chucking up. Smell of it. Warm night out in the street, Farringdon's air full of onions from a hotdog stand, newspapers, crisp packets swirling lazily on the pavement. Clubbers gathering on the ticket concourse. Nick stopped, felt for the sachet of crack in his pocket. Hesitated, squinting at it, fingering the raised plastic seal, then tossed it in a rubbish bin overflowing with KFC debris, lager cans, other shit. He walked on, drawn by inescapable magnets of hope and foolishness into the direction of Ivy's, just to look and wish, exaggerated stride and effortful lurch of someone newly released into the community by pub landlord. 'Filth,' he muttered. 'Everything gone to fuck.'

• • •

Mesdames, messieurs . . . Jas waited at the arrivals gate at Stansted sipping latte with his back to the pillar, eyes above the rim of his cup scanning the swell of passengers, searching for platinum blonde, tired of the chime of the tannoy, the monotony of announcements. His heart upped its beat when at last he saw her, taking her time, luggage slung over one shoulder, jacket draped over her arm. He was about to wave, push his way through to meet her, but he could see now that she was chatting with another woman, and there were two men, too, alongside.

He took a step back, not hiding exactly, but trapped in a moment of not belonging, as if having gone through a wrong door. The taller of the men – jeans, denim jacket, careless, slept-in hair, undoubtedly this *Mark* – was saying something, the others inclined towards him now, listening with interested expressions that turned to smiles as he smiled. Stella laughed and touched his arm. They stopped at the barrier, just a few feet away from Jas, chatting, allowing the crowd to pass, the jumbled castle of their luggage on the floor between them. Then the woman and the shorter man – balding, less fascinating, not this *Mark*, for sure – picked up their bags. They were leaving, saying their goodbyes, which would mean Stella and this *Mark* . . .

Stella leaned across to embrace the woman, and was just about to do the same with the shorter man when she looked across the barrier and saw him. She blinked a blink of surprise. 'Jas?' The others turned to him too now, their eyebrows rising in synchronised curiosity.

Jas coughed, and spurring himself to an unfelt jauntiness stepped up to the barrier and kissed her on the cheek. 'Hello,' he said, sharing his grin with the others.

'Jas, what on earth are you *doing* here?'

'I came to meet you.'

'That was sweet of you, but we were just . . .' She paused. 'How did you know which was my flight?'

'I didn't. I was here for the earlier one too.'

She looked at him. 'Is everything OK?'

'Absolutely.'

'Sorry,' she said, 'Stuart, Julia, this is Jas.' Jas shook hands. 'And this is Mark.'

'Jas. Photographer, right?'

'Right.' He turned back to Stella, smiling for grim life. 'Are you ready? I've got the car outside. Sorry, I didn't mean to barge in on you guys . . .'

He *was* sorry, now that he was going to get rid of them.

'That's fine, we were just about to head off,' Julia said, raising her voice against the gonging announcements, the aggregate babble and movement of people, the smooth murmur of electronics, machinery, systems.

'Stuart and Julia are driving up to Cambridge,' said Stella. 'Mark and I were just going to get the express to London. But we could drop him in Stoke Newington, couldn't we, Jas?'

Mark and I. Jas gave a shrug, looking beyond Mark, as if distracted, towards the big glass doors. Looking at the sun's glare against the glass made him feel hot and damp and airless, despite the architect-built space above and the air-conditioning. The leather coat was a mistake, he felt, looking at the four of them, lightly attired, fresh Bolognese suntans from an afternoon's sightseeing perhaps. He just wanted to be alone with her, out of the noise and crowdedness of this place, on the road, the old Merc with the top down, the two of them resuming what they had, making whatever might be wrong between them better. 'As long as you're not in a hurry,' he said. 'The train's probably quicker. And more comfortable.'

Stella put on an amused cross face. 'Jas, you sound as if you're trying to put him off. Of course you must come with us.' She was touching Mark's arm again.

Mark smiled. 'I'm in no rush. If you're sure you don't mind.'

201

'That's settled then,' said Stella.

Jas took Stella's bag and they walked to the car park, Stella a pace behind, laughing with Mark about some mix-up with airport security in Bologna. 'I took my little telescope for the opera. I think they were looking for the rest of the gun. Lucky for me, Mark speaks Italian – I kept breaking into my terrible Spanish,' she said. 'I might have ended up in a jail cell.'

'I didn't know you liked opera,' said Jas.

'You probably didn't know I could speak bad Spanish either,' she laughed. It was a different laugh to the one he knew. She seemed to be laughing this new laugh for this whole other crowd he wasn't part of. She was right about the opera and her rudimentary Spanish, of course, and he felt a surge of resentment that Mark had discovered these things about her first, things that he now had over him. A usurper's advantage.

'Lovely car,' Mark said, when they got outside. '1970s?'

Jas, pretending not to hear, released the boot, threw Stella's bag in, shucked off his leather coat. Stella opened the back door. 'You'd better go in the front, Mark – stretch your legs out. I can squeeze in the back.'

They set off, Jas driving in silence while Mark chatted to Stella, half-turned, his arm resting on the back of the seat. Jas glanced up from time to time, tried to frame Stella's face in the mirror, strands of her hair snapping back in the wind, tried to gauge her responses to Mark, looking for signs of greater intimacy than their talk about faculty funding and falling student numbers suggested.

'Have you ever been to Bologna, Jas?' Mark asked at one point.

'Nope.' Jas busied himself with an unnecessary manoeuvre, lowering his head to squint critically into one wing mirror then the other – though there was nothing behind but the flatlands of Essex – then made a careful but pointless adjustment to the airflow before pulling into the outside lane with ample time to overtake a lorry half a mile ahead. In fact, Jas had been to Bologna, twice actually, including a school trip, but there was no way he was going to allow himself to be *invited* to be sociable in his own car, to be granted the opportunity to share someone else's personal space with his own girlfriend, to make everyone feel comfortable with the situation.

He had the idea of turning the radio on and twiddled with the dial until he found something suitably disruptive to communication. Eventually Mark leaned back and closed his eyes. No one spoke until the tailback into Hackney brought them to a standstill. 'Nearly there,' Jas said, with a cheerfulness that betokened the imminent end of Mark for the day and, perhaps, he hoped, also offset any inkling that he might have behaved badly, or was in a strop, a signal to Stella that he was perfectly sanguine about giving her colleague a lift and that any appearance to the contrary might be a simple misunderstanding ascribed to jet lag or premenstrual tension or a trick of the light. 'Upper Clapton . . .' he announced, looking right then left. 'Downs Road should do it. Half a mile? A mile? Can't be far.'

No one responded. At Stoke Newington High Street he pulled over at the lights, reached over to let Mark out, brushing his denimed leg with his bare arm. 'Dodgy door . . .' He said. 'Nothing personal,' he grinned.

'Thanks,' Mark said.

'See you Monday?' Stella said.

'I'll be there.' He closed the door.

Jas waited, watching until Mark was out of sight, then turned to Stella. 'Come and sit in the front?' he said.

'I'm OK.'

'You OK? You're very quiet.'

'Yes, I'm fine. I'm just tired, that's all.'

'You didn't seem tired when you were talking to Mark.'

He wished he hadn't said that. She didn't answer, but just closed her eyes. He drove her to her place in Mile End. A Victorian workman's cottage with a two-storey front room. She got out of the car before he had switched off the engine, hauled her bag out of the boot.

'I won't ask you in, Jas. I just want to get my head down.'

'I was going to show you some photographs I took while you were away. I'd value your opinion. It wouldn't take long . . .'

'Do you mind if we don't? I've got a bit of a headache coming on. It must have been the wine on the plane.'

'Also, I was wondering if you still had students looking for work experience. I might be able to fit someone in for a couple of weeks in the summer.'

She looked at him for a long moment, examining his eyes, a glimpse of something in her own. Disappointment, perhaps.

'Are you annoyed with me?'

'Let's not talk about it now.'

'Talk about what?'

Her sigh was inaudible. The worst kind. The kind that presaged not frustration or good old impatience but news that didn't want to be told. 'I'll call you, OK?' she said.

nine

A beautiful dilemma. A . . . a *thing* of such exquisite perplexity that it had stopped Bart's mind in its tracks – sent it off on *two* tracks, each leading to something bad – and made the tending of ordinary life unexpectedly laboured. It was a thing you didn't hit upon every day, questions of good and bad being more, well . . . *relative* than they were a hundred years ago, which made your moral choices not really moral in any universal way, one person's personal morality being someone else's offence against the order of God or nature, etc. And therefore – if you thought about it, which no one did any more, and who could blame them – it was not much more than your word against theirs. Life was only *that* complicated and, in the general run of things, it seemed to work pretty well without pissing too many people off. But not this. This was a moral thing of the old-fashioned, difficult, dispiriting, heartbreaking kind.

The weather was threatening to break at last, the sky outside darkening the office as Bart dialled the first four digits of Kate's number and put the phone down again. He had spoken to her twice. Once to put her off Jas's book launch and once to say he couldn't get out to see her on Wednesday night after all, due to emergency work. ('Two broken dates in a week? You sure know how to woo a girl . . .' she'd said, still good-humoured but with a speck of wariness in her voice – perhaps as if, against all the signs, he was after all the type to make his excuses and retreat. As if he were the kind of idiot who didn't realise you could conceivably have sex with a girl without having to take her home to meet the folks.) He tried to imagine what shadow of expression crossed her face as she put the phone down, what wrong conclusions were settling in her mind, what benefits turning to doubt.

He had to tell her. He had to tell *him*. Bart turned back to his screen, displaying Mortensens' website. A south Manhattan streetscape. Shots of various interiors, spec diagrams that came to brilliant life, a virtual tour winding up and down ornate staircases, dwelling on iron radiators and thick, opaque glass panelling, a hat factory with penthouse apartment, rooftop swimming pool. Mortensens was an escape that kept coming and going, but wouldn't come and go for ever while he decided whether escape was what he actually wanted. He gazed, distracted, at his desk calendar, ringed in black with the reference number for the purchase of the Citroën chevron badge he had ordered from a collectors' website. He took off his glasses, slowly polishing each lens on the hem of his shirt, frowning, entertaining a thought that should have come to mind late on Saturday night while he was lying awake in bed, Kate asleep beside him.

Jim was waving, saying something, on his way out to get teatime cakes with Ivy, taking care of her, showing her the important jobs. Bart swivelled his chair to face him. 'Jim . . .'

He turned on his heel. 'Yes, master?'

'Where did the Cambridge job come from?'

Jim's eyes rested on the ceiling for a moment. 'I think we were just asked to pitch for it. Hang on.' He moved briskly to his computer, released the window blind and pulled the job up on screen, scrolling through the details. 'Recommendation,' he said, looking out of the window as the rain started to fall. Thunder sounded somewhere far away. 'Listen to that,' he said. 'Ivy – the umbrellas!'

'So who recommended us?'

'We don't have the who, I'm afraid. We only have the how. Will that be all, sir? The caketh awaiteth.'

He was unusually skittish – excitement, perhaps, at his holidays coming up (Barcelona was it? Casablanca?), the changing weather, the absence in New York of the master builder Christian, the novelty of having a girl around the office to gossip and share manicuring tips with – though Ivy had never struck Bart as the type for gossip, and her grubby art student nails, he noticed, were gnawed down to the skin. 'Have you got the number there?' Bart said.

Jim gave the number. Ivy waiting at the door – careless, sleeveless, bra-less, no doubt happy to be earning money by shopping for cakes – smiled in an obliging way. They went off giggling about something together, letting the sound of rain and the sudden cool of the street into the office.

Bart picked up the phone again. He wouldn't ring

Tristram. He knew now where this was leading. He dialled Monty's number. Monty would see, when Bart explained what had happened. Once Monty realised his part in it, he would see.

'Montgomery Books.'

'Monty, hi – it's Bart. Just a quick one . . .'

'Bart, how are you?'

'Terrific. Well, you know, fine. Just a quick one . . .'

'Fire away, *mon brave.*'

'Right. It's nothing really. Just a bit of housekeeping. We got this job referred, some time ago – restaurant in Cambridge. Someone called Tristram? He asked us to do a conversion . . .'

'Tristram, yes, I know him. Catherine used to do a bit of work for him. He rang here a few months ago, looking for her. Said he'd bought an old factory or something?'

'Flour mill . . .'

'That was it. He said he was looking for an architect and designers and plumbers, etc., so I gave him your number. I think I must have told him you were conversion experts. You got some work out of it then?'

'Yes, we did. Thanks . . .'

'Good. I suppose that means you owe me a pint.'

'Yes, let's do that. Hang on a minute, Mont . . .' Bart looked out of the window. There was a wreck of a blue Transit parked on the kerb outside, rain bouncing on the roof, and two twenty-something mat-haired baggy types struggling to get up the steps, one with a box the size of a small armchair, the other loaded with electrical equipment of some sort. Bart laid the phone on the desk and went to open the door. The first of them reversed into the office, looking around, his fellow baggy behind him, foot against the door. 'Ivy around?' he said, turning his face to reveal an array of

208

eyebrow rings. He dropped the box at Bart's feet. His friend was pushing through with what looked like a battered, rolled-up screen, along with extensions and transformers and other junk. Brown cables trailed behind, a sellotaped plug snagging, then bouncing over the threshold. 'Shit,' he muttered, collapsing with the effort of keeping the load together, dumping it across the floor. He exhaled loudly and went out again.

'She's out of the office right now. What's the, er . . .'

'Can you tell her Jamie and Sean came with the stuff?'

'You're leaving this here for Ivy?' Bart said, watching his office space disappear beneath the 'stuff'.

'She said you'd be cool about it.'

'Well, I suppose I am *quite* cool, but I'd be cooler if she'd mentioned it.' He stood to one side as the second baggy reappeared laden with two smaller boxes. 'That's it.'

'Brilliant. Thanks.'

Bart went back to the phone. 'Monty? Sorry about that . . .'

'So, did he tell you?'

'Who?' Bart watched the van splutter off down the road.

'Tristram. Did he tell you I put him on to you?'

'Oh, right . . . yes, he must have done. I thought I'd just check, that's all. And, you know, say thanks.'

'No problem.'

'Listen . . .'

'I'm listening.'

'Why don't we go for a drink this week . . . have a chat.'

'That sounds ominous.'

Bart laughed as loud as he dare. 'Thursday OK?'

'Let's hope the weather holds.'

Bart put the phone down, sucking air through his teeth. 'Shit,' he said quietly. He remembered something Kate had said, that first day in Cambridge, when he'd asked if she believed in fate.

I don't even believe in coincidences.

It was barely ten to six, and still raining, when Jim gathered his rucksack and waltzed out of the office with a wave, leaving Bart idling over colour and lighting moods for a tapas bar – Kasparo – in Charlotte Street, while Ivy continued with a programme of clerical tasks so uncompromisingly menial that neither Christian nor Bart had ever had the nerve to bring them to Jim's notice, preferring instead to save them up for temps or students.

'New boyfriend,' she said, smiling at him with her green eyes.

'You have a new boyfriend?'

'No, no – Jim. Gays have such prolific sex lives,' she said. 'They're so . . . what's the word?'

'Promiscuous?'

'That's it. I wonder why.'

'Because they can be, I suppose,' said Bart, without looking up. 'They are, you know, men, after all.'

'Are all men promiscuous, if they get the chance?'

'I don't know. Um, listen, Ivy, what about all this equipment? Didn't you say someone was picking you up?'

'Yes, Jamie said he'd come. If he can get the van.'

'Is this the same Jamie who brought this stuff? Why didn't he just take it to your place this afternoon? Or why didn't he just come with it all this evening in the first place?'

'Because I wouldn't have been at my place this afternoon, would I? And Jamie had to get back to college, and he couldn't bring it here tonight because he knew he might not be able to get the van, and I need it for tomorrow. It's for my end-of-year show.'

210

'Oh. When's that?'

'Friday the third. Everyone's invited.'

'Hang on, won't you be here tomorrow – you know, *working*?'

'Of course. I might just have to take off a couple of hours in the morning, that's all. I've got a technician friend coming round to make sure I know how it all fits together.'

'Right. OK. I'm glad I asked.'

They worked for another twenty-five minutes, Bart trying to bring some life to his tapas bar, Ivy enthusiastically sifting through a mountain of cuttings from magazines and newspapers that Christian frowned at every time he opened the cupboard next to the coffee machine, but which he and Bart nevertheless casually added to daily in the hope that they would one day be carefully edited, scanned into the system and formulated into some sort of logical, time-saving, instant access, cross-referenced sequence that would be helpful to all in a way that hanging on to tons of otherwise recyclable paper was not. Ivy chatted as she sorted, blithely soliciting Bart's opinion on homosexual erotic literature for women, the disappointingly tepid conceptual art scene in Eastern Europe, and Pythagorean views of vegetarianism – subjects to which Bart was obliged to admit he had never previously given a great deal of thought, his mind drifting in any case, as the minutes ticked by, to the boxes and equipment surrounding them that Christian would come back to and be unfavourably surprised by in the morning.

'So what time did your friend say he'd be here by if he *was* coming?'

'Well, it was more of a loose arrangement.'

'Do you think you could make it a firmer one? It's just that I will need to lock up at some point.'

'I'll give him a call, shall I?' she said, as if this struck her

211

as a particularly bold idea. She keyed in the number and waited. 'Ah . . .' She grinned apologetically. 'His mobile's switched off.'

'Look, Ivy, why don't I just get you a cab?'

'It might be a bit tricky in this weather,' she said. 'Couldn't we just take it in your car? We might have to take it out of the boxes but I'm sure it would all go in. And it wouldn't take long.'

Bart sighed, looking out at the wet streets, jammed with traffic, the zero presence of taxis showing illuminated signs. 'But then we'd still have the boxes clogging up the office, wouldn't we,' he said, realising even as he said it that *what* he was saying amounted to an agreement in principle, requiring only the small print to be settled – as of course it quickly was – by Ivy simply suggesting they put the bigger boxes out back with the garbage.

'Fine,' Bart said. He brought the car round to the front and together they packed the equipment in the boot, in the end tossing only the largest carton into a half-empty skip they found two doors down. It took twenty minutes to drive the short distance to Smithfield, slowing at the crooked line of cars occupying the space near Jas's flat. 'There's nowhere to park,' he said. 'I'll have to drive round again.' He pulled up a hundred yards further down the street and switched off the engine, allowed the wipers one last sweep of the windscreen. 'This is where we get soaked,' he said.

'It's not that bad,' Ivy said. 'If we're quick.'

She took the long, rolled-up screen out of the boot and two flat canvas cases and set off walking. 'Come on,' she said laughing. Bart closed the boot and hurried along behind her, his arms encircling some kind of projector wound with a lasso of cable and a box that he was just able to tuck under his chin. He tried to lean forward to keep everything dry but the rain was lashing down now, hammering on the pavement, running down the lenses of his glasses, plastering the hair to his head.

'Dad's not home,' she said, looking up at the window. Her dress clung to her thighs and upper body. He waited for her to unlock the door and followed her up the stairs, water dripping down the back of his collar and inside his shirt. The corridor was cold. Inside her studio, Ivy laid the screen down, switched on a fan heater and lowered the blind. 'God, I'm wet through,' she said. She found a towel and started to dry her hair.

'I'd better get the rest of the stuff,' Bart said.

Outside, a lorry driver was climbing into his cab, about to vacate one of the spaces outside the front door. Excellent. Bart ran down the street and reversed the car back up to the flat. He piled the last two boxes on the pavement while he closed the boot then struggled back up to the studio with them, pushing the door open to find Ivy standing in the doorway to her bathroom . . . *entirely naked*.

'Bloody hell, Ivy,' he said, averting his eyes, his hands instinctively gripping the boxes tighter.

'What's the matter?' she said. 'Have you never seen a woman's body before?' She wrapped herself loosely in a green silk bathrobe and came towards him, obviously amused at herself, at the impact of greater closeness, a heavy magnet for those elemental stirrings – as conscious as him, it seemed, of the intrusive flexings of an erection, self-mustered from nowhere but now straining against what flimsy constraints his dignity could throw in its way as she stood within touching distance, looking up at him, a curiosity, waiting for him to blink and then maybe to start being promiscuous right here and now. His breathing had switched from automatic to manual, and he knew that if he looked – *if* he looked – his eyes would be drawn to the opening of her bathrobe, the pale

213

crescent moon of a breast sloping inside, the dark suggestion of a nipple just visible. Christ . . .

But this wasn't going to happen. Not because of Jas, though he vaguely felt that *ought* to matter – certainly it made what was looking like an open invitation to get out of those wet things and *go to it* with Ivy on her own bed more of a bad idea than a good one, a prospect that brought him suddenly into the mental orbit of Natalie, a person ever to shake her head with a pity bordering on contempt at the kind of sad *mess* other people got themselves into. But it was the more insistent image of Kate – and that other mess – that made him take the step back and put the boxes down on the floor. 'I *think* . . . this might be a good time to go,' he heard himself say.

'That's cool,' Ivy said, still smiling. She sat on the bed and crossed her legs, reached for her cigarettes and lighter, leaned on one elbow, regarding him through the rising smoke. 'I thought I might tempt you to stay for a while, chill out, maybe smoke a joint. What are you doing tonight?' She tossed back her damp hair so it hung down at one side.

'I'm going to see my girlfriend,' he lied.

'What's her name?'

'Kate,' he said.

Ivy narrowed her green eyes. 'Lucky Kate.'

He made his exit, taking the stairs quickly, smiling to himself, a man waylaid by adventure, relishing the frisson of escape, perhaps even cleansed by the experience, a correct answerer at least of *this* question of good and bad.

Outside, in the rain, stood Jas's old white Merc right behind Bart's car, hemming him in. Damn. He got in, switched on, revved up, inched backwards, then forwards, back again, up on the kerb, until he was clear of the car in front. He looked up at Jas's window, saw the silhouette of Jas looking down, watching. Bart rolled down the window to wave, but he was gone.

● ● ●

'Fuck *off*, Nick. Is that clear enough? Is that the bit you're not getting?' Ivy, beautiful when angry, though also ugly.

He took a deep breath. OK, so maybe she wasn't playing hard to get. No need to be so direct, though. She steamed off again, looking straight ahead as if he wasn't there beside her struggling to match her stride, trying to avoid the puddles, trying to avoid looking like he was being a sex pest. 'Ivy, Ivy . . .'

'What?' she barked sideways at him. '*What?*'

'Two seconds – *please*.' She halted abruptly, taking him by surprise, breathless with irritation now, looking at her watch. Late or pretending to be. There was nothing left to say really. 'How about a coffee?'

'How about *no*? Look, I'm late for work. I'm trying to get my head round my show. My mother is dying. I'm busy, OK?'

'Am I still invited to your show?' Pitiful.

She didn't answer. Just took a deep breath. 'I mean, even the stuff about the Porsche,' she said, calming, talking to him like a child who'd had to be given a spanking and now needed it spelling it out less physically. 'Can't you see how pathetic that was? Did you think I wouldn't find out it was Bart's? Did you think I wouldn't notice?'

'Well, you might not have. It's not as if you see that much of him.'

'I'm working at his fucking *office*. I was in his car last night, since you ask. But that's not the point. Forget the car. I'm talking about *this* – this fantasy life of yours. I'm talking about *you*, hanging around every time I come out of the flat. The mess you are. Why can't you see? It's so obviously over. It was so obviously never anything to start with. For God's sake, go back to your wife.'

'You were in Bart's car?'

She shook her head. Exasperation. Waved him away, ran for the tube, leaving him stranded at the fruit stall. Up at dawn, waiting three hours for two minutes of abuse. Eleven o'clock now.

Bart's car, Bart's office. What kind of boss let her start at that time?

Question answered itself.

On impulse he bought two cans of Special Brew and drank them on the train back to Stockwell, mind going in circles, sick for Ivy, wondering what next, Des being next to useless, himself now out on his arse at the agency, doing too much of the stuff himself, idle cunt. Fact it was that divorced men killed themselves more than non-divorced men. He'd always thought of people like Monty, people who couldn't cope with being free to play the field. Could happen to anyone though, had to admit. A woman could pull the chair from under you just like that. Life hits you on the back of the head. Finished.

He came out of the tube and walked up the high street, feet killing him. Gang of skateboarders scowling at him outside the off licence, eyes following him, idle scum. He held the loose change in his pocket, stop it jingling. Anything could set them off. Should be in school. In America they'd be playing basketball. He reached the corner, turned. Uh-oh. Police car on the street, light revolving on its roof, sort of pointless in the daylight, he thought. Officer behind the wheel, busy with the coffeetime crossword. Some poor bugger in trouble, though. Jesus Christ . . .

He slowed down, then speeded up, walked past Des's flat with its door kicked in, head down, casually clocking police in suits coming out carrying bags. Shit. Heart beating to fuck. Ari. He crossed the street to the newsagent. Ari stocking up choc display, box full of Toffee Crisps.

'Ari, what's going on?'

Ari looking up, frowning out of his pebbly glasses and jerking his beard towards what was going on. 'Took your friend away in handcuffs this morning. They been hanging about since then, in and out, in and out, in and out.'

'Right, right, but what happened?'

Shoulders up. Might as well ask him the fucking polo results from Buenos Aires. 'Varsha!' Ari shouted. Wife. Bit of sense. She came through the beaded curtain, bit on the fat side, beautiful eyes though, wiping her hands. 'What's all the shouting?'

'Where is the other box of Maltesers, woman?'

'How should I know?'

'Ari, Ari . . .'

Ari looked at him through the glasses. 'They come in here asking if I know Des. I tell them I don't know nothing. I ask if Des is in trouble. They say what's it to you if you don't know him? I say I don't know nothing. I ask if you're in trouble . . .'

'*Me?*'

'They don't know you, ask who you are. I tell them I don't know nothing. They say how you know this geezer if you know nothing? Said I'd better tell them if I see you. Better for you not to go back yet, mate. Wait till they gone.'

He nodded. 'Give me a *Standard* and twenty fags.' Dug in his pocket, counted out money. 'Better have some chocolate too. Flake. Thanks.'

He came out of the shop, closed the door quietly, belched quietly. Dog peeing briefly outside, sniffing at his leg. Quick glance. Uniform with notebook talking to the old crone next door always complaining about Des's noise. Doris or Gladys or somesuch with bad legs, bumpy and blue varicosed, relief map of the Andes. She was looking directly at him now.

Shit. Could she see him from there? He turned his face away quickly, walked, shook the newspaper open, casual. Walk faster. Don't look back. Wait, wait. Corner coming up, dry cleaner's. Easy. Soft belch. Special Brew. Car door banging. Wait . . .

Hang a left in a natural fashion and . . . *go*. Jogging, late for something. Shout somewhere behind. Faster. Run. Heads turning. Run like fuck.

● ● ●

Cherchez la femme . . . Jas stood at the sliding window of the office while the college secretary checked the timetables, inspecting the laughter lines on his face in the glazing, seeing his expression busy faking nonchalance as he waited. 'She's not expected in today,' the secretary said. 'If you'd like to leave a message in her pigeonhole, it's just down the corridor on the right.'

Knowing she wasn't expected in but hoping she would be, he now stared down at the portfolio of photographs he was holding with both hands. 'Yes, thanks, I will,' he said. He lingered at the window.

The secretary looked up again. 'Was there something else?'

'Is . . . Mark McCarthy around?'

'Mark McCarthy? Do you mean Mark McCaulay?'

'Yes, sorry, Mark McCaulay.'

She looked at him doubtfully. 'Are you a student, or . . .'

'No, no. It's just a personal call.'

She ran a finger across the timetable on the wall. 'No lectures this morning. I'll try his office,' she said, picking up the phone.

'No, no, don't bother him,' Jas said, smiling quickly. 'I'll call him later. It's not important.'

218

He walked down the corridor and scribbled a note, tucked it into the folder, which he pushed into Stella's pigeonhole, along with a handful of invitations to the launch party at Monty's. He stood for a moment. A group of students came echoing around the corner, high-voiced and jostling. He stood to one side to let them pass, Lois among them, wearing a sleeveless denim jacket and floppy lavender trousers, the baby-bare rump of her stomach sporting a glassy blue jewel at its centre. She looked at him for a second – enough time to give her a diffident smile and mouth a silent 'Hi' – but then she turned away, flicking her hair, walking past with her arms folded, laughing too loud at what someone else was saying.

He reddened and felt the lack of oxygen down here, as he had in the arrivals zone at Stansted, a furtive, alien outsider with local breathing difficulties. The stairs climbing to his left took him sweating back to ground level, to the neutral element of the car park. It had been raining again and was cool. He took his leather jacket off and started heading for the car when he saw Lois coming towards him again, fury in her eyes.

'Hi,' he said, slowing.

Her lips were pressed into a thin angry line. "*Hi?*" You are *such* a shit, do you know that?'

'Why, what do you mean?'

'I met your daughter, is what I mean,' she said.

'Who, Ivy?'

'OK, maybe I don't blame you for not mentioning you had a daughter who's like the same age as me and at the same college as me. But why did you think it would be a really brilliant idea to tell her about us?'

'Tell her what? I didn't tell her.'

'Yeah right. So how else did she know? She *said* you told

219

her. She said you always tell her everything. And this wasn't a quiet head-to-head we were having. It was right there in the union bar with all my friends sitting there, so imagine how nice that was.'

'Christ. Look, I'm sorry. I mean, about everything. It should never have happened.'

'Oh please, not *that*,' she said. 'That's not what I'm saying. I'm saying why did you have to tell her?'

'But I didn't tell her. She must just have seen the video you left at my place and guessed.'

'Right. She guessed. And I suppose she was lying about Stella too. You and Stella?'

He sighed. The leather jacket draped on his arm was a dead weight now, the inside of his collar cold with sweat. 'No, she wasn't lying about that. Me and Stella are, kind of . . . Look, I'm sorry. It wasn't supposed to happen. And, as for Ivy, I don't know. She's going through a bad patch. Exams are getting on top of her, I think. Why don't we get a coffee somewhere – let me explain.'

Coffee. Explain. What was he thinking of? A sudden weariness drained him of thought. Lois seemed too young to be having this conversation with, to have this shared history with. She shook her head and gave him a long look. 'You're disgusting,' she said. 'And pathetic.'

She strode off, flicking her hair. Jas went to his car and sat behind the wheel. How *could* Ivy do that? And then this mess with Bart. The rain started hitting the windscreen and the bonnet with oily explosions, and he saw his eyes looking back at him in the mirror, heard the sound of his own heart, like something ticking down, something that could just run out at any moment, without warning. Just stop.

ten

A beautiful rainbow, its colours fading into each other as it reached over into the empty white air above the dome of the church. Bart looked at the sky and wondered if he might risk walking. He came away from the window and pulled on a clean T-shirt. It seemed Kate had rung in the afternoon. Ivy had picked up his ringing mobile while he was out of the office for five minutes and told him two hours later when she was just leaving.

'You answered my phone?'

She gave a bright smile. 'Isn't that part of the job?'

'Why didn't you tell me before?'

'Sorry, I was in the middle of Christian's new system. We're about two-thirds of the way through it now, aren't we, Christian?'

'Indeed we are,' said Christian, beaming, avuncular, cool grey eyes.

'So what did she say?' Bart said, trying to put a bit of urgency in his voice without actually snapping.

'Oh, this and that. I apologised to her for the other night.'

He went rigid. 'You did *what*?'

'You know – for getting you soaking wet. I said it was all my fault. I told her what we'd been up to.' She grinned at Christian.

Christian grinned back, archly, over his monitor, joining in. 'Oh yes, and what might *that* be?' he said with unpractised Nordic jocularity.

'It might be *nothing*,' Bart said, turning back to Ivy. 'So are you going to tell me what she said?'

'Well, when I said I was sorry for holding you up for so long . . .'

Bart closed his eyes. 'Christ . . .'

Yes, that puzzled us both. Because she said – *Kate* said – she didn't see you that night, so whatever I was holding you up from it wasn't her. So I said, *oops*, it must be one of your other girlfriends.'

'Tell me you didn't say that.'

She wrinkled her nose. 'I didn't say that.'

He exhaled. 'So what did you say? Did you say I'd call her back?'

'No, she was on the tube somewhere, between stations, and I told her you were going out tonight, so . . .'

'*Ivy*, for God's . . . Hang on – you didn't say I was going out with Monty?'

She looked surprised, then smiled impishly. 'No. Is that a

good or a bad thing? I thought I'd let her guess.' She winked at Christian. He smiled and wagged a finger in her direction.

'Thanks,' Bart said. 'I'm glad the two of you hit it off so well.'

'Can I go now?' Ivy said.

The thought of Kate ringing – the thought of Kate revealing herself to others before he'd had the chance to sort things out – made him more anxious about Monty, whom he'd been trying to push to the back of his mind. Back in the flat there was a message from her. 'Hello, stranger . . . just to say I'm away for a few days. In case you're interested.'

He dialled her mobile number but it was switched off. Perhaps he should leave a message. But then he remembered her story about being pursued by her husband – Monty, as he kept having to remind himself – whenever she stepped out of the house, and decided against it.

Bird was miaowing round his legs. He peeled back the lid on a tin of cat chunks and spooned them into the bowl, took the umbrella he'd brought from the office and went out. It was just starting to rain again when he got to the Wren. Through the window he could see Monty at a table, a pint of Guinness, cigarettes, mobile phone on the table in front of him, some residual grief etched into his features. The pub was busy. Bart paused by the door, then walked on quickly with his head down, along Upper Street and across the road to a small bookshop. His heart was beating with panic as he browsed the shelves, looking blindly at the titles. There was no way of doing this without pain. There was no way that Monty was going to see what had happened as some kind of cosmic accident. Something *funny* had not happened on the way to Bart minding his own business in Cambridge – or the occasion before, the day he had first set eyes on her emerging from Monty's shop – just something brilliantly damaging.

The truth, he had imagined, would be enough, but now he had too much truth to deal with. He had knowledge of Monty that he shouldn't have, and that made things worse – the weirdness between Monty and Kate, the possessiveness, the mad stuff about calling her Catherine and himself Stephen, the sex-free marriage, her struggle to be free of it. And what if Monty went weird on him? Because, of course, there was another truth – a worse truth – that resisted being told. The fact that he had not felt the smallest twinge of real regret about falling for Kate. Regret and fear for the consequences, yes, but there had not been an instant in which he had considered giving her up to preserve Monty's hope that she might come back to him. Not that he believed Kate *would* have gone back to Monty – not after the business with the other girl, for sure.

The truth was that he couldn't contemplate losing Kate any more than Monty could. The difference – anyone could see it, surely – was that Monty had already lost. That was the reality. And though it was Bart's moral duty now to make Monty's loss worse, it was hardly his fault. No one could reasonably see it as a betrayal. No one could reasonably expect him to give Kate up. To do the thing that would make him feel a hundred times worse than Monty could hardly be described as the *decent* thing. Three people's unhappiness against one. How was that better?

And Kate – didn't her feelings count for anything?

Umbrellas bobbed quietly past the window like a silent film, a chaos of owners' heads tilted against the rain. For a moment it seemed like another world out there, sealed off from this place, whose sounds were distilled into the creak of his shoes on the wooden floor as he moved slowly down the canyon of books.

He hadn't got as far as fathoming Kate's feelings. There

was a fear of discovering bad things here too – perhaps that Kate would retreat once she found out, seeing this further heartbreak for Monty as one cruelty too many. Maybe calling the whole thing off wouldn't be too big a sacrifice for Kate. Bart sensed something special but you couldn't be a hundred per cent sure of a woman's feelings based on a couple of dates and a night of sex.

What it came down to, he knew, was that he was fully prepared to do the cruel thing – to sacrifice his friend, to win the girl and to hope for the best – because the alternative was to join Monty in his misery. But until he had done the cruel thing, he wouldn't be free to break it to Kate. But how to do that? Because his fear now was that Kate – if she was the kind of beautiful person he imagined her to be – was likely to have a different idea of what moral duty was. And it was this thought that now led him into considering a softening of the truth, playing a longer game, *not* saying – not straight away, maybe letting *her* eventually discover it for herself. Letting her be the one to tell *him*. Yes. OK, that would mean him now *not* telling Monty.

He felt an immediate flood of relief. It would mean stepping back and letting the truth unravel by itself. But, no, hang on. Think, stupid. She had *already* told him, albeit unwittingly, innocently, in the confessional of his own kingsize duvet. So, once it was revealed, in this absurd, hopefully accidental way, that he knew Monty – that, worse, he was a *friend* of Monty – she would immediately remember telling him about the husband, the name of the husband's bookshop in Clerkenwell and everything else about the husband. So he had to tell. To let it unravel by itself was not only a deceit; it was a deceit he had no chance of getting away with and it was a deceit that would get bigger, more glaring and more unforgivable the longer it went on.

225

The assistant walked by and gave a polite smile, said something about the weather. Bart smiled back, took a book off the shelf and inspected the index. There were three possible outcomes, or at least only three as far as he could see. There was the diplomatic solution, in which Monty (and therefore Kate) accepted that the situation had come about as an unfortunate juxtaposition of chance events (perhaps even helpfully construed as Monty's own tragic fault for sending Bart off on a job where he was likely to encounter his beloved, irresistible Catherine); the second, in which Bart emerged with perhaps two broken arms and the loss of one eye – a small price to pay (as he would come to see – well, half see – once the pain and inconvenience of not being able to earn a living had subsided) for Kate's immediate abandonment of what sympathy and compassion she might otherwise have held out to Monty; and the third, in which Monty fled the Wren in a flood of tears, deaf to conciliatory explanations, later to be arrested by police naked in the street outside Kate/Catherine's flat, emotions unleashed by drugs and drink, loudly lamenting his fate to the four winds. Bart wasn't sure what this last outcome would produce, but it seemed both the least favourable and somehow the most likely. He put the book – *Breastfeeding Africa* by I. L. Pitcher, Ph.D. – back on the shelf, and went out into the rain, leaving the umbrella hanging by its crook under non-fiction, a pathetic attempt, he acknowledged to himself with some shame, to present to Monty an image of bedraggled, apologetic humanity rather than dry, triumphant pragmatism.

He trudged back to the pub. Monty seemed not to have moved in the ten or fifteen minutes that had elapsed. He still had almost a full pint, and his eyes barely seemed to register when Bart came in and began exaggeratedly to shake the drips off his hair and wipe his glasses.

'Sorry I'm late. Bloody weather.'

'S'OK. Don't worry.'

'You all right?'

'Yep.' Monty turned his gaze to the window, to the cars edging forward in the drizzle, to the discommoded faces of the people waiting at the crossing.

'I'll just get a drink.' He went to the bar, watching Monty staring out – hardly breathing, it seemed, his hands in his lap, his face in profile, eye unblinking. Bart came back and sat down opposite. 'So . . .' he said. 'Cheers.'

Monty reached inside his coat and produced an A4 letter and documents, folded in half. 'That's it,' he said, placing it on the table between them. He started to light a cigarette, his hand trembling.

Bart's heart started thumping. 'What is it?'

'It's officially over. I'm divorced.'

Bart flattened out the stapled sheets and glanced at the solicitor's letterhead, the forbidding legalese of the first paragraph, his eye unwillingly taking in the underscored names – Stephen Charles Montgomery and Catherine Mary Montgomery (née Kiernan). Seeing those names together – connecting them for the first time in his mind with a living, breathing relationship that would be fused, as in all marriages, however soured, with a core of intimacy he had not yet reached with Kate, and might now never reach – he felt a surge of irrational jealousy as he folded the letter again, and made what he hoped was a sympathetic face. 'Sorry, old chum,' he said, leaning across to pat Monty's upper arm.

Monty said nothing, smoke rising between them from his cigarette.

'When did it arrive?' said Bart.

He took a sharp breath. Bart expected to see his eyes fill up but they didn't. He frowned and looked to the side as he spoke. 'It's been coming, I knew that, obviously. But it's still hard to believe when it happens. We weren't married long, but when you're with someone you love, you get bound up with them. You think it's for ever. And then, one day, when you realise it's not for ever, it's like someone dying.' He paused. 'Sorry. Of course, you already know all this.'

Bart was taken aback and then felt himself redden, not realising for a second that Monty was referring to Natalie. He nodded. He did know what Monty meant – how it felt – and yet found himself emptied of fellow feeling. He occupied himself by taking a long drink, which in itself felt like an act of desertion. Looking at the circle his glass had left on the table, his lips pressed together in a devout silence, he waited for Monty to say something else, preferably without touching on the importance of having the support of good friends at times like this. Monty was looking at him in a way that made him feel uncomfortable. 'Thanks for, you know . . . everything,' he said at last.

'Hey,' Bart murmured, giving a shrug. He took another drink to fill the next silence, and then another. He looked at his glass, which was now three-quarters empty. 'So . . .' he said. 'How are the preparations – I mean, for Jas's party.'

Monty's eyebrows went up and he nodded, as relieved as Bart was, it seemed, to find a subject that didn't need changing. 'Yes, pretty good. The publishers' PR woman seems to have got everything organised. All I have to do is clear some space and be my usual smiling self for the customers.' He smiled at his own joke. 'I spoke to Jas yesterday.'

'Really?' Bart said. Yes, really. Why wouldn't he have?

'He seemed a bit subdued. I think he was feeling a bit under the weather. Not his usual self. He did say he was looking forward to it, though.' Monty hesitated. 'Bart . . .'

Bart looked at him, holding beer in his mouth.

228

'I think I should tell you something. As a friend.'

'What?'

Monty gave a short, nervous laugh. 'It's Jas. He thinks you and Ivy are . . . you know. I mean, I know that's rubbish but . . .'

'Oh my God.'

Monty took a sip of his drink – the first since Bart had arrived. 'It *is* rubbish, isn't it?' he asked.

'Of course it is. What did he say?'

'Well, it was a few weeks ago . . .'

'A few *weeks*? It can't have been.'

'Why can't it have been?'

Shit. 'Nothing. Nothing happened. I just helped Ivy take some film equipment back to her place.'

'And?'

'And nothing. Well, OK, not and nothing exactly. I went out for some stuff and when I came back she was stark naked in the room. And she wasn't just being . . . arty, in that provocative way. She was definitely, you know, I think, *interested*. But nothing happened. I just made my excuses and ran.'

Bart was surprised to see Monty smile and nod gravely, as though he already knew the story. 'She's been working at your place?'

'Yes, she has. It wasn't my idea though.'

'Do you remember after the Chelsea match, remember me telling you what *really* finished it between me and Catherine? It was a little while after we'd split up – two or three weeks – and she dropped by at the flat one Sunday morning and found a girl coming out of the front door—'

'You're kidding.'

Monty shook his head. 'That was Ivy. She'd been working in the shop that week. We just went out for a drink after closing on Saturday. I'd been in a bad way about Catherine, and we talked about that, and she seemed really sympathetic. I mean, I know she's only twenty or something, but . . . Anyway we ended up getting a bit pissed, and she said she'd got some weed and why didn't we go back to my place. So we went back and I opened some wine . . .' Monty grimaced and shook his head again. He stubbed out the cigarette and lit another.

Bart was listening but at the same time trying to see the story from two angles. Here was Monty, who had made an untouched idol of his ethereal, virtuous Catherine, desperate to prove something, perhaps even hoping to re-educate himself in the ways of the flesh and win her back with a display of earthy passions. But what would it have looked like to Kate, unsuspectingly wandering down to the large flat above the bookshop, a bright Sunday morning, the church bells ringing, perhaps even thinking of reconciliation? What fury and humiliation and disappointment must she have felt? Monty, who couldn't get it up with her, getting it up after all, and with a girl young enough to be . . .

'The thing was, we didn't actually have sex,' Monty said. 'I did think we might – I was drunk and stoned enough – and we did get far enough into it for it to look bad when Catherine walked into the room that morning. I was still in bed, too fucked up to move. Ivy had just left and I knew straight away, even before she said it was over . . .' He leaned forward, his elbows resting on the tops of his legs, his chin cupped in his hands. The tears welled in his eyes now.

Bart looked at his drink, the wrong person to turn to for support. He drained his glass, thinking how to get out of this, wondering where this left him now, this fourth outcome. 'What will you do?' he heard himself say.

Monty issued a snorting laugh. 'I don't know. Shoot myself? There's nothing I *can* do, is there?' He seemed about to say something else but stared into the space between his feet instead.

'So what is it with Ivy, do you think?' Bart said.

Monty shook his head silently. The phone on the table was ringing. He picked it up and lifted it to his ear, turning away slightly as he thumbed the call button and listened. 'Ring you back?' he said. He slid the phone into his pocket.

Bart looked at him expectantly, then with a sigh picked up his empty glass and pointed at Monty's almost full one. 'Fit a half in there?'

'I don't think I'm really in the mood for this,' he said. 'Do you mind if we call it a day?'

'Course we can. Whatever you like.'

Monty found a sad smile. 'You're a friend in need.'

Bart managed a stiff grin. 'Don't worry about it,' he said, thinking about Kate, thinking about wanting her right now.

●●●

Fuck off, then, Nick thought, glaring, lighting a fag, willing him away. Wandering homeless beardo lurching past, looking back, giving him the eye, filthy duvet full of germs trailing behind him. You couldn't sit in the park for five minutes with a breakfast can of Special Brew without some scabby cunt mistaking you for a relative. *Fuck off.*

Ignore him. Nick turned his face up to the sky, as if just out soaking up a few rays. Winos at their worst if you caught their eye, like bulls or gorillas. Couldn't get rid of the fuckers. Still there, lurking, periphery of his vision. Nick peeked at his watch. Nice chunky Rolex. Well, Rolex copy. Odd to see it there, memento of something better. Lucky to still have it too after nightmare stay at hilariously named Delight Hotel, Paddington, courtesy of meathead Des getting himself locked up, police hanging about all day and night stopping him getting his legitimate stuff, including emergency personal weed/coke stash and five hundred cash hopefully still taped into empty electrical socket hole behind kitchen cupboard even Des didn't know about.

Nick, fag in mouth, brushed ash from his trousers, straightened one cuff, then the other. Yesterday's shirt. Start smelling like one of them soon. Hello, he's back . . .

'Spare a cigarette, pal?'

Nick looked at him. Palm out, ingrained with filth. What does he do all day – walk around on his hands?

'No problem.' He gave him a fag, lit it. Guy, probably same age as himself, looked a hundred years older, nose full of red veins, eyes like phlegm.

'Got any spare change?' Hand out again. Terrible nails.

'No.' Emphatic. He shook his head. Still there. '*No.*'

'Spare a drop of lager then?'

Stereotype thicko straight out of central casting for plucky but miserable mid-Eighties anti-Thatcher TV series. Bleasdale or the other one. Unindustrial north.

Nick gave him the can, saw his eyes light up. Christ.

'Thanks, pal. Sound.' He took a big gobful, offered it back.

Nick gave a tight-lipped smile. 'Keep it.'

'Sound.' He sat down on the bench, stinking to fuck, legs stretched out, holes in his knees, smoking Nick's fag, drinking his Special Brew. 'You lookin' for somewhere to stay?'

'Do I look as though I am?'

Shrug. 'No offence, mate. Nice suit,' he added.

Meaning suit buggered and crumpled to fuck. Not quite down to this guy's level yet, despite *SS Redundo* shipping more sea than the fucking *Titanic*. Must warn Livvy at some point. He lit another fag. Gave the poor guy another, what the hell. First conversation he'd had in twenty-four hours unless you counted the population of South-east Asia watching TV behind desk at the Delight Hotel, pissed off with him turning up after midnight, skinning him twenty-five quid ('You pay now! You pay now!') for the privilege of sleeping in his clothes above the noisiest street this side of Rangoon.

'Married, are you?' Wino's eye on Nick's ring. 'I used to be married. Still am for all I know.' He threw his head back and cackled loudly, showing a mouthful of stumps and craters yellow as popcorn.

Nick ran the rug of his tongue over his own unbrushed teeth and had a sudden thought of the early days, him and Olivia, when they were still proper lovers, how she sometimes used to fix her toothbrush bristles against his in the water glass, so it looked like a sort of embrace.

'Had a job an' all. On the bins. Good money.' He looked wistful. 'Blew it, though. This stuff's a killer . . .' He held up the can, took a swig, wiped his mouth on the back of his hand. Hawked, spat on the path. Pigeon strutting over to inspect it. 'Came down here in ninety-two. Seek my fortune.' That grin. Jesus Christ. Who was this guy? He shuddered.

Like one of those angels who comes as a warning.

Half an hour later he was on the tube south, rattling down the tunnels, staring at the ads. A switch to marketing was the thing. One good idea went a long way. Legalise drugs, for instance. Think of the opportunities. Coke nasal spray, keep it in your handbag. Coke-impregnated dental floss that sends you to work with a zing in your step. Salt-and-vinegar-flavoured cannabis seasoning that you can shake on your egg and chips. What else? LSD ice cream at cinemas. Blank screen, dream your own film. Spunk aftershave. Wank, slap it on your cheeks before you go out, get a girl to kiss you. Quite a turn-on it was supposed to be. Aphrodisiac. Tried it once on Livvy on an early date, straight out of the bank in her chalk-striped power suit. Didn't seem to notice. Definitely gave himself a frisson of something though.

Stockwell. Headache coming on as he emerged at the top of the escalator. Muggy, more rain on the way. He held the key tight in his pocket as he walked up the high street, past the Portuguese butcher, baker and candlestick maker, turned down Robbin Road, past the flat head down. Looked quiet enough, but first stop Ari's place. He jingled the door twice before Ari looked up from the counter, uninterested hooded eyes.

'Ari . . .' he hissed, 'what's happening?

'Your friend Des is selling drugs to children. You can't do this. Did you know he's doing this?'

'Absolutely not. I'm as shocked as you are.'

Ari shrugged, not especially shocked.

'Tell you the truth, Ari, I don't really know him that well. I'm just staying at his place while I'm getting a new kitchen fitted. But now I need to get in for my stuff. Can you keep an eye on the street for me?'

Ari stared at him for a moment before shifting his weight from behind the counter. 'Police have gone now.'

'They might come back. They might still be watching.'

'What do you want me to do?'

'Just give me a whistle if you see anything.'

'Whistle? I don't have a whistle.'

'Well, just shout – you know, as if you're shouting for a dog.'

Nick sauntered casually across the street, opened the gate, key. Pushed the door open, not stepping in straight away, as if the place might be full of lions. No. More of a pigsty than usual though. He picked a way across the room, sticky

234

underfoot, drawers pulled out, carpet rucked up at one end, kitchen cupboard in the middle of the floor, stash gone, along with the five hundred. Shit. He imagined Des at one of those tables in a bare room trying to convince the police that the stuff wasn't his, police now looking for him – this Nick, full name supplied – enquiries at the agency, ending up with Olivia, the children, everything. Sweating now, mind full of dreadful permutations, he found a laundry bag, stuffed it with what clothes he'd got left, folded a couple of ironed shirts from Suds & Co service wash into it. No shout from Ari. Sidling out. Ari nowhere in sight, back behind his counter, idle cunt. He closed the door quietly, tossed the key into the jungle at the front and headed back for the tube.

Find a pub, he thought. Time to think. He travelled to Green Park, walked down to Piccadilly Circus and up into Soho and Covent Garden. Day warming up heavily, stifling. He bought a *Standard* and found a big, dark Victorian pub off Long Acre where they didn't mind unshaven scruffs with laundry bags. Crow and Flag. He smiled. *Crown* presumably. Bit of the sign dropped off. Friendly Oz bar staff, couldn't give a fuck. He sat for the afternoon in the smoke watching the racing, nursing one pint then a second, then a half, watching the odd tourist stumble in, take one look, and stumble out again. Two or three raddled old blokes in old clothes dotted around, drink-blotted faces, grubby morning papers folded at the sports pages, nothing to live for but this.

Going back to Jas's would be pushing it, at least till Ivy cooled down a bit. He scanned the ads again, leaning back, knees bent, feet up on the chair in a shaft of dusty sunlight. Marketing and Sales. Biroed round a couple of possibles that an hour ago he'd passed over as chickenshit.

Man requires situation. No fixed abode. Anything stupid or demeaning considered. Good shoes, one recent scuff.

Sober up a bit. He walked to Holborn, leisurely pace, looking in windows. Clerkenwell was about a mile, two at the most. He carried on, blood full of false energy. Alcohol that was. Turned left when he got to Farringdon Road, past the fish and chip shop. No time to waste money on food. Five to six. Church, CHRISTO LIBERATORI. Christ something.

Monty's. He waited for a moment. Assistant at the back of the window, leaning in, making some adjustment to the display, hair hanging down. Nick walked past, then stepped back smartly into the shop, watching her there, still bending over the panel, grunting to reach something. Spine on show, bendy ladder under the skin. Nice arse. 'I think your Hitchcock needs to be angled more towards the right,' he said loudly. She extricated herself awkwardly from the bowels of the display, stooping to avoid banging her head, flustered, armful of books.

'To catch the casual browser coming out of the pâtisserie,' he grinned. 'And of course the thing with cut-outs is you don't want to see the back. Spoils the illusion. Especially with the master of suspense, if you see my point.'

'Can I help you?'

'I'm Nick? We met once – friend of Monty's?'

'He's not here,' she said, looking at his laundry bag.

'Is he coming back?'

'No. I was about to lock up.' She laid the books on the counter and picked up the keys.

'Is he in the flat?'

'You'll have to go round and try the buzzer.'

'I'll do that.' He paused at the door. 'Hey, any more point-of-sale marketing tips, I'm your man.' Grin. 'What was your name again?'

'Gail. And it's not Hitchcock, it's Charles Laughton.'

'Is it? Are you sure?'

Poker-faced, she closed the door and turned the sign.

He walked round the side and pressed the buzzer. No answer. Tried it again. Shit. He was just moving away when the intercom clicked.

'Hello?'

'Monty, hi, it's Nick,' he shouted.

'Nick?'

'Yeah, sorry to surprise you like this. Have you got a minute?'

'What . . . right now?'

'Yeah, I'm outside.'

'Well, I gathered that.'

'I wouldn't ask, but I'm in a bit of a spot.'

There was a long pause. Nick moved his ear closer to the intercom and waited. The speaker crackled. 'Nick, give me fifteen minutes. I'll see you in Starbucks, OK?'

'Brilliant.'

Ten minutes later Monty arrived breathless, waving as he saw Nick in the window. Bounding with something. Drugs or sex. Drugs presumably.

'Sorry about that,' he said, smiling.

'No problem. I got you a latte.'

Monty sat down, clocked the laundry bag, peered at Nick. 'You look terrible.'

Nick bit his bottom lip, then looked at Monty, long gaze of frankness. 'I've had a bit of a shock, to tell you the truth. My flat got broken into and all my stuff's gone. I mean everything – apart from a few things I managed to get out of the fire.'

'*Fire?* My God, are you OK?'

'Yeah, they torched the place. Or tried to. The place was gutted more or less. I was up half the night answering questions with the police. Landlord thinks it's my fault of course so there's no way I can go back there. Spent most of today in a shitty B&B trying to get a few hours' sleep.'

'Bloody hell. Are you all right for money?'

'I had a lot of cash in the flat. That's gone. Got a bit in the bank, obviously, but all my credit cards are a bit . . . you know. Since I lost my job.'

'You lost your job?'

'Well, I went freelance. And now my laptop's gone up in flames, along with all my contacts books and paperwork.'

Monty nodded, firm-lipped, good sign. 'You're insured, right?

He took a sip of coffee for an answer. Tragic pause while Monty, frowning, thought about doing the right thing, grappling with something, some obstacle.

Monty firmed up. 'I'll put you up in the spare,' he said. 'It's not much more than a boxroom and it's full of junk at the moment but there's a bed and a chest of drawers.'

Nick felt a huge surge of love, but unexpected shame too, choked for a minute at Monty's generosity in the face of his own wheedling, Monty usually being the flake, the needy one, the one lost in life. He blinked a real tear away and looked down at the floor, unable to speak. Jesus Christ. Cigarettes. He lit one, hand trembling, blew smoke out violently. Monty patted his arm. 'Don't worry.'

'Thanks,' Nick said at last. 'It'll just be for a few days. Just till I'm back on my feet. Prefer it if you didn't mention it to the others. Feel a bit of a twat, to be honest.'

'No problem.'

They walked back to the flat. 'Have you eaten?'

'Tell you the truth, I haven't thought about it.'

Monty got on the phone and ordered food from the Bangkok while Nick made the bed up with sheets from the airing cupboard and put the contents of his laundry bag – one pair of jeans, four or five T-shirts, a jumper, socks, boxer shorts – into the drawers. He hung the two ironed shirts, now wrinkled, on a metal rail rigged up by the window, and took off his jacket. He sniffed at his armpits.

Monty came in with towels. 'If you need a shower or anything, the bathroom's through there.'

'Great.'

'Let's just clear some space for you.'

There were a few boxes – mainly books – piled up in the middle of the floor, along with a few tins of paint and varnish, a stepladder against the wall, an old cottage armchair loaded with newspapers and brushes and packets of sandpaper. Together they managed to stow everything beneath a trestle table under the window. 'Most of this stuff was Catherine's,' Monty said.

'Nice bit of wood,' Nick said, stroking the smoothed arm of the chair.

'She restored that,' he said. He disappeared into his own room and came back with a photograph in a frame knocked together from oddments of unmatching timber. 'This is her,' he said. 'She made the frame too.'

'Nice,' Nick said. Classy-looking woman, short hair, standing in the street outside some kind of business premises holding a brush. 'This is her place?'

'It's her workshop in Camden.'

'Lost and abandoned,' Nick said. 'Sounds like me.'

Monty smiled. 'Me too.'

'Right. Are you OK, now? I mean, you know . . .'

'Final papers came through yesterday. I'm dealing with it. Sometimes you have to go through hell to find what you're looking for.' He grinned.

Nick nodded. 'Right.' Under different circumstances, Monty's cheerfulness would be starting to spook him, but here, right now, it looked like the best imaginable omen.

The courier with the food arrived. 'I can't stay and eat with you, I'm afraid,' Monty said. 'I've got a previous engagement. But help yourself to anything. Watch some TV or a video or something. Put your feet up. There's some wine in the kitchen.'

'Don't worry about me. I'll be fine. And, you know . . . thanks for this.'

'No problem. Anyway, now you'll be able to give me a hand with Jas's party.'

'Course. When is it again?'

'Tomorrow?'

'Shit, I'd completely forgotten.'

'Put it down to post-traumatic stress. Or just impending middle age.'

When Monty had gone out, Nick watched the news while he ate, then stood up to smoke a cigarette by the window, looking out on the quiet drift of evening drinkers and passers-by on the street below. He opened a bottle of red wine and sat through a video of *Moulin Rouge*. Afterwards he fell asleep on the sofa thinking about Bart shagging Ivy, and woke in the early hours, light blazing, TV still on, not knowing where he was.

● ● ●

Jas patrolled the outskirts of his party with a glass of champagne, greeting and chatting, glancing expectantly out into the street. Since six-thirty, successive taxis had arrived and departed, unbundling features editors, picture editors and their researchers, fellow photographers, one or two columnists and diarists from the dailies, as well as advertising and marketing people, publishing executives and some shiny-looking girls plucked from their sales and accounts departments. The publishers had done well to attract the right mix of guests. The caterers had come up with perfectly edible canapés, the fizz was nicely chilled, Monty had ingeniously found a CD of

New York themed music in Leather Lane market and put together a tasteful arrangement of books featuring New York architecture, design and films to complement the main display with its satisfyingly squared-off piles of Jas's handsome new tome, *Finest*, and blown-up facsimiles of the cover – a grainy close-up of an NYPD detective's shield being thrust forward, the owner's thumb and fingertips around the edge of the wallet, the leather-hemmed sleeve of his houndstooth sports jacket revealing a shirt cuff and the thick gleam of a wrist-watch.

This was a good party. But Stella wasn't here. Or Ivy. He'd rung Stella's house and her office and her mobile but had just been forwarded to her various answering machines. Some of her students had turned up. Everyone had turned up. Bart had arrived and was talking to two women at the counter. Nick was circulating with a bottle of champagne in each hand, topping up glasses. 'Hi, champ,' he said, coming up. 'How does it feel?'

'Stella's not here,' he said.

Nick looked round. 'That's a pity. We were all looking forward to meeting her. Maybe she got held up.'

'Ivy's not here either.'

'No, I noticed that. She will be coming though?'

'Supposedly. She didn't actually say so.' He was staring hard at Bart, who saw him and waved. Jas looked away, and drained his glass. 'Better give me some more of that,' he said.

'Yes, *sir*.'

It was pretty decent champagne, *actuellement*, and the buzz of talk got louder before it got quieter and Jas felt himself looking sideways at things by the time the last of the guests were drifting away, two or three having kindly bought the book and had it signed. Bart had been over to congratulate him, bearing his copy, and Jas had been obliged to sign, though with a perfectory scribble rather than the jocular message Bart was no doubt expecting. Fuck him, thought Jas, who now found himself blaming Bart for the non-appearance of both Stella and Ivy. Certainly the Bart factor would be why Ivy hadn't turned up. He was probably meeting her later at his flat. You could tell he was itching to get away, and was only hanging on because Monty was keeping him gassing.

'So where do you think she is?' Nick was saying, somewhere to his right.

'Fuck knows,' he said. There was a certain dinning reverberation in his ears now as he spoke and an exaggerated edge to his movements. He had already splashed two of Monty's display books with champagne and was trying hard now to get champagne into the glass without any hitting the floor. He saw Bart and Monty making their way over, Bart with that fucking self-deprecating, butter-wouldn't-melt business, Monty at least pretending to be happy, like a proper mate. Good man, Mont, lovely. Nick, too, upfront in his way. No frills.

'We were just thinking we could all go to that steak and chips place on Upper Street for some steak and chips,' he heard Monty say, his face swimming in front of his eyes. 'To celebrate some more.'

'Who was thinking?' slurred Jas.

'Me and Bart.'

'If Bart wants to go, then we must go!'

'We just thought it might be fun,' Bart said.

'Fun? Well, you'd know all about that.'

Yes, something registered in Bart's eyes. Guilt. He knew all fucking right. He knew exactly what he was saying.

'Well . . .' Bart started to say, but Nick had a taxi waiting outside now, saying something about it not hanging about all night. Gail could lock up, Monty said, making a joke about not setting the shop on fire and whispering sorry to Nick for something and clapping him on the back, laughing, before they all piled in the cab. He didn't feel well, rather queasy, but they were soon at the restaurant, Nick ordering more champagne with whose money was anyone's guess. Everything was happening quickly, digging into the food, atmosphere heating up and ending with liqueurs and some circuitous argument Nick started with Bart about sex and loyalty and what was OK and what wasn't, bastard looking really sheepish now, Jas thought, as if he'd been caught having nothing to say, changing subject to Ivy's end-of-year show and what kind of Freudian slip was that? The bill came, everyone insisting on paying, except Nick.

'No, but if you were still married,' Nick was saying, pushing it, 'and you thought nobody would find out, would you then?'

'Well, I never did,' Bart said, rubbing his glasses and putting them back on, flashing that smarmy grin. 'So, no, I suppose not.'

'So, what you're saying is that that's a superior moral position . . .'

'No, I'm just saying it's not right for me.'

'So, loyalty to other individuals, say, is more important than individual freedom? You're saying that I'm in a mess because—'

'No, I'm not saying anything about you being in a mess. I'm just saying that, you know . . . all things being equal, I'd rather not fuck other people around. By fucking around.' He looked around at everyone. 'How did we get into this?'

Jas hadn't planned to get the photographs out unless forced into it by Bart, the fucking hypocrite, but here he was, fumbling to get them out of his pocket quick as his fingers could grasp them, three prints shot in admittedly not brilliant light but clearly showing one figure, then two, at a window. 'What do you call this then?' he said, throwing them down in front of everyone, though he hadn't actually mentioned Ivy by name. Didn't have to. Bart knew all right, pretending to look puzzled, bemused look. Monty across the table about to say something but glancing at Bart instead.

'Just admit it,' Jas slurred, banging the table with his fist, photographs wet there in the pool of beer, Bart peering at them, Monty biting his tongue, not getting involved, waiter materialising to see what the fuss was. 'S'fine, s'fine,' Jas said, waving him off, trying to focus on Bart, puzzled expression, playing the innocent.

'Is that my flat?' He looked up at Jas, coming on the defensive, caught out. 'That's Ivy . . .'

'*And* . . .'

'Well, so what – she just came up to see the flat. I mean, what is this?' he was saying. 'Did you take this picture?' The one of him bare-chested under the light, Ivy leaning against the window. He blinked at Jas, mouth open, mister fucking incredulous, guilt written all over him.

'Evidence,' Jas said.

'I was changing my *shirt*, for God's sake.' Whole place looking now. Bart got to his feet, looking for the waiter. 'You're mad,' he said, shaking his head.

'Right, and I suppose you were changing it the other night you were in Ivy's room.'

'OK. There are things I could tell you. But I don't think right now is a good time . . .' Bart took his credit card off the plate, grabbed his jacket.

Jas followed him to the door, and out into the sudden cool, snatching at his sleeve, then felt himself wheel round on the pavement and hit something, and then, somehow, he was down on one knee, throwing up against the window, Bart holding *his* sleeve now saying *help me with him, someone*.

'Fuck off and help yourself, you cunt . . .'

'Steady on, Jas, I think you ought to . . .'

Jas got up, other hands gripping both his arms now, trying to shake himself free. Monty, trying to calm him.

'BECAUSE HE'S BEEN FUCKING MY DAUGH-TER!' he heard himself roar to some interjection, now halfway across the street with traffic coming both ways, Nick behind somewhere taking his side for sure and shaking his head at Bart and saying that was right out of order, and Bart throwing his hands up and striding off into the distance and Monty hailing a taxi and saying *whoa*, *whoa*, for God's sake get him into the *cab*, Nick, get him in the *cab* . . .

eleven

A beautiful headache, and it wasn't just the champagne and beer and Calvados. The weather was fit to burst again, the clouds sitting heavy in the air, keeping the heat in and soaking up all the oxygen and replacing it with something less breathable. Bart unfastened a third button on his shirt. He was sitting in a café in Fitzrovia with a late breakfast in front of him – orange juice he had gulped down, a gluey almond Danish he already regretted having bought and black coffee, which he sipped as he looked out of the window on to the street. It was just gone twelve. He had been up since before seven, waking to an obscure bluegrass album Aunt

Marian had given him, the flat too muggy to allow further sleep and his mind pulsing with the effort of putting everything off that was important – seeing Kate, speaking to Monty, having sex with Kate, getting back to Christian who was pressing him on the New York offer, falling asleep with Kate in his arms, clearing things up with Jas, who seemed to be having some kind of breakdown, telling Kate at some point soon that everything wasn't as bad as it looked and that though he knew he shouldn't be saying this so early in their relationship he was in all likelihood crazy about her and wanted to have her babies because there were at least some things in life you were a hundred per cent sure about.

So he had spent some quality time with the cat, got dressed and was at his desk early, diverting his wandering attentions to the work. He left the office at ten, just as everyone else was arriving, and took the bus to Tottenham Court Road. From there, the new tapas bar job – Kasparo – was a few minutes' walk, on the site of a former legal practice in Charlotte Street. Bart liked jobs when they were still new, that period of optimism and creative purity before the inevitable complications set in. It was easy to absorb himself in the project for an hour or so, going over his designs with Luis, the owner, who walked him again through the dusty oak-panelled offices that would be knocked through and fitted with a long curving bar and fans overhead for days like today and tall, folding windows opening on to the street to let in the noise of the lunchtime crowds.

But now that was over, everything else seeped back into his head. Obviously, he would have to see Jas, reassure him that he was completely in the wrong about him and Ivy, perhaps without mentioning the naked episode in her flat, and accept his apologies for being drunk and disorderly. It would have helped to have Monty backing him up, but Monty had his own Ivy story and, judging by last night, was happy to distance himself from this one.

Staring distractedly at the almond Danish, he called the office. Ivy answered. 'Someone called Natalie rang for you,' she said. 'She said it was kind of urgent.'

'Oh. OK, thanks.'

'I didn't mention Kate, before you ask.'

'You must be getting the hang of things,' Bart said.

'Are you coming to my show?'

'I'm not sure. When is it?'

'The third. You have to come – everyone's coming.'

'I'll try.'

He pocketed the phone and went to the counter to pay his bill, Natalie niggling so much that the waitress had to call him back for his change. What could be so urgent? He'd ring later. After he'd spoken to Jas. He'd got as far as the pavement outside the café before he punched in her number, his heart beating.

'Natalie, hi, it's me.'

'Hi,' she said. 'Where are you?'

He looked round. 'Charlotte Street.'

'Have you got time to come up here to the flat?'

'What, now?'

'If you've got time.'

'Are you OK?'

'Yes, I'm fine.'

He took a cab to Finsbury Park. She was waiting at the door to meet him, offering her cool cheek to kiss. 'Suzanne's here,' she said.

'Suzanne?' His heart started up.

'I asked her to pop over. She's between surgeries.' Natalie led the way through into the living room. He felt as though he was about to be interviewed. Suzanne was standing by the window in her doctor's clothes – skirt, blouse, flat shoes – hair up, smoking a cigarette. 'Hello Bart,' she said, coming forward to give him a hug. 'How are you?'

'I don't know,' he said, settling on the edge of the sofa. 'Why am I here?'

Suzanne looked at Natalie and sat down in one of the armchairs. Natalie perched on the arm and took a deep breath. 'This isn't going to be easy,' she said. 'And if I'm honest, it's only going to make one of us feel better.' Suzanne stubbed out her cigarette and positioned herself as if to listen impartially, her ankles crossed and hands in her lap, focusing her gaze at a spot on the solid beech floor he and Natalie had triumphantly laid together one bank holiday weekend five years ago.

'I'm asking my solicitor to go ahead with the divorce,' Natalie said. 'I know we said there was no rush but . . .'

'That's OK. I did kind of expect this at some point.'

'Hang on. The other thing is . . .' She took another breath. 'I'm seeing someone.'

Bart nodded. He tried to gauge how he felt.

'His name's Andy.'

'Andy,' he repeated, still nodding.

She paused. 'And I'm pregnant.'

He looked at her. He found he had to swallow before he could speak. 'Congratulations,' he said.

'Eighteen weeks,' she said.

He could tell that she saw what was in his eyes now. He could tell in the way she bit her bottom lip and took in another sharp breath through her nose. For months he had been resigned to at least one thing – that the moment had long passed where the two of them might go back to where it went wrong and make things better. But he realised that, actually, *this* was that moment right now, and he felt the pull, the unexpected weight of it. Where before he had managed to keep a calming, residual memory of what they'd had – some sense that it had had some meaning, that it had at least left each of them with something to show from each other – now all he felt was its destruction, that it had all been a waste of life.

He scrutinised her furtively, noticed that her body seemed more rounded, her ripening breasts, and felt a wave of regret. 'I'd like to be pleased for you,' he said, 'but I can't. I can only feel crap about it. Why are you even telling me this? Why couldn't you have just . . .'

'Suzanne told me you'd spoken to her . . .'

'Oh brilliant, thanks. What happened to confidentiality?'

Suzanne looked up sharply. 'You rang me up at home, Bart, remember? You appealed to me as a friend, not your doctor. And then Natalie came to me, after you saw her. Which made things difficult, but under the circumstances, we – Natalie – felt she owed you an explanation, and . . .' She was holding Natalie's hand now, which seemed odd in this setting, among the things he and Natalie had once shared.

'And you thought you'd both get me up here to—'

'What you thought was true,' Natalie said quickly. 'About the abortion . . .'

'Oh Christ, no . . .' He felt a sudden, sickly emptiness, not believing his senses, as if some treasure had inexplicably gone while everyone's back was turned, leaving the velvet hollow where it had nestled amid the useless criss-crossing of invisible beams. A blue egg or a precious jewel. He felt himself filling up, flooded with the bewilderment of it, the humiliation and slow pouring of anger – anger at her for the thing itself, for her lies, anger at his own credulity. He felt his face crumple into ugliness. 'How could you, Natalie? You mean, all that time we were fucking *trying*, and *talking* about it, you were—'

'Bart, *Bart*,' she interrupted. She looked at him, stopping him with her eyes, now full of tears. She hesitated. 'The baby wasn't yours.'

He said nothing for a moment, then stared at her, disbelieving.

'What? What do you mean, not mine?'

'I'm sorry. I'm sorry.' Her voice was a whisper now.

'Well, whose *was* it then?' He had raised his voice, but his soul was already warming to this lesser hell, that of a baby conceived and dispatched but no longer his to mourn.

She blew her nose on a tissue. 'It was Andy's. I met him when you and I were together. It started as just a fling.'

He shook his head. 'This just gets better and better.'

Suzanne was watchful, a finger pressed against her lips.

Natalie cleared her throat. 'It was at a time when you and I hadn't been getting on too well. Pressure about my not wanting children. You were working quite a lot. That didn't help.'

'Oh, right, I *see*, so . . .' But even as he started to get angry again, he knew it wasn't anger now, just sorrow in costume, sorrow putting on a show to distract him from the general, inevitable now, sense of collapse – sorrow deciding that anger was the best tool for the job, so that if there had to be tears they would be hot self-righteous tears and not those of self-pity.

'No, I'm *not* saying it was your fault,' she said, banging her hand on the coffee table.

'OK, OK.'

There was a silence between them. Suzanne uncrossed her legs as if signalling an end to it. He felt a moment of clarity. Whatever he said couldn't change anything. Nothing seemed to matter now. There would be no tears from him. In one sense, he was breathless from these new blows from the old life, but at the same time, for the first time, oddly, he felt unmoored and set adrift from it, from its myriad particulars, from Natalie herself. He saw her from a distance, explaining in semaphore, getting smaller and smaller.

'Andy went abroad for a few months and I thought it was over,' she was saying. 'I really wanted to believe it was, I swear.'

He nodded automatically. 'So why agree to us trying for a baby? I mean after sleeping with someone else?'

'I don't know. How can you tell about these things? I suppose I felt guilty about everything. I stupidly thought it might give us a fresh start. I'm sorry, Bart. The truth was, I was already having big doubts and I couldn't bear to tell you. I was getting depressed and trying to hide it from you. And then Andy got back in touch. We saw each other a couple of times. By then I'd stopped using my cap. I got pregnant.'

'And did that help?'

She continued. 'Andy said he loved me. He wanted me to keep the baby, leave you, but I couldn't. I couldn't do it like that.'

'That was very gracious of you.'

Natalie closed her eyes. 'I know I behaved badly. I know that. *That* is not in question here.'

Behaved badly. Right. That was Natalie dealing with the ragged edges, making it neat, cleansing the wound, leaving the appearance of a single, streamlined cut, a work of art. He turned to Suzanne. 'And of course you assumed the baby was mine.'

'Of course.'

'This isn't to punish you, Bart,' Natalie said. 'I just don't want to start the rest of my life with a lie. I just don't need that kind of mess.'

'Well, thanks for passing it on.'

'It's hard for me too.'

'What, the idea of a baby?'

She frowned, unconsciously moving her hand to her belly, and the new life in there. 'I don't know. It's a decision, isn't it? It's different. I feel more positive about it. I know I should be ashamed for feeling this way, because of us, but I don't. Maybe if you and I had decided to have one early on it would have been different. Maybe it was just too late for us.'

He nodded. He wondered if she was talking about passion. Passion she probably had now with this Andy. Passion that was blind to fear and consequence. Passion that had once consumed Bart and Natalie themselves before contentment and the easy rhythms of habitual love had established themselves, as happened with all couples sooner or later. And that easy, habitual love would have been enough for most people to start thinking about babies late in their relationship. It was the way everyone did it these days. But he and Natalie were different. For them, not wanting babies was too big a thought to turn around with easy, habitual love. And it was that that had died in the effort.

'I'm sorry, Bart,' she said.

'Me too,' he said.

●●●

Fuck. All in all, horses were pretty unpredictable, except the fast ones and you couldn't get decent odds on them. Nick folded his paper and finished his drink, winked at the new barmaid. One last glance at the screen as he passed the assembled red-eared sots, and out into Long Acre. No point going back to Monty's. Never in, or forever fucking off out somewhere when he was. Always left him something nice in the fridge though from M&S. Thoughtful like that.

Nick was feeling a bit fitter, more presentable now. Haircut, suit dry-cleaned. Getting used to the suit. He'd spent yesterday morning improving his CV on Monty's computer and sent it off to a couple of marketing firms. Risked turning up at Jas's early evening. No Ivy in sight, Jas still in a state of ill-humour after the barney in Islington, though Bart had rung up apparently to say it was all bollocks about him and Ivy. 'And you believe him?' he'd asked, accepting Jas's offer of a sundowner. Tall vodka, ginger beer, squeeze of lime. Moscow Mule.

'I don't know,' Jas had said sighing, sort of general troubled air about him, face on him like last Nazi in the bunker and the Russians coming down the street, standing over the drinks with those tongs, dropping ice in like lumps of cyanide. 'I suppose I'll have to believe him.'

'Well, I wouldn't,' Nick said, waiting for Jas to rise to it. He didn't. No point carrying it on at present with Jas, international man of misery. Find out for himself.

He crossed the road from the pub to a call box, rang Jas's number. 'Jas, hi, it's Nick.'

'Nick, what's up?'

'I tried to catch you earlier. You been out?'

'Lunch with Stella.'

'Nice.'

'What's on your mind, Nick?'

'I meant to ask you about Ivy's show. Is she in?'

'I heard her go out a second ago. What did you want to know?'

'Tomorrow, is it?'

'Yeah. Starts at about seven. You know where the college is?'

'Yeah. just about.'

'So, what have you done with your ticket?'

255

'Mislaid, I'm afraid.'

'I'll make sure you're on the list. Ivy wants us all to be there.'

'Excellent. So, what happens to b&s?'

Jas grunted. 'Cancelled. Maybe just as well.'

'OK, great, thanks.'

Shit. He dug out Bart's number and called it. Bart on the other end. 'Hello . . .'

He listened for a few moments, no particular reason. Bart saying *hello* again twice, some gloomy music in the background. He put the phone down and flagged a taxi. Ivy wouldn't have had time to get to Bart's yet anyway. He could beat her there if she was walking. Cabbie pulling up, head half out of the window for instructions. He got in and settled back. Lovely rumble to them, taxis, unaccustomed luxury these days, apart from the other night, Jas throwing up like it was a dying art. Gave the driver something to moan about though, mad cunt going on about West Bank, Gaza, Palestinians, suicide bombers, towelheads. Shoot to kill, he was saying, only fucking solution, pardon my French, he said.

'Haven't they already tried that?' Nick had said. Cabbies. Must spend half their lives reading the fucking paper to half-know so much about everything, he thought. This one was quiet enough though.

He asked to be dropped off at Rosebery Avenue, just short of Bart's place. He walked up to the square, aim of hanging around out of sight, so if Ivy was walking up this way, he'd spot her. But the first thing he saw was the silver nose of Bart's motor poking out of the side street, indicator blinking. Shit. He looked around. His cab was still there, driver fucking about with his clipboard. He dashed across, risking being seen by Bart but needs must. He rapped on the window. 'You still free?'

'Bloody hell, mate, that was quick,' the driver said, stowing his clipboard neatly above somewhere, readying for action.

Good man. Some cabbies kept you waiting just for fun. 'Follow that Porsche,' Nick said, climbing in. Cabbie chuckling, challenged by the unexpected lark, swinging the cab round and putting his foot down, Bart way in the distance but his brake lights already flaring at the junction. 'Don't worry, he won't lose us. He never does more than forty in it. That car's wasted on him.'

'Mate of yours, is he?'

'Yeah, I just want to surprise him.'

They followed the Porsche to Euston and from there to Camden Town. He was slowing up, indicator flashing.

'This'll do,' Nick said, leaning forward.

'You sure this time?'

He peered out through the windscreen. Bart, getting out, locking the car. Obviously meeting her at a bar or restaurant, not taking any chances near his own place. Nick counted out money to the cabbie then started to follow Bart up the street towards the canal bridge, keeping a safe distance. Ivy must be arriving by taxi, he thought, watch for her.

He saw Bart turn off to the right ahead of the railway bridge and hurried after him. He reached the corner. Where the fuck? He scanned the little shops, the nearby café. There he was, standing in front of an old junk shop, looking up at the open window, Bart talking to someone up there. The window closed and after a minute a little door clanked opened in the big metal gate next to the shop. A woman. Nick moved to one side to get a better view. Bart was kissing her now. And serious hugs. Not Ivy. Short black hair, very cute. The gate clanged shut, leaving nothing to look at but the big front window, lit by the falling sun, full of old furniture. He stepped forward and registered the sign above the window for the first time. Lost & Abandoned. It took a few more seconds for it to sink in. Christ. He moved forward to make sure, recognised the setting now from the picture, the red and gold frontage. All that was missing was Monty's missus standing outside in the sun with a brush in her hand – now presumed upstairs in the dark with Bart's dick in her hand. Nick smiled to himself, almost laughing, almost rubbing his hands as he fled gleefully from the scene.

Monty's wife. Fuck!!

•••

Jas watched himself without pleasure in the bathroom as he shaved, flossed his teeth and tweezered out two rogue nose-hairs, both white. He sighed. His eyes looked terrible. He went to the bedroom, shed his bathrobe and stood in front of the long mirror there in his boxer shorts. He'd lost weight, but in a bad, unhealthy *hors de combat* way. His legs and arms looked thinner and the pallid breasts and folds of belly fat matted with hair, which had always seemed affirmative and bursting with life, now sagged on him like marsupial protu-berances that evolution had left behind. He got dressed, discarding one shirt after another, eventually deciding on the neutral linen. His skin seemed so clammy, too, these days. The flat was hotter – even sleeping with the window ajar, he was waking with night sweats and having to get up and take a shower. Napping during the day on the sofa had cost him two deadlines and a missed appointment.

He sat in the kitchen ready to leave, though he wasn't meet-ing Stella till one, and it was only eleven-thirty. He made a pot of coffee and read yesterday's paper. He spied a glinting sword of glass on the floor under the table and carried it carefully to the bin. It was from the smashed frame of his old laughing pirate print, now scrolled on top of the fridge gathering dust, evidence of his emotional homecoming three nights previously when – and he could not fully reassemble the reasons for this in his mind – he had hurled a copy of his excellent new book at it.

At twelve he went out. He hadn't felt so nervous in years.

Stella was on the phone when he tapped on her office door and peered in. She was laughing about something with someone, her voice a register lower as she talked, with a gossipy, conspiratorial edge, discussing some colleague or student, some minor scandal. Jas leafed through an art magazine while he waited, his ear alert to the voice on the other end of the phone, a man's voice. Her glance registered him and she held a finger up to indicate that she wouldn't be long, but seemed in no hurry to finish her conversation. It was the first time he had seen her since Stansted and he had an urge to kiss the back of her neck and to reach down to feel her breasts while she was on the phone, to hold on to her – assert his claim – as he had done once before, but that had been at her place, and here she was behind the desk, and it would be awkward and he didn't feel as free with her now.

At last she put the phone down, a smile still on her lips that belonged to whoever she had been talking to. 'I won't be a sec,' she said. She busied herself for a moment straightening a stack of papers, scribbling out a Post-it and sticking it on the top sheet.

'I thought we might go to a restaurant for lunch,' he said.

She looked at her watch, made a doubtful expression. 'Do you mind if we don't? I've got an appointment at two-thirty.'

'Can't you get out of it?'

'It's a student,' she said, picking up her bag and looking at her desk and frowning as if she might have forgotten about something. She pushed her hair back. 'Exam worries, final crits, tutorials, end-of-year shows. It's an anxious time. I have to be here for them.'

'You're the boss,' he said.

They went to a pub that Stella suggested, round the corner from the college, the Mariner – large, purpose-built, badly lit and full of office workers, gaming machines flickering and ding-dinging amid the nautical memorabilia. It was the kind of pub you might choose because it was the nearest, or because there would be no one in there you knew, where the food was overpriced and unimaginative and produced at speed. They found a table up the stairs on a mezzanine level, done out to resemble the deck of a ship. Jas didn't feel like eating, but he ordered the steak and ale pie, like Stella.

They made small talk while they ate, or at least Stella did – about current things, an exhibition she wanted to see, a day at Wimbledon. She didn't say who with. She ate quickly, he noticed.

'I thought you would have been too busy for tennis,' Jas said.

'I am. But someone got some tickets,' she said, pushing her plate away. 'Mmm,' she said, 'that was quite horrible.' She shook a cigarette out of a pack of Camel and lit it.

'Stella . . .'

'Mmm?' She looked at him expectantly.

'Are we . . . are we OK?'

She blew smoke out from the side of her mouth, frowning heavily. 'I don't know – are we? It depends what you want.'

'What do you mean?'

She shook her head impatiently, though it was obvious, he thought, that she had something on her mind. 'Look,' she said at last, talking quickly, waving the cigarette, 'if you want to sleep around with my students, fine. You're a grown-up. And so are they, technically. I don't have any expectations of you.'

He felt himself unexpectedly redden. 'This is Ivy who's been talking to you.'

Stella brushed a fragment of pastry from her wrist. 'Actually, it was Lois. I don't know what her motives were – perhaps she was just showing off, perhaps she needed counselling. I tried not to be too shocked. Anyway, I don't need anyone to tell me what you're like, Jas. It's not a secret. It's written into your life. And that's fine. I suppose.'

'Stella, I . . .'

'No, no, really. I knew all that when I met you. And it suited me well enough that that was the life you wanted. What I like less is you trying to come between me and my other friends, trying to curtail *my* freedom. Because *then* it starts to look like you want something else.'

'When you say "friends", you mean this Mark.'

'What I mean is that episode at the airport, and all the way home in the car. That's what I don't need. I didn't enjoy that. Not at all.'

Jas sighed. 'Are you sleeping with him?'

'That's not a question you're in a position to ask.'

'I know. I know. I'm not, but . . .'

'Then please don't.'

'Supposing I've changed what I want,' he said, looking at her.

She shrugged. 'Changed? Is that what you're doing when you suddenly ask if I've got any students looking for work experience?' She looked away. 'I assumed you were hoping I'd send Lois round for a second helping.'

'That's not fair.'

'Isn't it? It seems like a reasonable assumption to me.' She gave a thin smile and put her cigarette out.

The waiter was at the table, scooping up the plates, wiping the table. Jas waited till he'd gone. 'We can talk about Lois if you want,' he said. 'It was a mistake. I don't know what I was thinking.'

'That's your decision to make, Jas. Like I said, you're a grown-up. You are what you do.' She cupped her hands in front of her as if holding two spheres, her long fingers curved in the air. 'Look, what is all this actually about? Those photographs of the river you left for me to look at – what are they supposed to mean? Do you think I don't know you can take photographs? Of course you can. That's not in dispute. But they're not really you. They're nothing to do with you. For goodness' sake, do the advertising work that earns you money. There's no shame in that. By all means carry on with your open lectures and tell your war stories to young photographers if you like. I mean why *not* be yourself? What's wrong with yourself all of a sudden? What more do you want?'

'I want you,' he said.

She looked away again. 'People can't really have each other,' she said. 'I thought that was something we both understood. You can't go through life second-guessing somebody else. You can only do what's right for yourself and hope for the best.'

'So how do you explain happy marriages?'

'Yours wasn't happy.'

'But some are. How do they do it?'

'How would I know? By coincidence maybe. When what a man wants for himself coincides with what a woman wants for herself. A coincidence of two people's selfishness. I'm not saying it guarantees happiness but at least no one gets disappointed.'

'And what about trust?'

'*Trust?*' She gave a cold laugh. 'Well, isn't that just another way of expecting someone else not to do something you don't like? It's coercion by other means. I'd hate to have to trust you.'

'You could.' He felt a tightness in his chest as he said it. He felt the dizzying warmth of the room for a moment, but didn't want to leave it.

She shook her head, and left a long pause. 'You've lost weight,' she said. 'That's not like you.'

'I love you,' he said.

She sighed. 'That's just the fear talking,' she said. 'Come on, I've got to get back to work.'

'What about us?'

'There's never been an us,' she said. 'Just a me and you.'

'OK, what about me and you? Stella?'

She didn't say anything, just walked. At the gate she stopped to move a wisp of hair from the corner of her mouth. 'So . . .' she said.

'Will I see you again?'

'Will you be at the show tomorrow?'

'Of course.'

'See you there then.'

twelve

A beautiful thing. She had rung him the minute she'd got back to Camden, her van still warm from the drive from the Eurotunnel terminal at Folkestone. She'd invited him over for dinner. The *minute* she'd got back. Obviously she was tired from the journey but equally obviously she wanted to see him. She had to see him.

'You must be tired,' he'd said, smiling into the receiver.

'Mmm . . . not *too* tired,' she said.

The wonder of it. His heart, defeated and sunk by Natalie, had risen, fluttered to life and thundered anew to hear that *not too tired*. 'I'll cook for us,' she had said. 'I brought an absolute ton of mussels back from Dieppe – they need eating and there's too much for one.' The way she had backtracked on her eagerness like that, by bringing necessity into it, made him love her all the more. 'I'll make some *frites* to go with them, French style,' she said.

Once he had loved Natalie and now he loved Kate. And she loved him. Why would she bring a ton of mussels back from Dieppe if not for the purpose of having too many for one?

'Isn't it illegal to smuggle mussels in from Dieppe?' he asked.

He wondered if he would tell her about Monty.

'Do we care?' she laughed.

But that was yesterday. Today Christian was talking about New York, two cups of strong coffee between them in the conference room, Ivy out there alone watching the phones, magenta hair tied up in rags just visible above the high sills as she moved around, making and receiving calls about her show tonight. It was muggy, and she had switched on all the office fans, setting papers rustling and flittering as Christian was saying that the moment of truth had come.

Bart was nodding, to keep away the moment of saying no, thinking of Kate and how, before the food, while the *moules* were steaming and the *frites* deep-frying, they'd tumbled into a furious, thrusting bout of route-one sex in her small sitting room, in her big tweedy armchair, her long, floaty cream dress up round her waist, her unbuttoned breasts spilling into his hands, how she'd looked into his eyes and kept on looking until she half closed them, in one of those synchronised Hollywood climaxes with the girl on top moaning and the man hardly believing his luck. And then later, after the food and a bottle of champagne – when he had told her not about

266

Monty, but the Kasparo tapas bar on Charlotte Street – they'd gone to bed and done it again – long, slow, fucking into the night beneath a seascape of St Malo, thrown in with a Victorian armoire she'd bought in that town, she said, as they lay afterwards, he in her arms, staring into space. She asked if there was something on his mind. 'You seem to have made yourself a bit elusive recently,' she'd said, stroking his hair, taking his glasses from the bedside table and trying them on.

After a short silence, as if in reply, he told her about Natalie and the two babies, one dead, one living, neither of them his. She listened and brought him closer to her. 'I thought there was something,' she said.

He got home at seven in the morning. Two dustbins over-turned in the courtyard, rubbish strewn across the asphalt. He righted them, puzzled, but too happy and full of vigour as he came up to the flat to wonder too deeply. Bird there in the rising light, curled up on the futon, an album of Japanese electronic jazz playing quietly and the answering machine blinking. A short, incoherent message, made in the small hours, Monty's accusing voice lost in the smudge of alcohol and tears, pitching between anger and sadness before the click of the phone being replaced . . .

Some friend you turned out to be.

I can't believe you could've.

You fucking, you fucking . . . *hypocrite.*

Since then Bart had been waiting for the rush of the real hurricane, one that would really blow his dustbins away. 'It is an excellent opportunity, Bart,' Christian was saying. 'Mortensens are not to be sniffed at. It really is a very impressive package. A first-class opportunity.'

Bart was aware of the door swinging open, or shut, or the

sound of it, a jarring of some kind, a flicker of movement or
sound that caught his senses by its exaggeration – in the way
that the sound of someone fainting or breaking into a run will
turn heads in a public place, not for the volume of the sound
but for its unexpected quality of turbulence. He looked up
and saw Ivy, wearing a strange expression, walk to the main
door and peek out. Christian, glancing over his shoulder
momentarily, carried on talking, more animated now.
'Mortensens—'

'Hang on a minute,' Bart said. Ivy was making a face at
him now through the glass. She came round to the door.

'What is it?' he said.

'Someone just arrived for you. But then she—'

'Give me a minute, Christian. Sorry.'

He hurried out into the office and to the door, Ivy following, talking in his ear. 'This mad woman took one look at me
and raced back out again. I mean, I know I'm not at my best
in the mornings but—'

'Which way did she go?' He leapt down the stairs and looked
up and down the street. She was fifty yards away, half running,
flagging down a taxi. He sprinted after her. 'Kate, Kate . . .'

She turned and saw him. 'Get away from me!' she
screamed, her face a mess of tears. The taxi was pulling into
the kerb just ahead. She strode quickly after it. Bart caught
up with her, touched her arm. 'Kate, wait, talk to me.'

'Fuck off. Fuck *off*.' She pushed him away. 'What did you
think? It was some kind of game?'

'What do you mean? I don't know what you mean. Tell me
what you mean.'

'The two of you. Some kind of pathetic revenge. You getting out of my bed, while YOUR FRIEND Stephen leaves a
message on the downstairs phone. *What's it like fucking my
best friend? How does it feel? How does Bart do it to you? I hope*

268

you're happy now. I'm telling you, the man needs help, seriously. He is sick. And so are you if you think this is—'

'Look, I don't know what he said. Let me explain.'

'Right, and you don't know what that girl's doing in your
office either.'

'What? Oh Christ, no. Listen, Kate, please, calm down for
a second, will you.'

'What – are you saying you *don't* know him? He's *not*
your friend?'

Bart took her hand. 'Look . . .'

'Get *off* me,' she screamed.

She got into the taxi and slammed the door. He watched
the cab pull away, the driver shaking his head, seen it all
before. Back at the office, Ivy was sitting on the step, fanning
herself with a sales brochure. 'Wow, who was *that*?' she
said.

He didn't answer but came back into the conference room,
sweating from the heat and the effort of running. Christian
was smiling, cradling a coffee cup. 'So, Bart,' he said. 'Do we
have a deal?'

There was no point following her. And he knew she
wouldn't answer her phone. Not right now. The best he
could do was leave a message and hope she would listen to it
all the way through. He went up to the flat. Even as he keyed
in the number, he thought about the times Monty must have
called this number, too, to leave messages for her, to plead
with her to listen. But then what about the calls Monty had
made last night – had he been outside Kate's, watching, seen
him arrive? He would have felt doubly betrayed, thinking that
Kate knew. Christ.

How, though, had he stopped himself rushing out of
hiding to intervene or kick down the door or throw bricks at
the windows? Instead he had waited till the early hours and

made those calls in a howling, drunken rage after drowning his sorrows somewhere alone.

Where was he now?

Kate's answerphone beeped. He left the message, not perfectly formed, but carefully detailing the truth as he saw it: that, however bad things looked, there was no horrible, weird conspiracy between Monty and himself; that when he had first set eyes on Kate – the fiasco with the taxi near Monty's shop – and later, when he'd met her at the Cambridge site, it was the result of them both independently knowing Monty; and that finding out about her and Monty had left him with a dilemma he'd been unable to deal with. 'I know I should have told you as soon as I found out, and I wish I had,' he said. 'But I didn't want to lose you. I didn't know how you'd react. I wanted to do the right thing. I promise you – Monty didn't have a clue about us. The trouble is, I couldn't tell him either. And then the longer it went on . . . the more impossible it was. The whole thing's been driving me fucking mad. I don't know how he found out. He rang me too. Christ, what a mess. I'm really sorry. I'm going to see Monty now and try and straighten things out. And then maybe . . .'

He paused, remembering the Ivy factor. Kate had been prepared to hear his side of the story until she had recognised her at the office. It was the shock of seeing Ivy there, cocksure, challenging, her magenta hair tied in those trademark rags, that had confirmed in Kate's mind some unforgivable deceit. But what Bart knew about Monty's wild night with Ivy had been told in confidence. He couldn't be expected to know about it. Even so, Kate would be adding together other connections and making four. She would be wondering whether this was the same overfamiliar young woman who had kept her on the phone with a long rambling apology about stopping Bart getting to his date at the cinema with her the day it had been bucketing with rain; she'd be wondering whether, somehow, she was being made a fool of even back then. He feared also what Monty knew about him. About him being in Ivy's flat standing there while she stood naked in the doorway of her bathroom, about being within touching distance – *breathing* distance – of something happening . . .

'What you said about the girl in my office,' Bart said into the phone. 'I don't know about that. She's just a student – she's the daughter of a friend, Jas, who I've told you about. Anything else – I really don't know. Whatever it is, it's nothing to do with us. All this is the truth, I swear. Please, please ring me.'

Not the whole jigsaw, but enough to see what the picture was.

Bart went downstairs and back though the office, vaguely aware of Ivy telling everyone in that generally announcing way of hers that Jamie was picking her up at three in the van, and of Christian approaching in his peripheral vision, about to say something but changing his mind. 'You will be coming, won't you, Christian?' Ivy added. 'Everyone will be there.'

Bart looked in vain for a cab as he walked to Monty's shop. Gail was busy with a customer and had two others hovering at the café counter. 'Is Monty around?' he asked.

'No, but if you see him before I do, you might tell him he's missed two reps this morning and I don't know who's supposed to be going to the bank.'

'Is he always here to see reps?'

'He's here to see everything – unless he tells me otherwise. It's my lunch in half an hour and there's supposed to be two of us after that because of the rush. Am I supposed to close up or what?'

'He's not in his flat?'

Two more customers wandered into the shop and she glanced at Bart impatiently, meaning, he supposed, that, actually, she *had* thought of that.

• • •

Fuck. Nick looked at his watch, shook it. Unbelievable. Fucking thing had stopped. Still, couldn't be more than half five, six tops. Couple of hours in the Crow or Crown scanning for jobs in the *Standard* and watching the tennis, bar staff whooping apeshit, rooting for the Aussies. Quick McDonald's afterwards to soak it up. Show started at, what was it – sevenish? He wandered around Soho looking in shop windows till it started drizzling. Fucking weather. Could do with a bit of rain though. Clammy. Trendy bar on Old Compton, past the oaf in the black coat on the door. Always a good sign. Paid an arm and a leg for a beer and sat in the window. He yawned, shook open the *Standard*, lit a fag, yawned again. He'd woken up at four in the morning on the sofa, having enjoyed some of Monty's best Cabernet and nodded off in front of the TV, again, or rather got woken, every bone aching, Monty bursting in from some club somewhere, happy as Larry, though pissed. Nick took no pleasure in giving him the news, though it had to be given. Sat with him for a while, brooding over it. A man confused. Then, before he knew it, off he'd fucked. Cab presumably back out somewhere. Then he must have dropped off again. Monty deserved better. Fucking Bart, shagging everybody's women but his own. Just wait till Jas found out. Confirmed suspicions in a way, in terms of character. Exonerated.

Right, he thought, flicking through the ads again, less fussy now. Job, job, job. Daren't show up at Olivia's till he'd got one. He'd done the right thing at last and rung to explain why the funds were drying up and ask after the kids, maybe make an arrangement for Sunday. No way, Nick, she said. Heart ached for the little loves when he thought about them. The in-laws ought to be helping out. 'Come on, Livvy,' he'd said. 'What's the point of having a millionaire dad if you're not prepared to touch him for a few quid every now and then? Come on, just a few thou to tide us over.'

'You just don't get it, do you, Nick?'

'What?'

Click.

Couldn't blame her. He thought of her pregnant with Matthew. Massive. Ditto with Lucy. Took a while to shed it afterwards. Sex life disappeared for a while too. Tired. So was he, but he was still up for it. You didn't let *that* go. Otherwise who were you married to – the kids? Much as you might love them. And he did love them. He did. Loved her too, still. Just wished she'd given him a bit of attention back then. No. Couldn't blame her. Him really. Him. Nick. Nicholas Murrow, married, father of two.

He refolded the paper, looked at his useless watch again. He left the bar and wandered off in the direction of Covent Garden. He meandered slowly through the piazza, past the jugglers and fire eaters and string quartet and the idiot who painted himself white and pretended to be a statue. What kind of a skill was that? He stood for a moment to stare at him, try to make him blink. He walked on, unsuccessful. Sweating inside his jacket. Six-forty by the tourist clock. He wandered into a bookshop, Jas's new one on display. New York cops. Acclaimed, it said. He leafed through the pictures. Had to envy that. Body of work. Something to be remembered for. Vicarious pride, knowing someone who'd done it. Friend of mine, he thought, looking round. Girl next to him, browsing. 'Friend of mine,' he said, pointing at one of the pictures. 'Photographer, I mean, not the policeman.' He grinned.

The girl looked at him as if she'd like to be helpful, but gave in, shoulders up. 'Soray, no spee Inglay . . .'

Just as well. Making a cunt of himself. Though what she's doing in a fucking Inglay bookshop not speeing Inglay.

He walked as slow as he could down King Street. Still a minute early but he could see the gate was open, people in and out. Big sign, End of Year Private View. He walked up the steps. A few people circling, waiting for other people. Students. Parents looking like parents. Woman at the table selling programmes, fiver a shot. Avoid her eyes, he thought.

'Excuse me, do you have a ticket?' she asked.

'Oh, sorry. Actually no. I should be on the list. Murrow? Nick?'

She looked in the book. 'Ah yes. Would you like a programme?'

'Yes, why not?'

He traipsed in. It was stifling inside. People wafting themselves with programmes all over the place. He took his jacket off and pulled out his shirt-tails, grabbed a glass of red from the table, started wandering. Still pretty deserted. Inspected a couple of abstract canvases, walked through a bigger gallery, stuff made out of hoover parts and bicycle tyres. Took all sorts, he thought. Conceptual. You couldn't be too critical. College. Four years pretending to be talented before you got down to the real business of having to work at CopyKwik or flogging rubbish over the phone. He looked at the programme. Ivy Hamilton. Right, her mum's name, he thought, remembering it from the cancer whatsit up in Norfolk. Fine Art Film, it said, 'Work 5 in Black and White'. Exchanged his empty glass for a full one, then up a floor. Place was filling up a bit now. Room H12. Where the fuck was that?

Along this one. He turned the map upside down. Fine Art Film, it said. Two blokes coming towards him carrying what appeared to be a full-sized bull. He stepped comically sideways to avoid a horn, smiling. Took a top up from someone circulating with a bottle.

Then he saw himself. It took a second, seeing himself projected big on to the wall. Walked towards it, jaw dropping, not quite believing. Himself sitting up in bed – *a* bed – not his. But hang on. No. A blur, transforming itself into a topless Ivy, arriving suddenly next to him in the bed – *her* bed. Jesus. He went cold. One of Jas's old war posters protruding at the periphery. Ivy smiling at the camera. Offering him a fucking *crisp* from a packet. The picture was fading out, the next image coming up, mesmerising him for a second but it was coming slow and he suddenly felt the urge to run. He glanced around. People were looking at him as he started to edge back. That was *him* there on the fucking wall, they were thinking. He glugged the wine down, legged it down the hall, getting lost, nowhere an exit. Sweat running inside his collar. Stairs leading down. He swung round to the left. Jas at the bottom, pausing, about to come up.

Holy, holy, fuck.

•••

Nausea, from the Greek *naus*, ship. Jas, holding a glass of white wine by its stem, forgot where he was for a moment and blinked at the light. He thought he saw Nick but there was no one there now. Students and visitors surged past him as he mounted the wide stair slowly, his mind returning. He wasn't sleeping well. His fingers tingled in the night. The cab driver had had to wake him when they'd pulled up at the college gate. He'd been back in Beirut, long ago. He couldn't

275

work out why. Why now. There was no residual fear of the shelling and death that took him back there. It wasn't that kind of dream, though a British photographer in his hotel had been killed – Leonard Hill. And it wasn't the addiction to danger that he couldn't shake off. He'd never had that. Very few did. Chasing bombs had the appearance of an obsession, but the truth was mundane. If you photographed war, you went where the wars were, in the same way that paparazzi pursued celebrities. It was no different. What was different were those you left behind. They feared for your life. And, oddly, with that, you feared for theirs.

Jas had been in the bar with other photographers and journalists when one of the street teams stretchered Leonard Hill into the lobby, grey dust and blood from the blast on his face and in his hair. They ran out to help but he was dead. One of the older correspondents covered Leonard's face with a bath towel, which seemed wrong somehow. The rest of them stood round the body, drawing on their cheap Lebanese cigarettes, not knowing what to say, until the paramedics came and took him away, to be flown to Britain – to his home town in Northumberland where his parents still lived. Someone volunteered to call the paper Leonard was working for. The evening was sombre, he remembered. They played cards.

But it wasn't remembering the end of Leonard Hill that haunted Jas's dreams now. Though it was near to that. It was connected but harder to see, even for himself.

At the top of the stairs he waited for a moment, lost, glass in his hand like a lantern. The first gallery was swarming with people, students, college visitors, academics and parents like him – though not like him – flushed as they were with wine and the gaiety of the occasion, newly arrived from Hull and Southampton and Carlisle to embarrass their children – self-

276

consciously grubby, rough-fledged, creative – with politeness and undisguised pride. There was no sign of Stella or Ivy. He still felt weird, outside himself. Room H12. He looked at the guide and made his way past the exhibits, occasionally stopping to peer at a piece of wire sculpture or a flickering screen or a painting.

He saw Ivy before she saw him. She was glancing around, arms folded, holding her breath nervously. 'Hi,' he said, coming towards her. 'Is this it?' He indicated the three rows of seats laid out in the darkened space between two bigger galleries, people getting up to leave, others taking their places.

'Dad, quick, hurry up.'

'Have you been waiting for me?' he said, his spirits stirred.

'It's just about to restart,' she said. 'Go and sit down,' she ordered, pointing to the middle of the second row where Stella was waving him over. Ivy stood on her toes and kissed his cheek.

'Well,' he said. 'You're in a good mood.'

She ushered him through.

'I saved you the best seat,' Stella said, standing up.'

'Aren't you staying to watch?'

'Bit warm in here. I ought to mingle. Anyway, I've already seen it.' She smiled, put her hand on his shoulder and made her way past the row of spectators. The film started, projected against the white wall. He looked to the side and saw Ivy still there, stationed at the entrance, and turned back as the title came up. 'Any Friend of My Father's'. He read the words and tried to take on their meaning, the irony they intended, but his mind was now drawn to the first image, monochrome but bleached with light. An oldish woman, frail and sick, hair cropped short, seen from a distance, sitting up in bed, staring impassively into the camera. The image flickered with the varying speed of the film. He was absorbed by the face, which, though indistinct, its gradations of shade reduced by the editing to blocks of black or white, seemed familiar. His eye was distracted by a pixilated blur to the left, and then, abruptly, Ivy was in the bed too, T-shirted, smiling. From the right, the ghost of Stella strolled into shot and out again, unconcerned, holding a paintbrush, wearing her painter's overalls. Ivy, younger she seemed, turned and kissed the cheek of the older woman, who melted away to be gradually replaced by a man, bare-chested, unshaven, holding a teacup. The scene was nearer now and it was a different room – Ivy's room. Jas leaned forward to scrutinise the man's face, not quite believing. *It couldn't be . . .* Roger Flowers, a fellow veteran photographer, a one-time close acquaintance, a b&s old boy who had moved on. Jas felt anger. Was that the connection? This friend of his, Roger? Was this some kind of terrible joke . . . The shot lingered, crackly, Roger's lips moving in dead slow motion. Ivy was now vanishing from the picture, but abruptly reappeared, as if in a puff of smoke, again from a blur, sitting up in the bed. She was topless. The shock of Ivy's breasts, almost surreal here, in public – though he knew he shouldn't be shocked – only intensified his apprehension now as Roger, slowly and grainily atomising, was replaced by . . . He watched, his hands trembling slightly, waiting for the next fresh hell as the picture composed itself, one person made into the next, fashioned from the same gathering sooty fragments. *Jesus Christ.* He squeezed his eyes closed and opened them again. Monty. Monty, sitting up in bed with Ivy, passing a joint. Christ. Jas looked quickly across to the arched doorway where Ivy had been standing but she had gone. He hardly dare look back at the projection. But when he did, what he saw was Nick being offered a packet of crisps by Ivy, both of them naked from the waist up, presumably from the waist down too. Jas averted his eyes from her breasts, angry, mortified, saddened. It was Bart's ghost now flitted across the picture, fully dressed but frowning, as though looking for something. Ivy was smiling now, saying something, but then her face was morphing, slowly, very slowly, to another, earlier or later, image of her, wearing a jumper – he was thankful for that – sitting now beside the old woman again, the old woman's fingers gripping the bed-covers like claws, the delineation of her features coming clearer now, an almost skeletal face, hair hanging down in wisps, soft wrinkled purses sagging under the dead, cratered eyes. Jas looked into the eyes and saw Ivy. And then he saw Barbara. Barbara, his wife, Ivy's mother. And then, unexpectedly, uncontrollably, he began to weep.

The film was coming to an end, but his sobs sounded an alert to those around him as he pushed past them, felt their eyes on him and heard their murmurs as he stumbled out and away from this, through the jubilant crowds of the outer galleries, trying to retrace his steps but erring into a second darkened chamber. Here he froze, saw the colours first – the turquoise of the pool and the deep lavender – and then the tumbling movement of the water and the swirling patterns made by the girl's dress as she swooped and turned. Seven or eight people occupied the seats. She wasn't here, Lois. He stood and made himself watch, conscious of enacting a drama in which the flawed protagonist is forced to witness his own past transgressions. Then he retreated, pressed on, glancing round as he walked, only now realising that he was looking for Ivy. But what did he want? Perhaps simply, gently, to ask about her mother. Perhaps to draw out of himself an apology, like poison from a wound. To ask forgiveness. To listen. To confess all. To do whatever was required.

But Ivy would have made her escape, he was sure now, stranding him with this new knowledge of her. He found the

279

stairs down and the pavement outside, the heavy warmth of the evening. There was a taxi at the gate. He spoke to the driver and opened the door. Someone was shouting his name. There was Bart, across the street, an urgent expression on his face, waving furiously as the traffic surged by, looking both ways, waiting for it to clear. Jas hauled himself into the back of the cab, lowering his head as it pulled away. Seeing Bart, he was angry again – not at Bart but at Monty, Nick, at Ivy (that kiss on the cheek – a token of betrayal to announce her theme), at himself. At Stella, too, for holding those secrets with such cruel ease. He felt sick. He was shaking, light-headed, afraid he might black out. He stared out of the window, tried to focus his eyes and control his breathing.

The flat welcomed him with an unfamiliar quiet, as if it hadn't been lived in for a time. He dropped the blind in the bedroom, lay on the bed in the half-light, pulled the duvet up around him, shutting out his thoughts. But the thoughts crowded in as he closed his eyes. Of Leonard Hill, of the memorial service in a village church in Northumberland, of Leonard's wife, his mother, his brother and two sisters.

He had lost what youthful appetite he'd had for photographing war, risking its dangers, though he returned from time to time – even now he still returned – to catch the back-wash of conflict, the debris it left, to exploit its hellish splendour for immoral purposes. Art had no morals. Stella said so. But what he made wasn't art. Ivy said so. Be yourself, Stella said. Be someone else, Ivy said.

It wasn't Leonard's death that scared him. It was Leonard's young wife. That day, seeing her face – crumpled, hollowed out, made old with grief – scared him. He realised for the first time what love was. But he wasn't thinking about Barbara. He wasn't putting Barbara in Leonard's wife's place. He was putting himself there. That's what happened if you got too close to a person, he thought. That's what love could do to you. That's how terrifying it could be. He drifted away . . .

In his sleep the fear was physical, stifling him, smothering and full of heat as the noise gathered, the baaing and lowing of a million driven beasts out there, the slaughtered ghosts of Smithfield, sluicing the gutters with their running blood, the hot smell of their panic filling the black world of his dream, their glassy, fearful eyes seeking him out. He was trapped by the darkness itself, which pressed against him, holding him down and crushing the life out of him, and he opened his mouth to shout out but nothing came, held out his arms but found only empty space. He woke instantly from the dream, gasping, his heart hammering inside him, his chest tight with pain, his clothes soaked in sweat. He couldn't breathe properly. The fear from his dream was real, pressing against his ribs, crushing him. The fear was to die here and die alone. He shouted out loud, heard his own voice calling Ivy's name, heard it echo faintly in the bare corridor and stairwell that led to her flat, and he saw the glow of street light marking out the window frame, aware of the rain outside hitting the pane as he reached for the phone, his whole body shaking like an engine gone wrong, about to break and burst.

thirteen

A beautiful opportunity, Christian called it, but now he had to push Bart for a decision, he said. This morning it had seemed a matter of courtesy to hear Christian out one last time if only to decline his offer with suitably humble thanks. Everything Bart wanted now was here. He knew that. And even if he couldn't have it, the prospect of a new start in New York would feel too much like running away from something. There had already been too many changes. And yet he hadn't said no. 'Look. Give me a ring at home,' Christian had said. 'I can see you've got some personal issues to deal with.'

'I'll get back to you,' Bart promised. But he hadn't.

Kate was not answering her mobile. He'd left another message, saying that he was worried about Monty, that he hadn't been seen all day and wasn't responding to his mobile – that Monty's assistant Gail had had to recruit one of her friends to run the café and watch the shop while Gail took the weekly receipts to the bank. 'Kate, I'll be at the Temple Art College in Covent Garden. There's a show Monty is supposed to be coming to. It's a long-standing thing. We're all supposed to meet there. Monty, me, Jas, Nick. So, I don't know, he might turn up. I'll be outside at . . . quarter to eight? Meet me. I really need you. I need you to help.'

Bart got out of his cab and saw Jas across the road about to climb into one. He shouted, but Jas seemed not to hear. The cab moved away, Jas slumped in the back. Where the hell was he going? Bart crossed the road and stood at the gate. If Kate was going to come, she would have called. He waited fifteen minutes then went inside. The show was set on two floors. He weaved a path through the revellers. Monty wouldn't be difficult to spot. He checked around the long tables set out with polished glasses and wine bottles in formation, figuring that if Nick was with him they wouldn't be far from the drink. Seeing Jas leaving was puzzling, but also worrying. Perhaps he had heard something about Monty and left in a hurry. Maybe that was why Nick wasn't here – and, come to that, Ivy.

He called Jas's mobile but it was switched off. Nick was still incommunicado. He called home and checked for calls. On the second floor he found the room showing Ivy's work. There was no sign of anyone. He looked in at the handful of people seated in the dark, glanced up at the images on the wall and saw Monty sitting up in bed next to Ivy. He went cold. He immediately understood what was happening, seeing Monty and now suddenly very afraid that this had something to do with him. He looked over his shoulder in panic, half expecting to see Kate standing there. But she wasn't. Just people coming in and out, peering closely at the paintings and sculptures, the cloud of small metal household items suspended in mid-air, as if at the core of a domestic explosion. He moved to the back of the room, watching the pictures appear and disappear one by one, checked his breathing as he saw a cameo of himself flitting across the screen – felt his jaw fall open as he saw Nick, followed by a sick, elderly woman. The film restarted . . . the woman again, some bloke he'd never seen before, an unknown see-through woman crossing from right to left, and all the time Ivy floating in and out of the scene. How much of it was real? He knew about Monty and Ivy. Nick wouldn't have posed much of a challenge. He reminded himself that he himself had not taken the bait, though he waited with rising alarm for his own image to materialise up there again (perhaps shirtless in his flat), his hand gripping the chair in front of him, until the first image of Monty returned safely to the screen of the white wall. He exhaled audibly. It explained what Ivy had been doing, though not why she did it – some unfinished father–daughter business no doubt, a comment on betrayal, perhaps, or desire. And the woman? A statement about something, to be sure. Whatever it was, Bart was happy not to have featured more prominently. But he felt for Jas, slinking off in the night when he should have been celebrating his daughter's talent. Did he deserve that?

Outside on the street, he took a cab to Exmouth Market. From the car, as it slowed up, he could see a lamp on in the flat above Monty's shop. The sash window was up a few inches and the curtain was moving. He paid the driver and ran across the street and round the side to the door. He looked up and pressed the buzzer. There was no sound. He rapped loudly using the iron knocker. He tried again. Someone was coming. He hadn't thought what he would say when he found Monty, only that he should be here making sure he was OK and getting his explanation in before things got volatile. But now he was apprehensive and stood back as he heard the lock being released and turned. The door opened a little, the security chain tightening across the gap.

'Monty? he said.

'Bart?'

'Nick? What are you doing here?'

'Is Jas with you?'

'No, Jas isn't with me. Where's Monty?'

'He's not here. I'm staying here.'

'Are you going to let me in or what?'

Nick unhooked the chain and opened the door. Bart followed him up the stairs, Nick in heavy suit trousers, no shoes, his shirt hanging loose as a concession to the weather, the scent of body odour carrying in the air behind him like an invisible cape.

'This weather's unbearable,' he said. He switched the TV off, straightened the sofa cushions. 'Do you want a beer or something?'

'No. Listen, have you seen Monty today?'

'Today? No, not today.'

'Have you spoken to him?'

'Well, I haven't really been in. The phone was going when I got back tonight. Maybe that was him. They didn't leave a message. Why, what's the problem?'

Bart heaved a sigh. 'I think he might be depressed.'

Nick nodded. 'Really? I'm going to have a beer.' He pointed to the kitchen. 'Sure you don't want one?'

'No. So, when did you last see him?' He followed Nick to the kitchen.

'Who – Monty?'

'Yes, *Monty*. Did you see him last night?'

'Ah . . . let me see. Yes, he was here. For a short while. Then he went out somewhere.'

'How did he seem?'

'Bit preoccupied, I'd say. That would be a good description.'

'Upset?'

Nick stopped in the act of opening the beer. 'You don't think he might top himself, do you?'

'For Christ's sake, don't say that, Nick. Are his clothes still here?' He went into Monty's room, peered into the wardrobe nervously. Everything looked normal, though the bed was a mess and there was an open bottle of Scotch and a glass. His mobile lay on the bedside table. 'Hang on. Have there been any other calls tonight?'

'No. Good point. I'll try 1471.' Nick hurried back into the sitting room and put the beer down on the phone table while he dialled. He listened and took a pen from the pot. 'This was the last person to call,' he said, writing the number on the pad.

'Try it,' Bart said.

Nick dialled the number and waited. 'No one's answering. It's switching to an answerphone. Some woman . . .'

'Give it.' Bart took the phone off him, listened to the message, frowned, put the phone down. He pondered for a second, Nick watching.

'Where are you going?'

'I don't know yet. Better stay near the phone in case Monty rings. Tell him I really need to talk to him. And then ring me – here's my mobile number.' Bart scribbled on a corner of newspaper and tore it off, pushed it into his hand.

'Talk, ring, right, no problem. Bart . . .'

'What?'

'Did you make it to Ivy's show tonight?'

'Yes.'

'Did you speak to Jas?'

'Yes. He said he was going to kill you.'

Nick nodded. 'Excellent. Thanks.'

Bart walked home, his head churning. Crossing the car park behind his building, he heard a noise near the dustbins, a disturbance too noticeable to be made by a cat. He flinched and halted in his tracks. A fully grown fox emerged, a chicken carcass clamped in its jaws. It stopped when it saw him then walked quickly, though not in panic, to the surrounding fence, found an exit and disappeared into the lane. He didn't know why, but the sight of the fox, appearing like a magnificent sign, unexpected and wondrous, filled him with unexpected elation. In the flat, Bird came to greet him. He stroked the cat and fed him, then hung his jacket from the head of the couch, jacked up all the windows and opened a carton of tropical fruit juice, wishing he'd taken up Nick's offer of a beer. He ejected the Pulp album that had been playing all day and put on a Marvin Gaye, closed his eyes.

Who was the woman, he wondered? He picked up the phone and tried her number again, listened to her voice again. At the last moment, he decided to leave a message: 'Sorry, I don't know who you are, and . . . and you don't know who I am . . . but I'm looking for Monty – Stephen Montgomery. I know this sounds stupid but if you get to him before me, could you ring me back and speak to me – Bart. I'm a friend of his. I'm worried about him. And, if you see him, tell him . . . Well, just tell him *I didn't know*. Neither of us knew. Tell him we met at Tristram's in

Cambridge. He'll understand. Sorry about this. I'm rambling. Thanks.'

He slumped down on the rug against the couch with the carton of juice and opened a packet of corn chips and set the packet down beside him. He sat eating, his jaw working hungrily at the chips, dry in his mouth, munching mechanically, his legs stretched out in front of him, crossed at the ankles, suede-booted feet pointing at the ceiling. From his jacket pocket the sudden fluting of canned Mozart filled the air. He leapt up and fumbled to dig out the phone, sending chips skittering over the floor.

'Damn . . .'

'Bart?'

'Kate!'

Pause. 'I got your message.'

He was kneeling on the floor now. Kate . . . 'Which one?' he said gently into the phone.

'Both of them.'

There was a silence, in which he felt the growing emergency of Monty dissolve suddenly and take on a different, more hopeful shape. 'Kate . . .'

'I went to the art show and looked around for you but you must have already left, so I rang Stephen's number. Someone called Nick said you'd just left there so I'm guessing you haven't found him yet.'

His stomach unknotted a fraction, sensing a freshness of purpose in her concern for Monty that carried, too, some promise, some prospect of reconciliation through this shared enterprise, like people thrown together in a train accident or a stalled elevator. 'Not quite,' he said. 'Where are you now?'

'I'm outside your house.'

'Outside?' He stood up quickly and ran to the window. The Citroën was parked on the other side of the street, sidelights on in the growing dusk. He waved, though he could barely make her out from here. 'Wait there,' he said.

He grabbed his jacket and went down to her. The window was open at the driver's side and she watched him as he crossed the road. He gave her a penitent's smile. Her hair was scraped back, held in place by a headband and she wore no make-up. There was paint on her T-shirt.

'I was out on a job when you called,' she said, drained and fragile-looking, barely repossessed from a day of unwanted surprises. There was a sheen of sweat on her forehead. She had one hand on the wheel, the other resting on the windowsill. He wanted to touch it but daren't.

'Are we on kissing terms?' he said, leaning on the van.

'We're not even on you-touching-my-vehicle terms,' she said.

'I'm sorry,' he said. 'About everything.'

'So, what about Stephen?'

'I don't know. Someone rang him tonight, though. A woman at this number. Listen . . .' He dialled.

Kate held the phone to her ear. 'Oh my God,' she said. She looked at the number displayed.

'What is it?'

'Well, there's no way this woman called him. This is his mother – who is very much dead. Which means he must have called the flat from her house. Which I imagine must be where he is now.'

'At his mother's house.'

'Well, obviously it's his house now. We were doing it up to sell it.'

'So you know where it is?'

'Of course I do. It's just off the Holloway Road.'

'You're a genius. I think we ought to go there.'

'Is that wise?'

290

'It might be wiser than not going and then wishing we had.'

'I suppose you're right. You'd better get in. It's a bit noisy. I've got a table and six chairs piled up in the back there.'

They set off, rattling up through Islington to Highbury Corner. She swung left at the roundabout.

'The house must be worth a fortune round here,' said Bart.

'Yes, that did occur to us.'

It was still strange to him, the idea of Kate and Monty being an 'us'. He watched her as she drove, the concentration in her eyes. She made a left, and chugged slowly down a terrace of tall Victorian houses and pulled into the kerb. 'It's that one,' she said, jerking the handbrake on. 'Sixty-eight. That's how old his mother was when she died. Stephen said she should have bought one further up the street.'

There was a light on in the living room glowing against the drawn curtains. Bart got out and stood in front of the house. Kate joined him. She shivered despite the heat of the evening. 'What do we do?'

Bart touched her arm. 'Here goes.' He stepped up to ring the bell then stood back, Kate behind him. No one came.

'What now?'

He rang the bell again. 'He might be . . .'

'It's only just got dark, though – why would the light be on?'

'See if you can see in the window,' she said. 'There, look. There's a gap at that side.'

He found an upturned milk crate at the side of the steps, and he stood on it, cupping his hands against the glass.

'Can you see anything?' Kate was saying.

'There's a jacket on the armchair – and some kind of bag—'

The door opened suddenly to his side and Monty was on the step, his tallness comically wrapped in a short white bathrobe, his hair standing on end and alarm on his face. He was staring at Kate. 'Catherine?'

'Stephen, I'm sorry. We didn't know if. . . .' She looked at Bart, diverting Monty's gaze to where he stood, frozen to the crate.

Monty almost leapt in the air. 'Jesus Christ.'

'Hi,' Bart said, his mouth suddenly dry, his own heart going.

There was a booming rumbling above and the three of them looked up for a second before becoming aware, only as its echo died, of a secondary thudding, that of footfalls on the carpeted stair and the sound of someone calling Monty's name, entering the picture behind Monty, and a voice – 'Who is it?' A face appeared, lit by the glow from the hall, puzzled at the disturbance but open to whatever novelty it might hold, a face accustomed to welcoming strangers. Monty, frowning, bit his bottom lip, as if bracing himself for something. Bart stepped down from the crate and moved forward, his head craning out of the shadows in disbelief. '*Jim*?'

'Ah. Bart . . .' Jim, wearing only shorts, stood transfixed, apparently caught between gravity and misplaced amusement.

Bart glanced from one to the other, waiting for Monty to decide whether this *was* what it looked like, or in fact some other scenario that might reasonably explain why he, Jim, was here and not in Barcelona or Casablanca.

'Is someone going to introduce me?' asked Kate, bewildered by the way Bart was looking at Monty and this new person, and the way they both looked at him unable to speak.

Monty closed his eyes. 'I'm sorry . . .' he started to say.

Lightning flashed, bisecting the sky and illuminating the

clouds with arc light, followed by the slow break of thunder, the swift cooling of air and the first flat smacks of rain on the pavement. Bart glanced up. When he looked back, Monty was holding on to Jim's hand, gazing at Kate.

'Oh my God,' she said.

● ● ●

Fuck. Bloody phone ringing somewhere. About to turn over but then he thought about Monty, what Bart had been saying, though whose fault *that* was if not Bart's, pushing him over the edge, fucking a man over when he's down. Nick switched the light on and staggered across to the phone, gingham boxers swaying out in front, courtesy of elephant's-trunk-like semi-erection. Phone ringing its fucking head off for *fuck's* sake, can't you see I'm coming. 'Hello?'

'Hello, WHO is this?' Woman barking at him, Third World credentials of some description.

'What do you mean who is this? It's the middle of the night. You're supposed to tell me who *you* are. What is it – minicab, pizza? You've got the wrong number.' He looked at the window. Raining out there, lashing the pane.

'I'm sorry to disturb you,' the woman was saying, 'but do you know a Mr James BRAILLING?'

'What? No, of course I don't know a James . . . No, hang on, yes, yes. Jas, yes. James Brailling. Why?' Nick blinked the sleep and lager out of his eyes, focus.

'This is St Bartholomew's Hospital. Mr Brailling was brought in earlier tonight. He has this number in his phone.'

'Jesus, what's happened?'

'Are you a relative?'

'No, I'm his . . . yes, I'm his cousin, yes.'

'Mr Brailling was brought in complaining of chest pains.'

'Christ. Is he, is he . . . has he had a heart attack?'

'They're doing tests now. Does he have closer family?'

'Hang on. Yes, let me get her number.' Shit. Ivy. He ran back to his room, scrabbled through his sock drawer for his useless mobile. Unpaid, but should be charged up. He tried to switch it on, but it was drained down like everyfucking-thing else. Shit. He ran back to the phone. 'Let me get back to you. No, wait. I'll find out where she is and get her to come back to you. It's his daughter. Hang on, did you say you had his phone? Maybe her mobile number's in there somewhere. Under Ivy.'

'Ivy?'

'That's her name. But I'll try to find her anyway.'

'All right, thank you.'

What now? What? He hadn't got anybody's fucking number. No, he had Bart's. What the fuck had he done with it? He found his trousers in the bedroom and dug the crum-pled triangle of newspaper out of the pocket as he ran back to the phone, keyed in the number. It was ringing. He started to count out the rings with rhythm. And. The. Chances. Of. You. Having. Your. Mobile. Switched. On. At. This. Time. Of . . .

'Hello.'

'Fuck, you're up! Where are you?'

'Nick? Ah, right. Don't worry, we found him.'

'What?'

'Monty. He's fine. We spoke to him. Briefly.'

'No, fuck that, listen. Jas is in hospital. He's had a heart attack. He's at St Bart's. Have you got Ivy's mobile number?'

'Jas? You're kidding. Give me time to get down to the office. We've probably got it on file. I'll ring you back.'

Nick, still holding his trousers, sat on the chair arm and pulled them on, went back for yesterday's shirt, found his

294

shoes. Kettle on for coffee, get his head together. He could walk it to Bart's from here – hospital that is, not Bart's the person's house, he thought, wondering at the coincidence of it. He found his joke Rolex down the side of the bed, miraculously working now, snapping the bracelet on to his wrist, fag in his mouth. Quarter past four. He sat by the phone until Bart rang again. 'Nick, hi, I called Ivy's number and left a message. I'm going down to the hospital now. Shall I pick you up on the way?'

'Ready when you are.'

He was on the step when the Porsche rolled up, headlamps blazing in the rain, wipers going. He ran across and got in and pulled the seat belt across his chest. Weird being strapped in with Bart, like his date or something. The trip with Ivy came into his mind; the night she had clung to him at her mother's house. But then he thought about Jas, made him feel bad about the whole thing. 'So where were you?' he said. 'Tonight, I mean. When I rang. Why were you still awake?'

Bart hesitant, looking both ways in the zero traffic instead of answering. 'There's this girl I've been seeing. We were at my place just sitting up talking.'

'Yeah, I spoke to her earlier. So she knows Monty, does she?'

'What makes you say that?'

'You said *we* earlier. When I rang, you said *we* found Monty.'

'Yes, well, we tracked him down at his mother's old house. He's fine. That was his mother we heard on the voicemail. She died last year.'

Nick let it go. 'What about Jas's girlfriend – this Stella?'

'What about her?'

'Don't you think it's funny none of us have met her? It's like Jas has us and he has her. Don't you think that's funny?'

'Maybe he wanted to keep her away from you, Nick.'

'Ha, ha.' He lit a cigarette, waited for Bart to object, but he didn't.

'I think that was her in Ivy's film,' Bart said. 'Not the old woman, the other one. The ghost one. The ghost one who wasn't me.'

'You were in the film?' Nick said.

'I had a walk-on part. Ivy made a rogues' gallery of us all.'

'What do you mean, all of us?'

'Well, you know, Monty too.'

'Monty? He was in the film?'

'You didn't see him?'

'No, I left pretty quickly. So, him and Ivy . . .'

'She suckered him into bed, that's all. For the film. Nothing happened.'

'It wasn't like that with us,' Nick said. 'Me and Ivy.'

'I know it's none of my business, Nick, but doesn't that kind of make it, well . . . *worse*?'

Nick wanted to say something about shagging Monty's wife making things *worse* for Monty, but something else told him that would make things worse for himself. 'So what's the story with Monty?' he said.

'He's just taking some time out.'

'What kind of time?'

'You'd better ask him.'

'I never see him. Since I moved in, he seems to have moved out. Maybe he's trying to tell me something.' He laughed.

Bart said nothing. Impatient. Touched a nerve mentioning Monty, Nick thought. Probably feels like a cunt. Nick looked out of the window. Bloody rain. They pulled into the hospital grounds and halted. Bart reversed the car over the pitted surface into a well-lit spot by the wall. 'Staff only,' Nick said.

296

'It'll be all right.'

They splashed across the car park. Reception was dim and yellow, handful of drunks and undesirables slumped on plastic chairs, others just outside the doors smoking in the shelter of the roof-felted overhang. Nick shuffled from one foot to another waiting for Bart to find out where they were supposed to go, then followed him to the lifts. 'I hate hospitals,' Bart muttered, looking up at the changing numbers.

'All the more funny you living in one, then,' Nick said.

The lift doors opened on to another waiting area with nurses gliding around, another in a blue uniform behind a desk. Bart spoke quietly to her. 'Yes,' he heard the nurse say, 'the lady over there is waiting.'

They turned to see a woman sitting, a blonde. She looked at them and stood up. 'I'm Stella,' she said. 'God, I'm glad you came. Ivy doesn't know yet. She's out of town.'

Nick stepped forward and introduced himself. 'And this is Bart.' They shook hands. She looked anxious, folded her arms.

'How is he?' Nick said.

'They don't know yet. They're doing tests.'

'I left a message for Ivy,' Bart said.

'I don't think she'll come,' Stella said, tears springing to her eyes.

Nick glanced at Bart.

'She got a call last night,' she said. 'Her mother's died.'

● ● ●

Uno, dos, tres . . . He counted. He was conscious in the ambulance. They asked him questions to keep him alive but didn't hear the answer and called him Chas instead. He tried to tell them but he had the mask on. In the hospital, nurses came and went, rigged him up. A doctor came and asked questions and shone a light in his eyes, pumped his arm with air. They gave him something to make him feel relaxed. He wasn't dead. He could avoid that while he was alive, he thought. Compos mentis. The beating in his chest had stopped. He opened his eyes and saw Stella, and then later Monty and the others. He was so tired. Stella was holding his hand. Someone from Bart's office was there.

fourteen

A beautiful piece of waxed English elm, rosewood panels. With the sunlight behind him, Bart ran his finger along the pale grain and saw how the colours from the rippled glass sent deep diamonds of red, green and burnt yellow fanning lengthways across the white wall. Kate, at the other end of the screen, warm with the effort of hauling it out of the van and up the stairs, squared the end to line up with the soft zigzag made by the hinged folds, and took a step back. 'It's post-war, brilliantly crafted – I don't know who by. It was just a lot in a house sale. They'd had it propped up in an outbuilding for years. It did need some work.' She turned to him, delighted at herself. 'Do you love it?'

'I love it,' he said. 'I do.' He looked at her for a long moment, loving her too, but afraid to say so – afraid that such an avowal might be a portent to her now, one freak whirlwind followed by another; afraid, too, that the words were too smoothed by the shape of a previous owner for any meaning of his own to cling. Everything Kate had said about Monty eleven days ago in this room, leaning against his couch, sipping tropical fruit juice in the early hours, seemed to come down to him saying those words, as if saying them more and more made it more true. 'From day one Stephen was determined to love me,' she'd said. 'I understand that now. I understand why he had that intensity about him. Loving me meant not having to face up to the real Stephen. Loving me like he did put an end to other possibilities. It freed him of that responsibility.'

Bart wondered whether we all didn't do that sooner or later. He wondered whether it wasn't natural to trade the uncertainties of freedom for the reassuring captivity of making a decision and fashioning a life out of trying to hold to it. Freedom seemed to him nothing but an allure to keep you occupied while your secret heart pursued narrower designs. Jas and his jolly tars. You looked like you were at sea: you felt the wind in your hair, you heard the shouts of your shipmates, you joined in their salty revels. But you were still *going* somewhere, still up that pole spying for land, looking to be anchored. He had said no to New York. He had said yes to having Kate splash his walls with her colours. No. Yes. This way, not that. You hoped you made the right choice, as Monty had hoped – as they all had. It might be the wrong choice but you had to point your sail at *something*.

'Obviously, you can put it where you like,' she said

quickly. 'You're the expert. And – of course – it's your house.' She turned back to examine and admire the screen, picking a snagged speck of lint from the leaded surface of the glass with her finger and thumb.

It's your house. The words seemed to resound in the air, drawing attention to themselves by being the last things said. He left space for them to hover. He wondered whether he and Kate would both live here with furniture, flowers in a vase and a fridge with food in it. Or whether they'd have those things somewhere else. Somewhere not his but theirs.

'It should be movable, I think,' he said, stirred to enthusiasm with the thought. 'Depending on what you want to divide off.'

'That's what the wheels are for,' she said. She had fixed it with neutral translucent rollerballs that made it look modern and old at the same time. Classic.

'I love it,' he said.

Unbreakfasted apart from coffee, on the way to the memorial service they stopped in a hot little concrete smudge of a town and bought cold fizzy drinks and a sweet pastry each at a stall next to the river. They sat on the wall next to the bridge watching a pair of swans marshalling three grey cygnets, the water fresh and green, the eddying surface bright with the yellow of submerged reeds pulled by the undertow like horses' tails in the wind. Bart threw his last sugar-crusted crumbs on to the water. He asked what had been worse – finding Monty in the arms of a woman or . . . He lifted his hand to shade his eyes against the sun-struck ripples.

'Or a man?' Kate said. She looked down at the swans. 'I always felt bad about our splitting up. Because he was the one so full of rage, it always seemed I was the one to blame – that

I hadn't given us enough of a chance. I don't mean it was my fault that he couldn't bring himself to have sex with me – my self-esteem wasn't that bad.' She smiled. 'I don't know, it just seemed wrong to kick a man when he was trying so hard. But we were both trying hard – trying everything. I suppose I thought that if we could get *that* right, then everything else would follow, that all the other stuff – the possessiveness and obsessive behaviour – was just a symptom of the sex thing.'

'That was probably true.'

She nodded. 'Anyway, seeing the girl – Ivy – coming out of the flat that morning made it OK for *me* to be angry. It made it less my fault. It certainly made it easier for me to walk away from Stephen – even if it now looked as though it was just *me* he had trouble having sex with.'

'I suppose,' Bart said, 'it seems more likely he's never had sex with a woman. And the thing with Ivy . . . well, that was pretty complicated. Ivy's pretty complicated.'

'I'll say.' Kate swigged from the little plastic bottle. 'But then finding out that Stephen is . . .' She gestured with her hand. 'Whatever he is. Of course it was a shock – it still is – but at least there's some kind of an end to it that makes sense. It means he can stop fighting. To be honest I don't know how I feel about it. Sad, I suppose. I loved him and he loved me. I'd like to think it wasn't completely wasted, but I'm finding that hard.'

Bart put his hand out for her crumpled wrapper and took it with his own to the yellow bin by the kiosk. They got back in the car, and strapped themselves in side by side, an intimate twoness. They drove slowly over the crown of the bridge, the two swans fussing below, a last glimpse of their impatient grandeur, their overgrown chicks paddling between them.

• • •

302

Fuck. 'Where are my cufflinks?' he called.

Olivia came into the room, pointedly not answering the question, busying herself with bed linen. 'Is it really necessary for you to take my car?'

'Sorry, babe. It's in the middle of nowhere and anybody who might have given me a lift is either recently bereaved, or a homosexual, or only has two bloody seats.'

'Dad swore,' Lucy said, standing at the doorway.

'Homosexual isn't swearing, poppet,' said Nick.

'Stop being such a ridiculous bigot,' Olivia said, 'and give me a hand with this. You know you don't mean it. You never had a problem with Gareth and Tony.'

'They were older and settled. You know what it's like with people who've just started getting groovy and gooey with each other. I'll probably end up in the middle of a conversation about fisting.' He glanced at Lucy. 'Whatever that is.'

Olivia shook her head and carried on stuffing pillows into pillow cases. She loved him. Wife.

Clean shirt, proper shave, new shoes, pressed suit with darkish tie, congruous with sombre occasion, unlike mood, which was upbeat and rising. Whistling down the path in the fresh London air, two twenties and a ten in his pocket. He got into the car and fired the engine. Gave her a wave, waiting there on the doorstep for him to go, habitual frown as if he was making the whole thing up. She turned to go in. Trust. You couldn't buy it.

First gear, manoeuvre, radio, seat belt, second gear, mirror, accelerate, fag, seat adjustment for person with longer legs.

He smiled. Olivia. He could kiss her. Surprisingly receptive to having him back, second time lucky following sudden difficulty of Monty dropping hints about needing space and privacy to facilitate establishment of centrally located love nest for Him'n'Jim, and who'd have thought *that*, living a lie, a shirtlifter after all the fuss he'd made about the missus, though come to think of it there was the occasional telltale sign in the flat – Pet Shop Boys CDs, preponderance of clean towels, plug-in air fresheners – on top of reportedly schizophrenic history of violence and voluntary work.

Best thing though. Return of the prodigal. Return of Odysseus to Mrs Odysseus following a long odyssey. Round the world and back. Adventure. Honey, I'm home! That day on the step, her face like Medusa, dressed in Saturday morning T-shirt and joggers, J-Cloth in one hand, Mr Muscle in the other. 'You've got a bloody nerve,' she said.

'Can I come in?'

'How does "No, fuck off" sound?'

'Friendly chat?'

'Did you bring money with you?'

Sitting perched on the edge of his own sofa, sipping tea from ironically selected orange mug (World's Best Dad), her standing up, the better to glare down at him, kids safely at grandparents' for the day. 'So, let's see, Nick,' she said, 'you're unemployed, skint, homeless, and no one will have sex with you. So, *obviously* you thought you'd go back to that idiot Olivia . . .'

Contrite pause, gazing at the carpet, chewing on lower lip. 'I miss Matthew and Lucy,' he sighed, then, looking up, adding, 'and you, of course. I thought we could give it another shot. You and me.' His eyes followed her to the window, her back to him. 'Livvy?'

Incredulous snort. 'Not a chance.' Which meant, as it turned out, thinking about it. Left it to ripen. Three days later (though it seemed longer, Monty and his beau whispering in and out of the flat, measuring up for new stuff, like a pair of fucking newlyweds), she rang, proposition being her going back to work – doing some highly paid job she'd somehow been miraculously headhunted for since they last spoke – while he looked after the kids during the summer holidays. 'You can have the spare room,' she said.

'So I'm the nanny.'

'I *think* you'll find you're the father.'

'Right. And after the summer holidays?'

'Depends how good you are at it.'

'Do I get paid?'

'We'll see.'

Fulfilment in children, but a trap to run from too, the hamsters and cornflake mess of it. Escape though, freedom or whatever, was a trap in itself. All the love was back there. Fuel for life. Like a car running out of petrol, he was. Ivy, putting nothing but sugar in the tank. He found the North Circular and headed east, sun high in the sky, shining down on him, a blessing it seemed like. Funny, being in the same bedroom just now, if not yet in the same bed, though he found himself aching more and more for that as Olivia moved around the house, sometimes urgently sweeping past in her sexy businesswear looking for something important, sometimes pottering, watering plants in her evening bathrobe before going off to bed with a book. Same person seen through new eyes. That was it. Mystery. Women.

●●●

Memorial services were about life, not death, Ivy said. She wanted all of them to be there, in the same way she'd wanted them to see her show, as though in connecting through art her father's life and her mother's death she was somehow getting everything squeezed into the picture at the same time – as though all things actually *were* just the one big thing, and not only for her but for everybody. Jas, for all his hurt, could see how it might be mixed up in that way. He could see how Ivy might consider herself free to make a grotesque of his life, not only in return for the way he had felt free to unhook himself from his wife and infant – allowing his own freedom, as Ivy saw it, to put shackles on her mother – but because Truth, as Art saw it, was worth more than the vanities of personal privacy, the petty questions of who deserved what.

Life having overtaken art again, he and Ivy did not speak about the show, and perhaps in not raising the subject he felt he was showing due acknowledgement that, whatever Ivy did, he wouldn't expect his approval to be a consideration. That way it was nothing personal, even though, in this case, it obviously had been. He even wondered, less fearfully, if his near-death experience might one day be commemorated in her tapestry of unfolding events – though, disappointingly from the point of view of drama, the doctor at the hospital pronounced his experience nearer to anxiety than to death, and had supplied him with beta-blockers and helpful literature listing panic attack support groups in his area. It might happen again, they said. Or it might not.

Ivy had called and spoken to Stella on the afternoon following his emergency, but it was two days before she had completed his own small *tableau vivant* of concerned parties by arriving to weep in his arms – not for him, of course, but for her mother.

Monty, Nick, Bart, Stella came and went. Whether forgiveness or apologies were called for, the moment now seemed to demand that he imagine himself somewhere without its own constant pleasures, its starry heaven and 360-degree views, perhaps on the lower floors of other people's lives, each leaking and cascading into his own. Sex, loyalty, conflicts of interest, calculated misunderstandings and high principles tumbling and seeping through. That was nothing personal either. You couldn't get away from it.

The service at the crematorium had been for Barbara's immediate family and close friends, but Ivy had wanted him and Stella there too. The vicar spoke in a deep, tremulous voice learned in vicar school, a small choir sang and there was distress to be encountered. Ivy shook as she sobbed, and Jas held her close, but he remained dry-eyed himself as he watched the coffin move towards the curtain, condemned with the feeling of having escaped something while others perished. Stella, an immovable presence for Ivy, was attentive to Jas in a way she hadn't been before, perhaps reading his mind, seeing how it flickered with a parallel denouement in which some other Jas – more of a James, perhaps – had never fled the terrors offered by marriage and fatherhood twenty years before but had stayed to love and cherish in health and sickness; who now led the mourning for his wife, Barbara, forty-two, and shared the grief of his daughter. What he had feared had come to pass. Should he be grateful or ashamed? Heading back from the funeral in Stella's car, he had asked her to marry him. 'We don't need to do that,' she said cheerfully, glancing at him, as if they'd got some obstacle out of the way with a simple word.

At the crematorium chapel, Ivy – her unruly hair tamed by a black satin band, and wearing a black sleeveless dress made in advance for the occasion by a fashion student friend – had given Jas her hand to hold, and they had sat heads bowed in silence together in the front row alongside Barbara's father and brother. But here, today, in the Hall of All Hearts, a friendly non-denominational spiritual facility in the small Norfolk town of her birth, Ivy roamed with her camera, as friends and family and neighbours arrived for songs, poems, readings and a film of Barbara, on the beach, in the kitchen, playing with a kitten, asleep in an armchair. And when, afterwards, they walked from there the short distance to Barbara's favourite pub on the seafront to drink and eat quartered sandwiches and to reminisce, it was as if something had been lifted to let light in. His thoughts turned to Ivy's decision not to tell him about her mother, about her forbidding Stella to tell him, and all the while shouldering a burden that would have been his.

He wandered out into the front garden with his drink, followed after a minute by the others, Monty, his arm round Bart, Nick tracing the air with a glass of wine like a pendulum, trying not to spill it. Stella, unfamiliar in a long dress and a straw hat, stayed on the step talking to Jim and catching the last of the sun, low in the sky, its fading light deepening the sandy cliffs, saving its best colour for last. Nick sat on a picnic table with his feet on the bench, lit a cigarette and gave one to Monty. They looked out over the dunes, rippling in the wind like a second sea. 'We should have brought the cards,' he said.

'It's a bit late,' Bart said.

Jas sat up beside Nick on the picnic table. 'You could say that about anything,' he said.

He didn't know why he said it. It was one of those throwaway comments best passed over. But the others nodded earnestly, as if grateful for a gesture of agreement that spoke for deeper reconciliations. A death brought people together. Jas smiled and half closed his eyes, framing the scene before him out of habit, switching focus, medium to long, back again to short, seeing the double-A frame of the newly painted garden swing, then the soft geometric shadows it threw long across the trimmed lawn, and then, bringing the foreground to life, a dancing cloud of tiny flies. How you looked made what you saw. You made the picture change. You saw the trick. You saw how it worked.